Alisa Dana Steinberg

Text Me
A Tale of Love
and
Technology

TEXT ME, A TALE OF LOVE AND TECHNOLOGY
July 2010
Copyright © 2010 by Alisa Dana Steinberg
www.alisadanasteinberg.com

This is a work of fiction. Names, characters, places, and incidents either are the product of the author's imagination or are used fictitiously. Any resemblance to actual persons, living or dead, events, or locales is entirely coincidental.

Cover Photo: © Andres Rodriguez/Fotolia

Broadcast rights to *It's a Wonderful Life* are owned by Republic Entertainment Inc..,® a subsidiary of Spelling Entertainment Group. Republic Entertainment has not endorsed this publication.

For my big brother, Darryl, who sparked my "Aha!" moment that led to this book – and who throws a damn good barbeque!

***

BRIEF INTRO:

Once there was a girl who had no knowledge of texting, and so, when she moved to Manhattan, she bought her first BlackBerry without text service. This girl also had a brother in the city who (much later) informed her of the dire consequences of not having this modus operandi of communications in Gotham – including to her love life – prompting her to rush out and get the service and write a novel. And some days later, this girl had a revelation – connect her favorite movie, "It's a Wonderful Life," to her novel; after all, the girl thought, the two main characters, Penelope McAdams and George Bailey, had much in common.

Well, that girl was me and that novel is the one you're about to read.

On a last note, for all the Penelopes and Georges out there – chin up; we've all been Penelopes and Georges at some time or other and will probably be at least one of them again in the near and distant future. Technology moves on and changes and so does life, but still, the heart remains the same. Thank God.

> *Joseph: I want you to take a good look at his face.*
>
> *Clarence/Angel 2ⁿᵈ Class: Who is it?*
>
> *Joseph: George Bailey.*

One

NEW YEAR'S EVE 2006

Penelope McAdams stood in the AT & T store, hovering over the shiny cell phones and PDAs, eager to choose her first communications apparatus for her new life in New York City. Disregarding the technical descriptions, which she was aware that she knew nothing about (and why should she? Did they really matter anyway?), she marveled and drooled over the candy colored phones with their cute, teensy-weensy, black and silver buttons.

She moved closer and squinted at a hot pink phone with a metallic face. "Excuse me," said a deep, nasal voice, and Penelope was startled, not expecting the voice and the salesman attached to it. The salesman, a very tall stick-figure man with hollowed cheeks and a thin mustache that twitched at her in a condescending fashion, scooted an index finger over the cell phone in a wiping gesture. "Please. No saliva on the cell phone, Miss."

"I'm *so* sorry," she said to him in a pleasant manner indicative of the small Midwestern town she came from; in that farm town of Elmont, Illinois, where she had been born, raised, and just left at the age of twenty-seven, the most sincere "sorrys" were given out freely to everyone on a daily basis – to a man or woman that someone might've passed in front of on a street, just in case that someone's head had impeded the person's view *(sorry ... sorry* the view-blocker would say*)*, to the ant that this same someone might've stepped on to get out of the person's way *(sorry ... sorry)*. And then of course, there were the frequent and congenial "hi theres" and "how are yas" exchanged by the townspeople that she had grown accustom to throughout her life.

"Sorry?" the salesman questioned her, raising an eyebrow as a hurried man in a navy-blue suit sideswiped him on the way to the customer service counter. "You're not from around here, are you?"

She provided a sweet smile at being found out, figuring her accent must have given her away, and to think – she had worked on it nonstop since she had arrived in the city just the day before.

Trying to make a transition from a Midwestern accent to a New York one, Penelope started to listen to the people on the street walking to and from work and to those heading off to the gym or their neighborhood Starbucks, and she realized her older and only brother Cory was right about the city's vernacular. Cory, a rising attorney and Manhattanite for the past six years, made it a point to study New York language from the very start. It was all in the vowels, he explained, especially the letter *a* – like "talk" was *taawk* , not the Midwestern *tohk* and then "dog" was *daawg,* which they had always pronounced *dohg.*

"Nope, I don't come from around here. How did you guess?" Penelope asked, sure that the salesman would say it had to do with a messed up I or O. (And she had tried so hard!)

"Sorry," he answered.

She shook her head. "It's okay. I'm not offended. I just moved here yesterday."

"No," he said, "it was your 'sorry.'" The salesman moved his mustache again and surveyed the cute and pixie-like, brown haired girl with her little nose that had a smattering of freckles. "Nobody says it here."

Penelope was taken aback. "Never? ... *Ohhh.* You mean in the store."

"No," he asserted, "not just in the store. Everywhere. In the streets, in the offices, in the restaurants ... The other day I saw someone trip an elderly woman in the subway station. No sorry."

Penelope almost fell over, aghast at the idea of a gray-haired grandmother with a cane being thrown off balance by a malicious person and their foot. This person obviously had no moral values whatsoever. She gasped at the thought of it and pressed her hand at her chest, trying to calm down. "How dare they?"

The salesman shrugged and turned to the row of cell phones and PDAs. He pulled out a rag from his pants pocket and dusted them off. "That's what you get if you're blocking the subway door of the Lexington Express at rush hour."

"But a grandmother?"

"Did I say grandmother? I didn't say grandmother. And it wasn't even an elderly woman really. Some old guy in drag who retired from the queen shows some years back. Doesn't know what to do with himself except ride the subways all day," he explained and then looked her up and down as she screwed her face.

Drag? she thought to herself. *What did he mean by Drag?* The only time she had heard of *drag* really was pertaining to racing and NASCAR.

"Hey," he said, looking her square in the face, "are you sure that you want to move to New York?"

Penelope frowned. That was what her brother asked her, and now this stranger was asking her the same thing? What was the problem? If it was only a matter of not saying "sorry" then that wasn't an issue at all, she thought. Actually, it was kind of freeing! One less word to say. And she had said it so often in Elmont! What a treat to be done with it and to save some of her breaths for more important things like idle gossip, sipping martinis, and kissing handsome men, which was what she knew happened to all girls in New York City when she became an ardent fan of the hit TV show "Manhattan Nights."

She immediately recalled her Wednesday evenings in front of the television with some of her Elmont girlfriends, chomping down on popcorn and guzzling down Slurpees as she watched the three cosmopolitan women of "Manhattan Nights" stride across the screen and the streets of New York with couture bags at their sides as they left their fascinating, high-paying jobs to head off to their luxurious, trendy apartments to get ready for their dates with their affluent, hunky boyfriends.

Giving up the word "sorry" to become an upwardly-mobile, Manhattan woman was definitely worth it, she thought – *AWAY WITH SORRY!*

"Yes! I *definitely* want to be here!" she answered, standing up to the Salesman, who she felt was a symbol of downright pessimism, something she was sure she'd never turn into being the eternal optimist that she was.

She swiveled around on her heels to look at the cell phones again, and just at that moment, she knocked into a woman wearing huge, round sunglasses and a leather overcoat. "Sor-" Penelope said, having bit her lip before she said the full-word "sorry," and she scrunched her face up, afraid of what the salesman would say about her almost-faux pas.

"Good for you," he stoically complimented her. "You didn't quite say it. There's hope for you yet."

She furnished a smug smile.

"Now, what is it that you're looking for?" he asked, leaning forward and down a bit to get closer to her and appear more personal, but he found himself still taller than his diminutive customer, at about a foot's length. "Anything specific?"

"Why yes." She beamed and pulled at her coat to close it more; the store's door kept flinging open as multitudes of people scurried in and out, letting the chill of the winter air gush in. "My, there's *so* many people" she commented, still trying to keep her cheerful attitude intact in the middle of the boisterous and crowded room. The last time she had seen so many people in one room was during an emergency blood drive in Elmont after a series of tornadoes hit a neighboring town; everyone had their sleeves rolled-up ready to help their fellow citizen. And then there was the one farmer's meeting about the rising property taxes – that was pretty dense; there were about fifty people in a room the size of a public bathroom at an expressway rest stop. The AT & T store was a little bit larger than that and there were nearly sixty people lined up side by side, either examining the products or standing at the customer service desk where most were waiting to be called on. All seemed disgruntled.

"The store's about to close in an hour-it's New Year's Eve, y'know." He smiled, and it was the first time she had seen him do so during their five-minute conversation. "We have this deal that we're giving for a new cell phone that just came out, and people, especially in this city, are always eager to have something new."

"That's me!" she exclaimed, "I like new! I mean-what's more new than relocating to a new city? Especially from a small town like Elmont, Illinois." Penelope went on and on as the salesman's eyes drifted around the room. "And I have this great *new* job," she told him, beginning to enumerate the happenings in her life by sticking up one finger and then another.

He stopped her with – "What kind of job?"

"Account executive with this big public relations agency!" Her tiny frame puffed up with pride.

"Small-town girl from Illinois lands a prime PR job in the big city? How did you manage to do that?"

Instead of waiting for a reply, the salesman gave her his own take on it. "I know," he said, nodding and seeming assured, "the agency's doing a campaign on cow manure or Dairy Queens."

It was obvious to Penelope that he decided to resign her to a stereotype of Middle-American communities from circa 1970s movies involving people who tended to crops and cattle in their mornings and afternoons, and then cavorted at saloons, diners, and neighborhood food chains at night. Considering all that, Penelope was not happy with the truth that she was about to provide. "No, actually," she replied, tightening her lips and lowering her eyes. "I'm handling a campaign for a line of tractors. Henshaw Tractors."

"Hah!" He laughed and wagged his finger in the air like he proved something.

"And if it weren't for those tractors working the crops, the people in this city wouldn't be eating," she lashed out but kept her composed posture. "Although it looks like some *haven't* been eating." She eyed his emaciated body.

He cleared his throat and then pointed his once wagging finger right at Penelope – "Good! Sarcasm! Rudeness! You'll need it! … You learn fast! So what kind of phone do you want for your new life in New York?"

Penelope sighed and then curved her frown to a smile. "Well. I heard about something called a BlackBerry."

A man snickered from behind her.

The salesman repeated, "*Something* called a BlackBerry?" Penelope could hear an undertone of mocking in his voice, which, after being in his company for a while and being exposed to his attitude, didn't shock her in the least bit. "Miss, you don't know what a BlackBerry is?"

She shook her head, innocence radiating from her face.

"But how can that be?" he asked. "It's the most widely used communications technology around, and it's been out for years."

Penelope realized she was about to tell the salesman something she had already acknowledged to herself during the past couple of years but didn't want to openly declare– that she was absolutely, completely, and undeniably clueless about technology.

"I don't know anything about technology," she said, shuddering as though she was confessing under the bright lights of an interrogation room.

The salesman's eyes widened.

"But seriously, no one in my town really pays attention to it," she explained as he looked on at her with an expression of fascination. "The last *new* technology we got in our town was the Space Invaders game they put in the Main Street Candy Store." Suddenly, Penelope covered her mouth, realizing that she just gave additional credence to the salesman's thoughts about small-town people.

But instead of making jokes as he had done before, he tilted his head and his gaze softened. "Must be nice to live in a place that's so untouched," he said and then signaled Penelope with a crook of his finger and ordered, "Follow me," as he turned around and headed to a line-up of phones near a side window of the store. Through the pane, Penelope could see the people pouring down the streets, many of whom were dressed up. Some men capped their heads with sparkly hats – red, black, and white – and some women slid princess tiaras in their hair that had the upcoming year "2007" on them.

"Just remember," the salesman commented, "when you go to Times Square, those objects and people you see floating in the air-that's technology, too. They're signs - billboards. I think they're digital or something…Anyway, I just wanted to tell you that before you saw them and decided to pray to them like they were gods or something. Like a caveman would." Penelope grimaced. "Excuse me," he said, "cave*woman.*"

He gestured to a phone with a screen and a number of buttons in different, rectangular shapes. "This is the BlackBerry Curve. This is probably what you want."

"Yes!" She lit up. "That's the one my brother told me about!"

"Well, that's good, because it's the smart choice since the reception on these PDAs - which stands for 'Personal Digital Assistant' by the way - is outstanding." He continued, "And in PR you're sure going to be getting a lot of emails, and this BlackBerry will pick them all up. And of course, you'll be able to send them, too … You do know what emails are … right?"

She was again perturbed with the salesman. Of course she knew what emails were. She used them while working as the public relations manager of the Elmont "Meals on Wheels" chapter; for the first four of the six years she worked at the organization, she sent out press releases via the fax machine and regular mail, but shortly thereafter, all the area journalists requested that she should send their press releases and any other PR documentation by email. After all, paper came from the bark of trees, they told her, and trees were a big deal in Elmont, and if people didn't start emailing, how else would they hold their heads up high at the town's festive Arbor Day celebration?

"Yes," she replied, narrowing her eyes at him. "I know what emails are."

"Just checking," the salesman said, and she wrinkled her freckled nose at him.

He went on – "Anyway, with regards to the other details, it has quad-band edge, international roaming, a megapixel camera, a media player and …" He suddenly stopped what he was saying and stared into Penelope's eyes that were all glossed over with confusion.

She had no idea what he was talking about.

"Do you want me to tell you what these things are?" he asked.

"No," she answered, feeling both scared and inept. Penelope had no desire to become more aware of her technology shortcomings. "It sounds great. I can make phone calls and get emails. What else is there to know?"

"Okay," he uttered with some hesitance, seeming not sure that he should let the pretty country girl out into the jaws of the city, where holding a cell phone or PDA the wrong way at your ear or inadvertently having it snap a photo of someone on the subway, would be grounds for the city to swallow you up whole and then burp your bones into Trinity Church Cemetery.

The salesman moved his eyes from Penelope to the rest of the store. It was filled to the brim with people. "I really have no time to turn into a concerned citizen," he mumbled and then turned back to her. "What about text messaging?" he asked. "Unlimited text messaging is about ten-dollars extra. Another special right now."

She didn't know what that was either. "Text messaging?"

Nervous, he smoothed out a side of his mustache. "Yeah," he responded and then tried to make it simple. "You can write to people on the BlackBerry, and you can send it to them automatically."

Penelope let out a pleasant sigh. "Oh, forget that." She waved the idea away with her hand. "I can email people."

The salesman went cross-eyed. "Soooo you don't want any text messaging service on your BlackBerry?"

"That's right."

He gave her one more chance. "Are you sure?"

She squinted at him, not understanding what the big deal was, and then said, "Please. Don't add the text messaging service." She was firm. "I won't be needing it."

> *Clarence/Angel 2nd Class: There must be an easier way for me to get my wings.*

Two

NEW YEAR'S EVE 2007

"Cory, a year later and still no boyfriend! Nothing's happened! Nothing!" Penelope croaked to her brother as she sat in front of a cluster of eel and spicy tuna rolls at Ruby Foo's.

Her brother listened to his sister's now constant complaints while trying to get control of his girlfriend's precocious five-year old son, Jake, who was bouncing around his chair with his Matchbox cars in hand and jet black hair flopping about. His girlfriend, Sonia, an attractive brunette with a ten figure and always pleasant disposition, was also on the case, occasionally tackling her son when he made close calls with the waiters' feet or interrupted a childless couple's conversations about their next trip to St. Barts or Rome; but mostly, she watched him, commanding her son in short sound bites – "Jake, stop that … Jake, I'm warning you," and then longer ones – "Jake, leave that lady's hair alone … Jake, leave that man's private parts alone … Jake, leave *your* private parts alone!"

"Pen," her brother said as he used a firm hand on the little boy's shoulder, holding him down and stationary on the floor, "I told you-New York's a difficult city. It's going to take more than a year for things to fall into place."

Penelope stared at Cory, who, except for his towering height, she resembled – from the freckles spotted around his nose to his narrow frame. She began to pick some rice off the spicy tuna roll. Although she felt depressed about her situation and didn't feel much like eating, she needed to get rid of the grumblings in her stomach; she had spent her entire day slaving over the Henshaw Tractors account without as much as a snack break at the building's junk food machine.

Penelope had no idea when she began the job at Renquist & Renquist that talking to journalists about the plowing of fields and a vehicle that had basically been around since the turn of the last century would prove to be so difficult – who knew it would be so time consuming and therefore, exasperating? And then there was the once-in-a-while curve ball from a fledgling reporter from a small financial newsletter who always went off on a tangent, beginning with questions about tractors and always ending up inquiring about the strife of the American farmer, hoping to write an earth-shattering and provocative piece that would skyrocket them to a position at *The Wall Street Journal*.

On that New Year's Eve, at the table, the realization that her work, along with her frequent internet dates and fix-ups, and the numerous fundraisers she had gone to in her mission to find a successful Manhattan man, fall in love, get married, have a luxurious apartment with floor-to-ceiling windows, and have two-point-five kids, led to absolutely nothing, was getting to be all too much. And now there was this – she had done all that and still she was with her brother, his girlfriend, and her son on *New Year's Eve?* And of all places – Ruby Foo's? Not even the Ruby Foo's in the center of the city, she thought, not in the hustle and bustle of Times Square, but on the Upper West Side where people were older and settled, and threw diaper bags over their shoulders while clinging onto Bugaboo carriages as they hustled over to children's birthday parties, some so elaborate they'd put the

Presidential Inaugural Ball to shame.

If they were going to go for sushi, Penelope thought they should have at least gone to Nobu 57, a much trendier place where she could be seen in her new, black Calvin Klein dress (not the *most* couture of outfits, but according to a friend at work, a vast improvement from her once Laura Ashley attire).

She posed the idea to Cory and Sonia, but they didn't go for it. They knew that Nobu on New Year's Eve was no place for Jake with his carefree attitude concerning servers and patrons, and their chic and above-it-all attitudes that would cause Jake and company to be kicked out on the street the minute someone saw a Matchbox 1986 Camaro doing a ramp-jump in the lounge area.

The Upper West Side Ruby Foo's was always congenial to Jake – and Cory's huge tip. So there they were, and there Penelope was, taking a small bite of a spicy tuna roll after much deliberation on how she felt about eating and figuring – *what the hell? I might as well do something.*

Hauling the partially eaten roll in her mouth, Penelope commented, "I know what you said about the city being difficult. But I didn't imagine the city being *this* difficult," and then she watched as the waiters plopped down sparkly hats, tiaras, and noisemakers on their table.

She glanced at her watch. It was almost eleven-forty five p.m. and almost the end of her first year in New York. *Whoopee,* she said to herself, wrinkling her nose.

"What about work?" Sonia questioned her, having one eye on Penelope and the other on her son who vroom-vroomed a miniature police car around the leg of her chair. "That's how your brother and I met." Sonia's features gentled, and she turned to Cory with her pupils dilated and her voice smooth as silk and said, "Out of all the people at the firm, I had to run into your brother in the hallway. I mean actually *run into.*" She beamed at him like a sixteen-year-old school girl with a smashing crush, and Cory returned her amorous looks with a hint of bashfulness, a half-smile appearing on his face, lowering his gaze to his dish of rice noodles and sashimi.

"I know," Penelope said. She heard this story many times before, and although she loved Sonia and was filled with joy about her brother's loving relationship with his girlfriend, she really didn't feel like hearing the tale again.

But there it was.

"I had to go to the copy machine in another office down the hall," Sonia started. "I was trying to get some papers together for the monthly meeting between human resources and executive management – and the copy machine in our office was totally busted. Like always."

Penelope sighed. She realized that even with three-hundred-and-sixty-five days of tough, urban living behind her, she still didn't have enough moxie to stop Sonia's repeat performance – *Oh,* she thought, *the Elmont and Midwestern sweetness and niceties won't wear-off … What to do. What to do.*

"Yes," Penelope said to Sonia as she reached for another roll. "In human resources the copy machine is always down because there's so much paperwork. Human resources does so much paperwork with the employees and all." The words spilled out of Penelope's mouth as though they were her own, and yet, they were Sonia's words spoken numerous times before at dinners, happy hours, family get-togethers, and the occasional phone call when Penelope wanted to discuss her own love life.

Anytime Sonia had a chance to tell the story – there it was.

"That's right," Sonia said to Penelope. "Anyway, I was hurrying to the copy machine because of the meeting, and at the same time, your brother was rushing to meet an irate client in the office next to the one I was going to."

"Uh-huh," Penelope said with a tone of interest, trying to convey that she was giving Sonia her full and undivided attention, but in fact, she fell short of that endeavor by focusing most of her attention on a handsome blonde boy with a sunshine smile sitting two tables away from them.

"And well - we just ran smack into each other!" Sonia exclaimed, her blue eyes sparkling "And we fell in the middle of the hallway at the firm! And my papers went flying, and his briefcase went flying! And it was like out of one of those movies. Like … um …"

"Like a Tom Hanks and Meg Ryan movie," Penelope inserted, grabbing the line from a memory of when Sonia had made the analogy at a fortieth birthday party for one of her cousins who was newly divorced, dejected, and practically put on a suicide watch by the State of Illinois. Everyone there, including her mother and then her crazy Aunt Clarabelle – who wore decompressed hats from the 1950s and always seemed to put two sentences together that were never related (the bad coffee she had that morning and The State of the Union Address, her assembly job at the shoe lace factory and her husband's pattern of male baldness, global warming and the turquoise brooch she saw in the window of a California town she once visited, etcetra, etcetra) – gave Penelope a queer, put-off look as if Sonia was her responsibility, as Sonia told her story of "true love" and "soul mates" meeting while this poor relative opened her birthday presents with one hand while holding a razor and a noose in the other.

"There's no way I can meet someone at work," Penelope said as she peeked in between two people sitting at the blonde boy's table, only to see his arm around a ravishing brunette with breasts the size of torpedoes that exploded out of her halter top. Penelope noticed a majority of the men in the restaurant ogling the woman, and she peered down at her own Calvin Klein covered breasts. They were small but pert, and by her own standards and those of her two past boyfriends (the only one's she had), they were considered more than acceptable, but still, she suddenly felt that in the larger scheme of things, that they weren't up to snuff.

"*What are you doing?*" her brother yelled.

Jake immediately stopped plowing a car into a groove of the floor, and raised his pitiful eyes as if to find out what sentence was about to be handed down to him.

"Stop looking at your breasts!" Cory directed to his sister, and the little boy, realizing that he was off the hook, smacked a car into a taxicab.

"I can't believe you made me say that!" Cory exclaimed, picking up his napkin and wiping his mouth over and over again in disgust as both Penelope and Sonia looked on at him, stunned and concerned. Even the boy raised an eyebrow. "I can't believe you made me say *breasts* to you," he said to his sister, after drying his mouth to the texture of sandpaper. "But you sat there staring at them. I didn't know what else to do!"

I was comparing them to someone else's in the room."

"Well, don't compare anymore! It's disgusting when a brother has no other choice but to look at his sister's ... *things*! Forget about them! Pay attention to what Sonia's trying to tell you!"

"I am, but like I said before, there's no way I'm going to meet someone at work. They're mostly women," Penelope explained, pushing her plate away; the talk about her love life and her breasts made her lose her appetite – it had been thrown into a sunken abyss of discouragement. It was the same abyss that the image of her dream man had fallen into.

She continued, "The only single man in the office is my boss. And he isn't even that single. He's separated." Penelope thought of her wired, handsome boss, Alden Renquist, who spent his Monday mornings sputtering random ideas at his PR staff as he paced around the conference room with his hands flying in the air. He talked a mile a minute about these off-the-top-of-his-head notions concerning various accounts, and according to some tenured employees, some of the accounts he spoke of hadn't been with them for years. But still, Alden Renquist would abruptly stop an hour into their meeting, turn to the staff member of his choice and scream to him or her – "Did you hear what I said about the account? – *Do it! Do it!*" even if the account hadn't been in existence at Renquist & Renquist for eons.

Sonia said, "Separated? That seems promising," and she dragged her son up and onto her lap. He finally appeared tired and worn out after hours of playtime.

Before Penelope had a chance to react, her brother had done it for her. "Promising?" he commented, looking at his girlfriend as if she had gone crazy. "No. A separated boss is not promising." He pulled his BlackBerry from his jeans pocket." "That's it," he announced."Separated men. Breasts. Pen, I'm calling Mom. You're going home."

Sonia pushed the phone from his ear. "Stop it."

"Oh, that reminds me," Penelope said, yanking out her own BlackBerry from her Gucci-bought-in-Chinatown-bag. "My contract ends tonight. I think it may be time to get a new BlackBerry."

"What kind do you think you'll be getting?" Sonia inquired.

Penelope examined her BlackBerry for a moment, thinking about some of the girls in her office who walked around like proud peacocks with their PDAs that had flashy, colorful screens that Penelope knew nothing about. "I don't know just yet…But definitely not the one with the button."

Sonia squinted. "What button?"

"The one with the antenna looking thing." Penelope pointed to an icon on her BlackBerry screen – it was an image of an electric tower.

"Why not?"

"Well, I've been careful with this one," she explained, holding up her BlackBerry. "But I don't want to risk touching it with the next one. I don't want the phone to explode."

"What?" Sonia stared at her, furrowing her brow. "What makes you think that if you touch that icon the phone will explode?"

"Cory told me."

Sonia reached over to her boyfriend and slapped him hard on his shoulder.

Cory let out a resounding, "*Owwww!*" as he doubled over with laughter.

Uh oh, Penelope thought. *My lack of knowledge about technology – is it making me a fool again?*

"What? Who's hurt?" a voice questioned from behind them. It belonged to their friend Stacey, who arrived at Ruby Foo's with her silky brown hair done up in a loose bun, wearing a black velvet suit. She also had on heavy winter boots and pink dish washing gloves that were filled with Vaseline. This was part of Stacey's everyday dress code since she became a superstar hand and foot model after many long years of short stints as a receptionist at medical offices and massage parlors, a mover at furniture stores and fish markets, and on very few occasions, a dog walker for some elite residents of Manhattan. And it was as a dog walker that Stacey was finally discovered – taking a well-bred poodle out for a pleasant midday stroll and defecation in her open-toed Jimmy Choo stilettos, stretching her arm out to the sidewalk with pooper-scooper in hand, her finely tuned fingers and red nail polish basking in the sunlight as she went for the waste. "Dear God!" shouted a modeling agent from Queens. "Those feet! Those hands!" And the rest was history.

Stacey and her Vaseline made a sloshing sound as she hurried over to the table. "I heard an 'Ow.' Who's hurt? What's going on?" she asked as she landed in the empty chair beside Penelope.

"No one's hurt," Cory responded, "but I think there's been some damage to my sister's optimism."

"What?" Stacey asked, trying to pick up a vegetable tempura roll with a plastic glove. The roll consistently slipped from her fingers.

Penelope looked on at Stacey, trying to decide if she really wanted to divulge to her any misgivings she had about coming to New York or about the disappointments in her romantic life.

As much as she felt like pouring out her frustrations to anyone who would listen, desiring to purge her negative emotions, something she wasn't at all accustom to, Penelope still also desired to remain the wide-eyed and fresh representation of youthful hope to Stacey, who was the opposite of this model, being a disparaging character – referring to her own just-turned-thirty-year-old self as "The Wise Sage of New York." This so-called "Sage," having been a resident of the City for nine years without finding a man, was always quick to dispel any romantic notion of New York, and along with it, tossed away the idea that there were any good cleaning women in the city who could be trusted with personal belongings. ("Why did she take my aspirin?" Stacey would ask. "Everyone has aspirin. Even people in tribal countries who still sacrifice virgins at the altar have aspirin.")

Also, Penelope still had no idea about how she felt about Stacey since they had become friends through her brother – a complete default situation, with no roots in sharing similar backgrounds, interests or even a special event that happened at random that would throw two veritable strangers together.

The latter happened with Stacey and Cory. It was when he moved into his first New York City apartment that he met her. She just happened to live a couple of doors away from him. It was the morning, and Stacey was taking her trash out in her cocktail dress, when she spotted Cory trying to squeeze his couch through the door to no avail.

She gave him a big "Hi!" as he scratched his head, trying to figure out how he was going to get the couch through his window, but then Stacey set her trash bags on the floor and strolled over to him with an impromptu breakdown of her heritage, which was an interesting blend of contrasts – Irish and Filipino – and it was this unique amalgamation, the robust and the exotic, that would explain the strength and magic Stacey possessed that would, after a few seconds, result in Cory's couch falling into his apartment after she bumped it with one skinny hip.

"There," she told him with a smile that could melt many a heart.

And the rest was history.

No, Penelope thought to herself after mulling over Stacey's usual skeptical attitude, *I won't talk about my problems to Stacey.*

"Stacey, it's been horrible!" Penelope blurted out. "I haven't had a boyfriend since I got here!"

Stacey dropped her roll from her fingers – this time on purpose for dramatic effect. "I told you. This city is no place for single women looking for men. There are too many of us and too little of them." She glowered. "You want a man. You go to Alaska."

Penelope imagined herself in an igloo writing up press releases while her husband would be out in the wild harpooning salmon.

"No one's going to Alaska," Sonia chimed in, ready to save the situation. "And I differ with you, Stacey. A lot of single women have found men here in New York. It's just that Pen is so new still. A year isn't enough time."

Stacey grimaced and waved a pink glove around. "So? What does that mean for me? I've been in New York for nine years and I still haven't met anyone.

"Well," Cory uttered, "for the past year you've been submerged in Neosporin-"

"Vaseline," she speedily inserted.

"Whatever," he said." But I'm sorry to tell you this, Stacey, but wearing heavy ointments is not attractive to men."

"There was that one guy."

"Yeah – that one guy – the freak with the fetish. He doesn't count."

"What about the eight years before then? Before the modeling and the Vaseline?"

"Did you really want to make a commitment to anyone?" he asked. "'Cuz I remember some really nice guys that you briefly dated. And most of them you just kicked to the curb with your 'I'm part Irish and part Filipino, and so I'm tougher and more interesting than you' speech."

Stacey frowned at him and crossed her arms on the table. "Well, it was true, and the speech worked with you."

"No, it didn't," he said. *"I'm not dating you."*

Cory quickly reached over to Sonia and rubbed her hand. "And I never dated her, I swear."

Sonia rolled her eyes, and Stacey did the same.

"Thanks," Stacey said. "Thanks a lot." She then turned her attention to Penelope, whose nose was sniffling as her freckles were falling. "But Penelope, you've had a lot of dates over the past year, right?" Compassion threaded through her vocal chords.

"Sure," she answered, unenthused. Penelope cleared her throat and reached for a tiara. It was now eleven-fifty seven, and she realized it was getting closer to that time when the famous ball would plummet in Times Square, and the paired up City people would give their significant others smooth kisses over Cognac and Cosmopolitans while the Bridge and Tunnel twosomes from Brooklyn and New Jersey and other adjacent netherlands would plant slobbers on each other over beers and plates of stale nachos, leaving the single people, the black sheep of the love fest, to sit around licking their own deep and raw wounds.

Penelope gazed over at Stacey, who was busy cleaning up a drizzle of Vaseline from her wrist with a napkin. *This is it,* she thought. *It's just me and Stacey – the "Wise Old Sage of New York" and "The Foolish Girl from Elmont, Illinois"* … Oh, how she missed simple, uncomplicated Elmont.

"You didn't like any of the guys?" Stacey inquired as she went to grab a tiara with both rubber gloves.

Jake was full of glee as he watched her like she was a clown at a circus playing the role of klutz, trying to maneuver the tiara onto her head, until it dropped, and then he clapped and giggled, "Do Again! Do again!"

"Yeah, I liked some of the guys," Penelope answered. "But then they didn't like me. I mean, I guess they didn't like me because I didn't hear from most of them after the first date." Then she thought about it. "Maybe it's just the way I met them. Maybe they weren't the best places – bars, the internet." Penelope adjusted her "Happy New Year 2008" tiara on her head, and then suddenly, her face lit-up. "There was this one guy who I met on an internet dating site. He was so cute-wavy, brown hair, nice eyes, dimples." Penelope added, "Nice body."

"Uh," Cory complained, "do I have to hear this from my sister?"

Sonia commented, "I remember him. That guy you told me about a couple of months back-who looked like JFK Jr.? The guy who owned the shipping company."

"That's the one. He also owned an apartment in Chelsea," Penelope said with a smile.

"Wait," Stacey interceded. "He owns his own company? An actual *tangible* company? Not one that's just a web site? And he owns real estate-*in New York? In Chelsea?* So what happened to him?" Stacey's face scrunched up, and she chomped on a vegetable tempura hand roll that she somehow managed to get to her mouth (the pointy end seemed to be key).

Penelope's smile turned to a frown. "I don't know. He never called. We went out once for drinks and everything seemed to be great. We got along well and we laughed a lot, but I never heard from him."

It was nearing midnight, Penelope thought, and everyone was poised for the countdown, ready to break free from 2007 with their horns blowing and their noisemakers cracking, and their lips smacking.

"Quick," Sonia said to Penelope, "it's almost midnight. What's your resolution for your second year in New York?"

Before Penelope had a chance to even think about it, Sonia answered for her – "I know! Your resolution should be to *not* to look for a guy!" Sonia's eyes sparked. "It's so obvious, Pen. You're looking *way* too hard! That's the problem. When you look, you don't find. When you don't look…Well, it's like that saying about happiness…happiness - love- is like a butterfly that will come and sit softly on your shoulder."

Stacey stopped gnawing on the seaweed of her hand roll. "No," she adamantly stated. "No. You're screwed either way – whether you look for them or not. And I must say this," she said, directing her angst at Sonia, letting her roll plop onto the table cloth, "I'm sick…SICK… I tell you of hearing about butterflies! Everything is about a butterfly! Or there's a connotation about a butterfly-like if you love something set it free, if it comes back, it's yours, if it doesn't it was never yours to begin with – probably about a butterfly! And I say-if it doesn't come back to you, go find it and kill it!"

Sonia's and Penelope's mouth fell open in surprise at their friend's sudden outburst, and Jake covered his ears, but Cory laughed, "Now there's the girl I never dated!" and then, after his guffawing wound down to a chuckle, he turned to his sister and said, "I can tell you what your resolution should be. You should say 'sorry' once in a while!" Cory bent over the table towards Penelope. "Mom told me that she hasn't heard a sorry from you in a year! Even when you bumped into one of our neighbors when you last visited! Even when you almost ran over Mr. Foster, the grocer, with Dad's new Chevy pick-up – No sorry!"

Penelope gasped. She didn't want to upset her mother, but then there was her mustached-guru from the AT& T store from last year who communicated to her that "sorry" wasn't commonplace in Manhattan.

Feeling tugged by Elmont on one end and by New York on the other, Penelope burst out – "I'm just trying to assimilate!"

"No," Stacey joined in again, "I've got something better than that." Everyone leaned into listen, except for Penelope, who wasn't sure if she should be in wild anticipation of what Stacey had to say. After all, it looked as though just moments ago, after the butterfly comment, her head was going to spin around and that she was going to shoot vomit. This, along with her brother practically berating her about her decision to reduce the usage of the simple phrase – "I'm sorry" – from probably around fifty times a day to zero, was not a good omen for other suggested resolutions.

"You should return people's texts!" Stacey declared.

Penelope squinted, having no idea what she was talking about. "What?"

Cory and Sonia nodded in agreement, emphatic in their head gesture.

"I've tried to get you hundreds of times," Cory said, "to go out, to tell you something about the family, what's going on at museums. Constantly! And you don't answer my texts!"

Sonia added, "Me, too! I've texted you about so many Happy Hours, and I never heard back from you!"

Stacey concluded, "It's SO rude."

Penelope shook her hands in the air, the strap of her Calvin Klein dress falling off a shoulder, and yelled, "Wait a minute! What are you talking about?"

Suddenly, each of Cory's eyes grew almost as large as the ball that was about to fall in Times Square. "Oh my God," he said, "You don't have text messaging!" and all at once, the entire restaurant began to count down to the New Year, and over and in between the numbers, the chatter went on:

"TEN!" the crowd yelled.

Stacey and Sonia gasped in horror.

"No, I don't. So what?" Penelope said, still unaware of any dire problems, but having a flashback to her experience with the AT & T guru, and how he offered her the service, and what she told him (*Please don't add the text messaging service. I won't be needing it.*).

"NINE!"

"I don't need texts!" she proclaimed. "I have email!"

Stacey and Sonia almost passed out.

"EIGHT!

"But it's instant messaging!" her brother shouted.

"SEVEN!"

"Everyone uses it!" Cory's girlfriend bellowed.

"SIX!"

"ALL those guys who didn't call!" their Irish-Filipino friend quickly hollered.

"FIVE!"

"They've all been texting you!" the three cried out in unison.

Penelope began to sweat and her heart started to palpitate.

"FOUR!"

'Don't worry! Homeland security!" Cory shouted.

"THREE!"

"They can retrieve the texts!" he announced.

"TWO!"

"With the texts … !" her friends and family exclaimed.

"ONE!"

"YOU COULD HAVE HAD A WHOLE OTHER LIFE!" her brother yelled.

"HAPPY NEW YEAR!"

George Bailey: What is it that you want, Mary?
What do you want? You the want the moon? Just
say the word and I'll throw a lasso around it and
pull it down.

Three

It was the morning of New Year's Day that Penelope made a special phone call to AT & T.

Before that moment, Penelope spent most of her early morning hours sitting on her couch, wearing the same Calvin Klein dress (albeit it was disheveled), in her four-hundred square foot studio, as if she was in a fog, repeating her brother's tour de force phrase of the night in her mind over and over again – "You could have had a whole other life … You could have had a whole other life …You could have had a whole other life." Eventually, after an hour or two, this unremitting sentence in her head streamlined into a sort of chant and then grounded into a soothing hum that aided her in falling asleep.

But even in her dreams she couldn't run away from Cory's comment and her angst about her mistake that all at the New Year's Eve table agreed resulted in Penelope's catastrophic first year in New York City, and possibly, according to Stacey, the tragedy called "The Rest of

Penelope's Life" – "Just think of it," Stacey told her, "if you were meant to be going down one path, and then this text messaging glitch blew you right off. You can be in an alternate universe of which no one knows where your life is going to!"

In Penelope's dreams, or nightmares rather, the letters of the phrase "You could have had a whole other life" quickly followed her as she ran away from them through hills and valleys and beside streams. It was like one big sign ribboning through the air, straight at her, and then faces popped onto the scene – Stacey's face, Sonia's face, Cory's face, even little Jake's face – and they all murmured remarks about her ignorance concerning text messaging, her lack of sophistication of the modern day world, and then there was a finale – Cory would mention again the possible savior of the text messaging situation called "Homeland Security" – "Homeland security! They can retrieve the texts!"

At this statement, Penelope immediately woke up like a ball at a shot-put event being thrust out by an Olympian, sitting straight as an arrow on her sheets, although her rusty-brown hair poked out at different angles from her head. She glanced over at her wall clock; it was seven a.m. and time, she decided, to first dial the one who spawned the idea.

"Hello?" her brother answered the call. He sounded groggy.

"Did you mean what you said?" Penelope asked.

"What? ... Who is this?"

"Cory, it's Pen."

"Oh, Pen." He reacted casual at first as if they were having nice conversation about sunshine or the bluebirds of spring, but then his voice bolted through the receiver – "Pen! It's seven in the morning! What the hell are you calling me for?"

"Did you mean what you said?"

"Mean what I said? What are you talking about?"

"About Homeland Security-that I can get my text messages back?"

Cory sighed. "Oh, that."

Penelope could hear Sonia in the background inquire, "Who is it?" with a cough and a sniffle.

"It's just Pen," he told her.

Penelope thought, *well that's just fine and dandy* – *'It's just Pen.'* "Look, Cory. You're the one who brought up the Homeland Security thing in the first place. You're the one who said I could have had a whole other life." She began to ponder. "You know what? I could have been… I could have been …" Penelope scratched her head while she tried to figure out the end of her sentence. On the way, she found a patch of bulbous hair and patted it down, unaware of all the acute strands that sprung from her scalp.

Suddenly, a light bulb went off in her brain. "I could have been royalty," she said.

"What?" his voice bristled.

"I met a duke, once, and I gave him my number," she clarified as she grabbed her BlackBerry from her coffee table and shook it, hoping the jostling motion would actually cause the BlackBerry to light up like a pinball machine, when in which her text messages would miraculously appear through its tiny screen – its window – that would lead her into a different and more agreeable life. "I did," she continued, "I met a duke, and he probably text messaged me."

Cory moaned, "Nooo, you did not meet a duke. It was just a dream, and hey, guess what? If you go back to sleep right now, I bet you can catch up on that dream again. I think that's a great idea, don't you?"

"It wasn't a dream," Penelope retorted. "I met a tall, dark and handsome duke at the Four Seasons who had to leave the next day for his homeland."

"No you didn't."

"Yes, I did."

Cory groaned. "No. What you met was an Italian guy from New Jersey who was in the City for a sales convention." Then he added, "And he probably had to go back home the next day to be with his wife."

"Ohhhh," she said, perusing the idea. She remembered a name tag pinned to the duke's shirt that was nicely tucked away under his suit jacket until he stretched to put his arm around her. The duke told her it was an official tag given to him by his country's embassy that would award him certain unique privileges such as complete immunity, an uncapped amount of drinks for himself and his *special friends*, along with a mammoth deluxe suite, if he'd like – wink, wink; she thought he had something in his eye and offered him a q-tip, suggesting how he could gently pry out the gook.

"Dear God," Cory commented, "there should definitely be a handbook for small-town girls planning to live in big cities … Am I going to have to keep on worrying about you, Penelope? Are you ever going to be smart about things? Are you going to be all right?"

Instead of paying attention to Cory's older-brother criticisms, which she was getting tired of, Penelope blinked at her BlackBerry and started to shake it again. Only this time much harder and quicker. *I'm going to get those text messages out of you! I'm going to get those text messages out of you!*

"What in the name of…Sonia?" Cory inquired. "Are we having an earthquake? What's all that rattling I hear?" Then he asked, "Pen, what are you doing? You're not doing something with your BlackBerry are you? … You know what happens if you shake or drop your BlackBerry, don't you? They have a special police task force that'll come over to where you are and beat you senseless!"

Penelope heard a slapping noise through the phone.

"Owww!" her brother screamed.

"Stop that!" Sonia commanded.

Penelope stared at the screen. Still nothing – although she had no idea what a text message would look like, but still, she was pretty sure that her last ditch effort to somehow retrieve the messages on her own was unfruitful, and so she stopped her shaking and huffed to Cory, "Is it true about Homeland Security, though? Do you think they can give me my messages?"

"I can tell that you're going to obsess about this until I give you an answer," he said. "I can only say this - I think so. These days we're so afraid of terrorist attacks. There has to be some government workers out there saving the country's texts. Why not? I mean - they tap into our phone conversations, right?"

Penelope grabbed a pen and a Chinese take-out receipt from her coffee table. "Okay," she said to him, flipping the receipt over to its blank side, "give me their number."

Cory laughed and shrieked like a surprised but amused schoolgirl –
"*Give you the number? Give you the number?* I don't have the number!
Homeland Security wouldn't give out their number! Suppose someone
was a terrorist and they called Homeland Security to find out where
they were? …You wouldn't want to call them up and have them think
you're a terrorist, would you?"

"No, of course not!" Penelope quickly hollered, thinking that she
wouldn't hold up that well in Guantanamo Bay, and how she wouldn't
have known anything about it if it weren't for a manic rant her boss had
in front of the entire office some Monday mornings ago – "If you don't
get this campaign up and going, I'm going to make sure all of you
disappear!" her boss yelled. "How hard is it to PR zit cream? Call up
Seventeen magazine for God's sake! … That's it-I'm going to have you
all thrown in jail! Better yet- Guantanamo Bay! You girls will love that-
limp hair! Limp and frizzy hair!" The agency let out a collective gasp as
he slammed his office door behind him. Afterward, all the girls in the
office crowded around the computer of the firm's Account Supervisor
– Ginger – an attractive blonde with an all-American face and perfectly
conservative clothes; they questioned in hushed voices what the
particulars were of Guantanamo Bay as Ginger's Google search led to
an easy click and then, pictures of terrorist prisoners and their captors,
followed by the startled looks of the high-heeled and freshly-lipsticked
mob.   Ginger nervously tapped on her mouse, saying, "I thought-
Guantanamo Bay-maybe a new place to vacation in the Caribbean? It
sounded like it. Right?"

"So I can't call Homeland Security?" Penelope said to her brother.
"So what do I do?"

"It's simple," he answered. "Call up AT & T. They probably had
something like this happen before. You can call today even. I think
they're open on holidays. And they have 24-hour service."

Penelope read aloud what she was writing on the receipt – "Call AT
& T for text messages."

"Oh, my God," Cory said, sounding like he was pulling away from
the phone. "Sonia, she's going to be reviewing her text messages from
all last year. We're never going to see her. Never, I tell you," and then

he remarked, "See you next New Year's Eve, Pen. Ruby Foo's sound good to you?"

Penelope gritted her teeth.

***

It took Penelope a good ten minutes of calling AT & T to go through a series of numbers that first lead her to the recording of a woman's congenial voice that said, "Due to an unusually high call volume we're experiencing a long hold time," and then, to a menu of choices which had her press zero for customer service, which then put her smack dab again in the middle of another menu and then, as she wiped the sweat from her brow, another press of the zero for customer service. This eventually forced her into making the choice of taking a survey or not after she talked to a representative. By this time, Penelope became flustered and pressed any digit causing an opt-out of speaking to a customer service representative, going directly to the survey. Penelope sighed as she realized she couldn't possibly answer anything on the survey about customer service when she hadn't even talked to them in the first place. So she hung up on AT & T, but as light and politely as she could, concerned that any sign of rudeness that could be trailed back to her might be an impediment to her mission. She dialed once more, and then got the same messages, but this time, she didn't make the mistake of choosing the survey option, which brought her to a recording of the same friendly woman from all the menus, telling her that their offices were closed for the holidays, and that she should call back during business hours the next day.

The next morning, there was a woman's giggle on the other end of the phone. *"Excuse me?"* the AT & T Customer Service Representative asked.

Penelope's freckled-face turned a flush red – *What went wrong? Was there something funny about my question?*

She gathered all her courage to repeat her inquiry – "I didn't have text messaging services all last year, and I was wondering if I could retrieve the text messages that were sent to me. I heard that you might have them."

"Uh-huh," the Operator said, making a noise as if she was gasping for air.

Penelope could hear a muffled sound. It was obvious to her that the operator put her hand over the receiver. There was an audible mumbling, and then, when the operator took her hand off the phone, Penelope listened to the peals of laughter coming from the helpful customer service staff at AT & T.

Penelope decided to go on the offensive as she stood in the middle of her den-kitchenette area wearing her black, pinstriped skirt suit that she was quick to iron that morning, trying to get in enough time to call AT & T before she had to leave for work. *Hey,* she thought to herself, *I pay my bills on time. They should treat me better. I even pay them early.* "Well, I heard about Homeland Security," she asserted, posturing upright and tall, serious as a heart attack.

"And?" the operator asked.

Penelope could decipher an underlying mocking in the operator's voice.

Suddenly not so self-assured, she nervously pulled some strands of hair behind an ear, and added, "And I guess they're supposed to keep all the text messages … like in the country."

There was a deafening silence for a few moments and then – "Can you please repeat that?" the representative requested, her voice even and professional. "I don't think I heard you right, Miss." There was a sudden warm sort of jingling in the representative's voice that Penelope found very inviting. It reminded her of the happy intonations of saleswomen at Greely's, a local department store in Elmont, Illinois, who were always amiable to shoppers, especially during the cheery holiday season with all the comings and goings of the town's families and the families' friends.

But, unfortunately for Penelope, it wasn't the holiday season in Elmont at *Greely's*. Rather, it was the day after the holiday season had ended, in New York City, when everyone had to go back to work, many less than enthusiastic about starting another year at their job and disappointed about what happened with their New Year's Eve plans that might've involved eating chicken wings in front of the television while watching the ball drop with their unemployed boyfriend as he wiped the blue cheese dressing off of his chin (cheese and boyfriend as lumpy as a centuries old mattress), and some weren't too thrilled with their Christmas gifts that might've included moth-eaten socks dug out of a clearance barrel at a bargain basement or a toilet brush painted to look like a French maid.

It was possible that one of these profiles fit Penelope's AT & T Customer Service Representative, but too lost in the jingling voices of the saleswomen of Elmont, Penelope lost her sense of situation. "Yes," she said to the AT & T operator, being very agreeable as she became more relaxed with the phone conversation. "I'll repeat what I said."

Penelope went on and even included more information – "I want to get my text messages back, and I heard that Homeland Security would have them-so can you get them for me?" Realizing there had been a strange echo when she talked, Penelope bit her lip, not knowing what was going on.

Only seconds later, an inferno of laughter, which had a magnitude far more intense, and therefore, more humiliating than the simple "peal" of laughter she had heard before, filled Penelope's ear.

The AT & T operator had her on speakerphone.

Penelope furrowed her brow, perturbed beyond all measure. "Really," she growled, her tiny body shuddering and hopping in place as she spoke, "is it necessary to have me on speakerphone?"

There was an immediacy to the representative shutting off the speaker phone and claiming to be an innocent. "Miss, I don't know what you're talking about."

Deciding to get to the point, Penelope asked her question straight-out. "Look, can you or can you not get me my text messages?"

"Uh-no."

Penelope went silent and slowly leveraged herself to her couch, crushed by the operator's answer and by a future, heavy and looming with regret – *I should have taken the text messaging service…Why didn't I take the text messaging service? … It was all those services offered on my BlackBerry …*

What the heck?- I got confused … That's right … I got confused … It was that salesman. Then, she huffed, picturing the sinister mustached-man who decided not to inform her of the grave mistake she would make if she didn't have text messaging. *Ooooh,* Penelope burned as much as she could – a flickering aromatic candle (a scent of gingerbread) – and imagined pinching the salesman's mustache a bit with two of her delicate fingers. At one point she was so angry that she even pictured his mustache coming off as she tightened her grip on the coarse hairs, but then she quickly let go – the sweetness and niceties of her Midwestern, Elmont upbringing having won again.

"Would you like to order text messaging service now?" the operator inquired. "Because if you do, you'll only have to add on ten-dollars for the service. It's the special for today."

Penelope shirked off her unpleasant thoughts long enough to answer what was, of course, a no-brainer. "Yes, I'd like the text messaging service," she said and then suddenly realized something. "Hey," Penelope reacted, "weren't you running that same special about a year ago? Like almost the same day a year ago?"

"I don't know, Miss."

Penelope was enflamed with ire at everyone who worked for AT & T – the salesman at the AT & T store, the phone representative at the AT & T Customer Service Center, the AT & T Customer Service Center as a whole, and the woman on the dizzying and emotionally disturbing AT & T recordings – and she pushed the issue – "What do you mean you don't know? You should know, don't you think?" She yelled, "How could you say that you're having a special when it clearly isn't that *special* since you had it last year?"

The representative was silent for a couple of seconds, and then said, "I see that you're having a problem that I'm not equipped or trained to help you with. Would you like me to transfer you to a supervisor?"

"No! Whatever you do, don't transfer me!" Penelope spouted while her hands moved around in chaotic circles; there was no way she was going to chance being rerouted to another menu. "Just add on the service."

After a minute or so of the representative processing Penelope's order to finally have text messaging service (Yeah!), the representative said, "Now, there's just the matter of you paying your bill. You're about a week late."

Penelope shook her head in disbelief. "What? What are you talking about? I paid my bill! I pay early!"

"Yes. We know. You've paid your bills for January and February. But there's still the matter of March." She continued, "Our computers have reformatted your account to integrate your personal payment schedule with the rest of our customers' accounts. Which means it's January for others, but it's March for you."

This was all too much for Penelope to handle.

Feeling a huge migraine headache coming on, she began to rub her forehead and tried to remain calm. "I've never heard anything like this before," she commented, her voice a few octaves higher than an alto pitch.

"Well, Ms. McAdams, no one has ever paid their bill two months early," the representative snickered, and then again, there was an overflow of rip-roaring laughter, and even some snorts, streaming through the phone.

Frustrated not only with the conversation, but with most likely running late for work because of it, Penelope snidely remarked, "Your computers can do all that, and they can't get my text messages from Homeland Security?"

With swiftness, the representative replied, "Gee, Miss McAdams, you sure do mention Homeland Security a great deal."

Remembering her phone call with her brother from the morning before, Penelope began to hyperventilate. "I'm not a terrorist!" she exclaimed. "I'm just a single woman living in New York!" And she hung up the phone.

***

"You have a secret it. I know it," Wendy, Penelope's co-worker, commented, her bright blue eyes peering at her over the cubicle wall that separated their desks.

Wendy, a Manhattanite for the past five years of her life and a Long Islander for the rest of it, grew suspicious since not a peep came out of Penelope's cubicle the entire morning and afternoon as she stared at her computer screen for hours.

But then again, from the very first time they had met, Wendy always said and thought that Penelope had traveled from Elmont to New York with a suitcase full of secrets. It was Wendy's own estimation that anyone who came from a town where the population only reached into the thousands and didn't have an underground transit system or Loehmann's, had to be involved in unmentionable acts which periodically wound up on "Cops" or "To Catch a Predator" or were collected and thrown in a closet; it was not unlike how women in Manhattan treated their shoes, except that a scintillating pump would be taken out for some fresh air every now and then while these great secrets were always kept hidden, cloistered even. Scathing small-town secrets, she once told Penelope — the town mayor's murder that was covered up to look like an accident (strychnine in his pie, actually), the ice cream parlor owner whose parents were first cousins and whose aunt and uncle were sister and brother and grandparents (although Wendy never really thought that idea through to test its plausibility), the hundreds of dollars from the town's treasury allocated to build a road to a more civilized territory stolen by a ninety-year-old woman, who was the town's poet laureate and world renowned wood-whittler.

Penelope couldn't fathom how Wendy came up with such extreme conclusions (after all, it was a bad batch of moonshine that did the mayor in), but she accepted the reality of her weird mind, because beyond what she thought of small towns, Penelope felt that Wendy was the nicest person in the office, having been friendly, courteous, and polite to her from day one (*I have some extra post-its,* Wendy said, *I stole them from the account supervisor's desk — want some? ... Did you see the Bachelorette show the other night?* she asked. *I can't believe she chose him-they should call it an "unreality" TV show*).

So Wendy would constantly say to Penelope, "You have a secret. I know it" or "Come on. Spill it!" while she frothed at the mouth like a rabid writer for Page Six, spinning yarns around the spindle in her mind, while Penelope put up with it, sighing and smiling, but always eventually disappointing.

This time was no different, at least in the beginning, and Penelope sighed and smiled, "No, Wendy. I don't have a secret."

Wendy grimaced and propped her chin on the cubicle wall, still staring down at Penelope, running her fingers through her long and lustrous black hair. Penelope observed, as she had done many times before, how Wendy's hair curled up at her chin and around the length of her neck, and how attractive the color looked against her alabaster skin. Penelope always thought that Wendy was very pretty, naturally pretty, but she noticed that even though Wendy may have known about her attractiveness, it still didn't seem to affect her ego wise. She wasn't big in the head. If anything, she seemed to be little on the insecure side, wanting to keep up with the "Joneses" of the office, although she claimed she had less money than most of the women there. (*I'm from Long Island, yes, but I'm a Suffolk County girl*, she told Penelope, *from Hauppauge. These girls are from the Five Towns area – like Cedarhurst, Woodmere, and Hewlett. "Snootsville" in Nassau County.*)

"Hey," Wendy uttered, trying to get Penelope's attention that wandered back to her computer. "Did you see my suit today?" She tugged the collar of her jacket and whispered, "Donna Karan ... Loehmann's ... One-hundred dollars. Almost fifty percent off of the real price." Wendy nodded proudly; she liked to tell Penelope, and only Penelope, of her great clothing buys, trusting her not to say anything to the Long Island "Snootsvilles" or "Blue Bloods," as she called them, whose noses might look down at her for not shopping at a boutique or fashionista department store such as Saks or Bergdorf's.

Wendy considered it a personal triumph to obtain designer clothes at lower cost than if she purchased them at trendier places. She liked to beat retailers at their own game and then to share her good fortune with Penelope, seemingly thinking that if she herself was the only one who knew of her wonderful and fortuitous buys, that it wouldn't seem to matter as much. Penelope thought it to be akin to the old conundrum – if a tree falls in the woods, and no one is around to hear it, does it make a sound?

"Did you see my shoes today?" Wendy asked.

Penelope shook her head and then rested an elbow on her desk, languidly cradling her chin in her hand. She felt tired and still disappointed over the morning's phone call with AT & T.

Wendy looked like the proverbial cat that ate the canary. She was sly and quiet as she moved from her cubicle to Penelope's, squeezing herself in, and then stretching her leg out as if she was beginning to do a dance number from "A Chorus Line." She was wearing five-inch high-heeled, patent leather shoes that had shiny, silver buckles. They reminded Penelope of the buckles on the Pilgrim's shoes she had seen in some textbook pictures and museum paintings.

"They're nice," Penelope commented, not really looking at them, her eyes still fixed on the computer.

"They're Prada… How much do you think they cost?" she asked, playing a game that she frequently liked Penelope to participate in called, simply enough, "Guess How Much this Cost?" that made Penelope feel more assured that one day she would be ready to go on the "Price is Right."

But she was still a long distance away from that.

Penelope threw out – "Ten dollars?"

Wendy's eyes widened. She put her hand to her chest and made like she was about to fall backwards as if she was on the verge of having severe coronary arrest. "PRADA TEN DOLLARS? ARE YOU HIGH? … Hey. What's that?" she inquired, turning her attention to Penelope's computer screen.

It was a project Penelope was working on – a list of all the men she had gone on dates with during her first year in Manhattan that could have text her. The list included a brief description of each.

"It's nothing," she replied, but then had a second thought about it. *Well,* Penelope said to herself, *she does trust me with the prices of her clothing. I guess I could trust her with this.*

She also realized that she did possibly have a secret. *No one in the office would know.*

"I guess I do have a secret," Penelope said to her.

Wendy's eyes sparked, and she lunged toward Penelope, closing in on her personal space. She rested her elbows on her co-worker's desk, ready to hear the long awaited secret that only a small-town girl could possess.

Penelope suddenly went quiet.

"So tell me," Wendy pushed.

Penelope took a deep breath and then confessed, "I know nothing about technology."

Instead of the surprised expression that she expected, Penelope received only a couple of blinks from her co-worker's baby blues.

Wendy stood up again. "Well, I know that," she said. "We all know that."

Penelope wound up being the one with the surprised expression. "What do you mean *we all know that?*"

Placing a compassionate hand on Penelope's shoulder, Wendy remarked, "Honey, your weekly hours sheets and media pitch lists are in WordPerfect format."

"So?"

"So the rest of us - the rest of the PR world - uses Excel."

"Oh, that's nothing. That's not technology," Penelope disregarded.

"Sure it is. It's technology software."

Penelope crossed her arms, upset that Wendy's knowledge of her technological inadequacies was just coming to her attention.

Wendy continued, "And the text messages." She threw her arms up in the air. "I've sent you text messages before, and you never answer. And I've seen you look really strangely at your BlackBerry, and I kind of had the idea that you were confused."

Aggravated, Penelope asked, "So why didn't you tell me about all this?"

"I didn't want to embarrass you."

"But you should have told me," Penelope whined, "because maybe then I would have realized how important text messages were, and then I would have gotten the service."

Wendy again put her hand to her chest like she was only moments away from being swept off to the pearly gates where just beyond its majestic bars were myriads of sample sales.

"Are you telling me that you don't have text messaging?" she asked, loud enough for a cluster of account executives to look over their cubicles.

"Shhh!" Penelope put an index finger to her lips and pulled Wendy down to her face. "I don't want anyone to know."

"Are you shitting me?" Wendy asked, her eyes growing large once more.

"No, but I have it now. Since this morning. But I didn't have it then. Like all last year."

"Are you shitting me?" Wendy repeated.

Penelope insisted, "Stop saying that." She wrinkled her nose and curled her bottom lip as if she caught a whiff of a bad odor. "And all that cursing." Not like she hadn't heard it before around the office, the bars, clubs, and the streets of the city, but nonetheless, Penelope could hear her mother's disapproval in her ear and feel the bar of soap in her mouth.

"Sorrry," Wendy retorted with sarcasm. "I'm just surprised, that's all. How on earth did you survive in Manhattan without texts?"

Penelope shrugged. "I don't know. I just did." Her fingers started to tap on her keyboard.

After Wendy stared at her for a good minute, she finally announced, "Not having text messages in the city-the primary method of communications for the entire area-is like not having oxygen." She put a hand atop of their wall. "Do you understand what I'm telling you, Penelope? You've spent an entire year without oxygen. You haven't been breathing. By all accounts, you should be dead."

"Great," Penelope said, shaking her head, continuing to work on her computer.

Wendy placed her hand on Penelope's shoulder. "You are truly a mythical figure."

Penelope turned around and squinted at her.

"How did this happen?" Wendy asked.

"Never mind. It's not worth talking about. And right now I'm just looking at this list I made up of all the guys that I went on dates with that might've sent texts to me...I'm thinking maybe I should call them, just in case…Just to be polite."

"Uh-huh," Wendy said to her, and she stared down at Penelope's computer screen.

Penelope listed about forty men she went on dates with over the past year that she could drum up from her memory. She noted that about seventy-five percent of them she met on internet dating sites, ten percent at clubs or bars, eight percent at house parties, four percent on fix-ups, two percent in street crossways, and one percent on the line at Dunkin Donuts (the donuts were for the office or for when she was deeply depressed about the other ninety-nine percent).

The first five men on her list were Penelope's top dates:

1. Luke – mid-thirties, very handsome, wavy brown hair, cute dimples, broad shoulders, just the right height (5'10), owns shipping business, lives in Chelsea loft, pays for dinner, opens the door. Nice. (Met on internet)

2. Peter – mid-thirties, ophthalmologist and eye surgeon, pasty skin, some boils on cheeks, quiet but agreeable, has three-bedroom apartment on the Upper West Side. Long nose hair. (Met on internet)

3. John – mid-twenties, in record business, very attractive, great hair and smile, speaks well, very easy to talk to, has penthouse apartment in West Village. Very fashionable. (Met at questionable club – may be gay)

4. James – late-twenties, hedge fund manager, "jock" – muscular, light blonde hair, nice green eyes, friendly, constantly talked about the Mets and the Rangers and his salary. Brought his own dinner knife to restaurant – pretty big knife. Owns nice condo with balcony in the Meat Packing district (Met at sports bar)

5. Matthew – early thirties, accountant, average looking, had nothing to say, nodded a lot, had to pay for my own meal, owns

condo in Upper West Side and two buildings in Astoria, Queens (Note: met on internet, but he used his friend's photo instead of his own).

"Penelope," Wendy quipped as she read, "Luke. Peter. John. James. Matthew? ... I didn't know that you were dating Apostles."

Rolling her eyes at the list and throwing her arms up, Penelope declared, "I don't even know why I'm even bothering with this. I don't even think I still have any of these guys numbers, and even if I did have their numbers, I'd feel stupid if I called them and found out they weren't trying to contact me. Stupid. Which would make things even worse." She shook her head. "If I could only get those text messages back." Penelope told her sob story – "I tried to get the messages from AT & T. I thought they could get them from Homeland Security, but they told me they couldn't...Wendy, they laughed at me."

Before Penelope uttered another word, Wendy was practically on the floor, doubling over with huge chuckles, some fluid coming out of her nose. *She's snorting*, Penelope thought. *She's like those people at AT & T customer service.* "Stop that," Penelope ordered, trying to keep the volume of her voice to a minimum, not wishing to get fired.

Wendy wobbled in her discount Prada shoes as she worked on regaining a regular stance and tried to clear some of her throat of whatever giggles lay dormant that could slip out while she was talking. "I'm sorry," she relayed to Penelope, her eyes tearing. "I just can't believe you did that." Then, only a second afterward, Wendy couldn't help herself anymore, and the hundreds of giggles that she had held in, produced one loud squeal, setting a domino effect of heads turning and cropping up over cubicles, including the head of the last domino that belonged to the Account Supervisor, Ginger.

Ginger shot up from her cubicle and glared at both of them, letting out a big "Shhhhhh!"

Wendy bit her fist, holding back the chuckles.

"I don't think it's *that* funny," Penelope chastised, turning her back on her coworker.

Wendy pulled her knuckles from her mouth. "Sure it is. Getting back your old text messages? Homeland Security? It's all hysterical," she said in a lowered voice. She twined a thick wave of her hair on a finger and flashed a smile. "Homeland Security? What were you thinking?"

Penelope didn't know what she was thinking, but she recalled her reaction. "I told them I wasn't a terrorist."

"Oh," Wendy said, "I'm sure that'll be great for your FBI file." She leaned against the shared wall of their cubicle, suddenly deep in thought. "You know," she said to her, narrowing her sky-eyes, "I actually might be able to help you."

Penelope's chair swiveled round, her interest peaking, and she looked at Wendy's face – it was earnest. "What do you mean?"

Wendy crouched down to her and quietly explained, "Listen, you know my ex-boyfriend, Gary. The one I see every now and then."

"For the booty call," Penelope added, remembering she hadn't heard anyone ever use that term until she came to New York (and she still couldn't crack the case of what a "sex call" would have to do with boots.)

"Yeah, whatever," Wendy brushed off. "Anyway, he has this friend, they've been friends for the past three years, who's supposedly a genius when it comes to technology. Something like he went to one of those big tech colleges on a full scholarship…um…What was it called?" she asked herself aloud and then snapped her fingers, "MIT, that's it. And he lived in Washington, D.C. afterward. He was working for some big company doing some really difficult stuff like cracking codes and shit like that." Penelope heard the curse word and wiggled her freckled nose, getting ready to wrinkle it again. "He was big time," Wendy continued, but then a shadow of gloom fell on her features. "And then it happened… He walked in on his fiancé cheating on him. He was so devastated that he left her, the job, and Washington, D.C. and moved here." She shook her head. "Supposedly, he was completely heartbroken - almost had a breakdown."

At the end of Wendy's tale, Penelope's jaw dropped, her expression a muddle of shock and dismay. She knew that cheating happened, but in her heart, she couldn't see how someone could do that to another person. Especially if they loved them – at least at one time. "That's horrible."

Wendy nodded. "Now he works for himself," she said. "His office is in his apartment. Gary tells me he's not even doing half the things that he could do career wise, and that he's mostly alone."

Penelope frowned. Although she didn't know this individual on a personal level, she wanted to shed a tear for him. She understood how it felt to be "alone" since she left Elmont. Even with her brother residing in New York and with some of the friends she made – who were more like acquaintances, actually – and the millions of people she shared the city with, she still walked the pavement like a lone and wandering lamb trying to find her flock of sheep. "That's terrible," she said without hesitation.

"Yeah," Wendy agreed and then stood up. "I met him one time. At a party. He's a tall and scraggly looking guy," she told her. "Not very social. Said a few words to me and basically hid in the corner. Anyway, like I said before-he's a genius this guy… I think his name is Ted." She went over to her cubicle, saying, "If anyone could get back those text messages, he'd be the one."

"Okay," Penelope uttered, having to force a smile on her face after she heard the sad story, but then her body began to throb with excitement. "But how do we do this?"

"Leave that to me. I'm going to the movies with Gary tonight, and I'll discuss it with him. This guy and my ex are pretty friendly. They hang out together. I'm sure Gary can talk him into doing a favor." She added, "He sure talks *me* into doing favors."

Wendy suddenly giggled a bit.

"What's so funny?" Penelope inquired, her eyes lighting up at her computer screen – the project, her list, had now been resuscitated with the breath of hope. Ted would help her, she thought. Ted would be the answer. *Good old Ted.*

"Oh, I was just thinking," Wendy responded, trying to muffle her snorts. "This guy- other than the fact that he's a social outcast- would SO not be for you. Not that I was really thinking about it anyway." She asked, "You know what all those guys on the top of your list have in common?"

Penelope squinted at the printed words on her screen. "No. What?"

"They all have great living accommodations."

Penelope reviewed the first five men on her list. *By golly,* she thought, *she's right!*

"And this guy has horrible living accommodations. Gary told me he basically lives in a dungeon near the South Street Seaport. Like he lives in the underworld. Like a hobbit. Try not to be scared when you go over there."

"I won't," Penelope relayed but shook in her shoes.

"Good afternoon, everyone!" exclaimed their boss, Alden Renquist, his booming voice suddenly circulating throughout the office, his salutation more imposing than friendly.

The Armani-suited Renquist moved in between and around the cubicles like an agitated head mouse in a maze. His office was the endgame – the cheese – his final destination, and lucky for Penelope, it just happened to be right next to her cubicle.

I have some huge news for all of you!" he yelled out when he got to his cheese, flipping back his wavy brown hair and pushing up his spectacles. Everyone in the office stood up in their cubicles to watch and listen.

He announced, "We're taking on a new client in the tech industry! I won't tell you who, because we haven't made the official announcement yet, but I think it's safe to say that the CEO of the company makes more money than God! And yes, ladies-and maybe some men-he is married." Renquist cleared his throat and continued, "And this company makes the best technology equipment around, and I'm looking to put one of you, one of my *wonderful* staff, at the helm of the account!" Everyone in the office searched around for the lucky person. "Now, I don't feel charitable these days, but I do feel crazy! The position is open to anyone! That includes lower-level and mid-level account executives who can show me what they can do!" All the eyes in the room lit up. Renquist pushed a wayward wave off of his forehead and with vigor declared, "And for the person who's picked for the account, it will be a boost in position, salary, and they will have the benefit of a great deal of traveling!"

Penelope's ears perked up, and she grinned. *Maybe an office instead of a cubicle? Maybe a one-bedroom instead of a studio? Traveling around the world like some of those girls on "Manhattan Nights"? Wow.*

Suddenly, she heard a "Psssst" sound. Penelope turned around to where it was coming from to find that it was hissing out of Wendy's mouth. Wendy's eyes darted out of her head as she mouthed to Penelope – "Nooooo."

"If you want the job – dazzle me!" Renquist continued and then coughed. "But don't dazzle me today!" He warned. "I have to be in court with my ... ahem ...almost ex-wife tomorrow morning, and I want to be left alone!" Everyone looked on at him with surprise, but not too much of it since Alden Renquist's outbursts were legendary. He ended his proclamation with – "I am now going to go to my office to read my paper, drink a cup of coffee, and swallow some Xanax!"

Renquist was about to enter his office when he stepped back and turned around to Penelope. "Penelope," he called out, his voice calm and kind ("He's nicer to you than anyone in the office," Wendy often commented. "Are you two having an affair?"). "What's going on with the tractors account?"

Penelope nervously went through all her pitches in her mind – the ones sent to the features editor from the New York Times, the reporter from The Wall Street Journal, the senior producer from CNBC's "Squawk Box," and to a multitude of trade journals whose focus was on farming equipment and agriculture, including "American Tractor" – and still Penelope wasn't having any luck at getting her client any press coverage or even simple desk meetings with any journalists for the past three months. "Nothing yet," she answered him, her voice quivering a little.

Renquist neared her desk. Penelope leaned somewhat away from him, just enough for her not to feel all of his ire, but not enough for him to think she was being rude.

"Penelope," he said to her, still with all his composure, peering at her with unblinking eyes. "I know you can do this. I brought you here for this specific account. You're from the heart of the country. Middle America. Your parents are farmers."

Penelope bit her lip. "Actually, they're teachers," she corrected him.

Wendy gasped in her cubicle, and Renquist blinked once and only once, and asked, "How did your family get over here?"

"Excuse me?"

"How did your ancestors get to America?"

Penelope knew the answer right off. She had heard it from both sides of her family, maternal and fraternal, since the day she could understand her first word. "The Mayflower."

Her boss nodded. "Exactly. Someone in your family had to be farmers at some time," he remarked, appearing confident in his decision-making abilities. "Penelope. Most everyone here had ancestors that came through Ellis Island-they were fisherman, tailors, butchers. But this is not an account for sushi or couture or a red meat coalition. This is an account for Henshaw tractors. These are your ancestors. This is your baby."

Renquist then turned around to go back to his office, waving his newspaper in the air, shouting, "Be creative. Get a celebrity to endorse the tractors! Write letters to them asking for their endorsements! ... Brad Pitt and Angelina Jolie! Tom Cruise ... They own everything in the world and the world includes tractors! Maybe even Tom Hanks! He's a friendly guy! Just get the media coverage!" and he strolled into his office, and closed the door behind him with a loud bang.

Penelope sat down at her desk, wondering what kind of letters she could compose to celebrities about tractors that wouldn't incur the wrath of restraining orders.

"Wow," Wendy said, gazing down at Penelope, her chin, again, sitting on their common wall. "He is *SO* easy on you. If it was someone else he would've been so awful and..." Wendy stopped talking. She noticed that Penelope wasn't paying attention to her.

Penelope was too busy to listen to her co-worker. Too busy thinking of the new technology account that could be the answer to all of her problems – along with the text messaging solution. Along with the genius capabilities of the scraggily, loner, dejected guy – Ted.

"Oh no," Wendy uttered, "like I said before, Penelope - NO. You can't take on that account. You can't even try for it. What happened to that conversation we just had, huh? You know nothing about technology. Remember?"

"Yeah," Penelope answered, a smile creeping on her face. "But I could learn, right?"

"No."

"You heard what Mr. Renquist said – I can do this."

"No. He meant that about the tractors account. Not the new account. Not about technology."

Penelope wasn't listening again. Her mind was in a fog of great property in some form, for both her office and home.

She thought if she could somehow get the account, she wouldn't have to subconsciously pick her men by if they had a great pad in the Upper West Side as compared to a shared closet in Hell's Kitchen.

"Are you listening to me, Penelope?" Wendy asked, putting her hands to her hips, her forehead crinkling.

Just at that moment, a tune spiraled out of Penelope's BlackBerry – *Buffalo Gals can't you come out tonight- can't you come out tonight- can't you come out tonight-Buffalo Gals can't you come out tonight-aaand dance by the light of the mooon*; it was the ring tone her brother installed for her on her PDA – an old song called "Buffalo Gals" that was featured in her favorite movie "It's a Wonderful Life."

Penelope picked up her BlackBerry from her desk and pressed it to her ear. "Hello?" she said. "Hello?"

Buffalo Gals can't you come out tonight- can't you come out tonight-can't you come out tonight-Buffalo Gals can't you come out tonight-aaand dance by the light of the mooon…

"Hello? Hello?" she repeated into the phone with still no answer on the other end.

Wendy sprung out from her cubicle and grabbed the BlackBerry from Penelope's hand. She played around with the buttons and handed it back to her with raised eyebrows. "You don't have a phone call. You have a text message."

"Ooooh," Penelope cooed. She looked down at the BlackBerry screen and the text message that she realized, in amazement, looked almost like an email. "So that's what a text message looks like."

Upon hearing that, Wendy slapped her forehead and groaned, "Oh, my God," and slowly slid down into her cubicle like she was in pain.

Penelope read the text message:

Jan 2, 2008 3:23:05 PM

Pen, Are u getting this text message? Do u have the service yet? Did u get your old texts back? How many were there? Were there any from dates? How many weeks are u going to take off to read them? (How many months? Years?) Hey - did u know that if u don't answer a text message the BlackBerry will turn off and spray toxic nerve gas in your face in ten seconds? ... Ten ... nine ... eight ... luv, your grieving brother, Cory

Mary (to George Bailey): What are you doing?
Picketing?

Four

Penelope held a crumpled piece of paper in one hand and a friendly Hallmark card in the other as she stood in the bowels of the South Street Seaport area looking on at a broken-down dungeon apartment below.

She raised the paper to read Wendy's handwriting once more:

Ted Hollis
205 Front Street
Important: remember to knock three times and then wait ten seconds — and then knock once more — and then wait five seconds — and then knock twice.

THIS IS THE ONLY WAY HE'LL ANSWER THE DOOR!

Great, Penelope said to herself, twitching her nose as the amalgamation of the East River and city grime pricked at her nostrils. It had occurred to her while examining the door of Ted Hollis' apartment, hich from the looks of its peeling and browning coat had been last painted in the turn of the previous century (when the gangs of New York ruled the streets of downtown), and the dirty window with its drawn beige curtains (resembling a school boy's bed linens with prints of schooners and sailboats), that she should just turn around and walk away. After all, she wondered, should she be risking her life to get these text messages? Was it really worth it?

Penelope suddenly had an image in her mind of her mother trudging through New York City in one of her superbly pressed dresses and kitchen apron, spotting her eyes and tears with a handkerchief that she made during some free time at the neighborhood quilting bee, looking for her or any clue of her whereabouts. She imagined her mother kneeling and picking up a very fine thread of brown hair from the pavement that resembled her daughter's tresses and openly weeping. She thought of her father standing beside her mother, carrying his favorite instrument, a bugle, that he could never really play, and blowing into it, hoping that the sound would be a siren call for Penelope to find them. But in Penelope's mind her father only succeeds in scaring the city's pigeon population, causing them to fly off to another place (and no one cared where, just as long as they were gone and away from their windshields, windows and heads), because she was dead. Dead. Dead as a door nail. Murdered in the dungeon apartment by a crazed, loner, computer-techno geek who strangled her with a mouse cord and stuffed her in his closet, and then after a couple of days, when he got tired of opening the closet and talking to her decomposing and reeking body for company, put weights on her ankles and dropped her in the East River.

A fearful Penelope turned away from the dungeon but then stopped and *hmphed* to herself, realizing that her overactive imagination had gotten the best of her.

She immediately pictured Wendy's face and heard her assuring voice. "He's harmless," Wendy said to Penelope as she passed her the slip of paper with Ted Hollis' information on it. "Don't worry that he's a stranger – or a little bit strange. He's just different. That's all." Penelope remembered asking Wendy if she would accompany her to the dungeon apartment. "No, I can't," Wendy replied, "I have to do two booty calls this weekend to pay for *your* favor." But she didn't seem disgruntled; she even smiled when she said it, although Penelope noticed that still, like all winter so far, Wendy hadn't worn any boots. Not even a simple pair of galoshes.

After all the pictures of her loved ones and coworker dissipated, another image emerged that was nice and pleasant. It was the image, the face, of Luke Carson, the wavy-haired and dimpled, wealthy, shipping entrepreneur; he was smiling at her and asking in a yearning way – "Why didn't you text me back…love of my life….I've been waiting … And waiting … " His big brown eyes pleading, yet, somehow sensual. Penelope shivered, and she realized that her provocative private places and thoughts suddenly didn't want to be so private. *Not now,* she censured herself. (No Luke, no man at all, what was she to do? Go frolic in her skivvies down at the river and force herself on a homeless man?)

Penelope felt the Hallmark envelope in her hand that had the scrawlings "Ted, welcome to New York! – Penelope" on it. She purchased the card the day before, feeling bad for this man she didn't know, thinking there was a definite chance that when he moved to New York no one welcomed him in a proper way; so for three years he kept himself cooped up – or more appropriately down – in his apartment, rather than going out and being social, and maybe even finding himself a new fiancé or girlfriend or whatever.

Penelope felt her brother had welcomed her in the proper way; the morning she moved to Manhattan he handed her a Hallmark "welcome" card and took her out to a real New York City diner and bought her a stack of chocolate chip pancakes. But since she knew buying Ted Hollis chocolate chip pancakes would be going overboard, she just got the card, thinking it was enough of a gesture, and besides, she found the card to be funny – it had little goblins of all colors scattered across the cover, and when she opened it up, she noticed the same goblins hanging on the word "WELCOME," along with a tune that had no real rhythmic pattern coming out of it, singing: *Welcome – Welcome – Welcome – (two beats) – Wellllcome!* This made her laugh out loud in the store for some reason. *So silly.*

Penelope tapped the envelope as she stood in place, and then she turned around and hurried for the dungeon door, quickly trampling down the steps, afraid if she didn't move fast enough she would lose her nerve, change her mind, and run the other away.

"Okay," Penelope said aloud to herself, smoothing down her hair and coat – neatening herself up, and then she slowly knocked on his door…One…two…three knocks, and then she searched on her wrist for her watch to count the seconds, but quickly noticed she forgot to put it on. Only one thing left to do … "One Mississippi," she mumbled under her breath, "two Mississippi … three Mississippi … four Mississippi …" When she arrived at ten Mississippis, Penelope again slammed her fist on the door, this time once, sighed, said five more Mississipis, did two more knocks, and then waited, patient and wondering…if she would get out of there alive. But no one answered the door for a good ten Mississippis, and then suddenly, the door flew open, and a tall, scruffy looking fellow appeared before her, a mop of dark brown hair falling all around and over his face.

Penelope immediately noticed that other than his nose and mouth, the mop covered the entirety of his features. Half of his face was hidden. Half was a mystery.

"You Penelope?" he inquired. He leaned against the doorframe, his demeanor apathetic.

She stood in front of him with the Hallmark card at her side, giving the mess-of-a-man the once over. Along with his disheveled hair that she felt needed more than a trim – it sorely needed to be hacked at with some sturdy scissors – Penelope saw that the blue, faded t-shirt he was wearing was two sizes too small for his torso and that his jeans were completely washed out and tattered at his feet. Penelope looked into his bangs, where his eyes should have been, and became increasingly fretful of what she would find inside the apartment after seeing what came out of it. "Uh, yeah. That's me," Penelope replied. "Are you Ted…Ted Hollis?"

He nodded a little and then returned her scrutinizing glances with his own, as evidenced not by the eyes she couldn't see, but by his head moving down and then up in her general direction. "Gary told me you'd be coming," he said, his tone very deep, deeper than she expected. She guessed that the proclivity for shyness or for being a shut-in had no bearing on the pitch of one's voice.

With just a wave of his hand, without even as much as a smile, he gestured for her to come into his dungeon apartment.

Penelope slowly entered with trepidation and took in the whole of his abode that appeared to have been put together like a makeshift tent. "Utility" seemed to be the operative word for Ted Hollis' apartment – a simple desk with a computer and whatever thingamajigs (she couldn't fathom what the other machinery, as she called it, was) to the left of her, a simple wooden table to her right in a kitchenette area where a medium-sized flat screen TV was propped up on a stove, and straight ahead was a column of wide shelves with books, magazines, and an assortment of objects laid out in a singular, massive disarray.

A group of small dumbbells were cluttered in a corner, and Penelope found this to be odd – *He works out?* she questioned to herself. *He can't cut his hair or pull his clothes together, but he works out?*

Her feet planted to one spot, Penelope bent forward just a little bit, trying to be inconspicuous, and saw another door leading into a small room with a utilitarian bed – a mattress on the floor with strewn pillows and sheets on top and an enormous quilt bundled up at an edge.

Ted Hollis sat down on at his desk, facing her, and hung an arm over his chair. "So what's this about text messages that I heard about?" he asked.

"Uh…yeah, I'm trying to get them back," Penelope answered, being terse as she immersed herself in some of the sci-fi prints on his walls, curious about Ted Hollis and his no-frills dwelling. She realized the prints were movie posters, and as she recognized some of them, she went through the films in her head – *Star Wars…The Lord of the Rings…*Penelope smiled to herself – *2001: A Space Odyssey;* she remembered a number of lazy Sunday afternoons when she and her father were sacked out on a comfy couch watching it on television on Elmont's "Saturday Afternoon at the Movies" program.

Penelope was about to point out her personal memory of the movie to Ted, a stranger, when he reasoned, "So you didn't save some important text messages?"

"Not exactly," she replied. Penelope turned around to him and was suddenly taken somewhat aback by Ted Hollis' discernable facial features that she only previously took a glimpse of, too thrown by his hair, clothes and his depressing apartment. Penelope considered his strong, determined jaw (and was that a little cleft in his chin?) and attractively prominent, Romanesque nose. Then her eyes traveled down to his full and flush lips. They reminded her of lips saturated with the juice from cherry popsicles. *Well,* she thought, *he's got some nice points about him,* and then she looked at his hair and bangs, the dangling dark curls that still covered his eyes; he reminded her of a shaggy, spaghetti-like, English Sheepdog.

Penelope swiveled round to check out some more of her surroundings, only to suddenly find herself staring into a strange face. "Oh!" she shrieked at this face, this man with pointy ears.

"No-don't be scared," Ted said, "that's just Spock."

Dear God! she thought as she took in the human-sized, cardboard figure of Star Trek's Mr. Spock standing next to her; Mr. Spock was wearing his blue Star Trek outfit and held some kind of laser gun that pointed towards the apartment door. The notion of Mr. Spock possibly being the guard of Ted Hollis' home, his otherworld, was not lost on Penelope, but even with his obvious need for protection, she wondered about Ted being over the legal age limit for displaying fictitious television characters in his home.

Penelope returned to their prior conversation. "Here's the situation," Penelope commented, beginning on a path of which she didn't want to go down, but knew she had to, "I didn't have text messaging service last year-all last year." She quickly tried to save herself – "But now I have it, but um … I think a lot of people sent me text messages last year, and I'd like to get them back." She recoiled, being sure that Ted Hollis would start grinning in a matter of seconds. He would ask himself – "Did she really go without text messages for a whole year? And does she really think that I can retrieve those text messages for her? Does she think I'm some techno-cosmic wizard?" *He's going to laugh at me,* she convinced herself, *He's such a smart technology guy, why wouldn't he?*

But much to her surprise, Ted Hollis didn't utter a word. He just continued to sit there, looking at her with no readable expression. Penelope couldn't figure out if his not laughing meant that he could get the text messages, or that he couldn't get them and he thought her lack of smarts about technology rendered her unworthy of any reaction whatsoever.

She gulped and cut through the silence, saying, "And that's where you come in." Some brightness shone in her eyes and in a tiny, emerging smile.

Ted's plump lips parted, and to her astonishment, he breathed, "Okay."

Penelope's eyes widened, and she began to smile even more, her heart and mind filled with elation – she was going to get her text messages! She was going to find out who tried to contact her! Another vision of Luke Carson immediately flashed in her brain – "Why haven't I heard from you?" Luke asks with the vision. "I haven't dated anyone since we met…I've been heartbroken." Penelope went dreamy.

"Uh …" Ted tried to interrupt, staring at her while her eyes sparkled at the heavens and the cracking ceiling, grinning like the Cheshire Cat. "Just give me your name, number, and who your carrier is."

Penelope suddenly crinkled her forehead, confused. "Carrier?" she questioned him.

"Yeah. Carrier."

She sighed, understanding that this was some kind of technology jargon she didn't know about, again. *Well,* she thought, *he's sure to laugh at me now.* She tightened her grip on the Hallmark card, anticipating the worst, plainly stating, "I don't know what you mean." She peered into his bangs. "What's a carrier?"

But Ted Hollis still didn't laugh. He just tilted his head at her and lowered his voice in a gentle sort of way, replying, "It's the company that gave you the phone."

Penelope bit her lip and laughed. "Ooooh," she sounded, realizing it was such a simple thing. "That would be AT & T ... and my name is McAdams ... Penelope McAdams. She spelled her name and told him her number.

He nodded, turned around to his computer, and started to punch away at the keyboard. "This may take a little while." He cleared his throat. "It gets kind of warm in here...you might want to take your coat off."

Penelope unbuttoned her coat, starting to feel a bit more comfortable in the dungeon apartment and with its dungeon master, Ted, (Spock or no Spock) who obviously wasn't going to get his jollies from her technological deficiencies like the others. And *how funny,* she thought, that the person who probably knew the most about technology might find her the least ridiculous.

She pulled off her coat and folded it over an arm.

As Ted worked away at solving her texts problem, ever so diligently, he remarked, "If you want, you can hang your coat up in the closet."

Penelope froze in place ... The closet? Oh no.

His eyes still glued to the computer screen, Ted pointed to where the closet was. Penelope slowly moved in that direction, near the shelves, and when she finally made it over, she stopped and imagined her decomposing and reeking body shoved in the closet, in between the coats, jackets, and a gallery of skeletons.

"Uh...I think I'll just keep it with me," she said hanging onto her coat for dear life.

Ted shrugged as he furiously typed away, and Penelope looked down at the Hallmark card in her hand, wondering if she should give it to him considering he didn't appear to be an affable or happy type of person.

"You've got a lot of stuff," she eked out, not certain if she should say anything, perusing his shelves. The books on his shelves were basically science fiction themed, as well – Ray Bradbury's "Fahrenheit 451" and H.G. Wells' "The Time Machine" and "The War of the Worlds," and then there were other classics she had seen numerous times in her brother's bookcase when he was a teenager – "Dune," "The Hobbit," and everything else J.R.R. Tolkien, and then there was the occasional Hemingway lodged between tales of space aliens and apocalyptic

worlds – "The Sun Also Rises" and a "A Farewell to Arms." On the
bottom shelf she saw a plethora of different comic books featuring the
typical superheroes – Spiderman, Hulk, X-Men, and so on, and then
Penelope got to the middle shelf, which she thought was the most
interesting of them all, being filled with old-tech artifacts that even she
could see were extremely outdated, and she knew of these objects since
her father still kept some of them around in his garage – a gigantic
remote control from the 1980s, an eight-track tape player, a word-
processing typewriter, a box for Atari's "Pong," and along with other
archeological relics, she came upon an old Canon camera from the
1980s. She immediately grabbed it up.

"A Canon A-1 camera," she said aloud, joyful. "I remember this,"
and Penelope carefully maneuvered the camera in her hands. It was
sacred to her. "My grandfather had one just like this. It was his favorite
camera." *Before he died,* she thought. *His last favorite camera.* The memories
of her Grandfather Ben flooded back to her – his scruffy gray beard,
his laughing eyes (crinkling with merriment), his striped suspenders,
and him sitting with her on his lap under all the cameras he owned
throughout his life that were displayed on a shelf amongst his landscape
and nature photographs and the many awards he had won for
photography. Penelope, remembering the love she had for her
grandfather, traced the camera lens with a finger, as gentle as could be.
"My grandfather, Grandpa Ben, he was an award-winning
photographer. He did photographs like um-Ansel Adams." Penelope
sighed. She missed her grandfather.

Ted stopped typing and turned to her. "Really?"

"Yeah," she responded, nodding to him with a tinge of melancholy.

The corners of Ted Hollis' mouth curved upwards a little, which
Penelope took as the beginning of an actual smile, and she could see
that he had a couple of perfectly straight teeth before he shut his
mouth in mere seconds. *He should smile,* she thought, *it doesn't look like it
would be too bad.*

"That camera was my favorite. I used to be into photography a lot,"
he said, and then he went back to his computer. "But not so much
anymore."

With tenderness, Penelope put the camera back at its original spot, and then her sights veered off to a film canister and a picture frame that were close by. In the picture frame was a photo of a beautiful, young woman with her long, strawberry blonde hair blowing in the wind, in jeans and a cardigan, sitting Indian-style on the grass. She was laughing and holding a little boy in her arms. The boy, who looked to be around four-years old, had dark hair with fringes of curls (and was that a soft and tiny cleft in his chin?), and was smiling into the camera as the woman's arm looped around his waist. Penelope was immediately hit with the emotion that emanated from the picture. The smiles. The love.

Penelope became increasingly inquisitive as Ted paid no attention to what she was doing, still plugging away at her text problem, typing, she thought, what had to be more than one-hundred words a minute. She picked up the film canister and analyzed it. Wound around the canister was a sliver of masking tape where "Hannah and me at the park" was written in black marker.

"Y'know," Ted Hollis said as Penelope heard him bang away at the keys, "they have digital cameras now. I know I'm supposed to be some tech guy, but I still like some of the gizmos from the past." He sighed. "I still like the old cameras with the old film canisters…each one of them saving memories … important memories," he remarked, and just at that moment, he looked away from the computer and over at Penelope, who was still holding the canister.

Ted quickly leapt up from his seat and rushed over to her. He grabbed the canister from her grasp and swiftly made way to his closet, opening the door, and quickly placing it in on a shelf above his head. For a split second, Penelope could decipher that the shelf was filled with film canisters.

He shut the closet door and rotated around to Penelope.

"I didn't mean to pry!" Penelope exclaimed, now not only worried that she wouldn't get her text messages back, but that she completely and seriously invaded someone's privacy. "I didn't mean anything by it! I was just looking around … I didn't see anything!" *Or read anything*, she thought.

Ted didn't react to Penelope's wails of explanation.

Instead, he was quiet, strolling back to his computer, sitting down and typing once again. About a half-a-minute later, Ted's typing ceased and in a flat voice he asked, "You have your BlackBerry on you?"

Penelope quickly reached into her handbag and pulled out her BlackBerry. She was giddy with anticipation.

"Take a look," Ted told her, "they're all there."

Penelope pushed some buttons that took her to her inbox for text messages, and she saw that where it originally indicated that she had five texts, it was now telling her that she had one-hundred and two. She jumped in place and beamed at Ted who was watching her but not smiling back.

"So there you go," he said.

Penelope, although ecstatic over finally obtaining her year's worth of text messages (and there were so many!), suddenly felt bad that she had nothing of real compensation to give to Ted for his time and effort. She wanted to kick herself for not thinking about it beforehand, but she was so nervous about the dungeon apartment and Wendy telling her that Ted was strange, that his payment wasn't upfront in her mind. Also, she subconsciously thought she wouldn't have to give him anything since this might have been a favor that was due to Wendy's ex-boyfriend, Gary, and retriever of her booty-calls. But Penelope felt poorly about the situation just the same, especially after she had the audacity to peek at his private things and therefore, his life, while he was focusing on her text problem. How dare she?

"I don't know what to say," she said to Ted, full of shame and embarrassment as her freckles fell along with her mouth, turning into a sad frown. "I have a couple of dollars I could give you, but I need it for the Taxi back ... I could give it to you and just go to the ATM...I could even take the subway back. I have a subway pass. You'd just need to point me in the right direction-I don't know this area very well."

Ted Hollis waved his hand at her, shaking his head, his curls bouncing off his forehead and cheeks. "Forget it," he said and he stood up from his desk chair. "Gary's a good guy and he asked me to do it. So don't worry about it."

Very nice, she thought. *Ted Hollis, scraggily, strange, techno-geek – with nice lips and cleft chin- would have done very well in Elmont.* As far as Manhattan went, she didn't know how most of the residents felt upon meeting him (she could only guess that it wasn't good), but in Elmont, he would have been well received. She was sure of it.

"Oh, wait a minute," Penelope said as she put her coat on, the Hallmark card slipping through a sleeve. How could she have forgotten? "I have this for you." She handed him the envelope.

Ted just stood around for a couple of seconds, staring down at the envelope, as Penelope buttoned up her coat, and when he finally opened it up, he declared, "Pac-Mans. The little guys on the front here look like little Pac-Mans," and then he looked inside, and the card immediately sang *"Welcome – Welcome – Welcome – (two beats) – Wellllcome!*

Penelope searched his mouth for a reaction, but there wasn't any, and he closed the card.

Well, I tried.

Eager to get back to her apartment and review her once-lost text messages and realizing that there was no hope in getting Ted Hollis to be expressive in any way – to at least smile – Penelope said, "Good-bye," and then Ted and Penelope shook hands.

Penelope was only two steps out of Ted Hollis' dungeon apartment when she heard *"Welcome – Welcome – Welcome – (two beats) – Wellllcome!"* from behind her.

She could have sworn she heard a little chuckle.

Ma Bailey: Nice Girl, Mary.

George Bailey: Mmm. Hmmm ...

Ma Bailey: Kind that will help you find the answers, George.

Five

With BlackBerry in hand, Penelope belly-flopped onto her bed, eager to read her excavated text messages, but after a brief review, Penelope acknowledged that she was too quick in her excitement, surmising that probably only about half of her texts were of real importance - hopefully one of them being from Luke Carson. The rest of the texts were from people she was close to who she already communicated with in other ways on a regular basis, and Penelope figured since none of these people bothered to complain to her about not answering them, they couldn't have been all *that* weighty or serious.

Actually, as she studied their messages, she understood them to be contrary to weighty or serious. If anything, they were on the lighter side – like her brother inviting her out to Thursday and Friday night happy hours and various dinners at his favorite steakhouses. He also sent her some texts while having a grand old time at two or three American Bar Association parties, and in one of these messages, Cory seemed to have a ploy to motivate her into texting him by dangling cute lawyers in its contents:

Jan 28, 2007 7:04:02:

Pen – I text you about an hour ago to come over to Tao, but you never answered (like usual). There's a great ABA party here – and there are some sorta nice looking guys here for you to meet. And they're all attorneys (is that a good thing?). Where are you?? … OK … I'll just do some interviewing for you then … Cory

Penelope furrowed her brow. She would have loved to have gone to those parties! The potential for meeting many Mr. Rights at an ABA party was enormous, she was sure of it!

As she scrolled through her texts, lying flat on her stomach on her stiff and cheap mattress, Penelope crossed one ankle over the other and kicked herself (an American Bar Association party would have been so promising). Her brother's ploy would have definitely worked - if she only had her text messaging service!

Wendy also sent her a couple of texts, inviting her to go out clubbing and bar hopping.

Penelope was happy to know that her co-worker was reaching out to her beyond the office, perhaps seeing her as not just a fun and interesting coworker but also as a friend.

When Penelope didn't respond, Wendy's texts ran the gamut from simplistic and blasé to comedic and curious:

Feb 3, 2007 6:20:16 PM:

Hey Penelope. i guess you must be busy. See you at work. Wendy

March 23, 2007 8:41:08 PM:

Hey Penelope. Okay. i guess you're busy. I'll just go do a booty call. Wendy

April 3, 2007 7:20:32 PM:

Hey Penelope. Okay. i guess you're busy – what are you doing that's so bad that you can't text me back??? Tell me! Tell me!…i guess I'll go pick up the Daily News and look at the weekend sales. Start clipping coupons. Wendy

Sonia sent about ten texts in all, most of them querying if Penelope would like to join her for a girl's night out with her friends, and then there were a couple of other messages asking if she was available for babysitting duties:

May 28, 2007 8:00:10 AM:

Hi Pen! Do you think you can watch Jake? It's just a spur of the moment thing. It would only be for 2 days. Cory and I were just able to get reservations at a North Fork bed and breakfast and we're going wine tasting for the whole weekend! - Your indebted, close-to-being sister-in-law - Sonia (greatly appreciated)

Penelope grimaced. Sonia and Cory wanted her to spend an entire weekend babysitting Jake, the four-year old whirlwind, while they went gallivanting through North Fork, the Hamptons' wine country? *Really now,* Penelope said to herself, cocking an eyebrow. She was definitely glad she missed that text message.

Cory's friend, Stacey, the supposed "Wise Sage" of New York, also sent her some texts, most of them having been written after a date had failed:

June 1, 2007 10:11:03 PM

Hey, I can't believe I went out with that guy. It must've been really dark in that bar when we were introduced. Stacey

June 15, 2007 10:11:03 PM:

Hey, I think I went out with this guy be 4 but I don't remember.
Stacey

(This text was sent more than once on different days and hours concerning different men.)

Stacey also wrote unique types of messages that would've seemed strange if anyone else had sent them, such as:
July 25, 2007 2:33:06 PM:

Pen, he asked me to take my Vaseline-dish gloves off over brunch — Can u believe that?
Stacey

After her friends and family texts went unanswered for about nine months, she noticed irritation setting into sentences, as exhibited by one of Cory's messages:

Aug 10, 2007 6:22:01 PM:

Sister - what's your problem? You can't text a person back? Brother

Although Sonia never seemed to get angry:

August 11, 2007 5:32:41 PM:

Okay Pen, I haven't heard back from you. Catch you another time — hope that you're with some fantastic guy ... Hey did I ever tell you how Cory and I met? Sonia

Penelope rolled her eyes.

Strangely enough, among the remaining texts were communications from someone Penelope didn't know at all. The messages, numbering twenty altogether, were from a man named "DePeche" who was love-struck to the core. The object of his affection — a woman named

"Cassandra":

Feb 22, 2007 2:20:11 AM:

Cassandra Hottie: I'm crazy for U. U ROCK MY WORLD. Since I met U I can't think of any1 else but U. Yours 4 eva – DePeche

March 12, 2007 1:06:35 AM:

Cassandra SCORCHING HONEY - Did U git my flowers? I sent U 5 dozen rozez because I love U. Need U. Want U. Why aren't U answerin my texts? I would call U but I do better with messages. Y'know. Being poetic and expressive and shit. Yours 4 eva and eva - DePeche

June 22, 2007 3:17:02 AM:

Cassandra SEXIEST GIRL I EVA SEEN - I see U at the bling-bling club and U don't notice a brother. Whats up? Now I've been calling U and U don't answer. What did ariana say to U about me? I bust her up. I'm goin to die if we ain't together. - Yours 4 eva and eva and more evas - DePeche

Noticing that DePeche's texts ended a couple of days after, Penelope became worried. *Did he kill himself?* she questioned, and then she suddenly remembered how her BlackBerry kept ringing and waking her up in the middle of the night, or more correctly, the wee hours of the morning throughout that month of June. Most of the time she couldn't answer the phone quick enough, reaching over for the phone on her nightstand at a snail's pace with her eyes still shut, searching and knocking over her Hummel figurines in the process. Penelope would then check her voicemail, but whoever was calling never bothered to leave a message, and when she looked for the number on the BlackBerry, the caller came up as "unknown." A few times she was able to pick-up before the last ring, and when she'd say a drowsy "hello," no one would address her from the other end, but her ears always detected some quiet breathing, and then there'd be the inevitable click, a sure sign of the breather hanging up.

It must have been DePeche, she said to herself. Once Penelope read all his texts and recalled what she thought was a pattern in his gasps and pants, she started to feel as though she personally knew him and his heart – a heart impaled with Cupid's fiery arrow.

But at one point in June, when Penelope didn't realize who was making the calls and what was going on, she became so annoyed, she toyed with the idea of getting a new phone number, but thought differently when Cory explained to her, ever so plainly, that if she decided to change her number before the end of her cell phone contract, her credit report would go down five-hundred points. "It's in everyone's contract. Stipulated on the bottom," he gravely commented with his index finger pointing down. "You didn't know that? Don't you read what you sign?"

Five hundred points? Penelope remembered cringing. She certainly didn't need that.

As she continued looking through her messages, Penelope came upon texts from some of her prime picks from her dating list or as Wendy called them – "the Apostles."

This is what she had hoped for.

There was Peter, the ophthalmologist and eye surgeon with the five-bedroom apartment on the Upper West Side with the long nose hair and skin problems:

April 23, 2007 7:09:42 AM:

Penelope, I had a great time with you last night. I think you're wonderful and charming, and completely lovely, and I love your stories about your hometown. I'd like for us to get together again – how about today? Lunch? Or maybe tonight? Dinner? If not today or tonight, anytime this week would be fine (I'm always on call, but I can turn off my cell phone). Peter

Penelope shook her head. Peter was being too desperate, and no matter what gargantuan apartment he owned, she doubted if there was enough room for both herself and his nose hair.

She shuddered at the thought of him going in for a kiss, the protruding follicles and abscesses rubbing against her face.

Then there was James, the jock-hedge fund manager with the choice condo in the Meat Packing District, who, on their date, tried to persuade her into doing the acrobatic feat of arm wrestling while chugging down beers:

May 20, 2007 1:10:52 AM:

Penmeister! How ya' doin? Had a fabulistic time with you last week – you're pretty good at pinky wrestling - you think this time we can use all our fingers? (Hee-Hee) Sorry about dropping the bar nuts on your dress while watching the game. Got kind of excited during the scoring run. Hey-want to meet out this weekend? There's an amazing karaoke-sports bar on the Upper East Side. Hey – do you know the words to "We are the Champions?" Talk to you lata' - The Jamesmeister

"Oh dear God," Penelope groaned, suddenly thinking of the hand pain she endured for a good week or so after James forced her pinky down on the bar. She put up a good fight for about two minutes, and then ultimately cracked under the pressure of James' colossal pinky, definitely much mightier than hers, and the boisterous cheers and boos of onlookers who were spilling Budweiser on their shirts while gorging themselves with piles of nachos and hot, molten cheese dip. Penelope knew she should leave the "Jamesmeister" for another, more aggressive (and more brutish), woman.

And then – "Oh! Oh!" she cried out after spending an hour going through trivial text messages to finally find her golden treasure – "A text from Luke!" Hungry for his words, Penelope's eyes went to feast on his texts (she imagined – "Why don't you text me back…love of my life?" and "I haven't dated anyone since I met you…I've been heartbroken"):

July 1, 2007 2:41:03 PM:

Hi Penelope, I had a wonderful time with you the other evening. Want to go out on Friday night? Luke

Sept 19, 2007 4:16:22 PM:

Hi Penelope, I never heard back from you. Maybe I should've called. I don't know. It just seems that texting is so much easier and quicker these days, and you know we all have such busy lives. I don't know why you didn't text me back, but I figured I'd give it another shot...So if you'd like, when you get a chance – text me. Luke

A smile spread across Penelope's face.
She pressed the BlackBerry to her bosom.
It had been enough.

> *George Bailey: I'm shakin' the dust of this crummy little town off my feet and I'm going to see the world!*

Six

Penelope sat across from Luke Carson, her sights perusing his handsome, tanned face and broad shoulders as her nostrils flared from the spicy aromas of the surrounding Curry dishes.

She felt as though she should pinch herself right there in the restaurant. She couldn't believe that she was actually out with this wonderfully attractive, successful, and polished man – the epitome of the elite New York City man, she thought, like the ones that a lot of the girl's in her office dated who wined and dined them, sent them bouquets of long-stem red roses (always at least a dozen), bought them Gucci handbags when they went shopping together, and purchased diamond jewelry (not with diamond chips, but with entire diamonds!) on their birthdays, and Christmas and Valentine's day.

Penelope's switch was on day dream mode again as she pictured the roses being delivered to her workplace, the women in her office circling around the flowers, admiring them and fawning over her, telling her how lucky she was to find such a fabulous Manhattan man; Luke was definitely someone they would date, they'd announce. He was like most of their boyfriends. *Penelope McAdams*, she would say in her mind, *you have finally crossed over to being a full-fledged New York City woman.*

She gazed into Luke's sparkling brown eyes as they flashed around the room.

"This is the best Indian restaurant in the city," Luke commented, looking wonderfully fit in a button-down oxford shirt, pulled taut at the sleeves from the muscles in his arms bulging out in all the right places. His thick and wavy, sandy brown hair was swept away from his face, exposing a pleasant smile and widening eyes overflowing with enthusiasm. "Fantastic food, incredible service…And don't you love the smell of the spices?" he asked her. Luke waved his hand around, moving some of the potent air his way, taking in a big whiff.

Penelope was more than fine with Luke's gigantic inhalation. She hoped that it would pull some of the piquant atmosphere away from her.

Not being used to the hot smells of Indian food, which she never had before, or spicy food in general, and feeling as though her nose was about to explode, she tried to cut down on breathing through her nostrils as much as possible by intermittently holding her breath for a good ten to twenty seconds or so.

She only hoped that the smell would simmer down a bit before she turned blue in the face and passed out from self-induced asphyxiation. *Wouldn't that be swell on a date?* Penelope mused.

"I hope you're okay with the restaurant," he said. "Maybe I should have asked you first, but I'm really first-rate at picking them. You could ask anyone that I know. They always let me pick because they know I only choose the best places to eat."

Penelope shook her head. "It's fine," she answered and then immediately thought – *no, no, you should have said "it's better than fine"! What's wrong with you?*

"I pretty much know every restaurant in the city," he proclaimed.

Penelope nodded, trying to control the pulsations of her nose with some facial muscles, hoping that Luke wouldn't see she was havingproblems with one of the restaurants he picked with all his unabashed confidence.

Still ecstatic from the aromatic riches of his environment, Luke swooned, "Ah wonderful…And the spices - they don't just clear up the nasal passages. They clear up the mind. Y'know?"

"Uh, yeah," she responded, lying through the teeth she was smiling with. She actually didn't know. Not at all. But as long as she was with Luke Carson – strong, handsome and magnetic Luke Carson – Penelope didn't care. She didn't even care if her loss of air and therefore, lack of oxygen, would result in the untimely death of her brain cells, one by one. It was Penelope's estimation that she must have had a surplus of brain cells stashed away somewhere. And how many brain cells did she really need anyway to eat, sleep, and travel to work, and then to execute a public relations campaign for tractors? (Although even with all her brain cells alive and kicking, that campaign didn't seem to be going so well).

Luke dug a piece of pita into a bowl of hummus. "I have to say I was extremely surprised when I received your text," he said to her before nibbling. "It's been a while."

Penelope thought – *Oh, here we go* – *"I wanted you so much, Penelope,"* she imagined saying. *"When you didn't get back to me, I was so down in the dumps that I couldn't date anyone else."*

"I know," she said. "Honestly, there was something wrong with my BlackBerry. For a while I wasn't getting messages, and when they fixed it, I saw your texts." Honestly, she lied, not wanting to embarrass herself in front of Luke.

"A person can get missing texts back?" he inquired, a bit shocked, and then shrugged. "It's good that you didn't text me within the past couple of months," he said. "I was in Monaco for a business slash pleasure trip. I laid on the beach a lot." He touched his golden brown face, rubbing it actually, as she patted her now runny nose (*gee those spices are a killer*) with her napkin. "Got a lot of sun." He grinned and then activated his dimples, and once Luke Carson turned them on it was as if he set off beams of sunlight from his cheeks – bright slivers of charisma – and they struck Penelope. They struck her hard.

He reached for more pita bread. "It's beautiful in Monaco," he commented. "Have you ever been?"

Penelope recognized she might be able to get away with saying she understood what Luke meant about the spices, but certainly wouldn't get away with saying that she had been to Monaco. All she knew about Monaco was Princess Grace. And she only knew of Princess Grace from her mother who was beside herself with exaltation every time Princess Grace's face happened to be on television. "Oh that Princess Grace," her mother would sigh as she stared at the screen. "She was a classic beauty. One of a kind…The world is so much less of a place without her," and Penelope was sure she could see tiny tears welling up in her mother's eyes as her father would rush into the room and swipe the remote control off the coffee table, saying, without much notice, "Football game's about to go on."

As he changed the channel, her mother would shoot him a dirty look.

"Uh-no," Penelope answered, suddenly wondering what Princess Grace would look like eating Indian food – would she still retain her classic beauty? Would the spices floating in the air spiral through her tight blond bun, loosening it up to the point of it falling away? Would her porcelain face turn flush when her teeth sank into some dishes sprinkled with chili? *Stop being silly,* Penelope said to herself, trying to hold in her laughter, but not doing too good a job of it.

"What's so funny?" Luke asked.

"Nothing," she answered, "it's something I just thought of." Penelope was sure that Luke Carson wouldn't find her thoughts to be as humorous as she did. Yes, on their first date, and now this one, she found him to have a lighter side – he smiled a great deal and he told ironic, funny tales and tidbits from his life and travels – but she felt that he would possibly find her brand of humor immature and nonsensical. After all, she thought, he was a mature man of the world, obviously well-traveled and sophisticated, while she was none of these things.

With a grin, Luke urged, "Oh come on. Tell me."

"It's stupid," she said, but them she gave in. "When you were talking about Monaco, just right now, I thought of Princess Grace." Nervous,

Penelope picked up a small piece of pita from the breadbasket, feeling this additional action might act as a slight divergence from what she was saying. "My mother loves Princess Grace…Anyway, I was just thinking about what Princess Grace would have looked like eating Indian food. The spices." She sniffled a bit from the spices. She couldn't help it. "I don't know," she relayed, giggling at the end of her sentence, but quietly, so as not to show him that she thought the notion was more amusing than it might actually be.

"No. It's not stupid," he said, seriousness fanning out on his face. "Actually, if you think about it, you can equate people to food … or even beverages," he picked up his glass of wine and then put it down, becoming philosophical. "There are similarities."

Penelope was attentive to Luke while pushing some pita in her mouth.

She realized that he hadn't gotten the gist of what she was talking about – what was really going on in her head. He had gone onto a whole other unique theory of his own. But Penelope wasn't at all upset about it. She was more than happy that he wasn't laughing at what she said about Princess Grace eating Indian food. If he had laughed, Penelope thought, she would have died right there on the spot.

"Princess Grace…well, she's not so much like any food," he continued. "she's definitely a beverage. She's like the finest champagne." He grinned. "And you," he pointed to Penelope who was at the midpoint of the chewing and ingesting process of her pita, "you're also like a beverage." He leaned back, staring at Penelope, taking her in. "And you're like lemonade."

Lemonade?

Immediately taken aback by what Luke said, Penelope forgot about the portions of bread in her mouth she still needed to chew on and swallowed them down almost whole.

"Excuse me?" she politely inquired, clearing her throat, her nose still throbbing. *Lemonade? But isn't that boring? Especially compared to Princess Grace Champagne? And isn't lemonade yellow?* she asked herself, thinking about her own coloring, and then she duly noted that there was, in fact, pink lemonade, but that wouldn't have mattered in her situation (she didn't have pink hair or a pinkish complexion either) or with her self-esteem.

He lunged forward with a piercing stare, his face moving closer to hers, like a carnivore going after his succulent, meaty prey. "You're very pretty." Penelope's eyes lit up, and she felt a sudden heat starting to gush through her body. It began with her face that reddened by the second. He went on, "I just meant that lemonade is a very all-American and wholesome drink, and you're wholesome looking – pretty and wholesome looking. And it's very special."

Penelope could deal with that. He attached pretty with wholesome. And then there was the "special" part. She knew "special" meant one of a kind or at least one of the very few, and she could tell that it was a compliment since for that moment, Luke looked as though he wanted to devour her. Penelope shivered with excitement, suddenly feeling as though she was a waiting lamb in his lion's den.

"And you're from a very wholesome place, right?" he asked her.

"Yes. I guess you could say that. Small towns. I'm from Elmont, Illinois."

"That's right ...Where is that exactly? Is it near Chicago?"

"Oh no," Penelope uttered. She always found it humorous how people continually tried to locate her hometown by its proximity to Chicago, like Chicago was a planet at the center of the universe and all the other cities in Illinois orbited around it. "We're very far away from Chicago. Elmont is actually *way* far east, southeast of Chicago."

"Uh-huh."

"But my Grandfather, he was this big photographer, he lived in Chicago for a little while," she said, noticing his eyes veering down to his fork. "He was so wonderful." Penelope was about to tell a story about her grandfather when she was interrupted by a waiter dressed in full Indian garb carrying a tray.

"Ah, here it is," Luke announced, turning his focus from his fork to the food being served. As the waiter placed their meals in front of them, Penelope saw and smelled the curry and chili scents rising from their dishes. They wound around her and her dinner date, creating a gigantic and spicy cocoon that weighed heavy on and above their table.

"Oh my," Penelope said aloud what she thought by mistake.

"What's wrong?" he inquired. He motioned to her dish. "You don't like what I picked for you?" Penelope took a second to touch the side of a nostril of her burning nose, as if that would help in any way.

"No. It's fine."

She stared down at her dish, her heart skipping a beat when she thought of how Luke chose the entrée specifically for her out of the goodness of his heart, and then she blinked a little – Penelope suddenly found her dinner to be recognizable.

Gleeful, she picked up her platter that had a couple of pieces of meat on a stick, proclaiming, "Steak on a stick! My father makes this on the barbeque!"

He scratched his head. "It's not steak on a stick – that's Lamb Shish Kabob."

"Oh," Penelope replied, remembering him ordering it, and then she peered over at Luke's dish – chunks of chicken covered with some thick brown sauce.

"Well, dig in," he insisted, grinning from ear to ear, his fork stabbing a lump of poultry.

Penelope put her finger to her lip and wriggled her nose above the Lamb Shish Kabob. The spices catapulted from the lamb to her nostrils, almost throwing her back in her chair. She couldn't fathom how she was supposed to eat something that she couldn't even bear to smell. And then there was the matter of maneuvering the meal itself; she knew how to consume the "steak on a stick" that her father prepared (while wearing his big, white barbeque hat) on the grill in her backyard – with her hands. First blowing on it to cool it down and then sliding the chunks of steak off the stick and shoving them in her mouth.

She would have done the same with this meal if it wasn't for the fact that she was in an Indian restaurant, and so, she realized there might possibly be different protocol for eating what Penelope now called "lamb on a stick" (to herself) instead of Lamb Shish Kabob, and Penelope didn't want to appear as though she was an amateur in the methods of eating Indian food.

As Luke cut a piece of his chicken into a nice and neat little cube, Penelope took a look around, searching the other tables for "lamb on a stick" or at least anything with a stick through it, and how the other patrons, who were possibly more professional Indian food eaters than she was, ate it. But her eyes went from one table to another, and she couldn't find any meats on sticks. But she did see people eating other dishes with their hands, but then, of course, like Luke, there were also people using a knife and fork.

Penelope stared down at her plate again – *Eat with my hands? Eat with a fork and knife? ... What to do?*

Instead of plunging into her plate, Penelope decided to stall and continue with her story about her Grandfather Ben and Chicago, saying, "There was one time when we thought my grandfather was lost in a snow storm in Chicago. Well-"

Luke interrupted, "And did you know that Chicago is called the 'Windy City' not because of the actual wind, but because of the hot air coming from the Chicago politicians?" He slid a forkful of chicken into his mouth.

"Uh-yeah."

Really? she asked herself. To think, she'd been living in the state of Illinois for all her life, excluding her residency in New York, and she had the "Windy City" thing all wrong.

Penelope certainly wasn't going to tell Luke that she didn't know this factoid. What would that say about her?

Since she was on the subject of family – "So is your family in New York?" she asked him.

"Um. No," he answered, paying more attention to his food than Penelope's face, incising the chicken and dunking it into the brown sauce, even though the chicken was already slathered with it. "They're still in Connecticut where I was brought up."

"And they're in the same house?"

"Hey," Luke said, lifting his sights from his plate to hers, "you haven't touched your Lamb Shish Kabob. Is something wrong?"

"No. I'm just a slow eater."

"Well-dig in...Wait until you see what I'm going to pick for dessert."

"Uh-huh."

Penelope sighed – what was she to do, and what would Luke choose for desert? Hopefully the desert was cold, she thought, feeling that she needed to lower her body temperature, which at this point was probably up around two-hundred degrees Fahrenheit.

She watched Luke who was now concentrating on his chicken again, cutting it up, and she finally decided to follow-suit. After all, wasn't using a knife and fork at least more acceptable in the United States than using your hands? And even though they were in an Indian restaurant, weren't they in fact in an Indian restaurant in the United States?

Penelope remembered seeing some people in a New York City pizza parlor eating their pizza with a knife and fork, and then once, at a New York City deli, she saw people eating french fries with that same cutlery, and both times she was amazed – weren't these edibles supposed to be eaten with a person's hands? Weren't french fries finger food? They were thick deli steak fries, too, she thought. *Oh,* how Penelope longed for french fries and a corn beef on rye sandwich. Since she arrived in Manhattan, it had been her favorite meal – it was much better than the green peas and ham on white bread her mother always prepared for her in Elmont.

There was a rumbling in her hollow stomach. *Oh, what the hell,* she said to herself and planted her fork and knife into the lamb, cutting off a piece. Then she quietly placed the knife on the side of her plate, leaving a hand free for the pinching of her nose to stop any inhaling of spices. She looked over at Luke to make sure he wasn't watching what she was doing, and when she was sure, she squeezed her nose shut, and shoved the lamb into her mouth.

Penelope's taste buds immediately detected the chili on the lamb along with other spices that she couldn't identify by name. She scrunched her face. It was all right, she thought, but way too strong! Before Luke had the opportunity to see her reaction, she stopped pinching her nose and flattened-out her expression, and it was just in the nick of time, too, because only seconds later, he looked up and smiled at her, close-mouthed, since he was eating his chicken, his magnificent dimples showing. The dimples that could sink a million ships, she thought as she went to swallow the lamb.

Suddenly, Penelope felt something strange in her throat, and it was sharp.

She began to cough, trying to bring it up, and thinking that she might be choking, Penelope quickly placed her hand on her throat.

"Oh my God!" Luke cried causing everyone in the restaurant to stop what they were doing and turn around.

Luke threw the napkin on his lap onto the table and jumped up, rushing over to her. He moved behind the still hacking Penelope, ready to do the Heimlich Maneuver, when Penelope miraculously spit up what was in her throat into the palm of her hand – it was a long piece of stick.

Penelope had been so engaged in the way she was going to eat the "Lamb on the Stick" that she completely forgot about the "not eating the stick" part.

Shortly afterwards, Luke circled round and knelt down on one knee in front her. He lowered his eyes to the stick that Penelope was now analyzing, holding it between her forefinger and thumb. "The sticks - they can be tricky." He gently smiled and raised his eyes to peer into hers. "Don't ever be afraid to ask for help," he breathed like he was on the verge of whispering but not quite, his dark eyes smoldering and sparking, "I'm always here to oblige," and then he touched her chin, ever so lightly, and kissed her soft on the mouth, and Penelope, gushing with emotion from the tips of her toes to the top of her head, drifted off to an "other" place. An agreeably hot and spicy place, deep in a whimsical and magical forest where flutes played a sweet and flowing tune, fairies flew around with unicorns, a rainbow mist fell over the trees and woodland creatures, and where Luke was kissing Penelope in an Indian restaurant that she swore she would never forget.

George Bailey: You understand that? I want to do what I want to do.

Seven

"**H**ello? Hello?" Penelope said into her cell phone while she sat in her office cubicle early in the morning, tapping her desk calendar with a pen, still flying high from her date with Luke from the night before.

She smiled to herself thinking of what a good kisser he was and about his soft but assertive lips, and then she thought of the smell of his hair as he put his mouth to hers. She was so close to his hair, and it emitted a scent that she never encountered before – so masculine that it made her think of things much more than blush worthy.

"Hello?" came from the other end of the phone.

At the same time Penelope was thinking about Luke, she was also wondering if it was such a good idea for her to call the lovesick man who had text and called her throughout most of the summer, thinking she was his stalking interest "Cassandra." But here she was…

"Is this DePeche?" Penelope asked.

There was an audible grumbling at the other end, and then – "Yeah. This is Depeche." He sounded very much on the offensive.

Not wanting her coworkers to know that she was making a personal call, Penelope lowered her voice. "Hello, um, I'm calling you about your text messages."

He immediately reacted with a tinge of a drawl – "Whas up? You callin' me about my bill? Cause I pay my phone bill. I tell the lady before I'd pay it, and I pay it the other day. Ya' see, I have problems with my bills –like my internet and cable. And dang-man! I don't know who ordered those porn flicks, but I pay my cell phone last week!"

"Um …Well, that's great that you paid your bill…and I feel really bad about your financial problems and…um porn thing," she responded, having no clue about what he was saying. "But I'm not calling you about any of that, really. I'm calling because you have the wrong contact information for a girl named 'Cassandra.'" She explained, "See, when you thought you were texting and calling her, you were actually texting and calling me."

The conversation went quiet for a couple of moments, and then suddenly he blustered, "What you talkin' bout? Is this Ariana?" He was completely irate. "Ariana, you bitch! You talk bad about me to Cassandra! Now you make me a fool disguisin' ya' voice and shit and tellin' me that I've been textin anotha person and makin' calls to anotha bitch?"

"No, no," Penelope protested, cringing from his cursing, dropping her pen on her desk and waving her hands around as she spoke. "I'm not Ariana. And you've really had the wrong number all along. You've been contacting me. Not Cassandra."

"And who are you?" he asked, his anger seething through the phone.

"Penelope … Penelope McAdams."

"Oh, damn, Ariana, you bitch! What you give me a fool's name for?" he hollered and then hung up.

"Hello? Hello?" she said, and when she realized DePeche had truly left the conversation, she pressed the red button on her BlackBerry and slowly placed the phone down, next to her computer.

She mumbled to herself – "Fool's name? Penelope McAdams? …What's wrong with Penelope McAdams?"

Penelope's eyes rotated around and then up. "Oh my!" she exclaimed, startled by a pair of bright blue irises peering over her cubicle wall.

The irises belonged to Wendy.

"What are you up to?" Wendy asked, her eyes narrowing to slits.

First, Wendy had been intrigued about Penelope because she came from a small town that she was sure had big secrets, and now, after Penelope phoned her the other day to tell her about the miracle – that she got her text messages – she seemed even more interested in her and the goings on in her life; especially since she was the one who helped get the text messages back, having traded in a bundle of booty calls for a favor for a coworker and friend.

As Wendy stared at her, Penelope could sense she felt entitled to tidbits of information.

"Nothing," Penelope answered her while arranging some papers on her desk. "Nothing. I was just talking with one of the guys who text me."

"Really?" Wendy said, chomping at the bit. "Who?"

Penelope sighed, knowing she had to divulge some information. "This guy. DePeche."

"DePeche? I don't remember him being on your dating list."

"That's because he isn't," she said. "He had the wrong number. He thought he was texting this girl he liked, but he was really texting me."

"Uh-huh."

"And I just called him to clear up the situation."

Wendy set her chin on top of the cubicle wall. "So what you're telling me is that you called a guy who contacted you, but it wasn't for you, it was actually for some other girl?"

"Yeah."

Wendy burst out laughing.

"What?" Penelope asked, frowning and putting her hands to her hips.

Some of their officemates turned around to them, and Wendy quickly put the lid on her guffaws. "Nothing. It's just rich that's all."

"What? What's rich?"

"That you called a guy that you don't even know to tell him that he's been texting the wrong girl."

"So? What makes that rich?" Penelope still wasn't understanding the 'rich' concept very well.

"It's just funny that's all."

"Really? So what if I told you he was the guy who text me the most? Would you call that rich?"

"No," Wendy firmly stated. "*That* I would call pathetic."

Penelope shrugged her off, saying, "Be that as it may, it's the truth," and then she felt the need to clarify her position – "This man - or boy, rather, thought that he was contacting the love of his life 'Cassandra,' leaving all these messages, and he wasn't getting any response. I just thought I'd clear things up for him, that's all." She continued, "And who knows. Maybe because of what I just did, they'll eventually get together." Suddenly, out of nowhere, a nail file appeared in Wendy's hand, and she stretched her arms over the cubicle wall and proceeded to give herself a manicure as Penelope went on. "Although I think she might have given him the wrong number on purpose," Penelope remarked. "But who knows. Maybe Ariana was the one who gave DePeche the wrong number."

Wendy stopped filing. "Who's Ariana?"

"Oh, some girl who's friends with Cassandra," she answered. "She certainly doesn't seem to like DePeche much."

"So you know Ariana?"

"Nope. Only from DePeche."

"Who you also don't know."

"Uh-huh," Penelope casually answered as she fiddled with the knobs on her computer, trying to figure out which one would brighten up her screen.

"Mmmm," Wendy sounded, rolling her eyes, and then she started to file again with a smirk.

Penelope was confused by Wendy's reaction. "What?" she asked. "It was the right thing to do."

"Well. I don't know if it was the *right* thing to do, but it was certainly the *nice* thing to do."

"What does that mean?"

"It means that ninety-nine percent of the people in this city would never have done it," Wendy explained. "They would've shirked it off and said it was this guy's problem, not theirs, and what's the sense of getting involved? What would *they* get out of it? And what did *you* get out of it, my friend?" Wendy pointed her nail file directly at Penelope, saying, "Remember, Penelope. In Manhattan, it's each man for himself … or woman rather." She pulled her nail file back, noticing that her coworker had now become visibly distressed, shutting her eyes tight and rubbing her tiny temples.

It was all too much for Penelope that she still wasn't catching onto the attitudes of the metropolis, and what made it worse was that other people, such as Wendy, still noticed her small town ways.

Penelope immediately thought of Luke and the comment he made to her the night before, and stopped massaging her head.

"Do you think lemonade is nice?" she asked out-of-the-blue.

Wendy yawned and began to slowly recede into her cubicle. "I never really thought about it much. Why?"

"Because last night Luke told me I was like lemonade."

"What?" Wendy immediately threw down her nail file, and her head popped up over their separation once more. Her blue eyes seemed to expand from one end of the room to the other; a sure sign that Penelope had finally told her something interesting after more than a year's worth of providing her with dull stories about Elmont – the horse and buggy rides in the Christmas snow; how the owner of the town's sweets shoppe showed Penelope how to make homemade chocolate ice cream one summer; and how the town's fire department saved a cat that got caught in Elmont's oldest and tallest tree – and boy, were they surprised when they found out the cat had delivered kittens while she was up in the lofty heights of the branches. ("I had a nightmare last night," Wendy said one morning, "I dreamt I was being held hostage in a Waltons' episode.") "You went on a date with that Luke guy you were pining for?" she asked, but it came out more accusatory than questioning. "Why didn't you tell me?"

"I was going to tell you when you were in the kitchen, but then I saw you with that doughnut in your hand," she commented. "It looked like you were really enjoying it. I didn't want to bother you."

Wendy wagged a finger at her. "Gossip comes first. First and foremost," she informed. "The minute you came in and saw me you should have said, 'Drop that doughnut, Wendy. I've got some interesting shit to tell you.'"

Penelope wrinkled her freckled nose. "I would've never said the S word."

"Okay. You would've said 'I've got some interesting crap to tell you,'" she commented. "You are allowed to say the word 'crap,' aren't you?"

Penelope shrugged.

Wendy continued, "And gossip goes with the doughnuts, Penelope. Women have spent decades gossiping over doughnuts...Gossip and doughnuts. "Wendy held one hand up and shook it – "Gossip" and then held the other one up and shook it – "and Doughnuts."

Penelope nodded, expressing to her that she understood the gist – doughnuts and gossiping were to women as beer and swaggered talk were to men (she had overheard way too many male conversations at Manhattan bars over the past year).

"Okay," Wendy salivated, "tell me everything."

Penelope beamed and leapt in her seat. Just thinking of Luke Carson gave her goose pimples all over, so going one step further to talk about him, gave her goose pimples *and* made her feel like a Mexican jumping bean. "Well, we went to this Indian food restaurant in the Lower East Side," she said and then thought to herself for a second, and then rambled, "I don't remember the name really, but the food was interesting, and I guess it was good because Luke picked it, and he told me he only knows the best places in the city." Wendy screwed her face and rubbed her chin as Penelope chattered away – "But I was having a problem eating the food, y'know, because honestly, I didn't know how to eat it...and then, I thought of Princess Grace and Monaco ..." and then Penelope went on and on about the details of the restaurant – the middle eastern ambiance, the impeccable service, and the spicy meals – as Wendy listened, or at least tried to listen as she blinked at least two times per second, trying to keep her eyes open, fighting her drooping lids.

Finally, Wendy couldn't take it anymore. "Penelope," she interrupted, "I don't want to hear about the restaurant or the food or the company who made the chair that you sat on." Wendy poked at the corner of one of her peepers, cleaning out some crud that could only be sleep-induced. "Tell me about Luke," she implored. "What happened?"

A little smile crept onto Penelope's face. "It was great. I choked on a stick, and then he kissed me."

Passing over the "choking on a stick" part, probably realizing it wasn't significant since Penelope couldn't possibly be dead (because she was right in front of her talking in mundane circles and incomplete sentences), Wendy got to what she felt was the good stuff. "So he kissed you," she commented and then leaned forward. "And then what?"

"And then we ate and he took me home."

"That's it?" Wendy asked, disappointed, her lower lip protruding as though she was a little girl who just left the doctor's office without a lollipop. "That's all?"

Penelope's shoulders lifted. "What else is there?" she asked naively, thinking there couldn't possibly be more for a second date. "Oh yes," she added, "there's still that matter of the lemonade...He told me that Princess Grace was like champagne, and that I was like lemonade." She sighed. "He said that lemonade was wholesome, and that I was wholesome." She folded her arms and frowned. "Honestly, Wendy, now that I think about it, I don't really want to be compared to lemonade."

Wendy shook her head and groaned under her breath. "Penelope. The man is well-off, handsome, and single, and you're telling me there was only a kiss?" She elevated an eyebrow. "You're lemonade, honey." She nodded and declared, "Oh yes. You're lemonade."

Penelope was about to refute Wendy's comment when Ginger, the account supervisor, showed up in their little office huddle, in her pristine, navy blue skirt suit. "I've been watching the two of you lately," she said, tossing back some of her pale blonde hair, "and I can just swear that you don't want to keep your jobs. Why else would you keep talking like you do?"

Wendy quickly pulled her head away from her coworker's cubicle, and Penelope stared down at the floor.

"Now, I'm all for coworkers getting along and bonding," Ginger remarked, "but not on paid time. Leave it for the lunchroom, girls, or not only am I going to have to separate the both of you, but I'm also going to have to talk to Mr. Renquist, and I'm sure you don't want that."

Penelope and Wendy shook their heads, and Penelope thought about what would happen if she lost her job - the only thing worse than living in her small, capsule-sized studio, would be living on the streets, which is what would happen if she didn't have any income to pay her rent.

"Good," Ginger said, composing herself and straightening out her perfectly tailored suit jacket. She provided a narrow smile, which conveyed politeness without giving up power, and then turned to Penelope. "By the way, Penelope," she uttered, "I just got a call from the downstairs desk. Something just arrived for you, and they're bringing it up," and then she strutted away in her stilettos.

Penelope and Wendy exchanged puzzled expressions.

"Penelope McAdams!"a man cried out in their office area. He was clothed in a paper bag-brown jumpsuit and held a bouquet of long-stemmed, blush-colored roses in a crystal vase that had a gigantic, pink bow tied around it.

The office staff turned around – some to the roses and others to Penelope, who, at the sight of the incredible flower arrangement, went slack-jawed, but was able to move her mouth just enough to answer, "Yes. That's me."

The man strolled over to her and then dropped the roses on her desk.

Penelope and Wendy sat still, gawking at the roses, and then a crowd of women, which included Ginger, hurried over in their spiked heels for an up-close look at the wonderful surprise.

All the women went quiet as Penelope examined the unexpected parcel of roses and picked off a tiny envelope lodged between two of the flowers.

"They're beautiful," cooed one of the admiring women.

The crowd of females let out a resounding *mmmmm*.

Ginger, getting into the thrill of the moment, excitedly asked, "Well?

Who are they from?"

Collectively, the women created a huge collage of bug-eyes as they stood around watching Penelope in anticipation of finding out who sent her the glorious flowers.

Penelope felt the perspiration of pressure building up in the collar of her blouse (a no-name blouse, and she didn't think anyone would notice, but she pulled away from the women just the same), as she opened the envelope and card. She read to herself:

Dear Penelope,
I had a great time last night.
Looking forward to spending future nights and days with you.
Luke

"Oh my God," Penelope said, her eyes growing larger by the minute.

"What?" Wendy asked, and the women moved in closer.

Penelope shook her head, like she was trying to wake herself up from a dream. "It's from Luke."

Wendy jolted back. "*No way.*"

Penelope nodded, and all the women became chatterboxes (*Who? What? Where?* they asked), and then – "Who's Luke?" poured out of Ginger's mouth.

"It's this guy I just started dating."

Ginger matter-of-factly noted, "How lucky you are to find such a man."

All the Blue Bloods, as Wendy always called these women, nodded and there were more *mmmmm*s, and as Penelope touched the rose petals with delicacy, so as not to disturb any stem in the arrangement, something suddenly struck her – it was all happening the way she originally imagined (they would way say - *How lucky you are to find such an "elite" man*). A couple of more comments (like *Luke is someone we would date...He's like most of our boyfriends*), and she could bridge the threshold (*Penelope McAdams, you have finally crossed over to being a full-fledged New York City woman!*).

As Ginger opened her mouth, looking ready to talk again, Penelope smiled big and bright. She was enthralled with the moment and the giddiness about possibly crossing over – that was until a familiar male voice jutted out, "Hey, girls. Having fun?"

Alarmed at hearing the voice of Alden Renquist, the crowd immediately jerked around to see where he was and were disconcerted to find his head amongst their own, being a part of their event, and for how long no one knew.

They all stared at him with astonished mouths, not knowing what to expect.

"What's going on here?" he inquired, the tone of his voice at the breaking point of a roar.

No one moved, and then Ginger impressively stepped up to the plate, and with shoulders back and a confident gaze, answered, "We were just talking to Penelope about one of her accounts."

"Oh yeah?" he said sardonically, eying the roses up and down behind his spectacles, and then raising an eyebrow at Ginger. "Did Henshaw Tractors send her the roses?" He glared at the group. "Because that's Penelope's only account, and so, I'm assuming you're talking about them and not the flowers."

The room suddenly got hot, and everyone was completely mute.

"I'd like to have a talk with Penelope, that is - if you all don't mind," he commented, snarling, particularly at Ginger, probably figuring she should display better behavior than her underlings. He then turned to Penelope and said, "I want to see you in my office...You have two minutes," and then walked into his office and slammed the door behind him.

The women made clattering sounds with their stilettos as they rushed back to their desks, and Penelope was left alone with her thoughts; her mind wandered off to her inability to get any press coverage for Henshaw Tractors, her meeting with her boss and having to tell him that there wasn't any upcoming press coverage, and her previous fear of losing her job, losing her miniature studio, and then having to reside in the gutter, or worse, having to go back to Elmont, Illinois, dejected, never to fulfill the promise of living a new and better life.

As Penelope went to grab a pen and writing tablet for the meeting trembling about getting the heave ho, she couldn't help but look over at her roses. She took a second to think about the posies and about Luke. *Wow,* she thought, *he really likes me … Little old me.*

Wendy rolled her chair back from behind the partition, and stared at the roses, as well. "Not bad for lemonade," she said.

"Is that meant to be sarcastic?" Penelope asked her, defensive of her gift.

"No. I'm just saying," she reacted. "Sarcasm would mean I was jealous…and I'm not jealous…much." Wendy thought to herself for a moment while Penelope panicked about her occupational fate and erratically searched for her favorite ballpoint pen on her desk; she thought the pen would be some sort of comfort to her while her boss read her the riot act.

"You know what," Wendy said, "you should pick up the phone and thank him." She tittered, "Or better yet, text him."

"I'll thank Luke for the flowers after I get out of my meeting. I just can't think straight right now, if you know what I mean."

"I didn't mean, Luke. I meant Ted. You should call Ted Hollis."

"Who?" Penelope absentmindedly asked, rummaging around for her favorite pen under a pile of folders.

Wendy's jaw fell slightly. "Ted Hollis. The guy who got you your texts so you could go on your date and get your roses? Remember him?"

"Oh yeah," Penelope uttered, not paying too much attention to what Wendy was going on about as she continued to look for the pen, and then finally found it hidden – in her pencil and pen cup. *Duh,* she thought to herself as she pulled it out of the cup and cradled the writing tablet in the crook of her arm. "That reminds me. If Mr. Renquist doesn't fire me, I'm going to ask him if he'd be interested in me as a candidate for the Streamers Technology account."

Wendy jumped up and in a hushed voice said, "No. No, Penelope. And again, I'll say *NO* - I thought you got over that. You know nothing about technology, remember?"

"I told you - I can learn … And besides. How do I know you're not just saying this because you want the technology account for yourself?

Maybe you're just trying to hinder my success."

Wendy folded her arms in front of her and glowered. "How could you say that? I would totally be upfront with you if I wanted that account." She shook her head. "And I don't want it. It involves too much traveling, and I don't fly unless I have to go to my parents in Florida for a family emergency or there's a Loehmann's sale on couture bags in another state." Wendy squinted at her, remarking, "And don't get snotty on me, Penelope. Not you. Don't turn into one of those Blue Bloods."

Penelope blinked a couple of times, thinking about how she was acting, and she felt a sudden urge – a force of nature – pushing her to say what she always did when she had the inclination she was hurting someone's feelings – "I'm sorry." But she didn't. It had been a full-year since she said it, and she wasn't about to turn back now. So instead she commented, "You're the one who told me that it's every woman for herself in this city. What else am I supposed to think?" and then she turned on her heels and walked towards the closed entrance of Alden Renquist's office.

"Good luck," Wendy mumbled.

Penelope knocked on the door.

"Come in!" her boss exclaimed, and she tiptoed into his office as if he wasn't expecting her or as if the clomping of her feet on his nicely carpeted floor would disturb the football and baseball memorabilia he had on his walls and shelves.

As she sat down in front of his desk, she noticed a Giants football scribbled with signatures set in a glass box. She thought about Ted Hollis and the objects he surrounded himself with and wondered – *does every man collect things?*

Alden Renquist had his head down, his flipped-out bangs brushing the rim of his glasses as he busily wrote something. "So, Penelope," he said, "what's happening with the Henshaw Tractors account?"

"It's going well," Penelope answered. She was lying and panicking and working hard not to show it.

He looked up at her face for a brief second and then down again, doing long swipes on his papers with a pen like he was deleting huge things that he inevitably felt he didn't need anymore. Penelope wondered if she was one of them.

Her boss picked up a large cup of Starbuck's coffee, took a swig, and then put it down.

"Going well, huh?" he mimicked, cool as a cucumber, now paying attention to Penelope's presence, and she wasn't exactly sure she liked it. He leaned back in his chair and folded his hands, presenting a very professorial look that she wasn't used to. "Look, Penelope," he said to her with a timbre not unlike his now sedate appearance. "I know you're having problems with the account, and you must know, it must be obvious, that I like you ..."

You're fired, Penelope immediately thought while her stomach was tied up in excruciating knots. *That's what the end of this sentence is... I like you but you're fired.*

He continued, "So when I see you flounder like this it makes me sad."

And you're fired, Penelope repeated in her head as she held her breath, which made the knots in her stomach more painful. *Just say it already! Penelope-you're floundering, so I'm firing you! Say it!*

"But even though you're floundering, I still feel that you have great potential and so, I'm not going to fire you," he said. Penelope let out her breathe, and the knots in her stomach unraveled. "And also, I'm not going to fire you because of this," he added, and Alden Renquist pulled out a gigantic pill bottle from under his desk and set it next to his papers. "Good ole' Xanax." He patted the bottle cap like a person would warmly pat the shoulder of a good and close friend.

Penelope didn't say a word about her boss' behavior that, after working there for a year, she deemed be his normal state of being.

She was just beside herself with joy that she wasn't getting fired.

Alden Renquist continued, "Do you know what alimony is, Penelope?"

"Uh. Yes," Penelope answered, now concerned that she may wind up knowing more about her boss – specifically about his broken marriage – than she wanted to.

"But you've never experienced anything about it yourself ... I take it our parents have been married for what–thirty years?"

She hated to rub salt in the wound, but she was basically a truthful person. "No, Mr. Renquist," she amended, "they've actually been married for forty years."

"Forty years!" he exclaimed with an awed and amused expression, and he slammed his hand on his desk, almost losing his spectacles in the process. "That's incredible! Incredible! Have you called Guinness?"

"Excuse me?"

He waved his hands in front of him. "Never mind…But see, that's what I'm talking about. You have potential because you're fresh and down-home, and closer to the basics. You're not like the other girls in this office. You're the real stuff. You're down-to-earth, Penelope …You know what? You're not just down to earth – you *are* the earth," he declared, and then he slammed his hand on his desk again. "Wait a minute. I've got it." He pointed at her. "You're the salt-of-the-earth. And that's why I pretty much favor you in this office and picked you from that small, insignificant town in the South."

"The Midwest."

Alden Renquist slapped his hand on his desk for a third time, exclaiming, "That's right! The Midwest! Where your family were farmers!"

Penelope squirmed at having to correct him for a second time (or was it third?). "Teachers."

"Aren't we all teachers in some way, Penelope?" he questioned her with raised eyebrows, and he touched his bottle of Xanax once more. "And I do understand that you may be having a hard time, Penelope. It's difficult moving from a small town to a big place like Manhattan. I too lived in a small town once….for a couple of months. And I also found it wasn't easy moving to New York City after living there." His eyes widened. "Tell me, Penelope, have you ever heard of Cherry Hill, New Jersey?"

Penelope thought about it for a second, but before she could completely process the question, he jumped in – "It's not very far, and it's a pretty nice place, but the point is that I adjusted and you can too, and you can do this. I have faith in you. Have you started on those letters to the celebrities yet? To be spokespeople for the tractors?"

Penelope became nervous again remembering how she tried to write a letter to Brad Pitt and Angelina Jolie (or was that Angelina Jolie and Brad Pitt – which came first?), and the other stars he mentioned to her, but came up with nothing since she didn't know much about their lives having not read many gossip magazines. "I'm working on it, Mr. Renquist. I've started the one on Brad Pitt and Angelina Jolie."

"Yes, Brangelina," he said to her, and Penelope had no idea what he was talking about and was now even more confused about the celebrity couple than before.

He looked down at his papers and commented, "They've adopted a lot of kids. One of them must have come with a tractor." He flipped through some documents. "Well, Penelope – keep at it. We'll talk about this some more within the next couple of weeks, and we'll review the progress you're making."

Before the end of the conversation, Penelope gathered her guts together. "Mr. Renquist. About the technology account- the Streamers Technology account - I'd like to be seriously considered for the managing position."

Upon her request, Alden Renquist slowly moved his sights from his papers to Penelope's hopeful face, and then, with an extremely serious expression, said, "No."

Penelope's face dropped. "May I ask why? Is it because of the tractor account because I swear, when I get the letters going and make some more phone calls, I'm sure I can get media coverage."

"It's not about that, Penelope. It's just that the technology account isn't for you."

"No? But Mr. Renquist, I really think I can do it."

Her boss adjusted his spectacles on his face. "Penelope. Look, I see you around the office, and I see that you're no good at technology."

Penelope was horrified. Her boss knew as well? She could only wonder how much of a glaring example of technological stupidity she was. Was she the poster child for the technologically impaired?

"Really?" she asked him, her expression turning desperate, and then she remembered what Wendy said about her handing in her personal time sheets in a Word document instead of in Excel like the rest of the office. "Is it about my WordPerfect time sheets? I can do them in Excel if you'd like." She would find a way to do it, she thought.

"Penelope. It's not just about the time sheets ... You don't even understand the fundamentals of technology ... My God, you don't even know how to work the coffee maker."

"The coffee maker?" Penelope suddenly recalled a meeting when Ginger asked her to make coffee, and she just stood there, shell-shocked. But Penelope didn't know how to use the coffee maker because she never drank coffee. *And why did they have to make the coffee makers so intricate,* she wondered. *And what is it with the switches and the ridged cups and strainer?* And if there was a strainer involved, like with making pasta, was making coffee not unlike making spaghetti? Because she could make spaghetti ...kind of.

"Forget about the coffee maker," he said, waving his hands around. "Look, if you want the technology account, you can try for it like everyone else. But like I said the other day, anyone who wants it, is going to have to dazzle me. But Penelope, again, after seeing how you are, I'm suggesting that you should concentrate on the Henshaw account, and forget about Streamers Technology." Then, he punctured his statement with a "Really."

Penelope looked down at the floor and bit her lip.

"Time to end our meeting ... Time for me to go to divorce court." He grumbled, "For the millionth time."

Feeling wounded, she slowly got up from her chair.

Alden Renquist's mood suddenly changed from congenial to grumpy. "Go!" he yelled.

Penelope hurried out of his office, past curious faces, and plopped her pad and pen down on the desk and her bottom on her chair. She looked over at the roses that should have served as a reminder that not all was bad. Luke had come into her life again and in a big way – *looking forward to spending more nights and days together,* he wrote. How wonderful was that?

But still she was a bit glum as her fingers twined through the flowers and grazed the crystal vase. She pulled a little at the bow. She wanted to be taken seriously – she wanted that technology account.

"What happened?" Wendy asked from her cubicle.

"Nothing." Penelope was in a daze, thinking of how she could dazzle her boss into giving her the Streamers account. "We talked about Henshaw Tractors," she said, and then, it immediately became obvious to her – "I need to make coffee."

"But I thought you were all about the lemonade."

"It seems like all of a sudden everything's about a beverage."

"Did you ask him about the technology account?"

"Yeah," Penelope replied, "he said that I wouldn't be good for it."

"Hey, he's right." Wendy added, "it's really all for the best."

"Yeah," she said, but pursed her lips as she planned and plotted how she was going to learn about working the coffee machine and then about the subject that eluded and frightened her the most – technology. "All for the best."

Young Mary: Is this the ear that you can't hear on? ... George Bailey, I'll love you 'til the day I die.

Eight

Penelope hugged her Williams-Sonoma bag at her chest that contained her new Cuisinart 12-Cup Coffeemaker, which she would use to learn all the secrets of blending potent granules of caffeine for the sake of impressing Alden Renquist and legally drugging up anyone who came within five feet of her (*Ha! Ha! Why yes I can make coffee*, she'll say to whomever, *doesn't everybody?*). This was one of her present purposes. The other was to express her anger to the AT & T salesman who sold her the BlackBerry without the text service as she stood there in the cold and snowy weather with her coffeemaker, staring into the window of the AT & T store.

"Why are we stopping?" questioned Stacey with a scarlet nose, pulling up her collar as the flakes of snow fell on top of them. Her Vaseline gloves made a squishing sound as her hands grasped the neck of her coat.

Tugging at her white knit hat, Penelope went to cover an exposed region of her forehead and the top of her ears. "You see that guy over there?" Penelope asked, pointing with a fleece gloved finger to the AT & T salesman who did her wrong.

Stacey moved next to Penelope and peered through the window. "Yeah?

"That's the salesman who sold me the BlackBerry without the text messaging."

"The pole with the mustache?"

Penelope looked on at the bone thin man who went about his business of helping – or not helping, rather – customers as she sneered at him behind a plate of glass.

"So strange to see a man with a mustache," Stacey commented, "most men are clean-shaven these days." She sniffled, and they watched him cross the floor to a register. "I don't like him," Wendy stated and her face soured. "He looks devious. He looks like he's hiding something."

"I know what he's hiding," Penelope uttered. "He's hiding his guilt for not giving me the text service. That's what he's hiding," Penelope frowned and her eyeballs rolled from one side of the store to the other as she followed the salesman's every move with disdain.

Stacey turned away from the store. "Let's go. He's not worth it," she remarked. "Like all men."

But Penelope continued to stare and glare and crinkle her freckled nose as the salesman straightened a row of cell phones, unaware of her presence at the front window of the store.

"What's going on?" Cory's voice panted. He trudged through the snow in his heavy parka and plaid hunter's hat with earflaps looking as goofy as a cartoon character. On his shoulder hung a gold tote handbag that in the beginning of the day's escapades was worn by Sonia.

Sonia walked unsteadily beside him, trying not to trip in the mounds of snow covering the streets, carrying a bag with her new loaf pan – "Why did you get a loaf pan?" Cory asked her in Williams-Sonoma. "You've never made a loaf-anything in your life."

Cory, out of breath, halted at the curb. "Why did we stop?"

With a sly smile, Stacey informed, "Penelope's got a crush on an AT & T salesman."

Even though Penelope knew she was joking, just the thought of her saying that she had a crush on the AT & T salesman made her want to lunge at Stacey, wrestle her to the freezing ground, and pull off her oozy gloves and galoshes – "There's your hand and foot modeling career! Now, go get frost bitten in your extremities!" Penelope would yell.

"What?" Cory asked, bewildered. "I thought you said you were dating that guy Luke?"

Penelope sighed at the stupidity of it all. "I am," she said, her eyes still glued on the twig with an AT & T tag.

"So he works at an AT & T store?"

Penelope took a moment to sneer at her brother and say, "No! Luke owns a shipping company and he's wealthy! He isn't any AT & T salesman!" She noticed the handbag on his shoulder and thought he looked completely ridiculous.

"Well excuuuse me," Cory responded with raised eyebrows. "Aren't we high and mighty now?"

Penelope didn't say anything to him and turned back to the store window.

Stacey commented, "Pen's pissed off at the AT & T salesman who didn't give her the text service. That's who she's giving the evil eye to."

Putting his fists up in the air, the handbag swinging at his side, Cory said, "You want me to kick his ass, Pen, huh? Do ya?"

"Oh stop it," Sonia interceded, and she slapped his hands down. "You're just trying to act macho because you're wearing my handbag."

Stacey giggled.

Her brother huffed, "Why did you have to go and point it out for?"

"But honey," Sonia said, "I just couldn't hold it anymore, it was too heavy."

"Don't worry," Stacey joked. She smoothed out her shiny black hair that was being slowly masked by flakes. "I didn't notice-it goes so well with your whole outfi t...Where did you pick it up?" and she giggled some more.

Sulking, Cory started to walk away from them, complaining, "I feel totally emasculated! Totally emasculated!"

"Honey!" Sonia called out. "You're doing it because you love me! Remember?"

Stacey ran after him, as best as she could in her squishy galoshes, laughing and loudly mimicking Sonia, "You love me, remember?" *Ha! Ha!* "You love me!"

Sonia stood at Penelope's side, first eying her, concerned, and then she looked into the store and at the AT & T salesman. "Come on, Pen. We have to go to Best Buy."

Penelope shook her head. "I can't believe this guy has gotten off scot-free."

"Come on. All he did was sell you a BlackBerry without the text service. It's not like he murdered or maimed you or really ruined your life," Sonia said, "You still wound up with Luke," and then Sonia went quiet for a moment. "Although," she continued, "if he gave you the text messaging service, you would have been with Luke last year, and right now, we would've probably been planning your wedding," and she clomped away from a now even more angry and horrified Penelope – *he took away an entire year of my life! And now he took away my wedding! … That … that … (What word to use?)… that cad!*

Penelope was fuming, and she wanted to do something about it. She wanted to holler curse words (would her brother faint?), she wanted to throw hard, snow boulders through the window (would she wind up in jail and on the front page of the Elmont Picayune?), she wanted to make hot coffee with her new coffee maker and walk in and throw it in his face leaving him (a little, she thought) deformed for the rest of his life (a year…a couple of months tops).

"Pen, come on!" Sonia yelled as she tried to catch up with Stacey and her irritated boyfriend.

Just at that moment, the mustached AT & T salesman, who was now talking to a customer, caught a glimpse of Penelope at the window. He squinted at her, appearing as if he was trying to place her face.

Ooooh! He doesn't even remember me! You took a piece of my life, AT & T man! You took a piece of it and delayed my wedding! Penelope thought of how she might've had a wedding this spring if he had given her the text service. A spring wedding would've been so nice! And now it would be a winter or fall wedding maybe! *Ooooh!* She burned. *It's too cold to have a wedding in the winter - and a lot of people won't come - and in the fall you're always risking an early snow - people won't come!*

The AT & T salesman watched Penelope intently, now nodding as if he finally understood who she was, and he even smirked, which brought Penelope's tantrum to a head, and she was about to scream out the biggest curses she ever heard, beside herself with fury … but then she couldn't. She just stood there, stiff, her face scrunched up and all red, and her hands balled into fists.

Suddenly, a homeless woman came up next to her in ragged clothes wearing a red, white and blue pin that said "I LIKE IKE" and seeing how Penelope was so insistent in looking into the AT & T store, looked herself, and saw the salesman.

The homeless woman slowly raised her hand and gave the AT & T salesman the finger.

The AT & T salesman frowned, twitched his mustache, and walked away, and Penelope looked on at the homeless woman, beaming with gratitude. "Thank you," she said to her, "thank you," and passed her a dollar bill.

***

"Now, are you going to be all right?" Sonia asked Penelope in the DVD section of the Best Buy store.

Penelope squinted at her, wondering what she was getting at. "Yes," she answered," of course I'll be all right," and she spread her arms out, inquiring, "What could happen?"

Sonia passed her a wary expression. "Well. After what happened in the other store with the coffee maker, I just wanted to make sure you'd be okay." She glanced around, seemingly concerned. "After all, *this is* the mega store for contraptions."

Grimacing, Penelope offered up a *hmmph.*

Yes. It was true that Penelope had some issues in Williams-Sonoma with the coffeemaker on display. Okay. So maybe dropping the coffeemaker five times while Sonia tried to explain to her the mechanics of the apparatus meant she had more than some issues and could possibly join a circus clown show if her public relations career failed. But Penelope was sure that if it wasn't for the wave of anxiety she felt as Sonia told her of the ins-and-outs and specific features of the coffee maker – it's fully automated 24-hour programmability, brew pause, charcoal water filter and gold tone filter, the glass carafe for preparing twelve cups of coffee – that her fumbling and bumbling wouldn't have happened. As it was, her venturing off into the new world of technology, no matter how rudimentary, reminded Penelope of how her nerves had been when she first encountered a practice SAT test – they were twisted tight, sending mixed bursts of signals to her brain, causing her to mind to go blank – and in the case of the coffee maker in Williams-Sonoma – lose all manual dexterity.

Her brother shook his head while he watched his lovely girlfriend point out different aspects of the machine to his sister like a letter turner on a game show – "and you put the coffee in here," Sonia said, "and the on switch is here."

"But she doesn't even drink coffee," her brother commented. "And why is she getting one with so many buttons? … She's going to blow up the world with one press of a button." He shouted, "Kaboom!" and then one more for measure – "Kaboom!" and Sonia spun around and silenced him with a dirty look.

"I'll be okay," Penelope assured her with a straight face, "I just want to look around. I promise I won't touch anything."

"How about promising me you'll stay in the DVD section? It's safe here," she said, and then Penelope realized that Sonia asking her to go to the DVD section because she was trying to find a DVD on the art of knitting caftans, had all been a ruse. Sonia wasn't interested in knitting caftans or scarves or pom-pom hats or any other piece of clothing that's eventual destination was the bottom of a closet underneath some dirty, forgotten underwear or broken piece of luggage. All Sonia was interested in was keeping Penelope in the DVD section so she could stay out of trouble and hence, keep her boyfriend from complaining about his sister's unusual behavior, antics and attitude, as of late, in her ear.

Penelope rolled her eyes. "Don't worry. Okay? It'll all be fine."

A blend of skepticism and apprehension covered Sonia's face. "Okay," she said, sounding unsure about leaving Penelope to her own devices *anywhere* in the store and remembering how Cory tried to push Penelope into following him to the computer area ("if you get in trouble for mishandling something, I won't bail you out," he told her, "and then I'm sending you back to Elmont!")

"If you need us, we'll be at the computers downstairs." Sonia pointed to a staircase to the ground floor. "And Stacey will be downstairs, too. In the TV section." Sonia appeared dumbfounded. "I can't believe what she did to her old remote. And all because her cable went out." Sonia shook her head and commented, "I'm surprised she didn't get a bruise on her hand. Even with the gloves," and then she shrugged and walked away, leaving Penelope alone next to a rack filled with old comedy flicks.

Penelope picked up a random movie – "Space Balls" – perused the cover, cringed with complete disinterest, and then put it down. Quickly, she scanned her surroundings, making sure that Sonia or her brother weren't spying on her. Once she knew the coast was clear, she darted to the gaming aisle where throngs of men were situated at two of the store's gaming stations with most observing and a few playing, pulling at the handles of their control boxes and staring up at the vibrant graphics on the television screens like zombies. One of the zombies was playing a game where Ninjas flew out all over the place, jerking the handles around while drips of sweat streamed down the sides of his face, plummeting to his blue button down shirt, seeping in through the fabric. This caused the shirt to stick to his chest, providing spectators with their own little peep show, whether they liked it or not. And Penelope noticed he kept on going. Slimy face and adhesive shirt and all, he kept on going. *That's me*, she said to herself, *I'm going to persevere! I'm going to learn everything about technology, darn it!* and she looked at the gaming controls and thought – *but not here*, reasoning it was best to start with the something smaller – but what?

While rounding a corner with bag in hand, venturing even beyond the gaming section, Penelope saw a crowd of people in one area, and with curiosity as her guide, she ambled over to see what all the hubbub was about and eyed her surroundings, making sure there was no sign of Cory and friends.

"Wonderful!" Penelope exclaimed, standing amongst a pack whose eyes and fingers were entirely focused on a display of interesting devices that were small and thin with tiny screens; many were in vibrant colors and this was the focal point of Penelope's excitement – she was immediately attracted to a row that had some of these gadgets in apple green, bubblegum pink and lilac lavender. The lineup was like a friendly, technological rainbow to Penelope. Friendly, and also, non-threatening enough for her to dare to place her free hand on the bubblegum pink device and play with its buttons, looking to see if anything would show up on its screen, but nothing did. *Well,* she thought, *maybe it's some new fangled phone...Yes, of course, that's what it is!*

Wondering how a phone so tiny could fit at an ear, she thought about trying the device out, and pulled it away from the display.

Suddenly, an alarm went off throughout the store, wailing as though someone had just broken into the National Treasury. Everyone in the store looked around in a shocked daze, including Penelope, and it was then that Penelope glanced down at the bubblegum pink curiosity she was holding, and realized that a thin cord was dangling from it, and that cord had been connected to the display, and that display had been connected to an alarm system, which she, herself, set off by mistakenly yanking and breaking the cord.

Penelope shuddered, and a booming, male voice blared out of the store's speaker – "LET GO OF THE MP3 PLAYER! ... LET GO OF THE MP3 PLAYER!"

Aghast and frightened, Penelope fumbled with the device as if it were a hot potato in her hands, repeatedly yelling, "Oh my god! I didn't mean to! Oh my god!" until she was able to stop the device from popping in her hands and put it back in its proper place.

A flash suddenly went off, and Penelope quickly looked up and found an Asian couple politely smiling at her. The male of the duo was holding a camera and nodded and bowed to Penelope as if he was trying to tell her – "Thank you for the picture...You Americans are so much fun."

"Having some problems?" she heard someone ask. Penelope turned around and was immediately surprised. The question was attached to none other than the techno-geek, shaggy haired guy from the dungeon apartment – Ted Hollis – and he was grinning as if thoroughly amused. "Do you need some help?"

Penelope scrutinized the long bangs that still covered his eyes and the worn-out black pea coat and sneakers he was wearing, and she wondered if he had just dragged his clothes out of the closet and threw on whatever articles were on top of the heap.

Just at that moment, two security guards approached them, one looking tall and thin as a line, the other squat and round as a circle. The circle one had a toupee that kept flipping off his scalp onto his forehead; at each instance, he speedily tossed it back.

"Excuse me," the line said, "we're going to have to take you in."

The circle moved towards her with handcuffs, staring hungrily at her wrists.

Penelope's eyes began to tear, and she started to breathe heavy. All she could think of was her brother bailing her out, or as he warned her, not bailing her out, and then possibly shipping her back to Elmont where people would look on at her disparagingly after they saw her picture and read the Best Buy story on the front page of the Elmont Picayune. She also envisioned her photo and sordid tale appearing in the New York Post, and although it would probably be buried in a part usually unread and used for dog defecations, she imagined Luke Carson somehow finding it and reading that she was trying to steal something from the store; thinking that she was a hardened criminal, Luke would conclude that she wasn't fit to date him and would promptly break up with her – *Oh no!*

"Wait," Ted asserted, "you've got it all wrong. She wasn't stealing anything."

The orb security guard who was inches away from grabbing onto Penelope, itching to get at Penelope's skinny arms, ceased what he was doing.

The thin guard asked, "You know this girl, Ted?"

"Yeah," he said, nodding an affirmative.

"You can vouch for her?"

Penelope noticed Ted giving her the once over like he'd done before when she first met him at his apartment. "Yeah," he repeated.

The line shrugged and looked over at the circle who was working and failing at adjusting his toupee. "Come on, Frank," he said to him. "We'll find someone else to arrest."

The other guard responded, "But…this one was so pr-e-e-tty."

Penelope didn't know whether to thank him or not for the compliment. After all, he was about to send her up the river – and seemed happy about it.

"Yeah. Well. We'll find another one for yer," the line told him, and then he put his arm around his stout friend and led him away.

Somewhat impressed, Penelope turned to Ted and asked, "You know those guys?"

"Yeah," he answered, shuffling a bit from side-to-side, appearing uncomfortable with getting into any conversation. "I … uh … tend to hang around here." He put his hand on the display, leaned into it a little, and shook his hair a bit as if he was being filmed for a shampoo commercial.

Penelope found this action to have some boyish charm.

He continued, "I like to come here to keep up with the newest trends in technology," and he tapped a finger on one of the devices on the display. "But today I'm here for a new iPod."

Penelope provided a blank stare. She wandered through random materials in her brain, searching for the file marked "iPod" but couldn't find it.

Ted, most likely reacting to her expression, asked, "You do know what an iPod is…right?"

Rolling her eyes and grinning like the Mad Hatter, she answered, "Of course I do!" and she added, "Doesn't everybody?"

He then made a point of mentioning – "But I think I'll go to the Apple store to get the one that I want."

"Oh," she looked at him quizzically, "they sell them at a fruit store?" Penelope began to ponder the idea of a market only selling one type of fruit and how illogical it was and probably very unprofitable. But in the end, she thought, someone must have wised up at the apple store – they were selling technology!

"Uh…kind of," he uttered and then was silent for a moment. "Sooo … do you need any help?"

"No," she replied, still with a phony smile, "of course not." She grinned some more. "I know this stuff inside and out."

"This stuff?"

"Yeah…this…this…technology stuff," she explained, and she gestured with a fanned out arm in the direction of the display that was the starting point of her almost-incarceration.

He nodded. "Good," he said, "it's good that you know about this *stuff*," and then he looked on at the display and devices, adding, "MP3 players are great for making phone calls by the way."

"Yeah. I was just thinking about that."

"I know. I saw you trying to make one just a couple of minutes ago."

"That's right. I was. Kind of."

"But there's only one problem," he said. "You *can't* make phone calls on MP3 players."

Penelope turned red. She knew she made a big mistake and felt like a fool. "No?"

"No," he informed her, "it's mostly for listening to downloaded music."

"Huh?"

"Downloaded music," he repeated, and Penelope took a couple of steps away from him, wondering what he meant.

Ted shook his head. "I'm sorry, Penelope. I didn't mean to make you uncomfortable."

"Well, you have," she retorted and realized she might as well tell him. "Okay. You got me. I 'm just going to come clean - I know nothing about technology. There I said it," she uttered, embarrassed, her sights veering away from his face to a pimply teenager playing a solo air guitar performance at one of the play stations. "Funny. The last time I actually just blurted it out like that was to an AT & T salesman," she told him and then mumbled under her breath, "And look where that got me."

There was an awkward silence.

"Again, I'm sorry," Ted said. His arms spread out as he spoke, relaying honesty and compassion. "I didn't mean to hurt you. I meant to help you actually – to get you to ask for help. I know that sometimes asking for help can be difficult." He shuffled his feet. "I guess everything came out wrong, or I did it wrong or something."

Penelope looked back at him and smiled a little, and Ted cleared his throat. He went to brush his bangs away from his face, and Penelope tried to catch a glimpse of what his eyes looked like, but couldn't; the moment she searched for them was the moment his hair returned to its previous position.

Wait, Penelope suddenly said to herself, *he saw me trying to make a phone call with the thing a couple of minutes ago?* "Wait," she said to him, "did you say that you saw me trying to make a phone call? You were watching me?" *And for how long was he watching?*

"Uh. Sort of," he confessed, and his shoulders hung forward as if he thought he might have done something wrong. "It was only for a couple of seconds - until I realized you were you -Penelope." He changed the subject, "So are we okay?"

Penelope shrugged. "Sure. I guess," she said. "Anyway, don't worry about it. I'm just a bit touchy right now."

"Why?"

"Oh, it's just a work issue. I'm trying to get this promotion at the PR firm I work for. It's to manage a technology account, and I'm just completely lost. Like I said before, I *really* don't know anything about the world of technology."

"Y'know, I kind of figured that out before when you came to me for your text messages and told me you didn't have text service for an entire year." He then added, "It must be difficult."

She grimaced at him and huffed, "Hey. It's not like I'm ill or anything. It's not like I have walking pneumonia or leprosy."

"That's not what I meant," he reacted, and then began to express himself with his hands moving back and forth in front of her. "What I meant was it must be difficult not knowing anything about technology in a world that's so wired up." He shook his head. "Geez, everything is coming out wrong."

"Don't worry," she said, "I get it. And it is actually." She shook her head. "This is what I get for spending most of my life in Elmont. A town that doesn't care a smidge about the modern world." Penelope furrowed her brow.

"Elmont," Ted said aloud as if he were thinking to himself. "Elmont … That's the town southwest of Chicago. Somewhere in between Springfield and Alton?"

Penelope's eyes grew large, and she suddenly felt as though she'd been injected with a vial of happiness. "You know it?"

He smiled at her, and she was suddenly swept up by the same comfortableness she experienced towards the end of their last encounter. "Well, I've never been there, but it's a point on my map."

"You remember a point on a map?" she inquired, amazed, but then she recalled how incredible he was at getting her text messages back and then remembered how Wendy told her what a genius he was – MIT graduate did she say? *What was MIT exactly?*

"Yeah. Geography is one of my hobbies. It helps me make great GPS technology."

"Huh?" Penelope was lost again.

"Hmmmm," he sounded, seemingly giving her a second once over. "Never mind." The conversation quieted down for a few seconds as Ted looked like he was trying to figure out what to say next, or maybe, how to say it right this time. "Hey," he blurted, "did you say that you were in public relations?"

"Yes."

"I've got an idea," he said. "I need to promote my business more and public relations would probably do the trick. Why don't we strike a bargain?" and then he proposed, "You provide me with PR services, say like press releases, media pitching, forums for presentations, and I'll teach you all you want to know about technology."

Penelope stood motionless. She was completely shocked that in the end, she didn't have to go and try to find the answer to her problems. In the end, the answer found her (although the trip to Best Buy certainly didn't hurt) in the form of Ted Hollis! Grungy Ted Hollis!

She went to answer him when a tune promptly shot out from her handbag – *Buffalo gals can't you come out tonight – can't you come out tonight – can't you come out tonight-Buffalo gals can't you come out tonight – aaand dance by the light of the mooon.* "It's my BlackBerry," she said as she reached into her purse and pulled it out.

There was a text message from Luke:

Luke (Mobile)

January 12, 2008 2:41:02 PM

Hey Penelope - change of plans. Meet me at Riverside Park in the Upper West Side tomorrow at 3 pm and we can decide what we want to do from there…See you tomorrow. Looking forward to it. Luke

Penelope smiled at her BlackBerry.

"So," Ted said to her, "I take it from your reaction that your text situation is better? Unless, of course, that was an email you were looking at."

"Oh no, you were right the first time," she responded, "it was a text…" and then she didn't go any further than that.

Ted shined some pearly whites. "So? What do you think? Is it a deal?"

For a moment, Penelope couldn't remember what Ted was talking about, all her brain cells being thwarted by her sudden text message from Luke. *Wonderful Luke* – she surmised a winter wedding would be just fine (to heck with the AT & T man! To heck with regret!).

Ted was still waiting for his answer. "Penelope?"

Hearing her name, Penelope was startled out of her vision of her and Luke walking arm and arm down the aisle heading toward marital bliss. "Yes, Ted?"

"PR in exchange for technology lessons? Remember? You-me?"

She laughed, mostly at herself. "Oh yeah." She snapped out of it – "Oh yes! Of course! That sounds great!" Not only would she have a wedding, she thought, she would also have the platinum Streamers account! Fantastic!

"Great," he said, nodding and smiling. "Well. I need to go now." He explained, "Gotta go feed Spock."

Penelope remembered his human-sized, cardboard figure of the Star Trek character and laughed again.

"I'll call you and we'll set up something," he said as he started to move away from her.

"Wait. Don't you want my phone number?"

As he walked on, he replied, "No. I remember it from last time we met …And it's McAdams. Right?"

She nodded.

"Bye," he said, and he gave her a strange type of hand signal, separating four of his fingers into two separate groups.

Penelope looked on at Ted queerly as he strolled off towards the door, still giving her the same hand signal.

Just at that moment, Penelope heard Stacey's complaining voice, and turned to the direction of where it was coming from and saw her brother, Sonia and Stacey at the top of the staircase, about to step onto her floor.

Penelope quickly rushed to the DVD area, almost knocking over an adolescent customer who was perusing the World Federation of Wrestling section.

Without haste, she picked up a DVD from the rack, and pretended to read its packaging.

"There she is!" Sonia exclaimed at the center of the store, pointing excitedly at Penelope like she had just discovered an endangered species.

The three of them moseyed over to her.

"See," Sonia uttered to Cory, who was still carrying her purse over his shoulder. "I told you she was all right," and then she threw Penelope a sideways wink.

Sonia looked lovingly at Cory, who at this point was knitting his eyebrows, adding, "See, all you have to do is trust the ones you love," and then she turned to Penelope – "We heard the alarm go off."

Stacey put in her two cents, complaining, "For God's sake – they heard it in China! It was so friggen' loud."

Sonia paid no attention to Stacey's comment. "When he heard the alarm, he wanted to come up and check on you. But I said 'no-trust, Baby. Trust.'"

"Hmmm," Cory sounded as he contemplated his sister, narrowing his eyes. "We were told some girl with freckles was having problems at the MP3 section and set off the alarm." His eyes were now squinting. "Do you know anything about that?"

"Me? No," Penelope answered, leaning away from him, acting as if his question bewildered her. "Wait…Did you think *I* was that freckled girl?" She fought back – "Cory. I'm not the only freckled girl in the world y'know."

Sonia interjected, "And that's what I told him. Exactly what I told him," and Penelope's brother continued to stare at her with suspicion.

"And besides," Penelope said, "I haven't moved away from the DVD section." She glanced over at Sonia and Stacey. "It's actually very interesting."

Her brother noted, "You're in the adult movie section." He grabbed the DVD out of her hand and read aloud from the back of it – "Debbie Does Dallas and the Rest of the Universe While Doing Push-Ups with One Hand," and then he thrust the DVD in front of Penelope's face as if to say, "Here! See! See!"

Penelope waved it away like she would an obnoxious fly. "I told you. I've been in the DVD section the whole time."

"I don't believe you," he said, tossing the porn back on the rack.

Stacey clamored, "Come on! Let's go! I have no time for this!" and she held up her Best Buy bag. "I've gotta go home and beat up another remote … I'll use my fleeced gloves this time for extra protection." She informed, "And it's also time for my foot soak. My feet are actually going to be filmed for a movie tomorrow."

Sonia raised her eyebrows. "Really?"

As they walked away from the DVD section, Penelope turned to her brother and asked, "Cory? Do you know what this means?" and she tried to do the same hand signal that Ted had done, but her fingers wound up looking mangled as if she was having a fit of cerebral palsy.

He smirked. "Yeah. It means that even though I'm carrying a handbag, you're the one with the problems."

At that, Penelope laughed within, because, after all, she didn't have any problems anymore. No, she didn't.

Penelope felt quite assured that with Luke Carson and Ted Hollis in her life that she could kiss all her problems goodbye.

Mr. Potter: Oh yes, George Bailey. Whose ship has just come in – providing he has enough brains to climb aboard.

Nine

Luke Carson stumbled around the basketball court at Riverside Park in a Boston University sweatshirt and jogging pants, and knit cap and gloves. "That was totally a foul!" he screamed to a person on the opposing team. White orbs of cold air puffed out of his mouth as he wildly sputtered, "You fucking moron!" He seemed unaware that Penelope had arrived at the park and stood at the wired fence of the court with her nose poking through a space in the enclosure, watching him with her jaw dropped to the snowy earth.

The competitors called for a break in the game during which time Luke paced the area, circling the court like an irrational predator staking out its prey that was huddled at the center of the tarp. "You fucking guys cheat and you can't play for shit!" he hollered.

As shocked as Penelope was about his behavior, that's how un-shocked his fellow players were. "Shut up, Carson," a member of the opposing team casually and unflinchingly said, sticking his head out from the team meeting. "You've always got a problem. Just shut up."

Luke was about to give a retort when he caught sight of Penelope looking on at him, retaining her astonished mouth. He stopped in place and didn't say a word, and took off his cap and ran his fingers through his gorgeous wavy hair. He flashed a smile in her direction. "Ok guys," he said to his fellow players, calming his tone and disposition, "I need to go."

The same opposing team member yelled out – "Fuckin' A! I'm psyched!"

"Hey, hon," Luke said to her and kissed her freckled nose that was still protruding through the fence. The kiss was soft and sweet.

"What was that all about?" she asked him, wondering if she really wanted to know.

"What? That?" he reacted. "Oh-that's just guys being guys."

"All that cursing."

"Yeah. That's what we do."

She looked on at him. "My brother doesn't curse." She thought of what her mother's expression would be if she heard someone curse like that. It wouldn't be pretty.

"Not when you're around." He winked from the other side of the fence and put his cap back on. ""I'm coming over to you," he said.

Luke picked up his backpack, flung it over his arm, and then kicked the snow in his path as he hurriedly circumscribed the fence to where she was standing. He grabbed her arms and pulled her to him, and gave her a long, passionate kiss. So passionate that Penelope almost lost her footing. If Luke hadn't held onto her so tightly, she thought she would have surely fallen down and been embarrassed for all eternity – *Choking on the second date? Tumbling over on the third?* What was she going to do for an encore on the fourth? Get hit by a car?

Again, she thought of the introductions to her mother and desired to fix the problem before it actually happened. She smiled slightly and asked, "You don't curse a lot, do you?"

He stepped back from her, grinning widely, appearing caught off guard. "No. I don't think so. Why?"

"Oh nothing," she answered, realizing she probably shouldn't broach the subject so early on in the relationship.

"Nothing?" he mimicked. "Okay." The expression of surprise and jocularity disappeared from his face.

He lunged forward to give her another kiss, but Penelope blocked the kiss with more inquiries. "But really-do you?"

Luke smiled again, but with a screwed face. "What's this all about?"

"Just curious."

"Why?"

"Well. Back in Elmont hardly anyone curses," she told him and then stopped for a second "Oh, but there was that employee at the grocers that one time," and then she shooed the notion away, "but he was from out-of-town. Albuquerque I think."

"Are you serious?" He eyed her up and down. "Hey. You never talk about your hometown."

That's right, she thought, and until they'd get engaged and would have to go there to meet her parents, this is as much as she would divulge. "What's there to tell? It's a town like any other town."

"Not exactly," he said, "in most towns people curse. Some less frequently than others, but they curse."

"I'm just saying."

Putting his large, strong hands at his hips, Luke questioned, "Are you allowed to curse in Elmont? I mean-is it against the law or something? You seem so dead against it," and then he chuckled, asking, "Is cursing in Elmont like throwing garbage in the streets of Manhattan or like jay walking? Is there a fine? Some jail time?"

"No," she replied but wasn't absolutely certain.

"Look," he said, placing a hand on her shoulder, "this is New York City, baby," and his other hand pinched her cheek. "Everyone curses here. If no one cursed we'd all be walking around with machetes killing one another." He pulled her to him again, "You'll get used to it."

Feeling Luke Carson against her and looking up at his bright smile and engaging dimples, Penelope suddenly felt light headed. *Okay,* she said to herself, *let him curse.* She was getting somewhat used to it anyway having heard people scream curses at their significant others in the street each day either in person or via the cell phone. She recalled a specific afternoon when she went to hail a taxi in Midtown Manhattan and saw and heard a couple at a storefront cursing bloody-murder at each other. Able to flag a cab, more than happy to get away from the cursing, she headed for the Upper West Side to see her brother, but when she reached her destination and stepped out of the taxi, she ran into another couple at a storefront exchanging swear words like drunken sailors.

The point was she couldn't do much about it, so she should accept — to a certain degree — the cursing, especially in the case of Luke Carson, she thought, as he sensually brushed his lips against hers.

"Come on," he said to her, grabbing her hand, and leading her to a park bench. He then pulled out his BlackBerry from his backpack to check his messages. He looked up at her and affectionately poked her in her stomach, teasingly requesting — "Come on. Curse for me."

Penelope was flabbergasted. Him cursing was one thing. Her cursing was an entirely other matter.

She calmly replied, "No. I don't think so."

He tickled her side. "Come on."

"No," she laughed, mostly reacting to the tickles and thinking he was joking.

"Come on." He tickled her some more.

Penelope started to become irritated but kept on laughing anyway. "No."

"Come on," he said, a grin taking up the entirety of his face. "Just one curse. Just one swear word. Just say 'fuck.'" She shook her head, pursing her lips together. "And you can even say it quickly," and then he said, "Fuck," in a half-second. "See, I can do it. You can do it too."

She lowered her eyes. "Yeah, but it's easier for you. You say it all the time."

"Come on. I won't leave you alone until you do."

Penelope, although not altogether thrilled with Luke's cajoling, could see he wasn't about to give up. Maybe if she at least tried, he would.

She bit down on her lower lip with her two front teeth and blew — "fffffffffffff" she sounded with laborious effort, forcing her eyes wide open; they looked like gigantic saucers, and then she tried again. Luke stared at her in amazement. "fffffff … ffffffffff … ffffffffff-" she pushed.

"Okay!" he stopped her, shaking her arm. "God. I don't want you to hurt yourself ... How about shit? Can you say shit? You say 'shoes' a lot, don't you?"

"Doesn't every woman?"

"Okay. So 'shit' should be easy. It starts with the same consonants," he told her. "Go ahead, try it."

Penelope sighed. "Shhhhhhh ... Shhhhhhhh ... Shhhhhhhh-"

"Okay, let's forget it," he said, placing a hand on her shoulder. "For now... lemonade."

She was about to frown when he added, "Cute. Very cute," and he kissed her again, and this time his mouth and tongue melted into hers. Penelope, lost in his kiss, dumped her grimace to the wayside.

"That was good," he informed her, smiling with his million-watt dimples. She swore he could light up the entire city with those things.

"Uhummm," she agreed, appearing tipsy with love, as she went in for another kiss, and just at the time she closed her eyes and their lips touched, it began to snow. She noticed that the falling flakes came down from the sky gentle like floating feathers, and that there was just a pinch of wind in the air. *This feels so wonderful. Am I dreaming? Is this for real?*

She opened her eyes to find his weren't shut, and they weren't looking at her either. They were perusing the sky.

"Damn' snow," he complained. "I hate all this weather. Nature needs to be controlled."

Luke checked for messages on his BlackBerry again, and Penelope turned away from him and scanned her surroundings – the men were still on the court playing basketball and, in the distance, the gray buildings were shrouded in a cloud of white, snowy haze.

She flicked a flake off her nose as the snow continued to drift down. The corners of her mouth turned up. "I think this weather is perfect."

"I think I need to go to a warmer climate in the winter time." He gazed at his BlackBerry. "Boston," he mumbled.

"Boston? Isn't it the same weather or colder in Boston?"

"Oh - I didn't mean that. I'm just waiting for a message from a

Boston client."

They sat quiet for a moment until he frowned and then shoved the BlackBerry in his backpack. "Hey," he suddenly said, "let's go shopping." He put his arm around her. "You like Gucci?"

Uncle Billy [drunk] ... Where's my hat? Where's my ... [George takes the hat from Uncle Billy's head and hands it to him] Oh, thank you, George. Which one is mine?

Ten

It was the break of dawn, and Penelope stood at the coffee maker in the kitchen at Renquist & Renquist with hot carafe in hand, staring into space, waiting to pour Alden Renquist a cup of Joe, specially made by her.

But she noted there was a little problem – he hadn't arrived yet. In fact, no one had.

Penelope was in a daze. "I did it," she said to herself as the sun rose sending slivers of light through the blinds of the office windows. "I did it."

She reflected on the past days' practice sessions for preparing coffee, and decided the process had been a grueling one.

On day one with the coffee maker, Penelope spent at least ten minutes trying to pull the machine out of the box. Once confounded by the task and abound with anger that she paid a great deal of money for a workout she could have easily gotten at the Reebok Club (and with less of a cost since she could've swiped a visitor's pass from her brother), she drew in a long breath and used all the might of her bony but bendy upper-body to yank it out. Thrusting herself back with the force of a fighter jet, the machine finally wobbled out of the box while she practically ricocheted into the wall behind her – a good twenty feet. Sometime afterward, Penelope made a visit to the emergency room to check for broken bones.

In the following days, she saw her way through unchartered territories and rocky terrain as she reviewed instructions that she decided only a rocket scientist could understand and only a rocket scientist could have written (*Was there a lay off at NASA?*), yelled at the coffee machine for not working (only to find out that she didn't plug it in), and tried to figure out how to set the clock (*Why does it keep going off at two in the morning?*). It was on the fourth day of coffee machine ownership that the sacred moment had been reached – Penelope, decided she was sufficient enough in her knowledge of the design of the machine, the digital display, the knob that turned to choices ranging from regular (clock set, on/off) to daring (auto on, brew, and 1-4 cup setting), and the nuances of plugging it into an outlet, that she thought it was finally the right time to make coffee –*Yeah!*

So after following the manual's directive on how to pour in the water, Penelope dispensed French Roast coffee into the machine and pressed the "on" button.

Vrrrrr the coffee maker immediately rumbled. *Vrrrrr. Vrrrrrrr,* and then it began to shake. Penelope stepped back, sure that the machine was about to lift off like a rocket catapulting towards space, but instead of blasting off, it just coughed like an old car engine, took its last breath, and died.

"What the?" Penelope asked herself, and then reached for the instructions. She mumbled the words from the manual – "Add the amount of ground coffee that corresponds to the number of cups being brewed." She lifted her eyes from the pages. "Ground coffee." Penelope looked up at the ceiling, trying to think – why didn't that sound right? "Ground coffee." Suddenly knowing why, she turned around to the coffee bag and picked it up. She scanned the print. "French Roast...Whole Bean." *So that's it – it's not ground coffee.*

Now what do I do?

She went back to the directions – "If you choose to grind your own beans…" She stopped reading and thought – *okay, grind your own beans. Why not?* Considering it was already nine p.m. in the evening, which in her estimation was way too late to go out and fetch more coffee at the grocers, why shouldn't she grind the beans that were right in front of her? And what a feather in one's cap to actually go beyond the common, mundane practice of making instant coffee – she would get down to the basics! And okay, she knew that it had nothing to do with technology, but the show of effort and self-reliance had to be worth something, and maybe she could find a way to do it in front of her boss, and he would be so mesmerized he wouldn't need to take his Xanax anymore. My God! He would make her the senior vice president of the entire firm!

Excited beyond all measure, Penelope dumped the coffee beans from the filter basket onto a paper plate and rummaged through her drawers and cupboards for something that could be used as a grinder. When she came up empty handed, she wished she took her mother's potato masher before she left Elmont (*One day you're going to want to cook,* her mother said, waving the potato masher in her face, *and one day you're going to want to mash potatoes)* – who knew? But suddenly, a light bulb went off in her head. "Break the beans!" she cried out. "Grinding is basically breaking the beans! Of course!" Penelope bounded to her closet and pulled out a hammer. "Here we go!" she yelled, and she rushed over to the kitchen counter, wielding the hammer as if possessed.

BANG! BANG! … She hit a cluster of coffee beans with the hammer – *BANG! BANG!* … *CRACKKKK.* Penelope winced. "Uh oh," she said, shaking her head. There was a new and dark hairline fissure in the counter, and surrounding the fissure were the coffee beans – scattered and still intact.

She put her hands to her hips, staring at her mistake. "How on God's green earth am I going to pay for that?" she asked to no one but herself. "Now I'm *really* going to need that technology account."

Twenty minutes later, Penelope walked into the door of her

apartment with a can of French Roast "Ground" Coffee from the grocers. She covered the crack in the kitchen counter with a dishtowel and proceeded to successfully make her first pot of coffee, filled with glee, feeling a great sense of accomplishment.

Penelope poured the coffee into a series of cups and counted – "One, two, three, hmmmm …Twelve." Twelve cups, she figured, for twelve people – where to find twelve people to drink the coffee? What to do?

She shrugged and threw some milk and Splenda into a cup as she had seen the people in Starbucks and her office do, put her lips to her concoction and took a taste. "Mmmmm," she sounded with a little smile, "not bad," and then guzzled down the entire cup in one minute flat.

Wiping her mouth with the back of her hand, Penelope announced, "That was good." She looked on at the remaining eleven coffees and remembered what her mother always said – *Waste not, want not, Penelope…Waste not, want not* – and she drank all of them up, licking her lips between gulps.

That night, Penelope lay awake in her bed, not being able to sleep, her mind racing and hallucinating – *was that really an Oompa-Loompa in my studio apartment? Am I really in New York? Maybe I'm back in Elmont…Am I living or am I dead?* and at four in the morning, without as much as a second's worth of sleep, she sat at the edge of the bed, staring into space. "Time to go to work!" she announced…

"I did it," she repeated, her saucer eyes blood shot, her hand gripping the pot, waiting for Alden Request to charge in and see her with the coffee, throw back a cup, and proclaim it the best coffee he ever drank – even better than the coffee they served him on the coffee plantation he visited in the Andes – and what a splendid job she had done with the machine to create such superior coffee! The instant coffeemaker was a befuddling apparatus – but she managed to operate it like a pro! Yes, she had! "Kudos to Penelope!" he would exclaim. "Kudos!" even though she never actually heard him say that word.

Penelope was ready for that – all morning – she was ready:

6:15 am:

Glossy-eyed, Penelope stood in the middle of the kitchen while Ginger, the account supervisor, with hairstyle in mad disarray, no lipstick, wearing an eye gel mask, stumbled into the still empty office and then kitchen as if she just barely survived a bad night of Cosmopolitans and other Martini variations.

Giving no indication that she knew Penelope was present and staring at her with a wide-open mouth, Ginger felt around for the counter and then the cabinet from where she drew out a mug.

The account supervisor turned around and raised her mug to Penelope. "Deal with it," she demanded.

Mouth quickly closing, Penelope poured.

7:00 am:

Penelope successfully brewed another fresh pot of coffee.

7:30 am:

A trio of gossiping female account executives— a redhead, a blonde, and a brunette – formed a semi-circle a few feet behind Penelope, who was still positioned at the coffee maker.

"Well, she must have had her stomach stapled," the leggy redhead commented with a nod.

The blonde with her hair in a spiral updo added, "Well, I knew she lost some weight. You could just tell."

"She had a baby," the squat brunette remarked, the diamond stud in her nose quivering as she spoke.

"What?" the blonde inquired.

"She had a baby," the brunette repeated.

The redhead balled her hands into fists, stuck them to her waist, and asked, "I wonder if that would work for me?"

7:32 am:

"Well, can you believe that she was having an affair with him?" the redhead folded her arms, frowning.

The blonde sunk the tips of her fingers into her hair, adjusting her bun. "And I hear his wife is so pleasant."

"The married man," the brunette said, knitting her eyebrows, "an oxymoron."

"Well I wouldn't call him a moron," the blonde remarked. "He's quite bright."

The red head and the blonde filed out of the room with the brunette lagging behind. She held up her mug to Penelope. "And I have to work with those two," she sighed and rolled her eyes.

Penelope patted her on the shoulder and poured her some coffee.

8:00 am:

Penelope successfully brewed another fresh and steaming pot of coffee.

8:30 am:

"I think we can take care of this," the plumber said to Alden Renquist's secretary, his head stuck in the cabinets under the sink. "Just a few screws here and there. Some twists and tugs."

Her boss' secretary nodded, spun around and pondered Penelope for a quiet moment, and then walked out of the kitchen.

The plumber fiddled with the pipes – *CLANK. CLANK…CLANK.CLANK.* "Damn!" he screamed, and a gush of water shot out from under the cabinets, spraying him in the face and hitting his wrench; the wrench flew through the air and landed on the floor that was now drenched.

"I can't do this anymore," he wept, scooping up his wrench. "I try and I try. For years I've tried. But I'm an awful plumber," he groaned, looking right at Penelope. "My wife, she told me I wasn't good at this. She tells me I'm not good at anything. And she's right." He walked over to her with his head down and shoulders slack. "I'm going to lose another job, and it's another career down the tubes … She's going to leave me." He became teary-eyed. "And she's going to take the kids with her." Then he pulled out a hankie and sobbed into it – "I'm such a loser! I don't deserve anything!"

Penelope quickly handed him a Styrofoam coffee cup and poured him some coffee. He blew his nose into the hankie.

9:00 am:

Penelope, now an expert on the culinary art of coffee making, prepared another fresh, steaming, and aromatically rich pot of coffee.

9:10 am:

A box of assorted doughnuts arrived.

9:15 am:

Dragging out a frosted jelly doughnut from the box, Penelope turned her back on the coffee machine and her coffee for just a second.

"Excellent coffee!" Alden Renquist cried out. She immediately spun around. "You made this?" he asked Ginger, who was holding the carafe. She had sufficiently straightened up since Penelope had last seen her.

"Of course," she said.

"Excellent!" he exclaimed with briefcase in hand, fluffy hair sweeping around as he spoke. "Excellent!" he shouted again, and rushed out of the kitchen.

Not taking notice of Penelope or rather, not paying her any mind, Ginger simply threw her posture back, stuck her nose up in the air, and exited with a strut.

***

Penelope plopped down on her desk chair. "I can't believe it," she said aloud to herself. "I can't believe it."

"What can't you believe?" Wendy asked inside her cubicle.

Penelope didn't answer, still stunned, and shaking a bit, although she didn't know why.

"Okay. How about this," Wendy suggested, "you can't believe that people are spreading around rumors that you're leaving Renquist & Renquist to become a cafeteria lady. At least I can't believe it.'

"How's that?"

"I'm going to buy you a hair net for your first day on the job. What color would you like? Personally, I think fuchsia would be great. It would set you apart from all the others. But I'm just not sure if they make one in fuchsia. I mean, I don't know much about hairnets. It's not my thing."

"What are you talking about?"

"You. At the coffee machine. Serving people coffee. Explain."

Penelope sighed. "I'm making coffee so I can show Mr. Renquist that I can do the Streamers Technology account. I've practiced for days now. It sent me to the emergency room."

Wendy sighed. "Now I know what your secret is – psychiatric incarceration. You escaped from Elmont's loony bin."

"Ha, ha," Penelope wryly replied, not at all amused. "Meanwhile Ginger took all the credit for my coffee. She served it to Mr. Renquist and said it was hers. She didn't even flinch. No remorse."

"What do you expect from someone who's climbed the ladder? She's a bitch. How else do you think she got to where she is?"

"Where is she?"

"Making six-figures while she's looking like she's doing something, but she's really not. Having a boyfriend who's a bigwig on Wall Street and buys her everything she wants and takes her everywhere she wants to go." Wendy concluded, "That's where she is."

Penelope mused over the notion.

"Hey," she suddenly said to Wendy, "don't I owe you some money"

"The bag of chips. A dollar. Forget about it."

"No really."

"Forget about it."

"No *really*," Penelope demanded, "I can give it to you now."

Wendy gave in. "Fine. Whatever," she said and popped her head over the cubicle wall and extended her arm out with palm upturned.

Penelope reached over for her handbag, her hand shaking as if she was having tremors.

"What's wrong with you?" Wendy asked, her eyebrows raised.

"I think it might've been the coffee I drank last night."

"How much did you drink?"

"Twelve cups."

"Why?"

"They were there."

Wendy shook her head. "You are SO going to crash."

"I'll be fine," she assured her, and with more verve than one would think necessary when paying a debt, let alone the measly amount of a dollar, Penelope plunged into her pocketbook and pulled out her new heart-shaped, monogrammed coin-purse.

"Wait now," Wendy uttered, partly gasping and then talking – "Just you wait."

Penelope smiled and sat up straight. The coin purse had a key chain attached to it; she slid her finger through its hook and dangled the purse in Wendy's face.

Her surprised co-worker noted, "That's not just *any* coin purse-that's a *Gucci* coin purse!"

"You bet your bottom one dollar it is," Penelope reacted, grinning some more. "You- know-who got it for me."

"Who?"

"Come on."

"Could it be the ever debonair, gorgeous, successful-Luke?" Wendy laughed.

"You know it is," Penelope said. "Who else would it be?"

Wendy leaned against the cubicle, her azure eyes brightening with interest. "Wow. First flowers, now this." Wendy suggested, "You should forget about the technology account and just marry the guy, and let him take care of you."

"Maybe I don't want just that. Maybe I want everything." She opened her heart-shaped coin purse with the gentle hand movements of an archeologist who was about to open a crumbling sarcophagus. "Maybe I want to be like Ginger," she said as she searched for a dollar's worth of quarters and dimes.

Wendy raised her eyebrows. "You really want to be like Ginger? No."

"She's the epitome of the New York women. Successful, utterly cosmopolitan," Penelope said and then reflected on that morning when Ginger came into the kitchen looking visibly shaken and disoriented, but Penelope understood that there had to be some negative side effects to living the high life, but that they definitely didn't outweigh the positives. "She's like the women in 'Manhattan Nights.'"

Rolling her eyes, Wendy inquired, "You really believe that stuff?"

"Sure. Look at Ginger."

"Yeah, but you've never seen how Ginger lives exactly. I mean, like I said before, she's got it real good, but have you actually seen her spending hours at a swanky night club drinking martinis, meeting famous celebrities, being invited to jet-set here and there and what not like what happens on that show?"

"No."

"Have you ever personally experienced this since you've been here?"

"No." Penelope thought about it. "Actually, it's been quite the opposite," she said, "but I'm optimistic."

"Optimistic today, optimistic tomorrow – welcome to the real life of a New York Woman, which is the opposite of that show." She pointed at Penelope and asserted, "Welcome to the truth."

Penelope handed her four quarters, commenting, "Truth is a matter of perspective."

"Please don't get philosophical with me, Penelope," Wendy commented. "You're pushing tractors for God's sake."

"And you're pushing pimple cream."

Wendy raised her hand in a matador "ole" type of move, saying, "Touché." She continued, "But a point. Ginger and all those girls on Manhattan Nights would've never accepted the coin purse. They would've insisted on a handbag ... But it was your what? ... Third date? So I guess the coin purse is appropriate."

Penelope slowly leveraged the Gucci coin purse into her fake leather pocketbook. "He said he'll buy me the handbag when I curse for him."

Wendy burst out laughing. "Yeah, like that'll ever happen. That'll be a cold day in hell – excuse me – *heck*."

"All I need to do is say one curse word," Penelope informed her. "That's it. Just one. And I don't have to do it again." She added, "I've been practicing. It's just that I keep seeing my mother with her disapproving look every time I'm on the verge of getting one out."

"Good luck."

"So you don't think I can do it?"

"Do you want to do it? Is it worth a Gucci bag to you?"

Penelope didn't answer. She had to think about it. Silly me, she thought to herself. Of course it was worth it. "I guess it's no big deal. What's the harm of a little curse?"

Wendy lowered herself into the cubicle. "It's like Pandora's Box. Just lift the lid a little bit and the flood gates will open, and soon you'll be swearing up and down the street like some of those lunatics we see stomping up and down midtown screaming obscenities to their imaginary friends."

Penelope quietly chuckled. "I don't think so."

She looked at the writing pad in front of her and read what she wrote the week before – *Must write letter to Angelina Jolie and Brad Pitt about tractors. MUST.* Penelope picked up a pencil and dotted her desk with the eraser head as she tried to figure out what she should scribe to the Jolie-Pitts, the world's most famous couple, but who Penelope didn't know too much about.

"Wendy?" she began to inquire. She heard her co-worker typing. "What comes to your mind when you think of Angelina Jolie and Brad Pitt?"

"We are the World … Poor Jennifer Aniston."

Penelope thought aloud – "Now how could I fit that into a letter to get them to be spokespeople for Henshaw Tractors? Once I get that done, I can show Mr. Renquist my knowledge of technology and get that account."

"Are you still going to do that?" Wendy strongly questioned her, her voice vibrating through the cubicle wall. "We keep going over this,

Penelope…How do you suppose you're going to learn enough about technology to get that account?"

"Easy," Penelope said, suddenly shivering all over. "Ted Hollis is going to teach me. He's going to teach me everything."

"*What?*" Wendy asked, swiftly rising up from her chair, sticking her head over the cubicle.

"Crash," she said, looking down at Penelope whose head lay sideways on her desk. She was snoring. Wendy shook her head. "Twelve cups, man …Crash and burn."

George Bailey: You know what the three most exciting sounds in the world are? ... Anchor chains, plane motors, and train whistles.

Eleven

Text #1:

Ted Hollis (Mobile)

Jan. 15, 2008 2:00:52 PM

Hi Penelope - meet you over at Best Buy on Saturday for your first lesson and purchase.
How goes it with the coffee machine?
Text me. Ted

   Horrible, Penelope thought, *I'm now on my way to becoming a coffee addict.*

Text #2:

Luke Carson (Mobile)

Jan 15, 2008 2:11:02 PM

Hi sweetie. Just got an important call. Have to go to Boston for business. Will be back on Tuesday. Will call you on the weekend. (Hey, have you cursed yet?) Luke

***

Penelope went *sssssshhhhhh* to say shit and then *fffffffffff* to say fuck, and with both she was a failure. In exasperation, her usual expletives came out of her mouth like shooting darts – "Darn it! Fudge me!"

***

"Behold," Ted exclaimed, extending his arm out, his dark bangs flopping over his eyes, "the sixty-inch flat screen plasma TV!" and he made a sweeping gesture to the humongous television set before them in Best Buy.

Penelope's eyes widened, almost to the point of them falling out, as she looked at the mammoth but sleek TV. She had seen flat screen TVs at various sports bars and clubs but never one so … so … imposing. It was so large.

"It's pretty big," she said, nervously eying him, afraid he was going to push the TV on her. She thought of the size of her studio and her present television, a twenty-five-inch Zenith that was older than she was, passed onto her from her father and the workshop in his garage where he tried to fix old cars as a hobby (operative word – "tried") while watching episodes of Gunsmoke.

He smiled and said, "Yeah," and appeared as dreamy as she had been when she thought of Luke, misty and dazed and all.

Penelope waved it away, asserting, "I could never put that in my apartment. It's too big. There's hardly room for my microwave let alone a sixty-inch television." She took off her knit mittens and hat, and shook out her newly highlighted hair. Just a couple of brownish-blonde highlights she decided to get on the spur of the moment the day before.

Something to pick up her complexion ("You must brightn'," said the Parisian hairstylist, "espezially in de wintr."), and something for Luke to admire when he got back from his stint in Boston.

She turned around to find Ted's head veering in her direction – she couldn't be sure if he was staring at her or not since she still couldn't see his eyes behind his clump of follicles, but her intuition told her he was, so she took a leap – "What?" she asked him, pushing a side of her bob away from a cheek.

He shrugged. "Nothing."

"Look, honey," a thirty-something old man in a sweater vest and loafers came around to the television with his significant other, who, except for a North Face down jacket, practically wore the same outfit. She looked quiet peevish as he pointed to the TV. "It's a sixty-inch plasma," he told her, grinning like a child who just encountered his first toy. His significant other shook her head and pulled him out of the area.

Afterward, Penelope noticed men of all shapes, sizes, and ethnicities (it seemed that the meaning of "sixty-inch TV" crossed all social strata and nationalities for the male species) stopping by the TV, ogling it and dribbling, some not answering girlfriends or wives who called out to them in the store. "Harry!" a middle-aged woman yelled. She stomped over to a middle-aged man with a receding hairline who was hanging out at the sixty-inch plasma TV with a now colony of men, mesmerized and frothing at the mouth. It reminded Penelope of some of the men she saw on any given balmy summer night in Times Square when an attractive women passed them by wearing a blouse with a plunging neckline. "HARRY!" the middle-aged woman practically screamed in the man's ear. "How many times have I told you not to go even near this section? How many times?" Everyone, including the fan group of the sixty-inch plasma, turned around to the couple.

"But it's a sixty-inch plasma," he whined, his eyes still glued to the television.

"Harry. You're going to have to stop trying to compensate. Get over it. You have a three-inch penis and that's that," she plainly told him and led him away like the woman of the sweater vest and loafer couple.

The group of men courting the sixty-inch plasma gasped and quickly dispersed, scurrying far away from the television.

The only man left was Ted, who gazed at the plasma amorously.

Penelope gave a sideways glance to the crotch of Ted's blue jeans and wondered.

"What?" Ted asked her, staring at her staring at him.

At the sound of his voice, she immediately looked up at him. "Uh," she managed to get out.

"It's my zipper, right?" he inquired. "It's undone. It's always … "

And before Penelope had the opportunity to figure out what she was going to say, a young, middle-eastern looking man with a Best Buy tag clipped to his shirt interrupted the potentially embarrassing scene. "Ted!" he exclaimed, providing a fingers-paired-and-separated salutation, the same hand gesture Ted gave her only days before at the same store, and Ted responded with the identical "fingers" greeting. *(What does it mean?)*. Then they grinned at each other and shook hands like they were old friends from way back when. "How are ya'?"

"Hey, Raj," Ted said. "Long time no see!"

"No joke," the Best Buy guy commented, his mouth still upturned. "You haven't been in my area for a while. I heard you've been hanging out at the GPSes and laptops."

"Yeah, well, I have some ideas," Ted said.

Penelope watched her technology guru as he conversed with the employee and was taken by the quiet warmth that he displayed – laying his hand on the shoulder of the employee as they laughed over a mishap concerning a very private tape of a past employee fooling around with his girlfriend in Best Buy's breakroom – it was shown on all the televisions in the store – boyishly smiling as the employee questioned him about his love life. "So is this your girlfriend?" the employee asked.

"Oh. Um. No," Ted said, "I'm so sorry. I'm being so rude. Penelope this is Raj. Raj this is Penelope."

"Hi," Penelope greeted, shaking his hand.

"Hello there," Raj said with lifted eyebrows.

Ted tried to explain. "We're not together … we're um … friends. "

"That's too bad," Raj commented. "This guy's a catch." He aimed a finger at Ted. "And I'm not even ashamed of saying that being a guy. Do you know what a genius this guy is? Do you know the work he did in Wash-"

"Raj," Ted instantly said, "how's the wife and kids? The little one walking yet?"

While Raj went over the happenings in his family and the developmental stages of his youngest child, Penelope thought about what he said – *This guy's a great catch*, and thought him to be correct. Even with an eyeless face, mopped hair, and possibly a three-inch penis (she wasn't sure that Harry's wife's theory actually held, but she filed it away in her brain nonetheless). He would be a great catch for *someone*. A nice someone since he seemed to be nice. A down-to-earth someone since he seemed to be down-to-earth.

Her sights followed the line of Ted's body. Not too bad. Although she couldn't tell if he had much muscle under his bally sweater, but she remembered from the one time she had seen him in a t-shirt that he had some bulging biceps.

She eyed the ripped jeans he wore, along with his bally sweater and faded work boots. She immediately thought of how clean Luke's appearance was. Even when he was sweating on the basketball court that day she met him at the park, he continued to sparkle like a pristine penny.

Yes, Ted was a good catch, she decided, for someone who didn't care about appearances, who didn't mind living a plain, average life. Who wasn't looking to get ahead. Not like herself, she thought, changing and moving forward. Dating Luke, getting gifts, going after accounts, leaving Elmont behind – *goodbye*, she thought, *goodbye, goodbye…*

"So what are you looking for?" Raj turned to Penelope and then to Ted.

"*She*," Ted touched Penelope's shoulder, "is looking for a flat screen TV."

Raj gestured to the sixty-inch plasma. "Well then. This is perfect."

"I live in a studio. It won't fit."

"Everyone thinks the big TVs won't fit in their apartments. But they always do." Raj explained, "You just can't picture it correctly until it's actually in your apartment. But it will fit."

"I have a four-hundred square foot studio."

"It'll fit. We'll install it on a wall."

"But I doubt that I have a wall as big as this TV."

"Caddy corner."

She said, "I'm not kidding you about the size of my apartment. You have to walk in to walk out."

Ted chuckled, and Penelope rubbed her forehead. Creases in her brow seemed to be more apparent than when she first walked into the store. Penelope felt the aging process quicken as she went back and forth with the insistent salesman.

He finally asked, "What size were you looking for then?"

Did she dare to say it? "Twenty-seven inches," she answered in a meek, unsure voice.

"OHHHHH," Raj and Ted cried out in unison, stumbling backwards as if they were suffering from heart failure.

"What?" she asked.

Raj said, "I hope you don't mind me being a little bit sexist for a moment."

Penelope wondered what she should say to that. Of course she minded, but it was difficult for her to say so when he had been so polite about it – *I hope you don't mind, he said*…It conjured up more polite and simplistic, unthreatening statements – *I hope you don't mind me reaching over you to grab that lox and cream cheese smear for my bagel* or *I hope you don't mind me telling you that you have lipstick on your teeth*. Comments like that.

"But," he continued, "I find that women always want the smaller televisions."

Penelope, without mulling it over, blurted, "Because they don't have to worry about having three-inch penises."

The men were taken aback, especially Ted. Penelope immediately covered her mouth, surprised she could even utter such a rude comment – this was something Wendy or Stacey might have said, she thought. Was she finally turning into a New Yorker? Is this what it was

all about? If she immediately ran home, would she now find herself
able to curse? Would she soon be parading around with her Gucci
handbag?

She went to say, "I'm sorry," but remembered it wasn't the thing to
do, so instead, she kept her mouth shut, not saying a word, acting as if
all was forgotten.

Ted was silent.

Raj, the salesman, screwed his face. "Come with me," he said,
crooking his finger.

They all strolled over to a shelved wall displaying various sizes of flat
screen televisions. "These are the LCD HDTV Widescreen Flat Panel
TVs."

She stepped back and perused the television sets. They all blasted a
cartoon movie that whooshed through Penelope's eyes and enflamed
her nerves. Penelope suddenly developed a new fear – what would
happen if she fell asleep with the TV on and in the middle of the night
she woke up and the TV screen was so big and the images so bright
that she'd scare herself half to death? And no one would be there, she
thought. No one would be there to save her from her impending last
breath. Her expiration would be so untimely – *Goodbye, New York,* she
thought, *Goodbye...*

"Are you all right?" Ted questioned her, touching her shoulder again.

"I don't want to leave New York."

"What?" he asked, startled. "No one's asking you to leave New
York, Penelope. We're just looking at TVs."

The salesman looked on at her, perplexed, beginning to snap the pen
he was holding.

Penelope thought about how she would wake up in a nightmare with
a sixty-inch plasma or a sixty-inch LCD HD whatever-you-call-it right
on top of her, because it would have to be on top of her, she imagined
– with the size of the TV and the size of her studio – it wouldn't be a
far out idea. In fact, it would practically be expected.

"I don't want to be in a nightmare," she said aloud, gazing into
nothing but her fear, taking no notice of those around her who gawked
at her as though she had lost her marbles.

"What nightmare?" Ted asked, almost whispering, bending down to get closer to Penelope's ear. "It's just a cartoon. Look it's just *Toy Story.*"

"Good film," the salesman commented and questioned her – "Did you ever see it?"

Penelope didn't answer. She was just too stunned now thinking of Cowboy Woody taunting her in the middle of the night and in her own personal nightmare. And what would happen if she had coffee? That was too awful to imagine. She had already imagined Oompa-Loompas on her wall. Very. Very scary.

She began to perspire.

To Ted, the salesman Raj commented, "It must be the prices." He swiveled around to talk to Penelope. "Don't worry about the prices. We'll get you a payment plan if you need it. And if your credit doesn't pass-don't worry. I promise that we won't kick you out of the city."

She didn't say anything, still being in a trance like state. "I should leave you two alone. Let you decide," the salesman Raj said. "Excuse me." He gave Penelope a funny look and walked away.

Ted moved even nearer to her. "Penelope, what's wrong?"

"I can't have a sixty-inch TV!" she screamed and customers in all departments looked over. "I tell you – I can't do it!"

"Okay, okay," he uttered, putting his hands on her shoulders, trying to assuage her present temperament. "Okay, okay."

"No sixty-inch!" she yelled, only this time at a lower decibel level.

"Okay. Okay," he said now rubbing one of her shoulders. "If I knew that this was going to happen I would've started with something small."

Penelope was breathing heavy and then tried to control her pants, saying, "Yeah. Why couldn't we start with the MP2s?"

"The MP3s," he corrected her.

"You mean there's more than one type?" she said, fanning herself with a mitten, not thrilled over the prospect of additional technology gadgets being introduced to her at that very moment. "Why do I need this?" she questioned.

Ted wandered along the rows of TVs, analyzing them, his hands in his coat pockets. "A couple of reasons. One, you could probably use it.

Two, we're going to need it for the gaming system we're going to get you which leads to three, you'll need to know about both-Streamers is going to be putting out their own flat screens soon and after that their own gaming system."

"How do you know that?"

"I read it in PC Magazine."

Penelope extended her arm out to the televisions. "Okay. So teach me."

"All right. These are LCD HD-"

"I know that," she interrupted, "but what's the difference between the plasmas and LCDs' whatchamacallits?"

"Well. Let's start with the plasma." He twisted round in the direction of the plasmas and began his professorial lecture – "In brief, the plasma has a fluorescent light bulb, and the display has cells which have two glass panels. There's a thin gap that separates them," he said and physically described the gap by holding his hands up, palm facing palm, inches away from one another, "and within this gap neon-xenon gas is injected and sealed. The gas, at specific times, is electrically charged when the TV is in use, and the gas makes contact with green, red, blue phosphors and this creates a television image." He then added, "Each group of these colors of phosphors is called a pixel, which is another word for 'picture element.'"

Penelope's face turned white. "That's brief?"

"Okay," he admitted, "maybe that's too much. I'll write it down for you."

"Right," she said, only half-serious.

He turned to the LCD televisions and commented, "So I suppose you don't want to hear about the LCDs and their special polymer and liquid crystals."

"No."

"I'll write it down for you."

"Right."

Ted moved closer to a set of huge LCDs, "These are the LCD Flat screens. LCD stands for liquid crystal display," and he went down the line – "here's the Panasonic brand, the LD, the Toshiba, and-oh, this is the Samsung." He eyed the set on a middle shelf like a loving dog would eye his owner. "Samsung is a great brand and they make excellent LCD TVs."

"He's right," Raj said, showing up again. "It's the best. Many of the employees working here have one, and they say only good things." He scuffed the tiled floor on his way to the Samsung. "It has a great picture. Don't you think?" His index finger followed lines and swirled around and in the shaded areas. "Just look at the picture compared to the rest," he commented as he swerved his index finger at all the other sets, "the brightness, the clarity."

"Yes," Ted agreed.

While Ted and the salesman nodded, and the pictures burst out from the TVs, Penelope dropped her head to the right, and analyzed the Samsung in comparison to the other sets.

The two men copied her, all of them shifting their skulls to the right and looking as though they were devising personal critiques on serious works of art, perusing the visuals streaming and striking out of the televisions.

"You see it?" the salesman Raj asked.

"I see it," Ted answered.

"I don't see it," Penelope replied. Not only did Penelope not see what the salesman was talking about, but she found all the sets to be exactly the same – color, brightness – pixels – *what the heck was that again?* Whatever pixels were, in Penelope's eyes, the TVs seemed to have the identical ones.

"You can't see that?" Raj reacted with a condescending tone.

Penelope thought – it must be a guy thing again – a male species thing – sixty-inch flat screen televisions, three-inch penises, and now this keen talent for detecting the most minute details of TV graphics that could only be compared to one being able to detect the eye of a needle that's been placed on the top of the Empire State Building from below in the gutter – at least to this female.

"Ohhhhh," Penelope uttered, "now I see it." She acquiesced, desiring to get on with the day and afraid that the longer her head was tilted the way it was, the more she risked having to take another trip to the emergency room ("look," the nurses and doctors would say, "there's the girl who almost fractured her skull trying to work the coffee maker!). *Technology*, she thought. *Who knew it could be so painful?*

"I'll take it," Penelope said. "I'll take a twenty-seven-inch Samsung - they have that, don't they?"

"You don't want that," Ted commented. "It's really too small."

Raj interjected, "He's right."

"Okay," Penelope revised, "I'll take a thirty-inch…They make that, don't they?"

The men moaned.

"Forty," Ted said, "It should be at least forty-inches. Just think about it."

***

Penelope faced the Samsung TV – forty-inches in total – set on a new glass television stand that she squeezed in between her desk and bookcase after moving her bed a couple of inches to the left and her couch some feet to the back on a Saturday morning, exactly one week after she laid eyes on it. *It fits,* she thought. *I may not be able to walk too much in the apartment, but it fits.*

In the afternoon, Penelope was busy pushing through the pages of the television manual, maneuvering aspects of the picture via the remote and the screen menu, making sure the colors were to her liking. "The picture is too bright," she expressed as she tried to dim the hues of the TV image that showed a reality TV program where people were swallowing live mice and garden snakes. Before Penelope tried to switch the colors to cooler shades, she promptly decided to change the channel, being thoroughly disgusted by what she was viewing, and then she couldn't find her way back to the menu. "Too bright," she said again, not only feeling the TV was on top of her since it was so big, but that the colors and lines of the picture were reaching out to strike her blind.

"I don't have the patience for this," she continued, and then reached into an end table near her couch, pulled out a pair of dark sunglasses, and put them on.

In the evening, Penelope left her TV to go to the grocers, and then returned to her apartment with a variety of coffees thinking it would be a superb idea to watch her new flat screen TV and brew coffee with her new coffee maker all at the same time (what a coup that would be!). But when she went to turn the television on all she saw was a blank black screen. "WHAT?" she exclaimed, throwing her grocery bags to the side, grabbing the TV and cable remotes.

After a half-hour of problem solving by randomly and calmly tapping her index finger on the buttons of the remotes, she finally lost it.

"Darn it! Darn this TV!" Penelope yelled out to her empty abode and then "Darn it all!" spilled out of her mouth as she sat on her couch, pressing the buttons on the remotes like a mad woman, trying to get a picture.

Penelope finally understood how Stacey, her brother's pessimistic hand and foot model friend, could lose her sensibilities and sanity with her remotes. In her own frustration, Penelope tried every button she could think of, and was almost driven to flinging the television remote across the room – salivating at the thought of watching it hit a wall and disintegrate into millions of plastic and undefined pieces – and to pulling the cable remote apart with sudden supersonic strength (rooted in her extreme anger) – howling at the idea of it being sliced in half, looking like a disassembled casket with wires hanging out of it like strewn and torn intestines. "Darn the thing!" she screamed, not caring if anyone in her building heard her outbursts, still punching at buttons, switching from one remote control to the other, perspiring and then – she stopped. And she questioned herself – *maybe it's not a problem with the remote controls. Or with the cable box...maybe it's the TV. Uh-oh.*

Penelope slowly settled back into the couch, one remote in each hand; she thought they looked sad, as if they recognized that they were only a pummel away from permanent malfunctions. She closed her eyes tight. Scrunching her face, she prayed aloud, "Oh please, dear God. Please don't let it be the TV. Please. Please. Please. Don't let it be the TV. I can't return it. I can't lift it into the box to take it back." Her eyes suddenly flew open, and she scanned the room. She then closed her eyes again, and this time they were close to tearing. "Dear God, not only can I not I lift it into the box. I don't have the box to lift it into," she informed her maker. "I can't return it…Please God. Help me."

At that very moment, her cell phone rang.

"God?" Penelope immediately let go of the remotes and looked up at the ceiling. "Is that you?"

On the last ring, she answered, "Hello?"

"Hello?" a voice returned. "My name is Greta, and I've got this incredible offer for you for a subscription to Popular Mechanics-"

"No!" Penelope hollered and thumbed the phone's red "off" button as hard as she could. She raised her sights to the ceiling for a second time. "Thanks a lot," and then she bit the fingernail on her thumb, thinking about how bad the telemarketer must have felt when she hung up on her. Penelope quickly excused herself from any guilt from her action, citing technological duress. (Now, if she could only curse.)

Penelope wondered how she could solve her problem with the TV, and then she remembered what her father always told her – *Penelope, usually a solution is right in front of your face. Usually someone who could help you is most likely right there.* She debated calling her brother. No, she thought, not a good idea. She sensed she was getting on Cory's last nerve, probably a result of her trying to change into a modern city girl, she surmised, and her noticeable desire to obtain newfound knowledge that her brother worried would land her in the hospital (which already happened) or in jail (which almost happened).

Besides his fretting, she also didn't want to ask for his assistance and risk his reaction about her new TV; she didn't want him to know that she was learning about technology to clinch the Streamers account, not looking forward to him laughing at her or telling her to forget it, like she knew he would and just like Wendy, her co-worker, did.

And there was no possible way she could phone Luke. She didn't want him to see her small and vastly unimpressive studio, and to know about her technological ineptness and risk ruining the relationship before they had an actual solid commitment. Besides, he wasn't around. After he returned from Boston and they went out again (this time he chose a French restaurant with food that tasted fabulous going in, but had Penelope working on the "going out" part all night), he had to fly back to Beantown for an emergency concerning the same client he had left for in the beginning of the same week.

There was only one person left, and it wasn't Wendy or Stacey or Sonia. It was Ted.

Yes. It made perfect sense. After all, he was her techno-teacher, so to speak. This was his job. This was in his agreement – he would teach her about technology in exchange for her PR services, although she hadn't gotten to that yet. So if not Ted, who?

Penelope glanced at her wristwatch. "Ten-thirty," she commented to herself. "Probably too late."

She stared at the television and then the remotes knowing full well she would completely lose it and be admitted into a mental hospital if she didn't get the TV to work soon. She smiled to herself a little, reveling a bit in the idea – the one situation that her brother hadn't probably imagined Penelope getting into was being hauled off to screwball central.

A song cut through her mirth – *Buffalo gals can't you come out tonight – can't you come out tonight – can't you come out tonight – Buffalo gals can't you come out tonight – aaand dance by the light of the mooon...*

Penelope picked up her cell phone, the only technology she didn't feel like breaking with a stomp of her foot or the slamming of a sledgehammer.

Someone sent her a text message:

Text (mobile)

Jan 20, 2008 10:32.06 PM

Having fun? How's it going with the TV?
Text me.

Ted

Perfect, she thought.

She text him:

Not having fun at all.
TV doesn't work.

Seconds after she sent out the text, her phone rang again. This time, a voice was attached to it. "Hello? Penelope?" Ted inquired.

"Oh. Hi, Ted," she said, trying to sound cheery, but failing at it.

"What's wrong with the TV?"

Penelope's bottom lip began to tremble. She was on the brink again, all that stood in between her composure and sobs was her pride – *must be a tough woman. City girls don't cry. They shop when they're miserable, and they may scream, but they don't cry.* "I got the TV this morning, and for a while it was working, and now it doesn't work. There's no picture. No matter what I do, no matter what I try, there's no picture."

"Uh-huh," he uttered. "And everything is still plugged in."

"Yes. It's on but there's no picture."

"And you read the TV manual."

"Yes," she said, ready to hyperventilate. "And I keep pressing all these buttons on the remotes, and nothing seems to work."

Ted must have sensed the frustration in her voice. "Now calm down. Don't worry," he said, "and stop pressing the buttons. You'll wind up breaking the remotes, or at the very least, messing up what's programmed into them."

Penelope decided not to tell Ted about her almost-nervous breakdown and her wild urges to destroy the remotes. "There's stuff programmed into the remotes?" she asked.

"Sure."

She looked down at the remotes on her couch cushions and sighed, being close to certain that she deprogrammed everything.

"Now, I want you to pick up the cable remote," he advised.

"No."

"But–"

She reacted, "No," her stubbornness twined through the word and the airwaves.

There was quiet from Ted's end, and then he commented, "You can do it."

"No," she repeated, "I'm just going to mess up. I know it."

"No you won't. You're just being too hard on yourself...You can do it. I know you're a lot smarter than you think you are."

Penelope turned her mouth to his voice. "I am?" she responded, brushing her lips against the mic of the cell phone.

"Well...uh...yeah."

She breathed a heavy sigh. "Maybe you're right. But I'm just a little bit jittery about this stuff, and until I learn more about it, I'm going to be on pins and needles."

For a moment, he didn't respond, and then – "You want me to come over?"

Yes, she did. But then he had been so nice to her – *how can I ask him to come over at this hour?* "I wouldn't want you to come all the way over here this late at night. I don't want to put you out." She thought about it. "It can wait til morning, actually. If you can come by then."

"Yeah. I can't," he said. "I'm pretty much busy on Sundays."

"Oh," she uttered and figured since it was too late for him to come over, and he was too occupied on Sundays to pay her a visit, that she should drop the idea of Ted helping her solve this specific technology dilemma altogether.

"What's your address?" he asked. "I'll be right over."

Fifteen minutes later, Penelope was shocked when there was a knock at her door.

"Hey," she said to Ted as he stood in the doorway of her apartment in faded blue jeans and a parka. He had a big, toothy smile on his face and his straggly, long bangs still performed a vanishing act on his eyes.

He gave her the strange hand signal that she saw him do when they ran into each other at Best Buy, separating his fingers into two groups and holding them straight up.

Penelope, not knowing how to receive this salutation, just blinked a little and fanned her hand in the air, producing a small, unsure wave.

Ted pointed to her face. "What's that?" he questioned.

Penelope felt her cheeks, brows, and then eyes. "Oh," she uttered, pulling off her sunglasses. "I forgot I had them on. I put them on this morning because the TV picture was really bright." She placed the sunglasses on her commode.

"Oh. I thought there was an eclipse," he remarked. "I would've gone back for my telescope."

Penelope was still startled it only took him fifteen minutes to show up.

"Wow. You got over here real quick," she commented. "I hope you gave the cab driver a good tip for being so fast and still getting you here in one piece."

He shrugged. "I rode my bike."

Penelope's eyes flew open. "You rode a bike?"

She tried to sum the miles together in her head from his place to hers, and although she couldn't figure them out, she knew there were additional factors alone that added to the miraculousness of his venture to her apartment – diving in and out of potholes, almost getting plowed over by runaway buses, not to mention the sudden pedestrian who decides to cross in front of you when the light isn't theirs. "That takes a lot, doesn't it?" she asked. "I mean, coming from downtown to Murray Hill."

He raised his shoulders again, appearing unfazed. "No big deal." He looked around. "Nice place," he noted. "Bigger than mine."

Penelope rolled her eyes and grinned. "No it isn't."

"Okay," he said, studying his surroundings from the ceiling to the floor and then from her kitchen to her living room area. "Maybe it's the layout that's better."

"Come on. Yours is a one-bedroom and mine's a studio," she informed him like he didn't already know. "You have much more square footage than I do." She folded her arms across her chest. ""You're just being nice."

"Maybe," he acknowledged, heading for the cable remote lying listlessly on her couch (he didn't know that it had been beaten senseless), "but at least you're above ground."

She laughed. "Okay. Now that's true."

Ted grabbed the remote and sat down on the couch. "I actually don't mind living underground. There's something nice about being away from the world."

That's interesting, she thought.

He added, "I sort of feel like I'm running away from the law."

Penelope didn't want to take any chances. "Are you?" she questioned, knitting her eyebrows.

This time he chuckled. "No." He glanced over at the flat screen TV. "It fits. I told you it would fit."

Penelope reacted, "Yeah, well. Once I got rid of the dog."

He immediately turned around to her and seriously asked, "That's a joke, right?"

She smiled and threw back some strands of hair. She tucked them behind her ear. "Yes it is." She continued, "Ah, heck. I wasn't that close to him anyway."

Ted let out a deep and throaty laugh and pressed a button on the cable remote. The TV screen was immediately filled with an image. Suddenly, there was a moaning coming out of the TV and when Ted realized the image was one of a man and woman in a Jacuzzi, naked from the waist up, watering down each other's chests, he said, "Excuse me," and turned red as a ripened tomato and quickly changed the channel.

He scratched his neck a bit, which was also scarlet, and turned to Penelope. "I guess you have some premium channels, huh?"

Penelope didn't seem to have a clue of what he was talking about. She just stood there, clasping her hands together, grinning, in awe of the feat he performed. "How wonderful!" she exclaimed with glee, her hands still locked together. "How did you do it?"

"Just a simple press of the 'All Power' button on your cable remote," he said, flipping over the remote so it should face her, the tip of his index finger touching a rectangular button. "I knew that's probably what it was." He pointed the remote at her. "See? You could've done it."

Penelope crossed her arms in front of her and puffed out her chest. "Yes, you're right," she affirmed, nodding, "I could've done it."

Ted scanned the room again and began to unzip his coat. "You mind if I stay a-" Ted suddenly stopped talking and unzipping. He just sat there with his jaw dropped to the floor, gawking in the direction of the Samsung. "What the … ?"

Penelope rushed over to the television, concerned about his concern. "What's wrong? Is there a problem? Is it going to shut off again?"

Ted slowly raised his arm and pointed to underneath the television. *"What is that?"*

Penelope looked. "That's the cable box."

"No." He could hardly catch his breath. "Underneath that."

"Ohhh," she sounded, "That's my VCR."

He leaned forward, appearing dumbfounded. "That's not just a VCR. *That's a Beta VCR."*

"Yeah, I know. So?"

Ted put his hands over his face and bangs, held them there for a couple of moments, and then dragged them down to his chin. Finally, he asked, "Penelope, do you have any idea how long ago they stopped making Beta VCRs?"

Penelope bit her lip. "I'm guessing it's more than five years."

"Yeah, you could say that," he remarked, sardonically. "Let's me put it this way. If I was to submit that VCR to the Smithsonian, they'd put it in their archives."

"Are you making fun of me?" she questioned, nervous about her technology teacher thinking she was a lost cause.

Ted's body jolted. "No, no," he insisted, shaking his hands about. "I'm just saying."

"My parents passed it onto me," she explained. "It still works."

"Yeah, but what do you put into it?" he questioned her, his eyebrows lifting as he spoke. "They stopped making beta tapes way before they even stopped making the beta VCRs."

Penelope suddenly threw up her arms in a "cease talking" motion, jumped in place, and ran over to her tiny, walk-in closet. She opened the closet door and gestured to the top shelf which had large, beta tapes stacked atop of it. "Voila!" she exclaimed, grinning wildly.

"You're kidding me."

"We can watch one, if you'd like," she suggested, clapping, excited about entertaining her first guest in her apartment (family didn't count) and being extra-enthused that Ted had complimented her about her apartment – even if he was lying. But he couldn't have been lying too much, she surmised. He did want to stay a while. "There are a lot of neat tapes here." (*Neat?* What was she thinking?)

While Penelope practically launched herself onto the closet shelf to rummage around in her virtual treasure trove of tapes, Ted sat there, speechless, still seeming amazed at his finding of the once-thought-extinct world of beta movies.

"Here it is!" Penelope exclaimed, pulling out a tape box, her feet now on the ground. She swiveled around to him and held it up. "My favorite movie! The greatest movie of all time!"

"Revenge of the Sith?"

"No."

"Close Encounters of the Third Kind?"

"No."

"Is it a Freddy Krueger movie?"

Penelope put a hand to her waist, slumped to her side, and cocked an eyebrow. "No. It's not a Freddy Krueger movie," she said. "It's 'It's a Wonderful Life!'"

Ted passed her a puzzled expression. "It's a wonderful what?"

"It's a Wonderful Life!"

"So says you," he retorted with a smirk.

She walked over to the couch and sat beside him. "Haven't you ever seen it?"

"Does it have little green men with big heads?"

"No."

"Does it have huge spaceships landing on New York or Tokyo?"

"No."

"Does it have alien beings oozing out of human bodies?"

She shrank back. "Ewwwww! No!"

Ted shrugged. "Then I haven't seen it."

Penelope waved the box around. "I can't believe you haven't seen this! Everyone's seen it!" Ted shook his head, smiling. "Every Christmas they have it on." He shook his head again. "Oh-you just don't remember!" she exclaimed. "It's customary viewing! Your mother *had* to have sat you down at the TV to watch it when you were a kid!" Penelope reached for her cell phone on the coffee table. "Give me her phone number! I'm going to call her and clear this up!" Ted's smile faded away. He immediately took hold of Penelope's wrist, ever so gently, and then pulled it away from the phone. He slowly set her hand on her lap and then let go.

Ted jerked his head towards the television. "I knew it would fit," he said and crossed one leg over the other.

Penelope went on about her movie pick. "'It's a Wonderful Life' is fantastic. It's a story about George Bailey who lived all his life in a small town called 'Bedford Falls,' and all his life he wanted to leave, but all these things happen to him that he needed to stay in his town – he had obligations – and he's not so crazy about it. Along the way he gets married, has kids, has loads of friends, and then something happens – I won't tell you what – and he thinks it would be better if he hadn't lived at all. But then he gets a chance to see how life would actually be if he was never born through this angel and how it would've affected other lives, and in the end he realizes he actually had a wonderful life! ... Wait! Did I give too much away?"

"Uh-no," Ted replied. "Well, maybe just the beginning, middle and end."

She put her hand on his. "Oh-you'll still *love* this movie." She then frowned at the box. "I have it in color, though. It was originally made in black and white, and I lost that version, and I can't find it anywhere now." She laughed. "And there aren't any more beta tape dealers to buy one from."

"Did you try eBay?" he asked.

"E what?"

"Okay...So that's another lesson for another day." He looked over at her desk. It was occupied with bracelets and earrings and cosmetic samples. "And you don't have a computer. You'll need to have your own computer. A laptop."

Ted watched Penelope as she carefully and calmly opened the tape box. "Penelope? I was wondering," he said. "You didn't have a problem buying the TV, and you didn't flinch when I told you that you're going to need a laptop. Do you mind me asking you if you're independently wealthy?"

"Are you kidding me?" she asked. "Take a look around. Does it seem like I'm independently wealthy?"

"I just mean-"

"No. It's all right. I have some money saved for some extras. Actually, a good deal of money for extras. Although, it wouldn't have been enough for a fancy one-bedroom in Manhattan," she said as she pulled the tape from the box. "It's what happens when you live in a small town long enough. There's nothing to do there to spend on, so you wind up saving all your money."

Penelope handed him the tape with an expression that said – "See. Beta!"

He moved his fingers through his shag hair. "You sound like you're not so crazy about Elmont."

"I'm definitely not."

"So do you mind me asking why you didn't leave a long time ago?"

Penelope peered down into her lap where she fiddled her fingers, not offering a reply.

Ted filled in the silence for her. "Obligations?" he inquired, seemingly referencing to what she said about George Bailey.

Penelope rolled her eyes. "Kind of," she replied, not wanting to divulge any additional information, and then she got up from the couch and headed to the kitchen. "Do you want something to drink?" She eyed her Cuisinart 12-cup marvel on her counter and excitedly asked, "You want some coffee?"

"At eleven at night? Uh-no. But thanks for asking."

She searched her refrigerator and found a bottle of martini mix. "How about martinis?" That would be the chic thing to do, she thought.

"What did you say?" he asked. "Martinis?"

Penelope reached into her cupboard and grabbed the stems of her martini glasses with one hand and held the bottle of martini mix in the other, and stepped out of the kitchen into the living room area. She wiggled the martini glasses in the air. "Dirty martinis?" she inquired. "They made a lot of them in Manhattan Nights. I love that show."

"You mean that show about those New York City girls where all they do is drink, shop and have sex with egotistical rich men?" Ted patted down his hair and then peeled off his parka, keeping it behind him. This time he was wearing a nice and tight knit blue sweater (not bally like the last sweater she had seen him in), and she could see the curve of the muscles in his arms and his shoulders through the threaded material, along with the flat and taut plane of his stomach.

Penelope felt a sudden twitch in her body.

"What's wrong?" Ted asked, his head tilting up at her.

Penelope immediately implanted a picture of sexy and sophisticated Luke in her head. *Poor Luke,* she thought. *Holed up in Boston again.*

Ted. Great for some nice down-to-earth girl, she noted. Someone who doesn't care about getting ahead. *For some other girl.* She remembered what Wendy had once told her about Ted and his ex-fiancé, and how he was cheated on, and thought he would need a nice and genuine girl after what that other girl did to him in D.C. *Definitely.*

"Nothing," she answered, providing a slight smile, ogling his bangs, wondering if she could sear his hair with a look, so she could see his eyes.

His eyes had become a great mystery to her. First, what did his eyes look like? – What color and how big were they? Second, how was he able to utilize his vision under his slab of strands?

"So," she said with martini glasses and mix still in hand, "do you want a martini?"

"No thanks. But water would be great."

Penelope returned to the kitchen and while she put the martini glasses back in the cupboard, she found a bag of unshelled peanuts next to her salt and paper shakers. She recalled buying the bag a week or so ago when her brother told her that their father might be planning a visit. Her father loved peanuts. "I know this might sound strange," she yelled out, "but I have peanuts. Would you like some?"

"Are you kidding me? I love peanuts!"

"Okay. Water and peanuts. Coming up." Penelope thought it was all boring, yet comfortable, and she soon entered into the living room area again and dropped the bag of peanuts and a bowl for the shells in front of him, and then made another round trip and returned with two glasses of water.

Ted turned to her as she sat down on the couch and set the glasses of water on the coffee table. "So you love 'It's a Wonderful Life,' which is a story about a man who comes from a small town and finds out that he's got a wonderful life there-with his family, kids and friends-but you love Manhattan Nights, which is basically about living in a huge city-New York City-and is about women who have a collective of one night stands, meaningless relationships and who are alcoholics."

Wow, Penelope thought, *for a guy who's supposedly anti-social and quiet, he sure says a lot and a lot of what he thinks.*

"That's way harsh," she said.

"How is it that you love both of them? Which one do you love more?"

She shook her head. "I can't choose."

"Why not?"

"One's a movie and the other is a TV show. It's like apples and oranges."

"So? Let's say they were both movies or TV shows-what would you pick? The apple or the orange?"

Oh, here we go again, she sighed. *More with the fruit.* She automatically thought of the Apple company and lemonade. "Are there any lemons in this?"

"What? No." He squinted at her.

"Good." She was thankful.

"Well?" he pushed her.

She looked away from him. "It's so silly." She picked up a glass and took a sip of water.

"Mmmmm," he hummed, like he was doing a Freudian analysis.

"Okay," she said, "let me ask you a question. If you were so keen on me buying this forty-inch TV, why don't you have one?"

Ted was swift with his answer – "Because *I* don't have any money. It was drained in D.C." He sighed heavily. "Long story," he mumbled under his breath.

He picked up the 'It's a Wonderful Life' tape and stood up from the couch. "It will be my pleasure to put in the beta tape." He grinned. "I haven't done this in eons! Cool!"

Once he slid the tape into the VCR slot, he went back to the couch and began to crack the peanut shells, and one by one, instead of placing the peanuts in his mouth, he threw them up in the air and caught them on his tongue.

Oh my God, Penelope thought. *That looks familiar. Who does that? ... My father does that!*

Penelope stared at him for a good minute, and then the movie started.

"Wait a minute," Ted suddenly said. "You said that the picture was too bright for you before. Do you want me to change the colors? Mute them? I'll show you how to do it."

"Is this how bright it's supposed to be?"

"Yeah. It's the factory setting. But it's your TV. And it's your apartment. Ladies choice," he commented. "Always ladies choice."

She liked that. "No. If that's the way it's supposed to be, I'd rather get used to it."

"Okay."

Ted settled into the couch.

"By the way," he said as they watched the opening movie credits roll down the Samsung screen, "whatever you did to your hair, it looks nice."

Penelope was stunned that he noticed. "Thanks."

"And I also liked the way you had it before."

"Thanks," she said again.

Penelope suddenly noticed how warm and toasty the apartment was. In the corner of her eye, she saw snowflakes falling from the night sky. How nice it was, she thought, the now cozy feeling of her apartment. Maybe it was her new flat screen television. "This is great," she announced, "the winter time inside a warm apartment with this great TV. A girl could definitely think twice about leaving her home. She could definitely become attached to the TV."

"Sure," Ted said, his eyes glued to the beginning scene of the colorized classic, "if a girl doesn't have a boyfriend."

Ted turned around to her and smiled. "You have a boyfriend?"

She wondered if Luke was actually a certified boyfriend or if he was someone she was just "seeing" at the present time (not that she didn't want more).

And should she tell Ted about Luke?

Penelope smiled back. "Uh-no."

She decided to go onto another subject, and one that was gnawing at her. "Ted? What's that hand thing that you do?"

"What?"

"You did it at the Best Buy the other day with your friend Raj. The two finger thing. And you did it one time before." She tried to show him with her own hand, but she still couldn't do it.

"Ohhhhh," he said, nodding, "the Vulcan salute," and then he explained, "It's from Star Trek. Mr. Spock used to do it, because he was half-Vulcan." He elevated his hand and did the gesture correctly, digits parting at the ring and middle fingers." It means live long and prosper. You can do it when you're saying hello or goodbye."

Penelope smiled. "I like that." She mulled it over. "Live long and prosper," she said aloud to herself. "Hello and goodbye." She looked at him. "It's kind of like 'aloha.' You can say that for both, too."

Ted's head turned around to her as she tried to do the Vulcan salute; she could only do half of the gesture. She attempted it a second time – no good – and then a third time – no good. She felt a bit distraught and it showed on her face.

"No, no, don't worry," he assured her, "most people can't do it. It just takes a lot of practice. It took me years to do."

"*Years?*" She put her fingers down. "Forget it."

"It was important to me," he remarked. "Just like learning about technology is important to you."

She nodded at him and the analogy, and he turned back to the movie, and she tried to do the same, but found that she was having the same problem as before with the bright colors bothering her eyes.

All at once, she hurried over to her commode, grabbed the sunglasses, placed them on her face, and rushed back to the couch.

She glanced over at Ted, who was expressionless as he leaned back into the cushions, just inches away from her, unshelling the peanuts and popping them in his mouth.

Pinching the sides of her sunglasses, she slowly lifted them up and stole a peek at him, and then she quickly dropped the glasses on her face, and sat back with her eyes centered on the television, waiting for the young George Bailey to stroll onto the screen.

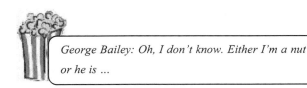

George Bailey: Oh, I don't know. Either I'm a nut or he is ...

Twelve

*(**D**ear Brad & Angelina - ?)*
(Dear Angelina & Brad - ?)
Dear Jolie-Pitts,

I am the media representative for Henshaw Tractors, America's most well known makers of tractors and tractor equipment since 1932.

Recently, I've read that you have adopted (2, 3, 6 - ?) many children from indigent countries who desperately need farming equipment and realized who better to represent Henshaw tractors around the world than the Jolie-Pitts?

Picture you and your entire family riding on Henshaw Tractors in the fields (in Ethiopia - ? New Guinea - ? Uganda-?) in the country of your choice, becoming the beacons of hope for millions of people who need to harvest their crops but don't have the equipment to do so.

*Additionally, if you do decide to become representatives of Henshaw Tractors, Henshaw will throw in two complimentary tractors — yours to keep!

If you're interested in representing Henshaw Tractors and being the symbols of charity for the world and its agricultural future, please phone me at our offices, or

you can email me at pmcadams@renquist.com.
Looking forward to hearing from you.
Regards,
Penelope McAdams, Account Executive
Renquist & Renquist Public Relations

***

Alden Renquist's fingers were hyperkinetic as he tapped them one by one on the draft of Penelope's "Jolie-Pitts" pitch letter that was lying on his desk.

As he looked on at Penelope with pursed lips, she looked on at him with eyes sparkling and hopeful, smoothing out some of the creases in her new Nanette Lepore dress as she sat in front of him.

"So. This is what you want to send out?" he asked her.

"Well. Not just yet. Of course, I wouldn't send it out with the question marks and ideas that are in parentheses. It would be a clean copy," she said, smiling, "and I still have to do some research."

"Hmmmmm," he intoned and not so pleasantly.

She noticed his expression of discontent and jumped in, "Of course, I would only send something out with your permission."

Renquist raised his hands to his lips in the form of a tepee, as if he was praying, and said, "I'm glad. And in this instance, I'm especially glad."

Penelope ceased the undoing of her creases. Not knowing what to say, she didn't say anything.

He continued, "Have you gotten any authority or word from Henshaw that they're intending to go global?"

"Uh-no."

Alden Renquist pinched a corner of the letter and flipped it up as if it he was airing out her words. "Then how did you expect to send this out? You can't promote global initiatives for a company that isn't global or isn't planning to be."

"Yes, I know," Penelope started, leaning forward with her pen, trying to make a point, "but I thought that if Angelina Jolie and Brad Pitt agreed to represent them that Henshaw would obviously be thrilled about it."

"Obviously."

"And then, if they were so thrilled about two major movie stars representing them, they probably wouldn't have an issue with going global."

Her boss inhaled deeply and then exhaled and nudged his spectacles up over the bridge of his nose. "I'm sure. If there weren't licensing and export issues involved, along with more money needed for financing, and then there's just the tiniest of problems-who would buy tractors in poverty-stricken third world countries?

Penelope wondered to herself and wanted to punch her own head for not seeing the apparent contradiction between marketing to third world countries and the purchasing of expensive tractors (*where has my mind been?*). She had to think fast. "The governments could probably buy them."

"Penelope. The governments would most likely buy the necessary food for their countries first. After all, if people dropped dead from starvation, who would be around to operate the tractors?"

She didn't have an answer, and sat there, now completely anxious to the point of her feeling as though she was out of her own body looking down at herself with a wagging finger, saying, "You should research your letters more!"

He veered his body to one side, crossed one leg over the other, and settled back into his chair. "Also, most of those people wouldn't know the first thing about riding a tractor. Even if someone trained them, they wouldn't have a clue. Take for example, a medicine man I once visited with my soon-to-be-ex-wife." Renquist reached over to his pencil and pen cup and pulled out a sharp letter opener. "We specially traveled to one of the places you thought of for this letter-New Guinea-for a special healing circle for her liposuction that went bad." He swung the letter opener side to side like a pendulum and for a second, Penelope twisted her head over her shoulder, looking at the door, speculating if she should make a run for it. She quickly unraveled her neck and head and went back to the conversation. "Come to think of it," he said, "it was only the three of us. So it was more like a triangle than a circle." He thought aloud, "I wonder if I paid for extra people…Anyway, between the Hopi dance, the goddamn annoying rattles, and having to wear paint on my face like I was a goddamn French hooker, I was not a happy camper." Putting down the letter opener (at this, Penelope had her own personal sigh of relief), he said, "But I digress," and his mouth stretched and opened to a smile, "the point is that in the midst of the Neanderthal nonsense and ritualistic hullabaloo, my cell phone goes off, and the medicine man jumps out of his skin, falls to his knees and starts to babble around in his native tongue. He thinks it's the gods giving him a signal. I tell him it's my bookie calling me with bad news about a not-exactly fortuitous point spread. He doesn't believe me. I tell him to concentrate on my wife's ass."

Alden Renquist swept a wavy bang off his forehead. It buoyantly landed in the perfect layers of his hair.

Penelope fidgeted – what to say or do when a boss mentions his soon-to-be ex-wife's posterior?

"Do you understand what I'm saying, Penelope?"

Penelope rolled her eyes to the ceiling, pensive in thought. "That you shouldn't give your bookie your cell number?"

"Besides that."

"I don't know, Mr. Renquist," she said, shruggingly.

Her boss reached over for his Xanax bottle and moved it into his personal space like it was a security blanket. He continued, "The point is that the medicine man had never encountered a cell phone, and thus, would never be able to operate a tractor. He'd think it was a space vehicle dropped down to the earth by extraterrestrial beings. Just like the people you'd be marketing the tractor to."

Alden Renquist suddenly stopped his discourse for a moment, just long enough for him to give birth to an idea from his harried mind. "Now that I think about it, he also didn't have a clue about how to get my wife's behind to shed more fat." He added, "She must have been crazy to think that would work."

An expression of enlightenment infiltrated his pupils, and his eyes blew up like two balloons, and with a swoop of a forefinger, her boss immediately pressed a button on his phone and talked to the intercom. "Ms. Shirley, can you pull up one of my divorce files labeled 'My Wife's Mental Illnesses'? Thank you."

He turned to a shocked Penelope. "Well. At least I can say two important things came about from your letter. One, I may have additional proof that my wife is mentally incompetent and therefore, suffering from delusions that I'm having affairs and hence, entitled to less alimony." A smile crept up on his face and then disappeared. "And I've gotten into the crux of your problem."

Penelope didn't know that she had a problem. "You have?"

"Yes, I have. You worked at a non-profit in Indiana before you came here – is that correct?"

"Illinois. Yes," she answered, adding, "Meals on Wheels."

"And it shows in this letter," he told her. "Penelope. You're not at a charitable organization anymore. This is a profit seeking, prominent PR agency in New York, and your client and your future clients are only interested in making money, as well. They're not interested in saving anyone, let alone the world. This letter," he remarked, picking up the draft, "reeks non-profit." He put it down. "Is this what your other pitches are like?"

"No. Not at all," she replied. "With the other ones I've primarily concentrated on the tractors themselves and how they would be of interest to the publications' readerships."

"Good," he stated, "Remember Penelope, you're not in Illinois anymore...What town are you from again?"

"Elmont."

"Remember. You're not in Elmont, Illinois anymore. Forget about the Midwest. Pitch from a New York point of view.

Confused, Penelope commented, "Forgive me, Mr. Renquist, for saying this, but I thought you put me on this account because of my Middle-America approach."

He picked up his pen and flicked it in her direction. "You're right," he gave her. "I'll tell you what. Average out Elmont and

Manhattan. See what you come up with."

She figured it out. "Cleveland," she muttered to herself. "I'd come up with Cleveland."

"What's that?"

"Nothing," she replied, and then, not having anything more to include, she said what first came to her mind. "I made the coffee," she blurted. "I've been making the coffee everyday for two weeks."

Renquist gave her a deadpan stare. "I don't drink coffee anymore. My doctor tells me if offsets the Xanax."

"Oh," she reacted, disappointed.

Narrowing his eyes and jutting out his jaw, he said, "But it's now my own personal mission to create a pill that is both anti-anxiety and stimulant-Hell," he raised his pen as if he was about to lead the cavalry with it, "if they can get a ninety-year old man to have an erection, they can do anything!"

Penelope's eyes bugged out – *did he just say "erection" to me after he just talked about his almost-former wife's behind and his gambling problem?*

"You're excused, Penelope. Just remember – Elmont and Manhattan. Average them together and you'll do fine."

Penelope got up from her chair, turned away from her boss, and then turned back to him. "So should I work on the letter some more?"

Her boss' phone beeped and he picked up. "Hello?" he said into the receiver and then glared at her, crumpling up her letter and throwing it in his trash basket.

Slogging back to her desk, Penelope plopped down on her chair with dejection written all over her face.

On the way to the copy machine, Wendy asked, "What's wrong?"

"Renquist didn't like my letter."

"What? He didn't like your incredible letter to Brangelina?" She smirked and pitched back her long black tresses with a glint in a single blue eye.

She didn't like the letter? "If you thought it was so awful, why didn't you tell me?"

Wendy placed a hand to her bosom. "*I* didn't think it was awful. I really wanted to see the Brangelinas riding off into the sunset on a tractor in Ethiopia, picking up kids in the crops along the way-orphans or not." She then supplied an addendum – "But I had my doubts if Renquist would like it. But you have to take your chances, y'know."

"He really didn't like it."

"But he didn't fire you."

"No."

"That man has a yen for you. I swear he does."

"No he doesn't. He has a thing for pharmaceuticals."

Wendy leaned against the cubicle wall, leisurely crossing her shins, and then thrust her arm out in front of Penelope's face, displaying a platinum plated watch. "Guess what."

Penelope moaned, her eyes swirling in their sockets. *Here we go.* "It's a watch."

"Well, duh," Wendy sounded. "But this isn't just any watch. It's a Movado," she informed. "Guess how much."

Penelope knew she always provided Wendy with monetary figures for her belongings that were way too low – even for discount stores – so this time she decided to take the "high" road. The very "high" road. "A hundred-thousand dollars."

Wendy reeled back, a look of shock spreading across her face. "Penelope," she said, "if I had a hundred-thousand dollars to buy a watch, do you think that I'd be standing here at this firm talking to you?"

Penelope changed the subject, reflecting on her conversation with her boss. "Have you ever been to Cleveland?" she inquired.

"No," she replied. "Remember? I don't travel much unless it's necessary." Wendy furrowed her brow. "Why? What's in Cleveland?"

"I don't know. People."

"Oh," she uttered. "People? Not interested." She pointed to a sheet of paper on the floor underneath Penelope's desk. "You dropped something," she said, heading towards the copy machine.

Penelope picked up the paper and read it. It was her print out from that morning – an article having to do with Ted:

September 30, 2005

The Peabody Firm, a renowned biotech company in Washington, D.C., has just obtained a new contract with the U.S. Department of Defense concerning the creation of DNA microarray chips to identify genetic predispositions for disease and physical reactions to specific environments and toxins.

The contract was acquired after the firm exhibited an impressive body of work by Peabody's top pair of bio and computer engineers, Ted Hollis and Dane Trask, who have been the operation's wunderkinds for the past three years.

During their time at the firm, Hollis and Trask, graduates of MIT and Harvard respectively, have been researching and developing a microarray chip that focuses on individuals' backgrounds for Diabetes, Type I and heart disease.

Trask stated, "A chip would be created at birth for each person. All that would be needed is a swab sample from an infant's mouth."

The firm would not go into the contract and project extensively, but did comment that not only were both engineers working diligently on the chip, but that Hollis was in the process of developing a computer program where scientists could take a closer look at the DNA and create personalized plans for immunization, medication and hopefully, proactive treatments.

"Ultimately, the focus is to help people before disease exhibits itself," Hollis commented. "It's all about preventative care to create a better quality of life for future generations."

The contract extends over a five-year period, and the government has allocated close to $10 million for the project.

Although she didn't understand some of the article's particulars, she understood from the information that Ted's achievements were impressive. *Very impressive.*

Penelope's eyes moved away from the paper, and she gently placed it on her desk.

She'd been doing a search on Ted for two weeks now. After all, it was the deal that he would teach her technology and she would do his PR. But Penelope wasn't getting anywhere in keeping with her end of the bargain. And it wasn't as if she wasn't trying. She had asked Ted many times over to sit down with her to talk about his past career and what he was doing at present, and he always seemed to manage to switch to another subject altogether – the weather, politics, science fiction movies, and books, how he couldn't put together a simple, polished outfit (which even Penelope could see was a valid point, even with her lack of fashion flair), etcetra, etcetra. "We can talk about it next time we meet," he would say to her over hamburgers at a diner or a banana split served at Serendipity's where he would then tell her about the origins of the microchip or the internet, or on a pleasant, crisp-cold day walking along the street of the city, following the subway routes, explaining to her the engineering history of the New York subway system – "Can you believe it? It took decades to construct. It all started in 1904," he would say, and he'd go on and on.

Through it all, Ted wasn't providing her with any information she could put in a press release to send to members of the media. So Penelope decided to take it upon herself to begin the process and do some investigative work on her own on *who* Ted was, and according to The Washington Post, The Washington Times and the MIT Technology Review, Ted was the virtual boy wonder of engineering, having received a bachelor's degree in Electrical Engineering and Computer Science from MIT, as well as his Master's from the school in the same subject area, along with a second Master's in Biological Engineering, graduating at the top of his class in all programs, and later working on important research at the Peabody Firm.

In the morning, she went through a variety of articles on his academic achievements and research accolades, searching for a photo of him, hopefully being one where she could get a look-see at his eyes – just because she was burning with human curiosity, following the tenet that anything hidden is probably worth seeing. As for the seeing possibly resulting in something negative – like he was a Cyclops or he was cross-eyed with a chronic and noticeable, oozing eye fungus – that was beside the point. Curiosity was curiosity, and it led her to madness as she printed out the articles – all nine of them – and there weren't any photos – well, there weren't any photos of him, she thought. There was a photo next to the Washington Post article she had just tossed on her desk, which just happened to be the last one written about Ted. But it wasn't of Ted. It was a picture of a co-worker at the Peabody firm named Dane Trask who had helped Ted work on one of his many projects – a cute blonde boy with cheerful blue eyes and smile wearing a short sleeved, pink polo, resting his hand on lab table filled with microscopes, slides and Petri dishes. But Ted was nowhere in sight.

Penelope had some sudden thoughts about the Washington Post article, and she picked it up again, turning it upside-down and then downside-up as if she was manipulating sand in an hourglass, trying to see if Ted and his thoroughly naked face would plop down next to his co-worker's. A part of her knew this was true insanity, but the curiosity was making her crazy.

"What are you doing?" Wendy asked having come back from her brief excursion with a small bundle of copies.

Quickly, Penelope put the printout behind her back. "Nothing."

Wendy went into her cubicle and threw down her papers. "The Blue Bloods shooed me from the copy machine after only being there for a minute. Damn them and their perfectly manicured nails and probably perfectly coiffed hoohas. Their hoohas probably have designer bags and jewelry, too."

"What?"

"Their hoohas."

"What?" Penelope asked, totally thrown off into oblivion by a term that she had never heard of – *hoohas*.

"Never mind," Wendy sighed. "Talking about designer stuff, how's Luke doing?"

"He's fine," Penelope answered and let her mind wander off to a night that week when he took her out to the posh supper club "The Waverly Inn" and greeted some of his friends there who all wore suits and ties and had tans in the middle of winter; the women at their side had French manicures and large diamond stones and begets wrapped around their marriage fingers, smelling like the perfume hub at Saks, with iridescent smiles gleaming from teeth whiteners. After Luke had introduced her to his comrades, who all seemed to talk like they were acquaintances since they only skimmed the surface of meaningful conversation (*Where did you vacation this past summer again? … Do you think their second home compares to the one he had with his first wife? … How could she serve that leek salad with rose centerpieces? It threw off the entire balance of the table*

…), he introduced her to the variety of wines lining the shelves above the bar. With an eagle eye, he pointed at each one, able to tell her their type and vintage. Penelope yawned for a moment, and then Luke captured her yawn with a plump kiss.

She swooned.

"Actually, he's more than fine. He's great," Penelope informed her, grinning to herself.

"You know who I heard was also doing pretty well?"

"No. Who?"

"Ted. I heard from my ex Gary that he's doing quite well."

"Really?" Penelope asked her, cocking an eyebrow at the wall that divided them.

"Yeah. Are you still spending time with him learning all about technology?"

"Yes."

"Well, maybe you're bringing him out of his shell. Gary tells me that he's been going out to more happy hours in the past three weeks than he has in the past three years he's known him, and that he even catches him with a smile – and sometime he cracks a joke."

Penelope was suddenly satisfied with herself that she had done some good for Ted. The possibility of her presence in his life lifting his self-esteem in some way served as a momentary replacement for the PR job that wasn't getting done (again, not that she wasn't trying). "Really?" Penelope tried to sound unfazed, even though she smiled with delight.

Then, Wendy added, "He's even been hanging around this one blonde girl."

Having a knee-jerk reaction, Penelope blurted, "What?" There was a crack in her voice in this one-word question. She composed herself, repeating her inquiry in a more hushed tone – "What?"

"I think she lives in his neighborhood and in another dungeon. He didn't tell you?"

Penelope didn't remember Ted talking about a blonde who lived in a dark hovel such as his own. And why hadn't he told her? What was going on? Then again, why hadn't she told him about Luke? Well, she reasoned, it was none of his business really, and the world that she spent with Ted and the world she spent with Luke were too different to merge together – the simplistic and then the adorned. An easy breeze and a rush of flames. What would be the point to meld the worlds and ruin equilibriums?

But what of the blonde girl? What delicate balance would Ted endanger if he had told her? Maybe he thought the blonde girl wasn't any of her business, as well.

But, Penelope thought, *I could help him out with the girl. Advise him a bit since he's been out of the dating scene for a while.* And she could also size the girl up for him-see if she was Ted-worthy or not. Penelope certainly didn't want Ted to wind up with another wretch like he had obviously been with in D.C.

Penelope shook her head. No. What was she thinking? Wendy didn't know what she was talking about – blonde girl! Wendy loved gossip and talking in general. She was most likely fabricating a tidbit of information that her ex-boyfriend-booty-call had passed onto her (the blonde girl was probably a standard poodle that Ted was walking for his dungeoned next door neighbor, who was not allowed to go out in public being that he was a grossly unattractive man with leathered skin and a peg leg).

"Ted and I don't talk about personal matters," Penelope provided. "Strictly technology." She then thought of a catastrophe. "Wendy? You haven't told your ex about me and Luke, have you?"

Dear God, please say no.

"Uh," she appeared as though she was thinking. "Uh, no. We kind of talk about Ted sometimes and then sometimes the weather and then go straight to the booty-call." She threw her a perplexed expression. "Why?"

"I just rather you wouldn't tell him."

"Why?"

"I really don't feel like talking about it right now," she said, and it was true since she didn't know what she would tell her – she was afraid that any explanation she would give wouldn't matter; she had an inclination that Wendy would make more of it than it was – maybe concluding that Penelope actually *liked* Ted.

I couldn't have that, Penelope thought, deciding that keeping quiet and being vague was the best approach.

"Well," Wendy commented, "I know that you not wanting me to say anything to my ex about Luke couldn't mean that you're involved with him."

Penelope suddenly became worried. "Involved with who? Ted?" Her face tensed.

"No, silly. My ex. Gary."

Ohhh. Penelope's features bunched up. "I've never even met your ex."

"That's beside the point. I doubt that you would give up Luke for Gary." She paused. "Hell, I wouldn't give up Luke for Gary."

Penelope laughed. "Don't worry," Penelope assured her. "It's just not serious enough to go into."

Wendy's pupils flicked up to the ceiling. "Okay. I won't say a word, but it's just more secrets," she remarked. "Can't you tell me anything?"

"Wendy, I told you, it's not serious. It's not even important."

"All right," she sighed. "So if you're not going to tell me any of your secrets, can you at least show me something new that you've learned about technology?"

Excited, Penelope exclaimed, "Sure. Come on over!" and pulled out her new iPod as her co-worker moved into her cubicle.

Penelope held it up. "See?"

Wendy looked at her. "It's an iPod … Ohhhh. I've seen one of those," she reacted sardonically.

"But Ted taught me how to put stuff on it-"

"You mean download."

"Uh-yeah," Penelope answered, connecting her iPod to the computer with a single chord. "We went out last week, and I got a lap top, and he showed me how to put music on my iPod via the computer."

"Great." Wendy rolled her eyes while Penelope enthusiastically switched her windows screen to the internet and began to Google.

"Penelope," Wendy said, "I don't think you should be downloading in the office."

"Oh, it won't be a problem," she said to her, clicking away at her mouse, exchanging one computer screen for another.

"But seriously, I think we were warned not to. Something about our shared drive."

"It's fine. Ted taught me how to do it."

Penelope hungrily looked on at her computer, searching for websites to download music from. "Oh-here's one," Penelope announced with a grin. "Jack's Potpourri of Music."

Wendy jumped a little. "I never heard of that site."

Penelope did a couple of clicks on the site's links, working on downloading some Bob Denver songs. "I don't like Bob Denver, really. It's just an example."

Wendy raised an eyebrow. "Sure."

Doing one last push of her finger on her mouse, Penelope exclaimed, "And - voila!"

Exactly six seconds later, there was a collective groan throughout the office.

Penelope's eyes grew large as her computer screen had gone from "Jack's Potpourri of Music" to a completely black screen with codes and letters and symbols she didn't understand, and they just stayed there, not moving, not changing, remaining perfectly ominous.

"WHAT THE FUCK?" Ginger, the account supervisor, screamed out to all. "WHO FUCKED UP THE SHARED DRIVE? WHERE THE FUCK ARE ALL OUR FILES?"

Penelope didn't breathe a word and neither did Wendy, who just shook her head and slapped her hand on her brow. She appeared to be in pain. "One word for you," Wendy whispered to her, "virus." Panic spread throughout Penelope's body and flowered onto her face. "Don't worry," Wendy assured her, "they won't find out you did it. Just too many computers. Too much time."

"WHAT THE FUCK?" They suddenly heard from their boss' office, and the air was immediately sucked out of the room by a myriad of gasps.

Alden Renquist's door flew open and his tie, as if a cyclone caught onto it, immediately picked itself up and wound around his neck. He stood there grimacing, gritting his teeth, with the eyes of a mad man pulsating and scanning the room from behind his spectacles. In his hand, raised up like he was ready to lunge, was his letter opener, sharp and shining under the fluorescent lights of the ceiling.

And then, as sure as he made his entrance, Alden Renquist slowly receded into his office and proceeded to slam the door behind him. Loudly.

Very, very loudly.

George Bailey [to Mr. Potter]: I know very well what you're talking about . You're talking about something you can't get your fingers on ... and it's galling you.

Thirteen

"**A**re you okay?" Luke asked Penelope as she felt herself being flattened against the wall of the bar at Asia de Cuba. Being that there wasn't one empty stool at the Friday night happy hour, it was inevitable that someone should become the restaurant's semi-permanent décor – on this evening, that décor was Penelope.

She adjusted the straps of her new and very red Betsy Johnson Dress and swirled her Merlot around. "Sure," she muttered, "I'm okay," and she took a swig from her wine glass.

Luke turned to her. She noticed he was wearing his hair differently. His waves were swept off his face revealing more of his well-defined cheekbones and strong, smooth forehead. He smiled a little, his dimples still showing in the dimly lit room. "Really? You don't seem fine." He took a sip of his wine.

Penelope's eyes gravitated from his face to his jacket. She couldn't help admiring him in it. It was a plaid, light-beige smoking jacket that was tailored to fit him perfectly and, she thought, the lightness of the color brought out the olive tone of his skin that remained from his tanning in Monaco.

"I like your jacket," she said to him, the corner of her mouth upturned as if she had a secret (Wendy would be so proud).

Luke's mouth followed suit, and he slowly reached for her shoulder, slipping his forefinger underneath the shoulder strap of her dress. "I like what you're wearing...Red is a very sexy color," he said to her in a breathy voice. "It looks great on you."

"Thank you." She smiled but looked away, trying to appear coy as if she was playing the starring role of temptress in a movie.

She waited for him to compliment her about the highlights in her hair. She had been waiting since he picked her up.

Finally, her patience took a leave of absence. "So, if you're liking the new dress so much, I can only imagine what you're thinking about the new hair."

Luke examined her follicles. "Nice," he said, "but you could probably go a little lighter."

What? Penelope's mouth dropped. She wondered if his comment was a jab that meant she didn't look as good as she ought to, or that it didn't really mean anything, and she was being oversensitive.

He quickly corrected his mistake with − "I just mean, if you went lighter, your hair would shine more, it would get more attention, and people would be automatically attracted to the pretty face right under it."

Penelope's mouth closed; she was partially satisfied and then decided to shrug the matter off.

The same masculine hand that reached for the dress strap started to rub her shoulder. "You haven't seen my place yet-have you?"

"No," she replied, suddenly feeling her cheeks heat up; Luke's touch, his low and deep voice, and the Merlot were taking effect.

"How about seeing it tonight? After we have some dinner, some more great wine ...," he whispered in her ear, still stroking her shoulder. She sensed the tenderness, but also, an underlying determination.

As innocent as he and others thought she might be, she knew what he meant. The question was – what to do about it?

She had pictured his huge loft apartment many times over in her head – the large den with the soft and artificially-weathered, leather couch, the dining room off to the side with a long oak table, and farther off in the distance, his spacious bedroom with a more than king size bed.

Suddenly, Penelope had a new vision – a balcony off his bedroom overlooking the city's skyline.

She felt faint.

But she knew better than to rush her relationship with Luke. After all, she wanted Luke for keeps, and what was that old saying? Why buy the cow when you can get the milk for free?

Penelope was determined to be the cow that held out.

"We haven't been seeing each other for that long," she said to him, trying to take get control of herself and the situation. Slowly, so as not to display pointed displeasure, Penelope reached for the hand that was making love to her shoulder, gently took hold of it, and brought it down between their bodies. She made sure to keep their fingers intertwined as she spoke. "It's been what? Five weeks?"

Luke moved closer to her, grinning widely. "Five weeks? Five weeks?" He then commented, "You know what that is in Manhattan time? That's five months."

She laughed. "How do you figure?"

"It's like how you figure out dog years. It's not the same as human years."

"But we are humans, right?" she teased, inching towards him. "So why are we talking like we're animals or something?"

Luke softly clipped her chin and peered into her eyes. "It's New York, hon. We're all in a zoo." He sighed. 'We're all animals here … Except maybe you still … eh?"

Penelope frowned. She decided to defend herself – "*I'm* an animal."

"Have you cursed yet?" he asked.

"No," she admitted, "but that doesn't mean anything." But in her heart, she knew what he was getting at.

Luke's mouth moved to her forehead. She could feel his soft lips brushing her skin as he said, "I bet I could make you curse if you come back to my apartment. All I would need is a third of a minute of your time tonight, and I could get you to do it. And believe me. You wouldn't be cursing because you were mad."

While Luke spent time at her temples, Penelope's face screwed up, and the mechanisms of her mind churned to a halt — *what was he talking about?*

"And then I wouldn't just buy you one Gucci bag," Luke said. "I'd buy you the whole damn store." His lips left her forehead, moving towards her mouth. "Just come back with me tonight," he said as he was readying to kiss her.

Just then, a familiar female voice yelled out, "Pen!"

Penelope stopped short of kissing him and turned around. It was Sonia, gleefully romping over to her through a scarce space in the crowd with Stacey and her galoshes sloshing behind her.

"Pen!" she screamed again, though she was only a few feet away.

"Hi, Sonia," Penelope answered the call with a slight smile and her voice wavering, not altogether thrilled about them being there. She waved to Stacey who was still at Sonia's back. "Hey, Stacey." Stacey returned the gesture with a dish-gloved wave, also appearing as though she was forcing a smile.

Penelope introduced them. "Sonia, this is Luke, Luke this is Sonia." They shook hands, and Sonia was bright-eyed as she gave him the once over. Penelope pointed to Stacey, "Stacey this is Luke, Luke this is Stacey." He proceeded to go in for another handshake until Stacey lifted her dish-gloved fingers to him. Luke quietly stared at the glove for a few seconds and slowly put his hand down. Stacey shrugged and withdrew her vaselined digits.

"Sonia is my brother's girlfriend," Penelope explained to her date, "and Stacey is a good friend of ours." She looked over at Sonia and Stacey and said, "Luke is a … a …" Penelope wanted to use the most appropriate word but got tongue tied trying to find it (he wasn't her boyfriend yet, but she didn't feel they were just "seeing" each other).

Stacey stepped in and saved her — "A *very* handsome guy," she commented, grinning, and admiring him up and down.

Stacey was never one to hold back, Penelope mused while Sonia mouthed to her *nice dress* and *nice hair*.

Luke's chest puffed out and so did his head. "Well, thank you."

"And this is the Luke that you were talking about before?" Stacey asked. "The one with the loft apartment in Chelsea and his own company that isn't a website?"

"Oh, but I have a website," Luke pleasantly corrected her.

Stacey grimaced, and Penelope recalled how Stacey felt about men who had their own website companies ("They're losers," she would tell her. "Losers."). Penelope was swift to elaborate. "The site is just an adjunct to his business. Just to explain what his company is about and to provide contact information. That's it. And the company's been around for a while."

Luke nodded. "Shipping. I'm in shipping," he stated, standing tall and proud. "Wow-you know about my loft. I guess word gets around in this town - especially about real estate." Luke nudged Penelope. "But Penelope hasn't been to it yet."

"What?" Stacey reacted, raising her voice and her hand as if she was making a gesture that said *what the hell is wrong with you?* "Penelope-you haven't seen the man's loft?"

Penelope squinted at her and gritted her teeth, trying to communicate that the issue shouldn't be discussed.

Stacey didn't catch on but Sonia did. "Oh," Sonia sounded, "there's always time for that."

Examining her surroundings, Penelope inquired, "Is Cory here?" *Please say no*, she thought.

"No," Sonia replied, and Penelope breathed a sigh of relief. She wasn't ready for Luke to meet the family yet without forming a good and solid opinion about her first. After all, her family could provide him with information about her embarrassing habits or her past in Elmont, maybe childhood stories that he might now judge her on, and she thought – *God knows that Cory would be the one to spill more than a bean or two, and his jokes about my naivety and lack of knowledge – such as with technology – would, at the least, have Luke making more of his "lemonade" comments.* She still found these comments to be a tad offensive in light of her trying so hard to move on and fit in.

Penelope pondered to herself for a moment and realized no matter what stage their relationship was in, she would have to prep her brother before his first meeting with Luke.

Now that she thought about it – Sonia and Stacey weren't exactly prepared for this present encounter.

Penelope looked at the three faces in front of her who were chatting away as she sunk deep into her paranoia, her fear not unfounded as she noticed Luke eying Stacey's gloves and galoshes while he spoke about his successes in the world of exporting and importing – fruit, dresses, art, manure, and missile hardware for the U.S. Defense Department and biodiesel fuel for the Environmental Protection Agency. "All in the same year," he told Sonia and Stacey. "Two totally different factions of the U.S. government. One's intent to destroy, the other to save. Big orders, too." He glanced over at Stacey's gloves again. Penelope knew what he was thinking – *"What is going on with those gloves and galoshes? What kind of strange friends does Penelope hang out with? What am I getting myself into?"*

Luke continued, "I guess when you're in big business you have to remain impersonal about things. That's the only way to do it. It's the only way to remain unbiased and get the job done."

Sonia interceded, "That's kind of how Pen has to be in her job," and she touched Penelope's arm in a caring, maternal way. "Right, Pen?" she turned to her. "When you pitch, if you have mixed emotions about it, you have to put your personal feelings aside?" Sonia nodded.

Stacey scoffed, "I can't imagine what'd be so controversial about tractors." Then, she added, "As long as it doesn't involve running over a cow or horse or something."

"Stacey!" Sonia exclaimed and then calmed her volume to a simmer. She gave her a dirty look and remarked, "What a pleasant point to bring up in the conversation."

Penelope was about to say something about Stacey's unique hand and footwear when Luke said, "Well, I'm sure she's had to face controversial issues before when she's pitched." He raised his wine to his lips, took a taste, and then lowered the glass. "I know from some of my friends in the field that account supervisors have to keep focused since they juggle so much. They have to spin and make sure that the people working under them spin and spin, as well."

Jaw dropped, Stacey asked, "Penelope, did you get a promotion that we didn't know about?"

"No," she answered and put her eyes on Luke. "I'm an account executive. Not an account supervisor." *But I'm going to be one* – she wanted to say – *just as soon as I get the Streamers Technology account.* But Penelope held back. She still wanted to keep it to herself. The only ones who would know for the present time would be Ted and unfortunately, Wendy.

Luke was quiet for a couple of seconds and then he reacted, "Oh. Okay. I just thought…I don't know."

Why? she asked herself. *Did this make a difference?* Penelope's innards shivered. She needed to change the subject. She pointed to Stacey and said, "Stacey wears those gloves and boots because she's a professional hand and foot model." The company of three immediately stared at Penelope as if they were wondering how her comment burst out of the blue. What made it worse was that she couldn't stop talking – "What I mean is that she doesn't wear them for fun or anything. She wears them for work."

"Oh, don't lie," Stacey said sarcastically, "this is how I get my jollies. It's all about picking up the guy wearing plastic and rubber." She raised a glove and kicked out a galosh while Penelope imagined herself passing out from the weight of tons of embarrassment. "And then when I pick up a guy, I take him back to my apartment, and I have him roll me up in saran wrap … Of course, I keep the dish gloves and boots on." She elbowed Luke. "After all, they *are* my signature items."

Luke shot her a queer expression.

"Stop joking," Penelope urged, grimacing.

Stacey gave in – "Okay, okay." She turned to him. "I am a hand and foot model. And I keep Vaseline in the boots and gloves to keep them silky smooth and soft."

Seeming sincerely interested, Luke asked, "And that's going well for you?"

Stacey grinned from ear to ear. "Yes it is. I'm one of the best. In fact, I may be *thee* best soon." Her face lit up like a megawatt bulb. "I have big, big news," she announced. "Tomorrow I have an audition for a huge movie. It's down to me and another hand and foot model, and my agent has the word that's it most probably going to be me!"

Penelope turned to her. "Oh! I'm so happy for you!"

"That's cool," Luke said to her. "What movie?"

Sonia, on the sly, whispered to Penelope, "You'll appreciate this."

Stacey announced, "I'm going to be a hand and foot model for the movie version of Manhattan Nights!"

Shaking with excitement, Penelope proclaimed, "I love that show!"

In unison, Stacey and Sonia said, "*We know!*"

"And I'm going to be Lorna Lufton's hand and feet," Stacey added. "I can't wait!"

Penelope commented, "Lorna Lufton plays Gina Sparrow on the show. That the main character! You're going to be the body parts of the main character!"

Stacey's smile expanded to the size of the city as she furiously nodded.

"What's wrong with Lorna Lufton's hands and feet?" Luke questioned. "Why would they need to be replaced?"

"Nothing, I think," Stacey replied. "But from what I gather she doesn't like them being photographed or filmed close-up. I guess there's supposed to be some close-up shots of her character's hands and feet in the movie."

Sonia looked at Penelope. "Your brother seems to remember some *close-ups* of Lorna Lufton's breasts-even though he hardly watched the series," she said. "He wanted to know if Stacey was going to be a stand-in for her breasts, as well."

Suddenly, Luke seemed even more attentive – "Did she have a stand-in for her breasts on the show? Those weren't her own?"

Penelope couldn't believe the conversation she was involved in.

"I don't know," Stacey answered, "but I would be her breasts if they asked me. I would do it." She paused and then added, "But I'd wish they would've told me months beforehand. I mean, I'd need to wear a good support bra for a while, for the preparation, and then it would have to be a cup size bigger for the amount of lotion or Vaseline I would have to put in it."

Luke gave her another strange look.

"Okay, okay," Penelope said, trying to put a halt to the subject of naked breasts and special bras filled with emollients. "Well, if you get it, it's great, Stacey. Good for you."

Just at that moment, Luke reached into his pants pocket and pulled out his BlackBerry, his eyes became glued to the PDA.

"I'm going to get it," Stacey stated, very confident, "and I can probably get you on the set of the movie one day, if you'd like."

It only took a second for Penelope to become completely thrilled and say – "If I'd like? If I'd like? Of course I'd like!"

Luke turned to Penelope. "Hon', I gotta take this. It's Boston again. They're having the same problems." He questioned Stacey and Sonia – "Do you ladies want something while I'm away? I see you don't have any drinks? Maybe some wine?"

"Not for me," Stacey replied. "I have to be good for tomorrow. I'm just out because Sonia thought it would be a good idea. That it would relax me." She frowned at Sonia. "But this place is ridiculously crowded. It isn't relaxing to me. It's stressing me out."

"Fine," Sonia reacted, apparently miffed, "we'll leave soon. But I'm going to have a drink first...A Pinot Grigio would be lovely, Luke. Thank you."

"You don't want that," Luke said. "They have a great Merlot here."

"I'm not really much of a Merlot person. How about a Chardonnay?"

"No, really. The Merlot is out of this world," he informed her, lifting his glass. "I know wine like I know restaurants. My taste is impeccable."

Sonia's face went blank with astonishment. "Okay...I guess the Merlot will be fine...I guess."

"Merlot it is," he said, and then he slipped away through the multitudes with BlackBerry in hand.

"Gee," Sonia commented, "he's as confident with his opinion as

Stacey is with her hands and feet."

"And breasts," Stacey included. "Don't forget breasts."

"Well, he's certainly good-looking," Sonia said.

Stacey's head went up and down. "I'll agree to that. But I'm surprised at you, Penelope. Telling him you were an account supervisor. Were you trying to impress him or something?"

"I didn't tell him that," Penelope reacted, swinging around her glass, spilling random drops of red wine on the floor and on an extremely tall, heavy-set man standing next to her wearing a baseball cap to the side and a long, gold cross around his neck. The man sneered at her before returning to his conversation with friends.

With an arched eyebrow, Sonia inquired, "You're seeing the man and he doesn't know what you do?"

"I told him what I do. I told him I was just an account executive."

"A man who doesn't listen or forgets...hmmm," Sonia noted. "I don't know." She folded her arms in front of her. "And I don't like how you phrased that – *just* an account executive. That's a wonderful job that you have, and it got you all the way from Elmont to New York."

"That's right," Stacey said, and she turned around, "and look what you have now," and she made a sweeping arm gesture to the Asia de Cuba crowd. Penelope noticed the room was inundated with men with neatly coiffed hair and fashionable, tailored suits trying to pick up women who were tossing their tresses around, acting tipsy and whispering in the men's ears as other women whispered in the men's other ears, competing for their attention.

She saw one blonde girl in hush-puppy loafers, jeans and a flowery blouse – totally hippy and out of character for the chic atmosphere of the restaurant – practically standing on the tips of her toes, trying to get the interest of some guy who readily supplied her with a big grin and laugh as she continued to talk in his ear.

Wait a minute, Penelope said to herself. *I know that smile.*

"Oh my god," she gasped," it's Ted." She recognized those floppy bangs anywhere.

"Ted? Ted who?" Stacey asked.

Sonia tittered and slapped Penelope's elbow. "Penelope McAdams! Are you seeing two men at once?"

Stacey's jaw dropped as she stepped back and sounded, "Naaaah!" and then she stopped for a second and seemed to ponder. "Yeah?" she asked, with an approving nod and smile. "So this is what happens when you can finally text!"

Penelope's eyes kept still on Ted who remained in his conversation with the blonde girl while taking intermittent gulps from his beer glass. "Cool down, guys. I'm not dating Ted," she explained, "I'm only dating Luke. I would *never* date Ted," and she emphasized her point by slicing the air with her hand as she said *never* with both eyebrows cocked.

"Again-who is Ted?" Stacey hungrily inquired.

Sonia commented, "Me thinks she doth protest too much."

Putting her hands on her hips, Stacey swiveled round to Sonia. "What the hell is that?"

"Shakespeare," she replied.

"Uh," Stacey moaned, "Shakespeare. A Friday night happy hour at Asia de Cuba and I'm listening to Shakespeare."

"And what's so wrong about Shakespeare?"

"I don't want to have to translate what I'm listening to on a Friday night," Stacey whined. "It's too much for my brain…And anyway, I'm an Irish-Filipino."

"What does that have to do with anything?"

"Shakespeare wasn't either."

Sonia's brow crinkled, and Stacey turned back to Penelope who was practically gawking at Ted (*Is this the blonde girl Wendy was talking about?*). Stacey asked for a third time – "Penelope-who's Ted?"

"Just an MIT guy," she said to them while watching him laugh and cavort with the light-haired vixen. "Who lives in a dungeon apartment downtown."

"Ohhhh," Stacey sounded, "just an MIT guy who lives in a dungeon apartment downtown. Well, that explains a lot."

Penelope took her eyes off Ted to glare at Stacey. "He's just a friend. That's it."

"Really?" Sonia said. "Then why don't you just wave him over here? It would be great to meet one of your friends. And it would keep Cory from worrying." She added, "He thinks we're your only friends."

Wonderful, Penelope thought. *My brother thinks I'm technologically inept and socially challenged.*

"I can't wave him over. He doesn't know about Luke."

"But I thought you just said that you're just friends," Stacey said.

Penelope observed Ted putting his arm around the blonde girl, pulling her next to him a bit. She felt some agitation crawl up and under her skin. *Wait,* she said to herself, *what do I care?* "We are just friends," she reiterated. "It's just that if Ted knew it might ... might ... ruin things."

"What things?" Sonia asked.

"Ted's teaching me-" and Penelope immediately stopped talking before she could say the word "technology," still not wanting anyone else to know about her goals, and tried to figure out what she could replace it with. Penelope glanced at the sweater Sonia was wearing. "Knitting." *That's right,* she said to herself. *That's a good answer.* "He's teaching me to knit."

Stacey squirmed. "Knitting? He's teaching you to knit?" She looked over at him. Ted's arm had left his gal pal's shoulders. "Well, then I guess you are friends. He's got to be gay."

Sonia displayed a disappointed expression. "Penelope. You could have come to me if you wanted to learn how to knit. I could've taught you."

Stacey interceded, "He went to MIT. He probably knits better than you do." She snapped her fingers. "I know why you're not introducing him to Luke-Luke's a hottie, and you're afraid that Ted will try to switch him to the other team." She paused. "But I don't know why you'd be worried about that. The guy Ted looks like he has a great smile, but what's with the hair and those bangs of his?" Stacey squinted in his direction. "Did you ever see his eyes?"

"No."

"At least you probably don't have to worry about him seeing you," Sonia commented. "He probably can't see much through his hair."

Penelope shrank back and then receded into their tiny huddle. She was so immersed in policing Ted that she completely forgot that he might be able to spot her as she had spotted him.

Penelope pulled Sonia in front of her, trying to block her presence from Ted.

Sonia frowned. "Penelope?"

Stacey sighed. "Well, this has been a lot of fun, but I'm really, really tired," she said. "Sonia, can we please go?"

Penelope gripped Sonia's sweater, desperate for cover. Sonia knitted her eyebrows and became stern. "Calm down…Yes. Maybe we'd better go. I'm getting tired myself." She looked at Penelope. "I'm sure you'll survive, Pen. But you should go home, too. You're acting awfully strange."

As they said their goodbyes and began to walk away, Sonia said, "Tell Luke it was great meeting him and thanks for the Merlot … You can drink it for me," and then the duo disappeared into the masses.

Penelope looked at Ted and the blonde and again wondered – *what's wrong with me? It's just Ted at a bar with a girl.*

She thought about it intensely, and she suddenly calmed down – *I know what it is*, she noted to herself. She'd just been caught by surprise, that's all. She didn't expect to see Ted at Asia de Cuba, and then the added shock of seeing Sonia and Stacey just sent her over the edge.

Yeah. That was it.

Just as Penelope made peace with her strange reaction, accepting her conclusion as fact, Ted unexpectedly turned her way.

Penelope immediately gasped and ducked and jumped behind the tall, heavy-set man with the cross, who she had previously sprayed red wine on. Again, the man sneered at her.

"Penelope?" Luke's voice rose over the crowd, and she could see him searching for her as he came upon the spot where they were originally standing. He held two wine glasses that were filled to the brim. "Penelope?" he called to the air, and as his eyes veered around, he found her. "Penelope-what the hell are you doing there?" The tall, heavy-set man now looked cross-eyed at Luke. "Where are your friends?"

"They had to go," she replied, lowering her voice, afraid that somehow Luke would hear her (he did go to MIT, after all. Maybe geniuses have better sensory perception).

"Oh," he said, his intonation declining, as well. "Why are we whispering?"

He went to hand her the glass of Merlot that was originally meant for Sonia. "Want to go two-fisted?" he asked, still hushing his vocal chords.

"Actually, no," she answered. All she wanted to do was make a quick getaway. "Luke, I don't feel like eating. Can we just skip dinner and go home?"

Luke grinned as if he had just settled a big account for shipping government missiles that used green-energy fuel to function.

He asked, "Your place or mine?"

> *Mary: It's full of romance that old place. I'd like to live in it.*
>
> *George Bailey: In that place? ... I wouldn't live in it if I was a ghost.*

Fourteen

Luke (Mobile)

Feb 8, 2008 10:20:02 AM

Last night was fun ...Wasn't I right about the wine?
Sorry that you weren't feeling so well. ☹
Don't worry about not seeing the loft – I'm sure you'll see it lots
of times in the future ☺

Ted (Mobile)

February 8, 2008 10:20:03 AM

A good morning to you! Ready for another day of learning about
technology?

I have something really cool for you today! But let me ask you – do you cook?

(This is not a sexist question, by the way. I have my reasons …)

Can you meet me over at my place today at around 2 pm?

Text me.

***

"Why is Mr. Spock wearing a chef's hat?" Penelope inquired as she stood in the middle of Ted's apartment, leaning against the cardboard Mr. Spock who was donning the hat while brandishing his laser gun.

Ted sat on the couch, looking on at her with a smirk, appearing amused.

She smiled at Spock, thinking about how his new piece of apparel nullified his intellectualism and wondering how Captain Kirk was now going to ask him for any advice (with a straight face, at least).

She imagined Captain Kirk shaking his head at him – *What's going on with you, Spock? I didn't know that you could cook.*

What would Spock say to him?

Penelope grabbed the shoulder of Mr. Spock and tried to throw her voice to the cardboard figure, speaking in a deep and rough tone – "Captain, let's forget about saving the planet from the Klingons. Let me whip you up some ham and eggs."

Penelope doubled over with laughter.

Somewhere in between her guffaws, Ted asked, "Are you done?" still grinning.

"Wait," she answered and giggled some more until she finally caught her breath. "Ohhhhh," she exhaled. "Okay, I'm done but," she continued, pointing to the head of Mr. Spock, "can I wear the hat?"

"Ah-hah!" Ted exclaimed, "that won't be necessary," and he whipped out two chef's hats from behind his back. "I've got one for the both of us!"

Her grin dissipated as Ted strolled over to her and slapped the hat on her head. It fell over her eyes. He pulled it up and angled it to one side and then giggled, doing a repeat performance of her titters from only moments ago.

"Wonderful," she said, unenthused. She felt completely silly.

Ted put his chef's hat on. The rim of it pushed his hair down even more, his bangs nearly dropping to the bridge of his nose.

Great, Penelope said to herself, *now Ted looks like a shaggy dog that's getting ready to make his own pet food.*

He beamed and stretched his arms out. "Well? How do I look?"

She stationed her hands at her hips. "If you really must know – you look like a complete goofball." *With a capital "G,"* she mused.

"Great!" he cried, "then we're right in the spirit of the lesson! Because I'm teaching you about gaming today!" He motioned to a white box under his television and then at a matching remote lying on his coffee table. "We're about to enter the world of Nintendo Wii. And we're going to play one of the Wii programs called 'Order Up!'" He tapped on his hat. "Hence the interesting garb."

"Ohhhh," Penelope sounded, "so this is what you meant when you asked me about the cooking."

"I was joking, though. I just thought this game would be fun to start with."

"But I don't know how to cook. Really."

"You don't need to know how to cook. I was joking. And this game is rated 'E' for everyone. Kids could play it."

Her attention span passed over what he said. "I really never cook."

"I figured as much when all you have to offer me at your apartment is peanuts."

Penelope's face soured.

He immediately jumped in front of his mistake. "Not that I mind the peanuts! I love the peanuts!"

Penelope composed herself. "My mother's a wonderful cook. She did all the cooking at home in Elmont."

"You mean in Bedford Falls?" he said, playing around with his hat.

Penelope immediately gasped. "Hah!" She shoved a finger in his direction. "You're making analogies to 'It's a Wonderful Life'! I told you that you'd like the movie!"

"Well, I must admit. It is a good movie. Even if Captain Kirk isn't in it kissing a voluptuous babe or Han Solo isn't blowing up an evil empire," he said. "It's a tug-at-your-heart movie." He suddenly started to look around. "Now where did I put that gaming disc, George?"

"What? What did you mean by that?"

"What?"

"Why did you call me George?" she questioned. "Did you mean 'George Bailey?' Are you inferring that I'm like George Bailey?" *The gall of it all!*

Ted continued to search around his apartment. "Where the hell is that disc?" he wondered aloud. "Yeah, I guess I'm inferring. Are you upset about it? Why are you upset about it?" He lifted up a couch cushion. The task left him empty handed, and he shook his head.

She huffed, "Well, first of all, George Bailey is a man and I'm a woman."

He immediately let go of the couch cushion and turned to her. "I know that you're a woman," he smoothly said, and she noticed keys in his voice she never heard before. "I'm not talking about your gender or that you bear some physical resemblance to George Bailey. I'm just saying your stories have similar aspects. Maybe your personalities, as well."

Penelope narrowed her eyes at him. "You're saying I'm like lemonade then."

"What?"

"People are saying I'm like lemonade."

"What people?"

"Just people. They say I'm wholesome like lemonade."

"I like lemonade," he said. "What's wrong with being lemonade?"

"I want to be champagne."

"Champagne has bubbles. It gives me a headache."

Ted went back to scouring the room for his disc, flipping over the objects and papers in his surroundings while Penelope left Mr. Spock and his chef's hat, wandering to Ted's shelves of memorabilia, trying to move away from him after being offended by his "George" remark.

He stopped what he was doing. "Are you upset with me?"

She shrugged. "Kind of." She slowly walked aside the shelves, glancing at his old techno gadgets and movie mementos. She halted at the old camera and the photo of the laughing little boy and woman she had examined with interest the first time she visited his apartment. "I don't think I'm like George Bailey," she whined, sweeping her fingers on the lens of the camera – *Oh, how I miss my grandfather. The talks. His warm arms hugging me …But then it was difficult in the end …*Penelope quickly shook her head, trying to rattle thoughts and images of her Grandfather Ben from her mind, not wanting to go to a place that was sad.

She switched her attention to what Ted once told her – he liked film canisters … each held important memories. *Intriguing.* She caressed the picture frame containing the happy boy and woman and remembered the canisters she saw in his closet and lingered to a different theme for the conversation. "Ted? How many film canisters do you have?" She gently dragged a finger along the edge of the frame.

"It's not important," he replied, his hand suddenly plunging in front of her; it grabbed and moved the picture frame to the top shelf, next to his row of sci-fi and fantasy novels.

"Who is that?" she asked him as he walked away from the shelves towards the television.

He didn't answer. "Penelope, let's concentrate on today's lesson, shall we?" Ted held up a disc. "I found it. He pointed to the box under the television and said, "This is the console. You put the gaming disc in here." He slipped the disc into a slot in the box and picked up the remote.

He started to click away at the TV. "You don't think you're like George Bailey?" he asked. "George Bailey desperately wanted to leave the small town he grew up in. Just like you."

"But he was held back," she added, glowering at him as she remained near the shelves.

Ted stopped clicking. "So? What held you back?"

"What?"

"All those years in Elmont. I'm sure you could have left earlier. Why didn't you?"

An image of her grandfather flashed through her mind's eye. "Nothing. Nothing held me back. I guess I just had to wait for the right time." There was silence, and then Penelope said, "Anyway, I'm not anything like George Bailey. He never got out, and he came to realize that he had a *wonderful life* in his small town." She elaborated, "And I would never go back to Elmont!"

There was a fierceness radiating from her pupils.

Ted resumed his clicking of the remote. "You can still live in a place and not be there."

"What does that mean?"

"It lives in you ... Never mind," he uttered. "Why don't you come over here, and I'll show you how this works."

Penelope tugged at her hat and "hmmphed" on her trip to the couch. She sat down next to Ted, and he pointed the remote at the television. "The Wii is an easy hook-up. And I got one for you, but I thought we'd try mine first - let you get the hang of it." He turned to her. "Then you can set it up at your place. I think you've become adept enough in technology that you can do it. What do you think?"

"I think I'm still mad at you."

"I didn't mean to make you mad," he said. "Look, just try to put your anger aside for now and focus." He gave her the remote. "Now follow my instructions." He gently grasped her hand that held the remote, and moved it up and down and sideways. Penelope noticed the arrow going in the direction of the remote on the screen, and she also felt the strength and heat of his fingers and palm.

Penelope glanced over at him, and then turned her eyes to his hand that was on top of hers. After a few seconds, she brought her vision back to the television and her Wii lesson. "It's motion controlled," she commented.

"Right!" he cried out. "Good for you!" He let go of her hand, and after a few more clicks, Penelope was on her way to picking a chef that would represent her in the game. She reviewed her choices that were flying in a cartoon airplane on the screen; she could either pick a cartoon man or cartoon woman chef.

Penelope reflected on her rousing conversation with Ted. He thought she was like George Bailey – who was a man – so she picked the female chef. After she clicked her choice, the female chef fell out of the plane and next to a diner. The chef then walked into the diner and was greeted by a geeky looking restaurant manager.

Immediately, Penelope began to click at the television with fervor.

"What are you doing?" Ted asked.

"I don't like the restaurant manager. I want to change him."

"Penelope, you have no choice with the manager."

"But I chose the chef."

"Yes, but you have no choice with the manager. The manager they pick for you stays the manager."

Penelope knitted her brow and kept clicking. "But he looks like he smells bad. Who would eat at a place where the manager reeks?"

Covering her hand with his again, he said, "Stop. Stop the madness. You can't change the manager."

A menu popped up on the screen to prepare a hamburger.

Ted instructed, "Now click on the hamburger, and you'll see the ingredients come on the screen-you'll have to flip a hamburger, peel lettuce, slice a tomato, and fry french fries, and you'll be doing it by pressing buttons to pick up the ingredients and to prepare them." Ted showed her the buttons and told her what they did, and Penelope clicked on the menu, all ready to go. "You'll also have to move the food around with the remote."

Penelope pressed a button that picked up the hamburger patty on the screen, and she dragged it onto the grill. After a couple of seconds on the grill, Ted said to her, "Now flip it. Just turn your hand over." Penelope went to flip the burger by twisting her hand and wrist, but it didn't work. The hamburger patty just stayed on the grill, coming close to burning, and she instantly feared that she might somehow set the Wii diner on fire. "Oh! Oh!" Penelope cried out, suddenly worried she would never get beyond the gaming part of her technology education. And she had come so far! *The coffee machine, LCD TVs (forty-inches, no less), MP3 players, iPhones, and various PDAs, and now this had to happen?*

"Calm down, Penelope," Ted said. "You just have to do bigger motions."

Lifting her arm up, she made a big swoop with the remote and then the patty started to flip.

She did it.

Penelope smiled and turned the patty over and over again until she was able to drag it to a picture of a dish and a cover that signified the preparation of the meal's ingredients was done with.

"See," Ted said to her, "you're doing great."

She proceeded to peel the lettuce. Moving her hand side to side. It only took her seconds to do, but she realized that it also took a great deal of strength from her arms and flexibility from her wrists.

She dragged the lettuce to the covered dish. *Done.*

"See," Ted commented, "you're doing great. Isn't this fun?"

"My wrists hurt a little, and I think I have a cramp somewhere." She looked down at her skinny arm.

"Really?" he reacted. "You probably just need to get used to it."

"I don't know, Ted. I have absolutely *no* upper body strength."

"Why don't you skip the tomato and try frying the fries," he suggested.

Penelope aimed the remote at the television, but before she worked on the fries, she said, "This could be fun. Is there a way to compete with this game? Maybe you can come by my place tomorrow and we can play against each other."

"I can't," he answered. "Remember, I'm busy on Sundays."

Penelope lowered the remote and stared at him. "Oh yeah," she said. "You're busy on Sundays … Uh-huh." She immediately thought of the blonde at the bar — *so that's what's happening on Sundays. He goes out with his hippy, blonde girlfriend.*

Penelope rested her hand and the remote on her lap and stared at the television, pursing her lips, posture like a straight edge ruler.

"What's wrong?" Ted asked, his mouth as tight as hers.

"Nothing. Why should you think something is wrong?" She couldn't figure out what he was talking about. She had seen him the night before (although he didn't know it), and she saw him with the blonde, and later on in the evening — once she reflected — she thought — "Good for him! Ted is going on with his life." So of course there wasn't a thing wrong. In fact, everything was peachy-keen, hunky-dory and whatever other cheerful, stupid saying she could come up with!

"Well, you stopped playing ... And you're so stiff."

Stiff. She perused the word. *Stiff-why not?* She shouldn't be sitting around so casual with Ted. This was getting too personal, she thought, and after all, their relationship originated from a business deal. "I was just thinking. About what we talked about in the beginning-you teach me technology and I do your PR for you." *Great. Time to set the story straight. Time not to lose focus. Time to reiterate what kind of relationship she and Ted really had.* "But you still haven't given me anything to PR about. Not even for a press release."

Ted turned to her, retaining a stoic appearance. "I've been mulling over a couple of ideas. I'll have to get back to you."

"When?"

"Soon."

"You always say that," she whined. "At least let me work on something." She paused. "Let me work on a name for your business."

"It already has a name."

"Really? What is it?"

"Ted Hollis consulting."

Penelope shook her head. "Ted. You need more help than I thought." Her eyes quickly ran up his snug fitting jeans and the new blue dress shirt he was wearing (she could tell it was new. The lines from where it had been folded in its wrapper were still fresh indentations in the cloth.). She wondered if she would ever know if the shirt matched or complimented his irises.

Ted shirked off her comment. "Focus, Penelope." He stuck his index finger out to the television. "Now, the french fries."

Penelope clicked on the french fries, dragged them to the frying basket, and then dropped them in bubbling, hot water.

"Okay. Now press the button to lift it up. You want to lift and drop the fries into the water to get it to cook right."

Penelope followed what he said, thrusting the remote up and then down, but found that it wasn't working. She did it one, two, and three times, and she still couldn't do it. The basket of fries was turning brown, and they were about to burn.

"What's wrong?" he asked.

"It's just not working for some reason," she whined. "I don't know why."

After a couple of more lift-offs with her remote, Penelope stood up, ready to finish with the fries and to go onto slicing the tomato. "Okay! I'm going to get this thing done!" she exclaimed, determined to take the Wii world on.

"Penelope, wait a minute!"

Ted bolted up from the couch as she threw up her arm that held the remote. The basket of fries immediately lifted, and to drag the basket to the "done" dish, like a lightning bolt, Penelope flung her arm to the right, in Ted's direction, her chef's hat taking flight from her head, and suddenly, she felt something hard hit her arm.

"That was great!" the restaurant manager complimented her from the television.

And then she heard a loud *kerplunk* on the floor.

"Ted? ... Ted?"

***

"So, Penelope," Wendy quietly uttered in the crowded conference room where they waited for their regularly scheduled staff meeting to begin. She raised a dark eyebrow. "What happened to Ted's eye?"

Penelope was immediately embarrassed. "What do you mean?"

"Don't play coy with me, McAdams," Wendy reacted, folding her arms on her chest. "It's bad enough that I haven't bothered you about your small-town secrets after you told me you didn't have any."

"But I don't have any."

Wendy raised an open palm. "Please. Tell it to the hand." She continued, "But you can't hide from this, Penelope. Word travels at the speed-of-light between me and my ex, and he said that he got together with Ted last night, and that Ted had a huge shiner. He told Ted that he looked like he was either bullied by a heavy weight champion or somebody shot-put an anvil into his face."

Penelope tried on her best poker expression. "And what did Ted say?"

"He went with the anvil."

Penelope smiled, giggling in her gut.

"But I know better," Wendy said. "I've never even seen an anvil-have you?"

"Uh-maybe."

"No you haven't, and I think you know something."

It had been a couple of days since Penelope last saw Ted, and Penelope felt the weight of guilt getting heavier with every passing hour. She needed to purge. "Ok. Here it is. I gave Ted the black eye."

Wendy's mouth flew open. "Did he get fresh?"

"No."

"Tell me," she urged. "He did, didn't he? Those recluses are weirdos, and he tried to have his way with you."

Penelope shook her head and thought it interesting that Wendy, who referred to a sexual escapade with her ex as a "booty-call" (she now understood what it meant after questioning Sonia about it and having her brother walk out of the room), would refer to Ted making advances as "having his way," as if he was a boorish, medieval ruler taking over another man's kingdom and wife, or as if he was a lurid character in a black and white movie grabbing the mistress of the film's hero. "No. He *did not* try to have his way with me," Penelope insisted. "I just got a little carried away with the Wii."

"The what?"

"The Wii."

"As in '*we* don't know what you're talking about'?"

"No. As in '*Wii* the Nintendo Wii.' The gaming system."

Wendy blinked a couple of times like she was having an optical spasm or tremor. "What were you doing playing with the Wii?" Then she rolled her eyes. "Oh yes. How could I forget? You're learning about technology, and this is a part of your education-isn't it?"

"Yeah," Penelope said. *And it wasn't too bad*, she mused. "It's actually kind of fun once you get the hang of it. It's motion controlled, and moving the program's remote takes a lot of doing." She continued – "And that's how Ted got the shiner."

"What do you mean?"

"I mean that I was trying to work the Wii controls, trying to lift some fries out of the fryer, and when I lifted it, I accidentally hit him in the face."

Wendy's jaw fell, and then she shut her mouth and said, "Okay. So I don't know what you're talking about with the fries and the fryer, but let me get this straight. What you're trying to tell me is that you were playing with the Nintendo Wii, and you accidentally punched Ted with the remote, and that's how he got the black eye. Is that what you're telling me?"

Wincing, Penelope responded, "Yes … well, that and a concussion. First, he had a concussion. He fell to the floor."

"What?"

Penelope figured she might as well divulge every aspect of the horrid story. "We wound up at the hospital. He got an MRI. But he's fine." Penelope thought about the hospital and claimed, "Y'know. They're much nicer in the hospital in his area. The staff at the hospital where I live isn't so friendly."

"When were you at the hospital?"

"When? A couple of weeks ago and then last night."

The eyes in Wendy's head popped out, and she scanned the crowd of coworkers, and said to Penelope, in a hushed voice, "Oh my God. What for?"

Penelope shrugged, trying to be nonchalant about her emergencies, saying, "I just had a mishap with the coffee machine and hurt my back, and then last night I was playing the Wii, and I suddenly couldn't move my arm. But they examined it and said it was okay. Just got to get acclimated to the Wii. Work out my right arm a bit, build some muscle, get some flexibility." She added, "I'm planning to join a gym."

"For an arm?"

"It's fine," Penelope assured her, using her functioning left hand to point to her listless right one and its arm that rested on the conference table; limb and fingers weren't moving a smidge. "Really it is. It's just a little limp."

Wendy looked down at the arm and hand in question. "Limp? It's like a dead fish." She shook her head. "You've got to stop this,

Penelope. You've got to stop this technology obsession."

"Why?"

"Why? You've been to the hospital twice in the past month after suffering from some technology debacle-and honestly, I don't want to know about what happened with the coffee machine. I just don't want to know. And now it's spilling over to innocents. You've put Ted's life in danger, as well." Wendy suddenly stopped what she was saying, and then she slapped her forehead. "And how could I forget?" She lowered her voice to a whisper – "You corrupted all our computer files-we almost lost everything with your downloading demo ... Penelope, you and technology don't mix ... You're becoming a danger to society."

Penelope turned her nose up. "Oh please. I think you're exaggerating."

"Whatever,"she commented. "But I'm requesting cubicle relocation."

Just at that moment, Alden Renquist flew into the room carrying a bundle of folders, his shiny blue tie flapping across his nose and cheeks, and his pupils steaming with intensity. His lowly staff swiftly sat up at attention, nervous and curious about what would happen next.

Penelope squirmed in her seat – would he finally mention something about Streamers? Since he mentioned the new position, there had been a couple of meetings, and he hadn't said a word about the illustrious opportunity at any of them.

He slammed down the folders at the end of the table and everyone jumped.

Grabbing the sides of the table, Alden Renquist bent over and dropped his head. Penelope couldn't see his expression, and from the looks of the fearful group sitting around her, neither could anyone else – was he grimacing? Was he smiling? Was he gritting his teeth and squinting with fury? What were they in for? And had he taken his daily Xanax yet?

Finally his head went up, and he grinned. "I'm in a *fantastic* mood today." He continued, "And I'm not on medication."

Everyone looked on at him in wonder as if he'd just told them that he had the ability to walk on water or communicate with a burning bush – what miracle was this that Alden Renquist didn't require little pills with a big punch to put him in such a satisfactory mood?

He resolved the question, sitting down while sweeping some springy hair from his glasses like a human windshield wiper. "The future of this agency was unknown for a while because of the financial and legal proceedings by the future ex-Mrs. Renquist," he said to his people, whose eyes popped out, "but that's all changed since the court is questioning her mental status." Suddenly, Alden Renquist turned around to Penelope, who innocently listened to her boss as she wondered if she would ever move her fingers again, and he winked at her.

Her coworkers looked at her quizzically, and Penelope gasped in horror; she remembered her last conversation with her boss about her career aspirations, about the Jolie-Pitts and third-world countries, and then a medicine man and Mrs. Renquist's liposuction, and how it somehow resulted in him mulling over the prospect of his soon-to-be ex-wife's psychological analysis that might have her diagnosed as insane in divorce court. Penelope quickly realized she had become an unwitting party in Alden Renquist's divorce proceedings. And divorce wasn't something she was used to. In Elmont, couples didn't get divorced, she thought. They may not talk to each other for years – maybe the wife would release her frustration by baking thousands of cakes and cookies for decades, becoming the town's equivalent of Mrs. Fields, and maybe the husband would chew tobacco every single waking moment of his miserable life, eventually creating the country's biggest ball of nicotine spit, the equivalent of a meteoric crater – but there was no divorce. And now she was somehow involved in one.

Alden Renquist proceeded to go about the business of the firm with a glint in his eyes and a rise in his voice. "Now about Streamers Technology," he said, and Penelope fixated on her boss' face and prize, "who are my candidates for heading up the account? Hmmm?"

Penelope's left hand immediately shot-up while three other account executives raised their own, although they did it slowly and with less determination; one account executive was in mid-yawn as her fingers spread above her head.

Wendy let out a quiet sigh that Penelope decided not to pay any attention to.

Their boss said the names of the candidates aloud as he pointed to each one, and Ginger, the Account Supervisor, wrote them down on her legal pad. "Simmons," he started. "Bernstein ... Gladstone, and uh ... McAdams." He emphasized the last consonant of Penelope's name, and set his eyes squarely on her. Then he went silent, only to recoup the meeting with a strange comment – "Penelope," Alden Renquist said, "did you make the coffee today?"

Penelope smiled and was utterly surprised. She had been making the coffee for weeks and with no notice of interest or gratitude from her boss or any other member of the office until that very moment.

"Yes," she answered.

"Good job," he said, and he winked at her again. "Why don't you write the minutes for our meeting today-give Ginger a break."

Ginger grimaced at Penelope.

Serves her right, Penelope thought. *After all, she did take credit for my coffee when I first made it in the office. And what's the saying – what comes around goes around?*

"Sure," Penelope responded, but she quickly remembered the problem with her right hand – she could hardly move it, and although she didn't want to admit this to anyone else since she didn't want to be a repetitive case at emergency wards, she couldn't feel some parts of it, as well (was she not supposed to feel her knuckles? ... *Maybe that's okay*).

Alden Renquist eased back in his chair, casual, like he didn't have a care in the world now that his wife might be close to being diagnosed with delusional hysteria. He pondered out loud, "I wonder what's going on at St. Luke's Hospital? If there's a special ward-just for ex-wives." He looked at Ginger and asked, "Is that illegal? A mental ward for ex-wives?"

While her boss mulled over special incarcerations that may not yet be in existence, Penelope tried to move her right hand towards the pen that was only a few inches away, but it might has well have been miles away since her hand and arm were like dead weights. They moved only centimeters, like one gigantic caterpillar trying to make its way across a large terrain.

Everyone stared at her.

"Penelope," her boss called out, ultimately escaping his own personal fog, "what's wrong with your hand?"

"Uh ... nothing," she replied and didn't have any idea of how she was going to rectify her paralyzing situation. Should she tell him about the Wii? Would he consider putting points in her column if he thought her learning about the Wii took some gumption and fortitude? Or would he minus some points or get rid of her column altogether if he thought she was a liability to the firm for not being able to handle a game that, according to the box, a pre-schooler could work.

Alden Renquist gave her a screwed look, and suddenly, Wendy blurted, "She's got a cramp in her hand. She's had it all morning," and she shoved a pen into Penelope's left hand. "You're ambidextrous-right, Penelope?"

***

"Thanks for the fast thinking, Wendy," Penelope whispered as they exited the conference room after the meeting. "You're a true friend."

"I was going to suggest that I do the minutes, but I could see that he had his mind made up," Wendy said. "And when his mind is made up, and he doesn't get his way…"

"Stark raving mad," Penelope said, "but he was already there."

"No joke."

"You couldn't even do your own notes," Penelope commented. "How long did he have you holding that growth chart?"

"Long enough for me to call in sick tomorrow with back problems, but not long enough for me to collect workmen's compensation." She added, "I swear that Ginger's hidden the tripod. She just wants to make us all miserable."

As they walked towards their cubicles, Wendy grabbed the minutes from Penelope's good hand. "Okay. You're going to need some help typing this up. Unless you're planning to do it all by your lonesome with that bum hand. But you're going to have to translate what the hell you wrote since you really aren't ambidextrous." She waved the papers around. "This is worse than chicken scratch," she informed. "But first you need to tell me why Alden Renquist winked at you."

Penelope shook her head. "It's nothing. I'll explain it to you later."

"You're having an affair with him. I knew it."

"Would *nothing* include having an affair with my boss?" Penelope said.

Wendy's azure eyes narrowed. "I knew it."

They were next to their desks when a BlackBerry went off – *Buffalo gals can't you come out tonight - can't you come out tonight - can't you come out tonight - Buffalo gals can't you come out tonight - aaand dance by the light of the mooon...*

Penelope, out of habit, went to grab her BlackBerry from her desk with her right hand, but found that she still couldn't lift her limb. "Uhhhh," Penelope groaned as she tried to gather all her muscle power to raise her damaged extremity.

"Oh, hell," Wendy complained as she scooped up the BlackBerry and pressed the green button. She handed it over to Penelope. "I think it's a text."

Penelope read the message:

Luke (Mobile)

Feb 9, 2008 10:32 AM

Hey cutie. Any ideas of what you want to do for Valentine's Day? … That's if you want to spend Valentine's Day with me … Do you want to spend Valentine's Day with me?
Maybe it's better if I call you...

Penelope grinned and thought – *Yes! Yes! Of course, yes!* And then her BlackBerry rang. Penelope answered, "Of course I'll spend Valentine's Day with you!"

"That's great!" returned a voice from the other end of the line. But the voice wasn't Luke's.

"I really didn't expect you to answer the phone like that," Ted commented, "but wow ... And here I was going to ask you if you wanted to spend Valentine's Day together ... I'm happy."

Penelope went completely silent for a few moments.

Ted then told her – "I'm happy...as happy as a friend could be ... Friend's getting together for what's basically a Hallmark holiday." She could hear him smile as he said, "That's cool."

Nervous, although she didn't have the faintest idea why she should be, she said, "Uh, Ted. I've got plans for Valentine's Day." She could feel Wendy staring at her, and then without thinking she added, "Aren't you seeing a bl-" and she was about to say "blonde," but she stopped herself. "A blank screen? ... Aren't you seeing a blank screen? On your computer? Don't you have a computer virus that you're working on this week - and on Valentine's day?"

"Uh, no," he answered. "Why? Do you have a virus? Because if you do, I can come over and take a look at your laptop."

"No, no I don't have a virus."

"Okay. Good," he said and then asked, "What plans do you have for Valentine's Day?"

Come on. Think fast, Penelope. "I'm spending it with my brother."

"Your brother?" He sounded surprised. "Doesn't your brother have a girlfriend?"

"Yes ... But it's a family tradition ... Actually it's an Elmont tradition. The whole town spends it together ... This way no one is alone. We all see each other and swap valentines and have dinner together at one big table in the town square."

"Well that doesn't sound very romantic," he voiced with a disappointed tone.

"Yeah. It's more about brotherly love," she added, wincing at the ceiling as she lied. "We even sing a couple of verses of Kumbaya. Just to get the ball rolling, y'know ... Some small town stuff." She couldn't believe what she was saying. "Anyway, Cory and I try to keep the tradition going while we're in New York. It's like having a piece of home."

Ted didn't say a word.

Penelope felt it best to end the conversation before her nose grew any longer. "Uh, Ted," she said, "can I give you call back? I'm kind of in the middle of something."

"Sure," he replied, and they hung up on one another.

Wendy stationed her hands at her hips and glared at her. "Luke? ... Our boss? ... And now Ted? How are you juggling all of them? And why on Earth did you pick Ted to juggle?"

"I didn't. There's nothing going on between me and Ted," Penelope responded, flustered and frustrated. She lowered herself into her cubicle. "And he's not that bad. And I really don't want to talk about this right now, okay?"

Wendy replied, "Okay," and sat down at her desk.

It was only seconds later that Penelope heard Wendy humming.

She could hear the lyrics to the tune rolling through her mind ... *Kumbaya, my Lord ... Kumbaya ... Kumbaya, my Lord ... Kumbaya ...*

George Bailey: Well, here's your hat, what's your hurry?

Fifteen

Luke wrapped up a wad of beef in a fragment of spongy, thin bread. "Like the place?" he asked Penelope, a meat thread hanging from his fold of food. "It's the top Ethiopian place in town."

Penelope smiled but wrinkled her nose. It was Valentine's Day, and she was spending her evening with Luke hovering over exotic smelling entrees, many of which were too foreign for her liking, making her stomach turn like a cyclone.

Even with her pallid face, the clearing of her throat (a sure sign of stalling an episode of acid reflux), and the intermittent pinching of her nose, Luke didn't seem to notice the subtle clues of Penelope's nausea. He especially didn't notice her wince as he explained that the large dish placed on their table, filled with various sauces and carnivorous treats, was for both of them. *Everyone would share from the same plate,* he told her. *It's cultural.*

Penelope thought she would be fine with the idea since she was never much of a stickler for table manners being that she grew up with her father and brother, who, more than periodically, would have burping competitions during dinner – the winner would get nothing more than the coveted title of "Burping King of Elmont" (this title was consistently passed back and forth between them), and then they would have a crown placed on their head – a gold paper crown, compliments of Burger King. There was always an objective judge – Penelope – who shrugged and rolled her eyes as she slurped her soup and took a bite of her hamburger and made calls on burping as if she was an umpire working a ballgame. So, she concluded, this shared plate situation was sure to be a cinch.

"I thought the atmosphere and view were perfect for the night," Luke said.

He was right about that, she thought. The restaurant had been dimmed, and red and white candles were scattered everywhere. The candle flames gave the restaurant the romantic ambience of a white tablecloth eatery. But more importantly, the restaurant had floor to ceiling windows that framed the most fantastic view of The Statue of Liberty that was standing in the rippling waters of the East River.

"The Statue of Liberty is nice," Penelope noted, gesturing over to the monument with a jerk of her head. She then rested her elbows on the table, folding one arm over the other, and observed him from across the table.

Luke winked at her, a grin and dimple blooming on his face as he plunged his meat fold into a dark and cloudy sauce on their communal dish. He proceeded to shove the meat in his mouth.

As he chewed, he mumbled, "It's good. Try it."

"But I did try it, remember?" Penelope replied with a coquettish smile, appearing as though she wanted to flirt, not letting on that she had no desire to have another morsel after her first taste when she nearly gagged from the strange flavor of the sauce and the exchanging of germs at the tables and the plates around her – and she quietly swallowed the food in spite of herself. In retrospect, she thought the swallowing of the food was better than the tasting of it. Maybe all she had to do was throw it back into her throat and forget about it in order to survive the night. That and gazing into Luke's handsome face while she imagined a life of success and luxury. Penelope noticed that these two factors helped her ease the pain of most of the restaurants he brought her to.

But Luke always said – *I know the best restaurants in the city.*

And once in a while, Penelope pondered if she had been erroneous in her private, scathing reviews of his culinary haunts. After all, she realized that Luke had spent most of his adult life in Manhattan and had probably been to every restaurant imaginable. She wondered if this resulted in the evolution of his taste buds, and if hers were still stuck in Elmont, savoring a chili dog at their summer fair.

Maybe, she thought, the evolution of his taste buds began earlier than in his adulthood. Maybe his parents brought him into New York City from Connecticut (she had checked proximities on a map – it wasn't very far) in his adolescence or even childhood, and like any cosmopolitan and in-the-know family, fed him Indian and Ethiopian meals and grabbed at food from the same dish (while some poor, small-town girl turned green at the next table).

Of course, she wouldn't know about this. Penelope took note that Luke was not one to talk much about his family.

"Luke? How did it come about that you have such great taste in restaurants?" Penelope inquired. "Did your parents take you into the city a lot when you were younger? Expose you to a lot of different foods?"

Luke peered down at the plate, grasping the bread and then the meat. "You mean Franklin and Rose?"

"Are those their names?" Penelope's face was aglow from the new information. "I had no idea."

He held his wrap at his mouth, asking, "Why should you?" and then heaved it in.

"Well, we're in a relationship ... uh ... kind of."

"And?"

Even though Penelope didn't want to push the issue, she could feel the words tumbling from her mouth – "In a relationship, or at the start of one, people learn about certain things. Such as each other's families."

His eyes narrowed into slits. "Okay, but I don't know your parent's names either."

Penelope knew he was right in what he said. Her reason, of course, was that she'd rather not get into her small town life and possibly ruin what she had with him, but she recognized maybe it wouldn't be so bad if she told him a little about her family.

"Touché," she gave him. "It's Simon and Anne...And you know about my brother Cory." Then she realized that she had no idea if he had any brothers and sisters. She just assumed he was an only child. It was something about his demeanor that she couldn't put her finger on. But maybe she was wrong. "Do you have any siblings?"

"Nope," he answered, taking a sip of his water. "Frank and Rose thought it wouldn't be a good idea to have more than one. It might've gotten in the middle of their golf game or country club Christmas party."

Penelope did a quick mental sketch of Luke's parents. She drew them as cold and possibly selfish.

Not having the faintest idea on how to broach the subject of his parent's personalities (or how he presented them to be), Penelope bypassed his statement. "What do your parents do?"

He tapped his fingers on the table as if he was bored and just passing time with their conversation because he had nothing better to do. "My mother was a banker and my father was in the shipping industry." He sighed, "How about yours?"

She could tell he wasn't interested but answered despite the fact. "They're both teachers. My mother teaches high school history and my father teaches science. They actually met during their first year of teaching at the same school in my hometown. They started on the same day."

He raised his eyebrows. "Interesting," he commented with a hint of sarcasm.

For the sake of their special Valentine's Day evening and relationship, Penelope also decided to bypass that statement. "You said that your father's in shipping-is your company your family's company or did your father help you out in some way?"

"My father hasn't helped me with anything," he asserted. Luke's eyes darkened. "It isn't a family business. I've done it all myself, without their assistance, and I like it that way." His voice was rough.

Penelope didn't know how to react. "Luke, I didn't mean to insinuate-"

"Look, forget about it," he said, composing himself. "It really isn't necessary for us to go into our families. Our relationship is between us. Not them."

Well, that's true, Penelope thought, and she knew she was a complete criminal when it came to hiding her own background in both her relationship with Luke and in her Manhattan life overall, but she also understood that at some point they'd have to divulge parts of their past if they were to move forward. It was a matter of emotional intimacy.

"But-"

"Penelope," he quickly interceded, throwing his napkin on the table. He rose from his seat. "Come," he gently insisted, reaching out to her.

She put her hand in his and got up.

Luke winked at someone in a distance, and in an instant, there was slow music streaming throughout the restaurant.

The surrounding patrons admired Luke and Penelope as Luke led her to an empty space in the middle of the restaurant, the luminosity of the Statue of Liberty highlighting the couple as he put one of her hands in his and the other around his middle. Once he looped his arm around her waist, they proceeded to step along with the romantic, instrumental melody that Penelope didn't recognize.

"What is this?" she asked as she put her head to his chest.

"I don't know. Just a tune they threw on," he replied and then whispered, "I asked them to put some music on, just for us."

Penelope looked up at him and saw the intensity growing in his eyes. She knew he wanted something. And she knew he wanted it bad.

He flashed a sexy smirk. "This is really nice," he said. She could feel the rise of his breath against her breast, but she remained calm and steady – *there was no need to rush things-right? After all, we've only been seeing each other for six weeks.*

"This is our first Valentine's Day together," he continued, his grip on her hand growing stronger and hotter. "I think it would be more than fitting if we'd go back to my place, crack open a bottle of champagne, and celebrate."

Penelope wasn't so sure about his suggestion, so she answered – "Mmmmm," to the idea.

She could hear Stacey's words in her ear – *What's wrong with you? Go to the man's apartment!* and what she imagined Sonia might say – *It might be too soon. But when true love calls, you must answer.* But when Penelope listened to herself, she heard – *It doesn't feel right yet. Maybe another couple of weeks …or a couple of months.* She questioned her own inner voice – *But why?* It could bring her so close to what she wanted – the life that she always desired – if she snatched up Luke Carson, just as the Blue Bloods in her office had snatched up their boyfriends, some having married them.

Luke pressed hard against her body. Penelope noticed her skin was cool. There was no fire prickling up and down her extremities and privates.

"Didn't you like the flowers that I got you?"

Penelope smiled. "Sure. I loved them. Who wouldn't love red roses?" she replied. She thought it was a shame they were delivered to her home instead of the office. She only wished her coworkers could see her receive a delivery for a second time. She did try to take out as much change as she could in front of them – providing money for lunch deliveries, for coworkers who desperately needed sustenance from the junk food machine, for a dollar, etcetra, etcetra – to show off the Gucci coin purse Luke bought her, but no one took any notice. It seemed as though a designer coin purse was a bargain basement item in the world of the upper class and upwardly mobile.

The roses would have been a reminder to all that Penelope was still dating a successful man, and at present, she had a gut wrenching sense that everyone might've figured Luke had just faded away.

"There were a dozen," he told her. "A dozen red roses."

"Yes. I know. I mean, I didn't count, but I know," she said. "But I didn't get you anything." And she hadn't because she didn't know if he would actually get her anything. She knew she would probably get flowers since he sent her a bouquet after their second date. But there was really nothing to purchase for a man that would be equal to flowers, so she was virtually empty-handed in the gift department ("But anyway," Wendy said, "a woman really doesn't have to buy a man gifts in the beginning. HE should be doing the buying.").

"You could give me something - later," he smiled and then laughed. "I'm *just* kidding ... not really." Penelope wasn't amused.

His dimples came out. "There is more, y'know," he commented. "Reach inside my jacket. There's a pocket with something in there for you."

What? she asked herself. What could've been small enough – that was a gift – to fit in Luke's pocket?

Jewelry maybe?

But it couldn't have been jewelry, she thought. She hadn't reached that part of the "Holy Trinity" yet; first, you get the flowers, then the designer bags, and then the jewelry. That was what happened to the girls in the office, or at least that was what she thought happened with the girls in the office. *Was there another way? Did the jewelry sometimes come earlier?* – Oh, this was all too confusing for Penelope! But exciting!

Penelope found herself practically panting as she put her hand in his jacket pocket while they kept on dancing.

She pulled out an envelope and they stopped moving.

"Open it up," he insisted.

She did as she was told, and in the envelope was a ticket. A plane ticket to Hawaii with her name on it.

Penelope was shocked – this wasn't in the Holy Trinity at all! She didn't know how to react. *Hawaii?*

She smiled nervously. "Thanks ... Hawaii?"

"Is that all I get?" he grinned. "Beautiful Hawaii? With me? The beaches, the mountains, sliding down lava?"

"What?" Penelope wasn't thrilled about the lava part. She already had enough trouble with her fair skin and freckles in the sun. She knew the combination of the burning sun, scorching lava, and her body would prove to be a huge mistake.

"What?" he mimicked her. "You should be saying 'fuckin yeah'!" He suddenly put his hand to his mouth. "I'm sorry. I forgot you don't curse."

"Luke."

"You should really curse now, Penelope. I mean-you might get a set of Gucci luggage out if it."

"Luke."

"What?"

"Don't get me wrong - I love this gift - it's wonderful, but don't you think it's too soon to go to Hawaii together?"

"What'd I tell you before about Manhattan years as compared to dog years? We might as well be celebrating our fiftieth wedding anniversary at an old folk's home playing bingo…But we're not. We're going to Hawaii. And for two weeks."

Penelope could now hear Sonia shouting in her ear – "*He said wedding! He's talking marriage-go for it!*" and yet, she still found herself saying, "But-"

"Besides. If you take another look at the ticket you'll see the trip is scheduled for the beginning of April. That's the only time during the next six or seven months I can take off," he said, and he grabbed her hand that was holding the ticket, and they started to dance again. "So that gives you about six more weeks to get to know me better." He laughed. "See my pad."

Penelope didn't know what else to say, so instead of speaking up about her concerns, she rested her head on his chest.

Luke bent down a bit and in her ear, in a hushed voice, he said. "It's in April. At least you know that I'm looking ahead. Long term."

"I've got to make sure I can take off those weeks," she told him, suddenly remembering work, and then wondering if that might be around the time that her boss would announce his decision about who was taking over the Streamers account. And then she thought about Ted and how thankful she was for the time they were spending together sharing ideas about technology (well, actually more of his ideas) … Thankful for the time they had together, period.

Penelope was suddenly misty-eyed, and Luke caught a glimpse of her face. "Hey, no reason to cry about it," he gently said, now hugging her body as they continued to dance around with the melody. "I know. I'm happy with you, too. I'm glad you fixed that text messaging problem you had. Otherwise, we'd never be here together."

Penelope smiled. "The fates. The fates brought us together."

"The fates?" He chuckled. "Or maybe whoever fixed your BlackBerry."

Penelope sighed, "Yeah, right," and asked herself — *What's wrong with me? This is wonderful! This is exactly what I wanted — what I've waited for!*

"What do you say, Penelope McAdams?" Luke whispered. "How's about that champagne at the Luke Carson loft?"

Mary: George Bailey! Give me my robe! Shame on you! ... I'm going to tell your mother on you!

Sixteen

It was the afternoon following Valentine's Day that Penelope was on the phone with her brother and accidentally slipped about owning the Wii ("Oh, you want to get the Wii for Dad's birthday? I have that," she stupidly said); that Sonia found out about Penenelope's Wii and came rushing through Penelope's apartment door with macaroni salad, microwaveable hotdogs, condiments, and a table cloth (as if she was setting up for a park picnic) with boyfriend Cory and son Jake in tow, and kissed Penelope's hand as if she was the Pope and hurried out, leaving her two boys in front of the television with startled expressions and astonished mouths ("What the ... ?" her brother sounded. "What's with the flat screen TV?"); and that Penelope posed a question to her brother that had plagued her since the evening before – "Do you think it's okay to be physically intimate with a guy before being emotionally intimate?"

Sitting on the couch with a forkful of macaroni salad in one hand and reaching for the Wii Remote with the other, Cory suddenly stopped in mid-action and responded, "Are you actually asking me that question?" He raised an eyebrow at her as she sat across from him, slumping on a kitchen chair.

"Yeah."

"Because you do remember that I am your brother, right?" he said to her as he shoved the macaroni salad in his mouth and grabbed the remote. "And brothers really don't want to hear about their sisters'- er - intimacies, let alone answer questions about them."

Penelope put on the expression of a sad, puppy dog and even threw in a boo-boo lip for good measure. "But if I can't talk to you, who else am I going to talk to?"

"I don't know. A girl friend, a coworker-a random stranger on the street."

Cory eyed Jake who was sitting calmly on the couch next to him, appearing interested and very mature with his legs crossed, looking as though he should've been puffing at a pipe and wearing a handsome smoking jacket.

"What are you doing?" Cory asked the little man. "And why are you listening that way? Who are you? Hugh Hefner?" Her brother dropped a microwaved hotdog into a roll on a plate and squirted some ketchup on it. "Eat," he ordered him. "Eat already."

Cory turned to his sister as he fiddled with the Wii remote. "So can you please tell me - and not that I'm complaining, mind you - why in the world you have this Wii and this HUGE flat screen TV? I mean, when you told me that you had the Wii, I literally had vertigo. I dropped the phone and went to pass out, but thankfully, Sonia caught me." He slipped a Wii gaming disc into its console. "And then, when I saw you had this flat screen television. This HUGE flat screen television, I swear I was going to have a heart attack." He added, "And I would've, too, if it wasn't for the fact that I was so hungry, and there was macaroni salad."

"I'll answer your question if you answer my *intimacy* question," Penelope replied, folding her arms.

"Forget it," he said and then exclaimed, "Great!" as he examined the television screen. "You have Wii sports! ... I think I'm going to play the boxing game!" He looked around. "I'm going to need the nunchuk that came with the Wii." He found it under the television, grabbed it, and then stood up with the Wii remote in his right hand and the Wii nunchuk in his left. He aimed the remote at the television screen and picked a cartoon character to represent himself – the Wii Cory – in the boxing match. "Yeah," Cory breathed excitedly to the Wii Cory," that's right ... You're really, really mean and a *tough* dude. You can do it."

Round one of the boxing match: Penelope glared at her brother as he swung his arms to and fro, punching the air with the remote and nunchuk. She watched as he jabbed his opponent one, two, three times, and then Cory's supposedly "tough" character was knocked out cold by his opponent. "Damn!" he hollered, anger sprawling on his face as the Wii referee counted down from the television – "Five ... six ... seven ... eight ...,"and Penelope continued to sit on the chair with a deadpan stare aimed in his direction.

On the count of eight, Cory's character got up from the floor and Cory shouted, "Okay! Now we're cooking," but then he gave his sister a sideways glance and stopped the game.

"Okay," he said to her. "This is your fault. You're making me lose my concentration with your evil eye."

Penelope didn't move or change her expression, but reacted with – "Until you give me advice on my intimacy situation..."

"Fine," he said, "ask me about drugs."

"What?"

"Go on," he insisted, "ask me about drugs."

"Okay ... What about drugs?"

"Just say no."

Penelope squinted at him, confused. "What?"

"Just say no," he repeated, his eyes widening. "Remember? ... *No always means no.*"

Penelope thought about it for a second and then finally realized her brother was trying to tell her not to have sex; Cory had figured out his own special way of getting around what he felt was an uncomfortable subject. "*Ohhh,*" she said, "I get it. So you're telling me not to have *intimacies* through a 'don't do drugs' conversation."

He grinned.

"So what happens if I want to talk to you about my crack addiction? What will we discuss then? The weather?"

Cory aimed the Wii nunchuk at her. "I'm sending you back home to Mom."

"You don't have to. She's already here. You're her, Cory. You sound just like her-'Don't do drugs! Don't have sex!'"

He grimaced. "Hey! Hello!" he shouted and pointed at little Jake as if to tell her that "sex" wasn't an appropriate word to use around him.

"Jake has no idea what I'm talking about! He's in nursery school for God's sake!"

"Please. Do you know what they teach in nursery school these days?" he inquired, his voice booming. "He's got one friend who's starting his internship with NASA and another who makes artificial limbs with Play-Doh … And I'm not Mom!"

"Yes, you are," she retorted.

"No, I'm not."

"Yes, you are!" Penelope cried out. "You're just like Mom, Cory! You think that I'm still a virgin, like Mom does, and I'm not. I'm twenty-eight, Cory! And even in a place like Elmont, a girl can lose her virginity if she wants to!"

"Next!"

Round two of the boxing match: Cory swung the Wii remote and nunchuk in the air. Penelope watched again, placid but amused. "Talking about Mom," he commented, "you'll have to give her a hug for me when you see her next month."

"What? What are you talking about? You'll be there for Dad's birthday, too."

"No, I won't. Turns out I've been handed a really big case that I'll have to work on that week, so I won't be able to go to Elmont with you."

Penelope sighed. She didn't want to face her parents alone and deal with all the questioning about her life in the city. It was bad enough she had to hear from her mother that she wasn't calling as much as she should or that her politeness had been eradicated by the city (as evidenced by her not saying "sorry" for more than a year, she was told), now she had to face them in person by herself? "Our tickets are non-refundable, so if you'd like, you can take someone on the trip."

"Like who?"

"Like that guy," he commented, still playing, striking the air with both hands, perspiration dripping from his nose.

"You mean Ted-er-Luke."

Her brother punched his opponent one and then two times, when his obviously ferocious competitor provided a harsh swing at his character's face, resulting in the Wii Cory dropping meekly in the ring for a second time. "ARE YOU KIDDING ME?" Cory hollered at the television.

"Five … six … seven … eight … nine …" went the referee, and on the count of nine, Wii Cory pulled himself up for a second time, and Cory cried out, "You're in for it now, buddy!" Her brother suddenly turned around to her. "Wait. Luke. Is that what your *intimacy* question is about? Have you and Luke…?"

She fidgeted and replied, "Yes, it's about Luke, and no, we haven't. I went to his apartment for the first time last night and he tried, but I didn't."

"Good girl! Too soon, I think," he said.

Penelope became dreamy, her mind wandering off to the latter part of the prior evening. "But his apartment was beautiful, just as I imagined it. Leather couch, balcony, full kitchen area, and big, expensive looking paintings on the wall." *But no pictures*, she thought. No photos of himself with others, no photos with himself just with himself, and no photos of people without him in the picture – and no photos of family.

He was about to go back to his boxing but instead said, "Wait. Who's Ted?"

"What do you mean?"

"You just mentioned the name 'Ted' before. Who is he?" Before she had a chance to tell him, her brother figured it out for himself. "Ohhhh. I know who Ted is. That's that gay guy from MIT who's teaching you how to knit. Sonia told me about him."

Penelope suddenly recalled the conversation she had with Stacey and Sonia that night at Asia de Cuba when they met Luke and then happened upon Ted. She felt bad that she hadn't eradicated the twosome's assumption about Ted's sexual orientation. "Uh, actually he's not gay."

"He's teaching you to knit and he's not gay?"

"Uh, he's not actually teaching me how to knit," she came clean. "He's teaching me about technology."

"Why in the world is he teaching you about technology?"

"It's a long story. I don't want to get into it."

"Fine," he shrugged. "Well, I guess that explains the TV and the Wii." He looked at her. "At least you're getting some supervision from this Ted guy." He paused. "But do me a favor, huh? Tell Sonia that he isn't showing you how to knit."

"Is she upset?"

"Upset?" He paused. "Well, I guess if you call turning over every picture of you in my apartment upset, yeah, then I guess you can call her upset. Very upset."

"I'll talk to her."

"Good," he commented, diving into the macaroni salad. "So … he's not gay. Are you dating him, too?"

"Ted? Noooo!" she replied and laughed. "He's just teaching me stuff. He's just a friend. Maybe an acquaintance even."

Her brother raised an eyebrow at her as he put his fork in his mouth. "Uh-huh."

Penelope sat up on her chair and shook her head. "Ted's got a sad story. He used to be this big engineer with some big firm in Washington, D.C., and then supposedly he found his girlfriend-his fiancé with another guy. And then he just left D.C. and everything and came here."

Cory furrowed his brow. His reaction to Penelope's news about Ted was palpable. "Well that sucks," he declared, "that really, really sucks … Has he dated anyone since then?"

"I don't think so. I don't know," she answered, thinking about the blonde and wondering if they were in a relationship at all since he didn't have any plans with her for Valentine's Day. But maybe she went out of town, Penelope thought. "There might be this blonde," she noted with a tinge of annoyance in her voice. "Maybe."

"That's a horrible thing to happen to a guy. Finding his woman with another man. Especially when it's the woman you want to spend the rest of your life with," he said. "I could only imagine what I would do if I found Sonia with another guy." Her brother grimaced and made a fist at his side.

He glanced over at Penelope. "Why don't you fix him up with someone? You must have a friend that'd be interested."

"All my friends are your friends. And Stacey saw him, and from her reaction, I don't think it would be a good idea to fix them up."

Her brother shuddered. "It wouldn't be a good idea to fix anyone up with Stacey. Anyway, her reaction doesn't mean much. She's a tough sell."

"Well, I can't say that I blame her. I mean Ted does need to be neatened up a bit," she commented. "And you never see his eyes. His bangs are so long." Penelope shoveled the macaroni salad into her mouth.

"Wait a minute," Cory said. "I think there's something that could help him …Wait …What is it called? … Oh yeah-it's called a *scissor*." He slapped his head as if to say *duh*, and then raised two fingers and made like they were scissors, incising the air. "You know about it?"

"Whatever," Penelope reacted, licking her fork clean. After spending some time prying Luke's hands off of her body the night before, she wasn't in the mindset to figure out how to tell Ted that he should cut his bangs. But she did take a moment to ponder the idea of telling him she was planning on doing some technology experiment with wires and scissors, and then falling on him with the scissors, claiming that splicing his bangs while descending was a complete and utter accident. No, she thought, she couldn't. An MIT guy would never fall for that. Although she would give anything to see his eyes.

Her brother looked at the Wii nunchuk and remote and then pressed its "power off" button," ending the boxing game.

Penelope grinned from ear to ear. "Why did you end the game?" she asked him, already knowing the answer.

"Forget it," he grunted, throwing the controls onto the couch. "I'm just not in the zone today!" he declared. "Just not in the zone!"

Penelope let out a peal of laughter. Her brother was never one for losing.

Just at that moment, little Jake reached over for the Wii remote control shouting "Wiiiiii!" and stood up and started to press its buttons and then assumed the stance of a Wii boxer – remote in right hand and nunchuk in the left.

"No way!" Penelope exclaimed.

Her brother was completely surprised. "You're kidding me! ... I didn't know he knew how to ...," and before he had the opportunity to end his sentence, Cory watched as little four-year-old Jake knocked his opponent out in the first round.

"WHAT THE ... ?" Cory hollered.

The opponent got up after a couple of moments, and in the second round, little Jake swung his arm around again and put his opponent out to pasture for a good half of the Wii referee's countdown. "Ten ... Nine ... Eight ... Seven ... Six ... Five ..." and the opposing character got up while Cory shook his head. "I don't believe this."

Penelope continued to laugh so hard that she thought she would die from lack of inhalation.

"Wait," her brother said as she tried to get a hold of herself, and Jake again assumed his fighter stance. "I know what this is, and it has nothing to do with Jake actually being better than me ... This is all evolutionary ... Like when humans were born with opposable thumbs ... so it made them different from apes." He explained, "The younger generations have played so many computer games, it had to have crossed over to Jake somehow when he was born. Some kind of manual dexterity that he can play these stupid games ..."

Now Penelope couldn't control herself, and she fell over, engulfed in her uproarious guffaws as her brother kept trying to make excuses while Jake pulverized his opponent.

Suddenly, Penelope's BlackBerry rang.

"Hello?" she answered, trying to hide her laughter.

"Hey, Sweetie," Luke said.

"Oh, hi, Luke." Penelope held her breath and stomach as she tried to talk to Luke while witnessing the spectacle of Jake destroying her brother's self-esteem as he destroyed his Wii opponent.

"Just wanted you to know that I was okay with last night," Luke said.

"I CAN'T BELIEVE IT!" Cory cried out as Jake's opponent dropped in the Wii ring. "I THINK THE GUY'S OUT FOR THE COUNT! THE ENTIRE COUNT! JAKE! JAKE!" And hence, Penelope doubled over with laughter, the BlackBerry falling away from her hand onto the floor.

Cory reeled around to his sister, who was now aching all over from her hysterical tremors, and exclaimed, "No, his opponent's up again!" and then turned back to Jake, who swiftly threw his strongest and farthest reaching punch since he started to play the boxing game, pummeling his Wii opponent to the floor, and in the process, plunging his fist into Cory, or more specifically, plunging his fist into Cory's groin.

Penelope's brother fell to his knees, right next to her BlackBerry, and he let out a loud, high pitched squeal – "FUCK!" – like a school girl who had just been whacked.

And from the phone, there was Luke's voice – "Penelope? ... Penelope?"

Young George Bailey: I wish I has a million dollars ... Hotdog!

Seventeen

"**I** don't know how it happened, "Penelope explained, "it just came out."

Wendy eyed both her and her set of Gucci luggage, caustically. "I can't believe you actually cursed," she said as the women passed by their desks and gawked at Penelope's special delivery. "Actually, I *don't* believe it." She put her hands at her hips. "Tell me the curse you used."

Hesitant to dive into her lie more than she had, and feeling bad that she was profiting from the injury to her brother's testicles, Penelope was defensive and uttered, "What does it matter what curse I used?"

Wendy crossed her arms and arched a dark eyebrow. "Just say it."

"Isn't once enough?"

"Just say what it was."

"What bags are *you* going to give me?" Penelope retorted with a sneer.

Wendy threw up her arms. "Fine. Don't tell me. It wouldn't be any different than other things you don't confide in me about," she said, examining the Gucci tags on the luggage.

"I swear, Wendy-aren't you ever going to listen to me? I have *nothing* to tell you."

Wendy pushed her long black hair to the side and bunched it up into a ponytail. "Like why Luke got you a set of Gucci luggage?"

Furrowing her brow, Penelope replied. "I told you. I cursed." Again, she was lying about what happened, and within seconds, Penelope tried to rationalize the lie in her mind to cure herself of guilt – *Yes. It was my brother who cursed. But he is a blood relative. Therefore, it's not too much of a stretch to say that I did the dirty deed … Was it?*

"But why the luggage? Why not just the bag? Did you just let a million curses rip all at one time?"

"No," she replied. "The luggage is for our trip to Hawaii."

"*Hawaii?*" Wendy exclaimed, her eyeballs popping out of her head along with a button from her discount blouse.

"Wendy!" Ginger, the account supervisor, yelled from across the room, providing an extreme expression of disapproval.

Wendy sat down. "Hawaii?" she practically whispered as she rolled her chair around the Gucci luggage to Penelope's cubicle. "He invited you to go with him to Hawaii? When?"

"On Valentine's day."

"No-when? When are you going?"

"Oh, in early April," she replied, admiring the Gucci insignia on one of her suitcases. She traced a "G" with her finger. "He showed me the tickets. He had the whole vacation set up. Dates and all."

With a muddled expression, Wendy inquired, "Why April? Why did he have the dates already? So soon?"

"I don't know-he told me that he could only take his vacation then. The dates must've fit into his schedule."

Wendy's eyes narrowed, and Penelope could sense her suspiciousness, it felt like a breeze moving between them. "Really? That's strange."

"What's the problem?" Penelope asked, annoyed. "You know what I think? I think you're jealous of my luggage, and that I'm going to Hawaii. That's what I think."

Frowning at her, Wendy reacted, "This city is really ruining you, isn't it? The Penelope I knew that first came toddling in here a year or so ago would've never said anything remotely like that."

Penelope felt her conscience creep up on her, including the phrase "I'm sorry," but she didn't breathe a word of it, instead saying, "Okay. I guess you're just looking out for me."

"That's right," Wendy nodded and one blue-eye sparked. "Just because I was never invited to such a nice place like Hawaii, where you can lie on the beach all day, sip tropical drinks, and get *leid* all the time, doesn't mean that I'm jealous."

Penelope looked at her.

Wendy's hand brushed against the leather of the Gucci cosmetic bag that was set on the suitcase. "And just because I never got couture luggage, let alone a single dowdy handbag, from any man, including my somewhat ex-boyfriend, doesn't mean that I'm reeling with envy." She added, "much."

"Couture luggage," Penelope said, rolling her eyes, "it's a lot. And it's not even part of the Holy Trinity."

"What? What are you talking about?"

"The Holy Trinity of a successful New York City woman when she dates," Penelope said, sticking up one finger after the other as she explained – "First, she gets the flowers, second, the handbag, and then the jewelry." She shook her head, confused. "There was no mention of luggage."

Wendy looked at her cross-eyed and then grabbed the cosmetic bag and stood up. "Look," she said, tucking the bag in her armpit. "A clutch purse." She strutted a small circle, throwing her hair back. "Perfect, huh?" she commented. "And you've officially reached the second rung of the Holy Trinity ... What do you think?"

Just at that moment, Wendy looked over to her side, and she quickly put the cosmetic bag back onto the suitcase. She informed, "The Blue Bloods are coming, the Blue Bloods are coming," like she was Paul Revere announcing the oncoming attack of the British soldiers, and sat down.

Ginger and two other Blue Bloods approached them with the click-clacking of their Jimmy Choo and Christian Lacroix stilettos below their Marc Jacobs and Ralph Lauren suits.

When the Blue Bloods arrived at the Gucci luggage, they looked straight at Penelope, turning their noses at Wendy (Wendy sneered).

Ginger started the discourse. "Penelope," she said, "what a nice set of luggage." Her fellow Blue Bloods nodded. "We were admiring the pieces as the delivery man brought them in."

Penelope smiled bigger than ever. This was worth her brother's testicular impairment, she concluded. After all, all he needed was a bag of ice and a series of moments to himself to review his privates. No real harm done, and anyway, she rationalized it was karmic retribution for the way he teased her for all those years – *yeah, that's it. That's it.*

"Thank you," was all that Penelope replied, still shocked and overjoyed over another reaction from the Blue Bloods after they had first acknowledged the delivery of flowers from Luke.

"From anyone special?" one of the Blue Bloods with flaxen blonde hair asked.

Penelope could hardly breathe but managed to get her words out. "That guy, Luke. The one who sent the flowers here before," she responded, her face filled with glee. "We're going on a trip to Hawaii soon. I guess he felt this present was appropriate."

All three of the Blue Bloods gasped, and Ginger announced, "I love Hawaii!"

"So do I," the other lovely Blue Blood with incandescent, spa maintained skin, chimed in. "Loved it."

"Me, too," said the flaxen-haired blonde, "three times I loved it."

"Have you ever been?" Ginger asked Penelope.

Penelope didn't know whether to tell them the truth or not. She was afraid that if they became aware that she had never been to Hawaii, they would consider her an amateur in the ways of being a successful and chic Manhattan woman, and therefore, unacceptable to their group. But she couldn't lie. She didn't know enough about Hawaii to get away with having a knowledgeable conversation about it, and besides, Wendy was sitting there, listening in, and knew that she was never "leid." Penelope had no choice. "No I haven't," she replied.

Unexpectedly to Penelope, Ginger beamed, "So this is your first time – we need to tell you all about it!" She then lowered her voice after everyone turned around to see what the raucous was about. "Oh my." She acknowledged, "*I* should be the one keeping the voices down. I guess I'm letting my excitement run away from me." All the Blue Bloods smiled, and Ginger continued, "Why don't you have lunch with us sometime, and we'll talk about Hawaii. We'll tell you everything you need to know."

"That's a fabulous idea," the skin-perfect Blue Blood added, "and you can tell us all about Luke."

They all nodded, and Wendy just sat there, jaw falling to the office carpeting.

Penelope's heart leapt. "Sure. That sounds great."

The Blue Bloods nodded approvingly and threw her a nice, smiley – "Toodles!" and turned their noses up again at Wendy, walking away without giving her so much as a simple nod.

"Well," Wendy said to them when they were practically miles away, out of earshot distance, "I didn't want to be invited to some crappy lunch anyway!"

A voice rang out, "Penelope!" It was the boss man, and he was yelling from his office. "Penelope McAdams! Can you please come in here?"

"Okay!" she returned.

Wendy smirked. "Better run now, Penelope. Your *other* boyfriend is calling you."

Shrugging off the comment, Penelope gathered what she was working on, including another letter to a celebrity couple to represent Henshaw Tractors, and made her way to Alden Renquist's office.

"Hi, Mr. Renquist," Penelope greeted him, "you asked for me?"

Her boss had his chin cradled in one hand, the elbow resting on his desk. His eyes rolled up to her. "Yes, Penelope. Do you have something for me?"

"Yes, I do." She took out a list, announcing, "I have placements for Henshaw Tractors," and scanned it. "I procured press placements in Farm Industry News and CropLife Iron for May, and Farm Equipment for July." Her eyes moved away from the list, landing on her boss' face. His lips had a slight upturn, which led Penelope to believe that Alden Renquist was pleased but not exactly overjoyed.

"And," she added, trying to throw some spices into the pot that was her job security, "there's some interest from BusinessWeek. They're looking to do a story on companies that have survived through recessions and depressions. And Henshaw Tractors is perfect for the story. So they're reviewing the materials that I sent to them, but they already seem to like the idea." She added, "They like that the company is connected to rural America."

A light went on in Alden Renquist's eyes. "Middle America. True America," he noted, puncturing the air with a fist as if he was cheering *rah rah* at a pep rally. He leaned back in his chair and pointed at her. "Like El Dorado."

"Elmont," she pleasantly corrected him.

"This is good," he said, "now I won't have to fire you." He had a straight face, but then let out a giant laugh.

Penelope laughed as well, although nervously.

"What else have you got for me?"

"Oh," she sounded, fingering through her documents. "I have another celebrity endorsement letter I'm working on." She pulled out a piece of paper and handed it to him. "This one is to Tom Cruise and Katy Holmes."

As he read the paper, he grimaced. "What's this?" he asked. "Who's Ted Hollis, and why are you writing a press release for him?"

Penelope quickly rose from her seat and grabbed the paper from his hands, frantic, realizing that she mistakenly gave him the press release she was working on for Ted. "Ohhh, that's not it."

"You're not doing any freelance projects at work - are you Penelope?"

"No, sir," she responded, shaking her head as if she was trying to hurl it off her shoulders.

"Because if you were, I'd have to fire you," he commented. And without a laugh.

Penelope found the letter. "Here it is," she said. She reached over his desk to give it to him.

He waved it away. "No. Why don't you read it out loud? I'd like to hear it."

"Okay." She cleared her throat and read:

Dear Mr. Cruise and Ms. Holmes,

I am a media representative for a company called "Henshaw Tractors," the nations' leading supplier of tractors and tractor equipment, and we thought you'd be interested in representing Henshaw and its mission to make our land a more positive and healthy place, not unlike the mission of your religion, Scientology.

In fact, we feel that the missions are so similar, that Scientology and Henshaw Tractors would be a perfect fit, with yourselves, of course, the most celebrated Scientologists around (and beautiful Baby Suri, if you'd like), being the spokespeople for a widespread campaign. This widespread campaign would include pamphlets on Scientology being distributed at every Henshaw establishment and/or outlet and an offering of one free Scientology orientation to take place at one of your temples with every sale of a tractor.

Please note that the above is only one of the many ideas that we have to spread the word about Henshaw Tractors and hence, Scientology. We would like to further discuss these ideas with you at your convenience.

To schedule a meeting, please phone me at our offices, or you can email me at pmcadams@renquist.com.

Thanks so much, and I look forward to hearing from you.

Sincerely,

Penelope McAdams, Media Representative, Henshaw Tractors

Penelope looked up from her letter and found that her boss was staring at her.

He reached for the bottle of Xanax on his desk.

"Penelope," he said, unscrewing the bottle cap, "do you have any idea what Scientology is?"

She answered, "A little I think," as he threw back a couple of pills and gulped down some water. "I probably should have done more research." She knew she hadn't done any research. She had become so fixated on her personal life and Streamer's Technology that she quickly wrote up the draft with only her assumptions about Scientology as her guide.

He was adamant. "Do-you-know-what-sci-en-tol-e-gy is?"

Penelope started to get the jitters as she stood there, and with meekness coating her voice, she replied, "Uh. It's kinda like Christian Science?"

"Noooo. It has to do with extraterrestrials."

"Huh?"

"Exactly."

"I don't understand."

"And neither do I and neither will the people at Henshaw Tractors." He leaned over his desk. "Penelope, if you proposed this to Henshaw, it would be a complete disaster." He chastised, "You should know better. You're generally from the same area. You're cut from the same cloth. They're Protestants."

"I'm Episcopalian."

"And I'm a Catholic," he informed her. "But the point is we don't pray to extraterrestrials."

"Is that what Scientologists do?"

"I don't know personally. I just heard." Alden Renquist clutched at a bottle of scotch on a shelf behind him while Penelope wondered if Ted would've known anything about Scientology since he was pretty well informed on the galactic and alien front. "Again. I wanted you to be on this account, because you're the same." Her boss guzzled down a couple of ounces of scotch directly from the spout.

Considering that she was a sober witness and therefore, possibly responsible for another individual's well-being, even if it was her insane boss, Penelope commented, "Excuse me, Mr. Renquist, but isn't mixing pills and liquor not a good thing?"

He released the spout from his lips. "No. Probably not." He put the scotch down on his desk. "But it doesn't matter really. I'm probably going to be broke soon," he remarked. "It turns out that there won't be any mental issue with my wife. No mental ward." The angles of his face tightened. "They changed the judge on me, and she's from New Orleans and she's Creole. Creole's believe in voodoo. Even practice it."

He rolled his eyes. "So it seems that the court doesn't think my wife is crazy … Not crazy for flying halfway across the globe to go to a third-world country to see a medicine man hopping on one foot to conjure up some spirit that specializes in facelifts and Botox injections."

Penelope sat still, her eyes glazed over.

He shook his head in disbelief. "I don't know. Maybe we're the crazy ones." He mumbled, "Maybe the medicine men and the women who get millions of dollars of work done on their faces, so they can look like cats, and the voodoo people and the Scientologists, should run the whole fucking world."

Penelope's mouth dropped.

"You know what?" he added, his voice becoming louder. "Let them have the fucking world." He flapped his hand around as if he was shooing away a fly. "I don't want it. Do you want it?"

"Uh …"

"You're excused, Penelope." He suddenly waved her away.

Penelope, not knowing what else to say or do, uttered the obvious – "Uh. Okay," but then stated, "so you want me to change the letter."

Alden Renquist moaned. "Yes, Penelope. I want you to change the letter … or think of something else." He slumped over and rubbed his forehead. "I've got a headache."

She turned around to leave, her knees shaking.

"Penelope," her boss suddenly beckoned. Penelope swiveled round. "Keep up the good work," he said and grabbed the scotch bottle. "Can you please close the door behind you?"

She nodded and walked out, shutting the door to his office.

Penelope sat down at her desk, astonishment still apparent on her face.

Wendy slid over to Penelope's cubicle, prancing around with a leather Gucci lipstick holder in her hand. "Like what I got at Filene's Basement?" She shook the holder in front of her. "Can you believe it? Guess how much?"

Penelope said, "Nice try, but I already looked in the cosmetic bag."

Wendy *hmmphed* and placed the lipstick holder on Penelope's desk.

"What the hell happened in there?" Wendy asked her, obviously noticing her coworker's agitated expression. "And why is it that every time you come out of that office you like you've been through some sort of shock treatment?"

"Because that's how it feels."

"And to think-he *likes* you," Wendy said. "Imagine what the rest of us have to put up with?"

Penelope changed the subject. "Wendy, how would you like to go to Elmont with me for my father's birthday? Get out of the city, get some fresh air?" she asked. "My brother can't go, so you can have his ticket."

"Is it a train ticket?"

"No."

"Then forget it. Remember what I told you? I don't fly anywhere unless there's a sample sale involved or someone's dropped diamonds. Like in a field or something. That I'd fly to."

"No one's dropped diamonds."

"Then forget it," Wendy replied. "Of course," she then said, picking up the Gucci lipstick holder again, "there are ways to persuade me."

"No way."

Wendy put the holder down for a second time. "Why don't you just ask Luke?"

"Because it's too soon." *Too soon for him to meet my family and to see where I lived*, Penelope thought.

"Well, then take Ted."

At first, Penelope thought she was being serious, that was until she burst out laughing, announcing, "I crack myself up."

Penelope glowered at her.

Her blue eyes mischievous, Wendy said, "But you know, I heard that Ted is looking good. My ex told me that he's actually wearing nice jeans and shoes – nice for Ted that is. He's supposedly even combing his hair more." She quickly put out her hand as if to stop herself from talking. "Although there's still those bangs."

"Yeah," Penelope included, thinking about some of the recent times she had spent with him. "He is looking more put together."

"Maybe it's the blonde. Maybe they are dating."

Penelope immediately thought about Valentine's Day and how Ted was going to ask her to be with him. Not the blonde girl. *Or*, Penelope wondered, *did he ask her first and she couldn't make it?* Maybe the blonde, like she had previously thought, had to go away for Valentine's Day. Is that why Ted asked her to spend the day with him?

Penelope's eyes bugged out.

She asked herself – *Am I a substitute?* She became puzzled about the situation and her reaction to it.

Turning her back on the Gucci luggage, Penelope stared blankly at Ted's press release lying on her desk.

> *Mr. Potter: Oh, confound it, man, are you afraid of success?*

Eighteen

"I'm glad that you suggested a 'Post-Valentine's Day,'" Ted commented to Penelope as they sat on a bench in Central Park, looking out at a pond scattered with remote control sail boats. "But I didn't expect you to pick this place to hang out at."

Penelope watched a tiny vessel drift by. Shivering, she burrowed her chin in the collar of her coat. "Why? What's wrong with this place?"

"Nothing," he remarked with a grin and still no eyes (but his bangs did seem more neatly combed). She noticed the stylish, dark denim jeans he was wearing (not a crease in sight), along with his new snug-fitting pea jacket and blue-checkered scarf. "The Conservatory Water. I've always liked it."

"The Conservatory Water - is that what it's called?"

"Yep," he answered. "This area was supposed to be a huge conservatory, but because of some problems with money they created the pond."

"Really?" Penelope tried to sound interested (another factoid of

Ted's to put away in a box of useless information). "So the place has merit. So why are you so surprised that I picked it?"

"Because you're so stuck on being *such* a woman of the city. A woman of elegance and refinery. I didn't think you'd want to brave the outdoors."

She laughed, gazing at her surroundings; there were children playing, adults strolling, and the water and trees were still in a solid calm. "Ted. I wouldn't call this rough terrain or anything."

"No, but for the chic Manhattan woman, sitting on a bench in Central Park in the middle of winter is unheard of." A cold wind blew past and he shuddered.

Penelope pulled her hat down to cover her chilled ears. "Well, that may be true, but when I need to get away this is the place that I go to."

"Hmmm," he sounded, looking at a bundled up little boy, maybe some months beyond being a toddler, who picked up his boat from the water after it capsized. The boy analyzed his toy for a couple of seconds and then placed it back on the water. It stayed afloat. The little boy clapped his hands, smiling and giggling.

Ted smiled himself, and then turned to Penelope to say something, only to find her watching the same boy with an identical reaction to his, a brightness radiating from her face. He looked back at the boy who was now jumping up and down. A man raised the boy up and gathered him in his arms for a big hug.

"There's that Elmont again," Ted noted aloud, glancing over at Penelope.

"Oh, now this is about Elmont? Just because we're in a place that has trees and water, and I'm enjoying it?" She chortled.

"Well."

"Oh, please."

"Fine," he said, "but I must tell you that even I would've wanted to go to the Central Park Boathouse." He put his gloved hands in his coat pockets. "It's pretty there, too. And it's freezing out here. We would've been inside."

"That would've been nice, but unfortunately I can't afford it. Especially since I bought all that technology stuff."

"Neither can I," he commented, "which brings me to my next order of business." Ted turned away from Penelope, reaching into his backpack.

"Oh-I have something, too," she added, unzipping her handbag, sinking her hand inside.

Ted pulled out two McDonald's bags. Penelope pulled out a piece of paper.

"Chez McDonalds, M'lady," he said, waving a bag under her nose. "A poor man and woman's caviar and crème brulee."

She caught a whiff. "I love McDonalds." Although Penelope didn't like to admit it, she practically couldn't stop eating Chicken McNuggets when they were put in front of her. "Do you have McNuggets?" she asked eagerly, her stomach beginning to growl enough for the fish in the pond to hear.

He smiled. "Of course."

"And french fries?" she clapped her hands, a bit like the little boy with the overturned boat.

"What do you think?" he answered her with a carefree air.

"Honey?"

"Honey?"

"Yeah. Honey," she repeated. "They have the packets of honey. I absolutely love to dip the McNuggets and fries into the honey. Especially the fries. The mix of the sweet and salt tastes *so* good." Penelope was licking her chops. Ted grinned and scratched his head, seeming amused.

"Let me see," he said, opening one bag and then the other. "I know I told them to put in a little of everythin- ah, yes. We've got honey." He took out a handful of packets.

"Great!"

"What's that?" Ted pointed to the paper in her hand.

"It's the press release I wrote for you.

He appeared startled. "A press release? Where did you get the information to write a press release?"

"Ala internet," she replied. "Aren't you impressed?"

He flicked his hand in the general direction of the document. "I don't need one."

"Of course you need one," she said as he set up a picnic on the bench. Ted placed some McDonald's wrappers and napkins between them, holding all of it down with his keys and a Star War's *Revenge of the Sith* eraser (which he said was left behind in his apartment by a little cousin who came to visit, but she knew better), and spread around the boxes of McNuggets, hamburgers, and fries, along with the packets of condiments.

"Everyone needs press, especially you," she said, grabbing up a packet of honey and peeling away the cover. "And if I can get the media interested in you, you'll have better projects and more money." She paused and then gestured to the picnic display. "You don't want to be eating McDonald's for the rest of your life, do you?"

"Why not? You seem to like it."

She realized that this was true, and she surely liked it more than the meals she had encountered and tolerated with Luke. McDonald's – *good ol' American food,* she thought. *Good ol' greasy, fried American food.* But that was beside the point. "But I'm not going to be here eating McDonald's with you for the rest of *your* life."

Ted frowned. "Put the press release away," he commanded. "I'll look at it later."

Penelope set the honey down and held the press release up in the air. "This *really* is important, Ted. Just take a look. Take a look now." Ted didn't answer. Instead he picked up a hamburger. Penelope paused. "You have a spectacular background. How is anyone supposed to know about your work?" she continued. "How are they supposed to find out about you?"

"Maybe I don't want to be found."

"Don't be silly. Everyone wants to be found."

"Not me."

Penelope's face screwed. "Then why are we doing this? We had a deal remember? An agreement. You teach me about technology and I do your PR, but I haven't done anything for you, yet, and I'm feeling guilty about it."

"Well don't," he said and then bit into his hamburger.

"You know what? I won't. Because it's not me that doesn't want to do your PR, it's you. I've tried, but it's all you." Penelope's eyes flared. "I don't understand this," she commented, "why did you make this deal with me in the first place?" and she stuffed the press release back into her handbag.

Ted swallowed some hamburger and said, "Okay. Fine. Just give me the press release. But let's look at it later. I want to enjoy this lunch. No work."

She pulled out the press release and handed it to him.

Ted slipped it into his backpack. "Is everything okay now?"

She shrugged and dipped a bouquet of french fries into the honey and hauled it into her mouth. "Mmmmmm."

"I guess that's a yes then," he joked.

Penelope started to chew on a McNugget and thought of what she really wanted to ask him. She knew his private life was probably none of her business. Yet, curiosity about the man she was spending so much time with, merged with some concern about his well-being, lured her into inquiry. "What did you do for Valentine's Day?" she asked, picking up a cup of soda, slurping away at a straw.

"Nothing."

She squinted - *What? Did the bohemian blonde go away? Did you not want to be with her?*

"Really? Nothing? ... Was there anyone you might've wanted to spend time with? Like in a romantic way?"

Like the throwback-hippie that I saw you with at that bar?

"Maybe," he replied, fidgeting. "I don't know." He then switched topics, pointing back and forth from her packet of honey to the fries — "Hey, how about the salty-sweet?"

Penelope didn't pay attention. "It's just that we spend so much time together."

"Ahmmmm."

"And I know that you don't want to be found," she noted, providing quotes around the "found" by raising two fingers from each hand in the air, curving them like claws. "But don't you think we should know more about each other?" she asked him. A pair of fingers that had originally been claws, closed, leaving a centimeter or so between them. "Just a little more?" She then looked at her fingers, and tried to do the Vulcan salute again, something she found herself working on in bed when she had problems falling asleep; she still couldn't do it. Only one pair of fingers would close, the other two digits being worlds apart from each other.

Penelope shook her hand around as if that would do her any good in performing her task.

Ted moved his head back and forth as if to say "stop driving yourself crazy."

"Penelope," he uttered, and just as that moment, her BlackBerry went off – *Buffalo gals can't you come out tonight - can't you come out tonight - can't you come out tonight - Buffalo gals can't you come out tonight - aaand dance by the-* she pressed a button and the ringtone came to a screeching halt.

It was a text message:

Luke (Mobile)

Feb 21, 2008 1:36:13 PM

Hey hon - Called you before but you didn't answer. Got to leave today for Boston and will be gone all week. Same problem with the same customer. Sorry about tonight. I'll take you out to the show you wanted to see when I get back. I'll call you when I land.

Can't wait to see you again and to smother you with kisses.

Darn it, she said to herself. *More trips to Boston.*

"Okay," he said, "If we're going to know more about one another … why New York now? Why didn't you leave Elmont a long time ago?"

Images of her grandfather went through her head. Penelope laid the BlackBerry on her lap. "Didn't you ask me that a while ago?"

"Yes. But you didn't give me an answer."

"And I'm still not going to give you an answer."

"I just don't understand," he said, continuing to pry. "I bet you were just itching to get out. Just like George Bailey." He put his hamburger down on the bench. "In fact, I bet your favorite part of the movie was when he was about to leave with all his suitcases. Ready to get out of town."

"Actually, you're wrong about that," she informed him, slamming her BlackBerry in her purse, aggravated. "It's the Zuzu's petals part."

"The what?"

"Zuzu's petals. Remember? It's when George Bailey comes back from his trip with the angel," she said. "Y'know. The Angel Clarence shows him what the world would be like if he never existed. And when he comes back to real life, when he existed, he finds the petals his daughter Zuzu gave him in his pocket, where he originally put them, and then he yells out, all excited, 'Zuzu's petals! Zuzu's petals!'"

"Why is that your favorite part?'

"Isn't it obvious?" She looked at him, bewildered by his ignorance. "At that moment, when he finds his daughter's petals, he completely realizes what's important."

Ted, at first, was quiet. "Is it obvious to you?" he asked.

She furrowed her freckled brow at him, confused.

"So - while you're throwing around the questions, why don't you answer one of mine? Why did you leave D.C.?" Penelope asked.

She already knew the answer from Wendy, but she wanted to hear it from his own mouth. She wanted to hear what was so awful that caused him to not only leave Washington, D.C. in a mad dash, but as far as she knew, resulted in him never going back. Note even for a visit.

"You know," he commented, "next time we'll go to *my* favorite place."

"Ted," Penelope reacted. He was steering away from her inquiry.

"No, really," he turned his face away from hers. He seemed to look at a cluster of trees in the far-off distance. Although Penelope couldn't really tell since his bangs still hung over his eyes like pulled-down window shades that were stubborn, never willing to unravel. "You know where my favorite place is?"

"Ted."

"No. Of course you don't. Because I never told you," he said. "47th and Broadway."

"What? 47th and Broadway?"

"Yeah. The Times Square area." He lifted his hand to the sky. "Those bright billboards looking over Duffy Square. The bursts of light. All that energy," he said. "Sure. Maybe it's not the most important technology, maybe it's not the most intricate, but it's beautiful. It's technology at its best." He paused. "Just think. It all used to be billboards that were flat images - and then they used bulbs. And now it's all digital. Spectacular." He looked at her. "When I feel low and just need to think. That's where I go ... And then somehow, it all doesn't seem so bad."

Penelope immediately felt guilty. No, he hadn't answered her question, but he had shown her a piece – a sliver – of himself, as indicated by the expression on his face – his easy smile and the warm flush of his cheeks. She could see a sudden, childlike innocence and bliss emanating from Ted Hollis as he appeared to gaze into a splendid nothing.

"I couldn't stand when some of my girl friends came home for the holidays," she blurted out to Ted's surprise and to her own. "I couldn't leave Elmont for various reasons, and year after year, when they were in college in places far away from town, they'd come back all different. With more experiences. Knowing more than I did." She sighed, looking away from him, towards the water. "Some went to schools in California, some went to schools in Wisconsin, others went to college in the Northeast. It was great for them. But me. I wound up going to Elmont College."

"An esteemed institution," he said with a kind smile, trying to make light of the subject.

She laughed a little. "Yeah. Well. Then after college, they went to big cities –mostly to Chicago, some to Los Angeles, and when they'd come back for Christmas or Thanksgiving, I'd notice how sophisticated they were. They had their big jobs with whatever law or accounting firm, big and bright diamond engagement rings from their successful lawyer or stockbroker fiancés, and wore designer clothing by designers I never heard of." She shook her head. "And all I kept thinking was how I wanted to be like them. How I wanted to be the posh woman, the woman everybody looked up to and said 'Wow. She made it.' It was so depressing. Eventually I just prayed to God all the time that someday he should send me somewhere. Somewhere I could start anew. Somewhere away from Elmont."

Ted put his hand on her shoulder. "And one day your prayer was answered."

Penelope showed half a smile. "Yes. But I didn't want it the way it happened."

A quiet purveyed the atmosphere until - "I left D.C. because of my ex-girlfriend," Ted breathed out of nowhere. "Or should I say ex-fiancé."

Taken aback by his sudden confession, she asked, "What happened?"

"I found her with someone else," he replied, his tone serious. "In my apartment. On my bed. On my sheets … On that damn duvet cover I got on clearance at Bed, Bath and Beyond … Cheap."

A gentle wind wove through his hair, lifting his bangs just a bit. Penelope searched for Ted's eyes, but still nothing. They remained hidden.

"Ted," she said, trying to figure out words of consolation.

"But that's all right," he remarked, his voice lifting. "I moved to New York City, I'm working on my own - and I don't have a boss to answer to."

Penelope realized he was holding back his emotions. For his sake, she went along with his phony demeanor. "What about Spock?"

Ted grinned. "Yeah. Spock can be a real pain in the ass boss. I'm afraid of that laser gun he has." Laughing, he said, "Hey, you know that sometimes when I get up in the morning, Spock freaks me out. I'm half asleep, groggy, and for a minute, I take him for a person who's holding me up at gunpoint." He added, "Sometimes I shove him in my closet before I go to sleep at night. That way when I wake up he's not there."

"Good to know," she commented, her eyes revolving in their sockets as if to say *do I really need to know about this?*

"Oh, I forgot," he said, "I got you something," and he reached into his backpack.

"You did?"

"Yeah. A Post-Valentine's Day gift."

"But I didn't get you anything!"

"No worries. I didn't actually buy it … Well not in its entirety … I made it for you with some parts," he said, rummaging through his belongings.

"Still …"

Ted pulled out a small, long box that looked like it came from a jewelry store. *He's giving me jewelry? Wait …but Luke hasn't even gotten to that yet!*

"Ted!" she exclaimed as he passed it to her. She opened the box. It was a watch. But not a typical watch. And it definitely wasn't jewelry made to be shown off." "What's this?" It was clunky and yellowish-green and definitely digital.

"What does it look like? It's a watch. But it isn't just any watch. It's a GPS watch. I looked for one for you in the stores, but right now they only make a GPS watch for runners, which only tracks running paths. So I decided to make a GPS watch for you myself." He asked, "Do you know what GPS stands for?

Penelope held the watch up, letting it dangle in midair. She scrutinized it with a wary eye. "Um. I've heard about it, but I don't know what it is."

"It stands for 'global positioning system.' It's a technology that lets you map anywhere you want to go and gives you directions." He took the watch from her hand and flipped it over so she could see what he was doing. One press of a button on the side of the watch and a map showed up on its face. "See?" She squinted at it. The image was small but she could make it out.

Ted pressed another button and print appeared on the watch. "These are directions," he said. "You just keep pressing on this button here and it will tell you every step that you need to take to get to your destination." He tapped its face. "I put in directions to where I live, just in case you forget."

"How can I forget?" she questioned him. "We practically see each other two or three times a week."

He went on. "AND I put an extra feature in here that a lot of the PDAs and GPS systems have nowadays," he said. "A GPS tracker. If a person allows it, you can track them on the device." He outlined the map with the tip of his fingernail. "Just follow the red blip that'll show up on the map ... For example ..." He pushed more buttons. "Just for today, I linked this watch to my BlackBerry, so you could follow me on the map. Just to show you."

He gave her the watch back. She smirked, thinking it was definitely interesting and would definitely be of use to her when she needed to find her way to department stores and restaurants, but it was too ugly to actually wear. Especially with a Gucci clutch (she had decided to take Wendy's advice concerning the transformation of the cosmetic bag).

"Now, watch the blip on the map," he ordered.

"Okay," Penelope said, looking at the blip that miraculously appeared on the watch.

Ted moved about ten steps away from her and the blip moved as well, although fractions of centimeters. "Wow!" Penelope exclaimed. "Cool! It works!"

"Now watch," he told her and strolled even farther away, enough for Penelope to have to call out to him– "Yep! Works great! The dot keeps on moving!" She crinkled her brow as she examined the map. "Hey!" she yelled, still looking down at the face of the watch. "There's something wrong! It won't stop moving! ... Hey!" Penelope lifted her sights from her new tech toy and found Ted many yards away from her, continuing to walk ahead in the opposite direction of their bench.

As he went on, he turned around to her, grinning wildly.

"Hey!" he cried out. "Now watch me go home! It's friggin' freezing out here!"

***

PRESS RELEASE

FOR IMMEDIATE RELEASE

Contact:

Ted Hollis, President
Hollis@aol.com
Penelope McAdams, Media Representative
pmcadams@yahoo.com

Renowned Computer Engineer Ted Hollis
Opens Consulting Firm

New York, NY – February 25, 2008 – Computer and bio engineer Ted Hollis has just announced the opening of his new computer consulting firm "The Hollis Group," which will provide top-notch problem solving services concerning computer programs and databases for companies and organizations. The Group will be focusing on a variety of issues that are both common and unique to personal computers, supercomputers, and all other modern systems.

Engineer Ted Hollis specializes in computer engineering, having worked with digital circuit designs, algorithms, software, database systems, embedded systems, and programming fundamentals. Additionally, he is a bioengineer, and has a background in biocatalysts, biomaterials, and biomechanics. Hollis previously worked at the Peabody Firm (Washington, D.C.), where he concentrated on creating a DNA microarray chip that would identify genetic predispositions for disease and reactions to specific environmental toxins, centering his research on Diabetes, Type I, and heart disease. He graduated from the Massachusetts Institute of Technology with a Bachelor's and Master's degree in Electrical Engineering and Computer Science and a second Master's degree in Biological Engineering. Hollis was the recipient of many scholarships and grants that would include the Coca-Cola Scholarship, The Jack Kent Cooke Foundation Graduate Scholarship, the Public Service Fellowship, and The Peter J. Eloranta Fellowship.

Hollis commented, "I'm applying the entirety of my computer engineering background to work with clients from varying companies and institutions, and I'm very glad to be on my own, so I can apply my expertise to differing and challenging subjects." He continued, "As for my background in biotechnology, in the future, I still may continue my research in improving and devising technology, such as with the microarray chips, to find treatments and cures for a variety of diseases, including diabetes and heart disease, and thus improving people's quality of life."

About The Hollis Group

The Hollis Group, a computer consulting firm based in New York, NY, provides a wide range of computer operations and systems management services for major corporations, small-businesses, and non-profits.

***

Ted's mouth dropped as if he lost a screw in his jaw. "I can't believe you put this all together," he said.

Penelope sat on his sofa, licking the honey and salt off her fingers. "Do you like it?" she asked with a sly smile, impressed with herself and her PR prowess.

"I don't know yet," he answered, continuing to peruse the totality of his career and education on paper.

Penelope frowned and Ted took notice of her reaction. "No. I didn't mean it that way. The writing is great. I like the quotes. I am thinking about working on some biotech projects in the future," he said. "And the information is correct." He paused. "Except for the release saying that I'm opening my firm now."

"What's wrong with that?"

"I started it three years ago."

"Did you send out an official announcement when you started it three years ago?"

"No."

"Then consider it a belated announcement," she said, stacking some empty packets of honey in a McNugget's box. "Anyway, *technically* you are opening up a new business. Before you were 'Ted Hollis Consulting.'" Penelope stuck her tongue out and off to the side with her eyes practically rolling back in her head. "Blech!"she commented. "And now you're 'The Hollis Group.'"

"Yeah, and how did that happen? Where's my group?"

Penelope pointed to herself and grinned.

He laughed. "Wonderful. Are you on my payroll?"

"Can I be?" she joked.

He went back to scrutinizing the release. "See, Penelope, it's just that I'm still not sure if I want to be out there. For all the world to see."

"Ted," she said, "It's not like I wrote that you're performing in some strip show." Although, she mused, that might make the press release more interesting. "So what are you so embarrassed about?"

"I'm not embarrassed," he replied, frowning. "It's just that after the breakup I sort of went incognito. Underground."

"You can say that again," she commented, looking around at his dark dungeon apartment.

"What happens if she hears about me? What happens if *they* hear about me?"

Penelope understood that *they* meant his ex-fiancé – the wretch – and the man she had an affair with. "So what? Who cares? They were the bastards!" she announced and then stopped, wondering if "bastards" was a curse; since she was so zealous with her statement, she forgot. *No*, she thought, browsing through her private, mental list of curses, *no it isn't.*

He laughed. "Well, if you put it that way," he said, "I don't see a problem with you putting it out," and he dropped the press release in front of her, aside the empty McDonald's boxes; there wasn't a crumb left over.

"Great!" she exclaimed, scooping it up. "You won't regret this!"

"I hope not."

Ted approached his computer. "Now to fix your GPS tracking system."

Penelope's eyes veered over to her handbag; she had thrown the GPS watch into it, next to a blush compact and a Tic Tacs container. "Why? What's wrong with it?"

"Nothing," he replied, his eyes centering on the computer screen and his fingers moving across the keyboard at hyper speed. "I just need to take myself off of it."

"Why?"

"Listen, silly. I don't want you to know where I am every single minute of the day."

"Ooooh," Penelope sounded. "And you don't want to be found."

"That's right."

She snapped her fingers as if to say *I got it,* and looked over at him, taking note that the picture of the laughing woman and boy had been moved to his desk, right next to the computer and pencil holder.

Quickly, Ted became agitated. He shook his head at the computer, saying, "Damn. Damn this computer. It's been having so many problems, lately. Even I don't think I can fix it. Maybe it's time to get another one." He crossed his arms on his chest and leaned back. "Forget it," he said and then slowly turned to her. Penelope was quiet as she flipped through his book on insects and mythology in movie making that was lying on his coffee table. "So," he started, "whatcha doing for the rest of the day?"

Penelope sighed, thinking of Luke and his millionth (it seemed like the right number) trip to Boston. "Nothing. Why?"

"Well then you can spend it with me," he leapt out of his chair. "We can go to a museum or two, the Museum of Modern Art has an interesting photography exhibit going on." She smiled. "And I know you have an inkling about that from your Grandfather."

"Just a little. But it sounds like a plan to me."

"And then we can ride the subways and I can tell you about the history of the L train," he uttered, heading towards the back of his apartment.

"Again?"

"What? Don't you like the L?"

"Sure. I like all the letters of the alphabet."

"Cheeky," he chuckled and disappeared into his bedroom. "I'll just need to put another sweatshirt on. It's freezing out there! ... Layering," he said, "layering is key."

Penelope walked over to his closet to get her coat. Upon opening the closet door, she found her parka where she originally left it, in between a musty baseball jacket bearing a Washington Nationals emblem on it and a holey, faded green sweater (the moths must have had a field day, she thought), and then she looked up and noticed the same film canisters she saw the first day she came into his apartment.

Penelope looked around. Ted wasn't anywhere in the vicinity.

She got on her tippy-toes and grabbed onto the top shelf to get a better look and gasped; there were piles and piles of canisters hidden behind the ones he had upfront. All had tape wound around them, and from what she could see, there was at least one other thing they had in common – the name "Hannah" was written on all of the tape on the canisters – one had "Hannah and me at Patriots Game," on it and another had "Hannah and me at Dee's wedding" as a label, and so on and so forth.

Unexpectedly, the shelf shook under her, and Penelope was afraid that she and the shelf might tumble down. As a last ditch effort to know more about Ted Hollis – before an accident would happen – Penelope quickly grabbed one of the film canisters for future scrutiny and dropped to the soles of her feet, leaving the shelf in place.

"Oh my!" she suddenly yelled out as something actually did fall on her. "Oh my!" she again hollered as she looked into this something's face, scuffling to push it away, only to realize she was fighting for her freedom with the cardboard figure of Mr. Spock, who was pointing his laser gun directly at her and the canister she was holding.

"What's going on in there?" Ted questioned from his bedroom.

"Oh, nothing!"

She pushed Spock's nose, hurling him back into the closet. *He doesn't know who he's dealing with!* she said to herself, and then her eyes traveled down to the tape on the canister. Penelope read "Hannah and me at the park." *Wait, this was the first canister I saw when I came in here. It's fate*, she concluded.

"You belong to me," she said to the canister and then reached for her parka and put it on.

"What?" Ted asked, entering the room, looking warm and toasty in at least three sweatshirts. He pulled some straggly hairs over his forehead and hence his eyes.

She swiftly slipped the canister into the pocket of her coat and thought fast. "I said you belong in an insane asylum for keeping a life size version of Mr. Spock in your apartment," she remarked and pointed to her pointy-eared perpetrator. "He attacked me."

Ted collected his coat from the sofa and went over to her and the closet. He eyed Mr. Spock and his laser gun. "Looks like he was trying to arrest you," he seriously commented. "What did you do?"

Penelope took in a deep breath and went white in the face.

He laughed, "Just kidding," lightly hitting her elbow with the back of his hand. "Come on!"

Ted went to leave and Penelope was right behind him, her fingers in her coat pocket, rolling the canister against her palm.

Uncle Billy: Nobody ever changes here. You know that.

Nineteen

Cory (Mobile)

March 14, 2008 9:26:11 AM

Give a big kiss to Mom for me. And don't forget my present!
Kudos on taking my suggestion (seriously) concerning a traveling
companion … Good luck.

***

The Elmont snow crunched under Penelope's Gucci luggage as she
dragged it along the short path to her parent's house.

She stopped at their bright red door. *My God*, she thought.

"My God!" cried Stacey as she pushed her Jackie-O glasses down the
bridge of her nose. She peered over the rims at the surrounding acres

of vacant land and the neighboring house, miles away in the distance. "I've never seen so much … so much … air."

"A problem?" Penelope inquired, turning to her and letting go of her luggage at the doorstep.

"No. My ancestors were Irish and Filipino, remember? They were used to it. It's in my blood."

Penelope nodded and wondered why the Irish and Filipino's would have more air than other ethnicities, and how her parents were going to respond to Stacey and her crazy comments that were probably more insane in Elmont than they were in Manhattan. *Whatever*, she thought to herself. *This should be interesting – at least it'll take some of the focus off of me.*

Penelope knocked on the door, and Stacey took in 'a big whiff of Elmont oxygen. "I'm positively euphoric!" she claimed.

In a pinch, the door flung open, and Penelope's mother stepped out wearing a huge smile on her freckled face. "Penelope!" she yelled. She quickly wiped her hands in her apron, moved the red flyaway hairs from her eyes, and gave Penelope a crushing bear hug, more worthy of a massive, muscular wrestler than a diminutive, small-boned mother.

Penelope pried her arms as much as she could from her mother's hold, so she could hug her back.

"Oh! I've missed you!" her mother exclaimed, still not letting go of her beloved daughter.

"I've missed you, too, Mom."

"It's been too many months, Penelope. You mustn't do this again! Staying away this long!"

Penelope sighed in the crook of her mother's neck. "Yes, Mom." She knew her mother didn't mean to give her a guilt trip, being as guileless as she was, but it felt like she aimed a shot of shame at her just the same.

A booming voice came through the entrance – "Penelope! My Sunshine!" her father shouted, his enormous, six-foot-four frame approaching her in overalls splattered with motor oil.

"Happy Birthday, Dad!" she cried out.

Penelope's mother finally released her into the open and yearning arms of her father, and although his embrace was mighty, she found it funny that her mother's hug was equal to her father's in strength. She attributed this to the longing her mother must have felt for her presence.

After some seconds passed by, her father pulled her away from his chest, and looked into her eyes, his own blue ones sparkling as he examined his little "Sugar Pop," as he sometimes called her (a term of endearment he picked up when he caught his once five-year-old Penelope in their kitchen with her entire head stuck in a "Sugar Pops" cereal box, wearing it like a combined hat and mask, searching for a prize – a plastic, blue ring embedded with a plastic "diamonette," as they phrased it, that she never did find). "Did you get the prize, Penelope?" he joked with her in a loving and corny way. "Have you found it in the streets of New York?

"Come on, Dad," she laughed.

All at once, he whispered in her ear, "I'll tell you the truth. Your brother took it. He gave it to his girl." Her father grinned, his face gleaming in the sun.

Penelope thought back to when she was five and her brother was ten. She finally remembered. "Jennifer Tyler?" *That wretch.*

He nudged her. "You think he's going to give a ring to that city girl we haven't met yet?"

"Sonia?" she said. Penelope knew that Cory had every intention of marrying her since they had discussed it a couple of times, and it was obvious he was out-of-his-mind in love with the woman, but she was also aware they were taking their time ("We're not in any rush," he would say), and this was something her parents wouldn't and didn't understand. She was about to enter dangerous terrain. "I think … uh …they're thinking it over," she told them and then pulled a safety move – "You should ask him. He doesn't really tell me anything about his personal life."

Her mother suddenly cleared her throat with a loud "Ahem," looking over in Stacey's direction.

Penelope turned away from her father. "Oh, where are my manners?"

Her mother grimaced. "I've been wondering about that for quite some time," she commented.

Penelope tried not to absorb her mother's jibe and gestured to the exotic bystander who looked on at them, smiling and misty-eyed. "Everyone. This is Stacey. She's a very good friend of Cory's and uh - a good friend of mine," she said, making the formal introductions even though she had informed them that she was bringing Stacey along for her visit, providing them with the particulars of Stacey's relationships with both of their offspring.

"Mom!" Stacey yelled and hugged Penelope's mother. "Pop!" she turned to Penelope's father and enveloped him with her skinny arms. Both parents had expressions of utter surprise as if they had been hit by a bolt of strange, otherworld, Manhattan lightening.

"It's great to be home!" Stacey proclaimed, stretching her squishy-sounding galoshes over the threshold into the quaint and unsuspecting house.

Penelope's parents stood dumbfounded at the doorstep, and then they both shot confused looks at their daughter.

"It's the air," Penelope said.

They proceeded to go into the house, her father at the end of the line, sniffing at the atmosphere.

***

Penelope sucked up her last morsel of birthday cake. "Great cake, Mom."

"Yes," Stacey chimed in with agreement, sweeping a napkin at a chocolate stain in the corner of her mouth, "absolutely scrumptious, Mrs. McAdams." Penelope looked at her approvingly from across the kitchen table after sneering at her throughout the afternoon and kicking her legs under the table at dinner when she called her parent's "Mom" and "Pop." Penelope was glad that Stacey finally got the hint and in turn, that her parents appeared to have more of a comfort level with their weekend border.

"Anne, you certainly outdid yourself," Mr. McAdams said, smiling at her in gratitude. He turned to Stacey and elbowed her in a congenial manner. "Do they have cake like that in New York City? Do they?"

Penelope held her breath, hoping Stacey wouldn't say something wrong or improper.

"No. I can't say that they do. It's completely delectable," Stacey replied with enthusiasm, nodding. Penelope's lungs were quick to deflate, as if they were two balloons popped by a newly sharpened pin.

"Oh. Thanks," her mother said above her own dish of cake crumbs, "but compliments aren't necessary. I just love to bake, especially for my family."

Stacey perused her face and then commented, "I think that compliments are always necessary. I mean – how would you know if you were good at something if it weren't for compliments?"

Mrs. McAdams returned Stacey's gaze, only hers was one of perplexity.

"You know, she's won hundreds of blue ribbons at the state fair for her baking!" Penelope's father exclaimed.

"Really?"

Penelope's mother blushed around and in between her freckles. "Well, I wouldn't say hundreds. But I've had my fair share."

Mr. McAdams continued, "She's won blue ribbons for her cakes and apple turnovers, but it's her pies that have really won most of them." He turned to his wife. "I swear Dorothy has it in for you this year. The summer fair isn't for months, and we haven't seen her since the beginning of winter. Not even for church." He waved a finger over the table. "She must be busy concocting a new pie recipe."

Penelope's head spun away from them. She was trying to hide her mirth and smirk. *Isn't this always the way it is in Elmont*, she mused. *People talking about baking as if it was like the act of creating a breakthrough vaccine.*

"Well, she doesn't have to be a heathen about it," her mother responded in an expected way, being an avid churchgoer since as long as Penelope could remember.

Not wanting her mother to ask about her own attendance at church, which was pretty much nil (she did go to services on Christmas and Easter with Cory and Sonia, but that was basically forced by her brother — *If you don't go, I'll tell Mom that you never go,* he threatened), she hid more of herself, now from just her mother's view.

Stacey had been quiet while she listened in on the exchange, and then she interceded — "Did Norman Rockwell live here?" she asked, her eyes wide with innocence. "Because when we were cabbing it through town, I thought I recognized buildings and houses that I saw in some of his paintings. And this convo we're having-about the baking contests and church-Rockwell loved that shit."

Penelope's mother raised her eyebrows at the mention of the word "shit."

Her father looked at his wife and cleared his throat, and Penelope stared into his eyes and shook her head. They both knew the situation couldn't be good.

Surprisingly, Mrs. McAdams kept her cool, seemingly brushing the expletive off to the side. "Stacey," she uttered, "I'm curious. We've been with you for a couple of hours now-don't you want to take those gloves off?"

"Oh no," Stacey replied, "I hardly ever take these gloves off. Except for when I blow dry my hair." She pinched at the bottom of one of her plastic gloves. "Flammable, y'know." Stacey suddenly put her hands over her mouth. "Oh, that's right. I didn't tell you what I do."

"Well, I would say that's our fault," Mr. McAdams suggested. "We were so busy catching up with Pen."

Stacey held her hands up. "I'm a hand *and* foot model. These gloves and galoshes have Vaseline in them. It keeps the hands and feet soft and young looking."

Penelope's mother looked authentically interested, which didn't surprise Penelope since she knew her mother to always be a good listener; she was always around to help and solve problems. "Did they tell you to do that?" her mother asked.

Appearing confused, Stacey responded, "They who?"

"Your managers, I guess."

"Oh. You mean my agent," Stacey shed some illumination on the conversation. "Yes. She told me to do it. And it's completely fine when you get used to it. It's just that people kind of look at you a little strangely."

Which is what Penelope's mother did for a moment.

"But people giving me strange looks doesn't bother me. It's when people don't give me strange looks that I start to wonder."

Mr. McAdam's let out a great guffaw. "You don't have to worry about that with us. Anyone who comes from New York or any big city looks strange to us."

Stacey laid a plastic glove on her bosom. "I'm from New York, yes, but my ancestors are from Ireland and the Philippines."

"Ohhh," Penelope's father reacted, "isn't that interesting?"

Penelope rolled her eyes and her mother just stared.

"Yes. I'm actually only first generation American on my Filipino side and second generation on my Irish side."

"That *is* interesting," her father again claimed.

Her mother politely interceded, "Excuse me, but is there a lot of work in that? Hand and foot modeling?"

Stacey's face lit up. "Sure!" she exclaimed. "In fact, I have some big news." She turned to Penelope. "I guess I was so tired on the plane I forgot to tell you."

Tired? Penelope said to herself. "Tired" was putting it mildly. Stacey slept and snored during the entire plane ride, which hadn't made her the best traveling companion in Penelope's eyes. Especially when she snored like a power saw that's engine was used for the launching of a space shuttle. All the passengers around them noticed Stacey's noises; five times Penelope was tapped on the shoulder by the people behind her to quiet her friend down, and seven times she was thrown dirty looks from the people in front of her. But no matter how forcefully Penelope nudged Stacey, she wouldn't rouse from her slumber or snoring or at least turn over to her side, which might've resulted in the ceasing of the nasal annoyances.

"Tired?" Penelope said to her, being sardonic. "No kidding?"

Stacey went on – "Well, the big news is that I've been tired because," and she stopped mid-sentence, seemingly trying to add to the suspense of her announcement, "I've been rehearsing for my new job as a stand in for Lorna Lufton for the movie version of Manhattan Nights!"

"Ahhhh!" Penelope screeched, and she stood up and so did Stacey, and they reached over to each other, grabbed each other's arms, and jumped up and down. "Congratulations! That's wonderful!" Penelope's parents looked on at the pair as though they both belonged in an insane asylum. "Why didn't you at least tell me in the cab?"

"Oh, I wasn't myself," Stacey said. "I was looking forward to getting some sleep on that plane ride, but I hardly got a wink."

Penelope squinted but let the statement go by - she recalled what Stacey had promised her before. "Do you remember what you promised me? That you'd get me on the set?"

Stacey smiled. "Oh, I think I can find a way to work that out. They're all so nice. The directors, the stagehands, the actors."

"Actors!" Penelope leapt and grabbed onto Stacey's hand. "Did you meet Lorna Lufton yet?"

"Yes, twice now, in passing. And she's so sweet! It's so surprising since she played such a bitch role!"

At the word "bitch," Penelope's mother, again, raised her eyebrow.

Penelope yelled out, "Oh, I can't wait!"

"Manhattan Nights," Mr. McAdams pondered aloud. "Isn't that the show you used to watch religiously every Tuesday night with the hoity-toity women - the fashion designer, the journalist and uh - the..."

"Plastic surgeon," Penelope's mother said, finishing his sentence.

"That's right- the plastic surgeon?" he continued.

"Yes, Dad," Penelope answered, a glint in her irises.

"Well ... doesn't that Lorna Lufton woman have hands and feet of her own that she can show?"

Stacey stepped up to the plate. "Yes, but they're not as pretty as mine. Thank God," she said, and she took a large galoshed step toward him and flapped out her hand.

"I never really did get into that show," Mr. McAdam's informed. "But I did get into 'It's a Wonderful Life' that Pen absolutely loves!"

"What's 'It's a Wonderful Life?'" Stacey questioned. "Oh wait. Isn't that a new show on HBO where the Amish parents are raising an entire family of transvestites?"

"Uh. No," Penelope's mother answered and then turned to her

husband. "'It's a Wonderful Life' is a movie, Simon, not a show."

"Oh, yeah. That's right."

Penelope's eyes widened. "Stacey, you never saw 'It's a Wonderful Life?' Why you're just as bad as Ted."

Her mother's ears pricked up. "Who's Ted?"

Stacey, still overcome with the glory of her new job, excitedly asked, "Isn't that the gay guy who's teaching you to knit?"

"No, no," Penelope replied, "he's not gay, and he's not teaching me to knit." *Uh oh,* Penelope thought, *I forgot to tell Sonia.*

Her mother put her hands up, a signal for everyone to stop. "Wait a minute! Wait a minute!" she cried out. "I thought there was a Luke!"

"There is a Luke, Mom ... I'm dating Luke. Ted is just a friend."

Her mother looked at her, suspicious.

"That's the guy that you can't see his eyes, because there's all that hair covering them, right?" Stacey chimed in.

"Still, hair over a boy's eyes is no reason not to date him," Penelope's mother commented.

"That's not it. I'm not dating him because he's a *friend.* Nothing more. Luke's the one for me. He's gorgeous, successful..."

Her mother inquired, "Is he the one who got you that luggage?"

"Yes. He's the one who got me the Gucci luggage. Why?"

"Very fancy."

"And what's wrong with fancy?"

"Nothing. As long as that's not all that your relationship is about."

"When did a set of luggage ever represent a relationship, Mom?" she scoffed, and her mother stared at her.

"As long as you love him."

"Love? I'm crazy about him ...We've only been seeing each other for about two and a half months now...Love? Probably soon."

"And Ted?" her father asked.

"I told you-Ted is just a friend." Penelope raised her voice. "Look! We're getting way ahead of ourselves with this conversation!" She took in a deep breath, trying to compose herself, and gestured over to Stacey. "And we have company. We shouldn't be going on like this. Have things changed so much in this town that we should be SO impolite?"

Stacey shrugged. "I don't mind," she said to them. "I'm used to angst. My ancestors were big on struggle."

"Would you stop with that already, Stacey." Penelope thought of an idea. "Hey, why don't we open Dad's presents? It is his birthday, right?"

Her father clapped his hands and rubbed them together. "I'm all for that!"

"Great," Penelope said, glad to escape the conversation, and she reached over to the kitchen counter, where a pile of wrapped presents were set. She grabbed a medium-sized box. "Here's one," she announced, and passed it into her father's eager hands.

"Wait," Stacey suddenly interrupted, eying the window that faced the side of their house. "Who's that?" They all turned towards the window, and Penelope immediately recognized the sweeping, shoulder-length blonde hair attached to the tall and immensely handsome and broad shouldered figure in blue jeans and a hunters jacket that was standing with a flashlight aimed at a tree – a tree that was thought to be one of the oldest in the town.

"That's Darvin Svendsen," Penelope's father said. "Used to be good friends with Cory. They graduated in the same class," he told her. "He's checking out our tree. It might be diseased. It might have to come down."

Penelope let out a resounding *Ohhhh*. "Dad, does it have to come down?" she asked. "I always loved that tree." She looked over at Stacey, whose eyes still hadn't left the window, and said, "Cory and I hung a tire on that tree, and we used to swing on it in the summer and spring." Stacey didn't pay much attention to Penelope, remaining fixated on what, or rather who, was outside of the house.

Stacey inquired, "So he's a tree doctor?"

"No," Penelope's mother answered. "Not exactly. He's a gardener. Like his father. But he's also a plumber and a carpenter."

"He's in business with his father," Mr. McAdams added. "He's like a Jack-of-all-Trades."

"Jack-of-all-Trades? What's that?" Stacey asked.

"They're people who fix things at your home. They're always around if you need something done."

Stacey turned back to the table. "We have that in New York. They're called 'Supers.' Except they're never around."

Penelope grew impatient. "Can we get on with this?" she whined.

"Penelope Abigail McAdams," her mother chastised her (she always knew she was in trouble when her middle name popped up), "what's gotten into you?"

Stacey silently mouthed, "Abigail?" to Penelope from across the table in a mocking sort of way.

"I'm -," Penelope blurted out, catching herself before she said, "I'm sorry." *I'm done with sorry,* she said to herself. *I've been done with it for more than a year now.* There was no need for her to turn her back on her commitment to being less of a "wimp," she thought, just because she was back in Elmont. "I'm just tired, Mom. That's all."

Penelope's mother grimaced, and her father rubbed his hands together for the second time that evening. "Well. I think I'll open my present. Who's it from?" He greedily went for the card that was taped to the wrapping paper.

Stacey peered out the window and quietly mumbled, "Darvin Svendsen."

"Nope," Mr. McAdams said, reading the inside of the card, "it's from Cory...and Sonia," and he smiled as he flipped it over, perusing the cover.

Like an eager child at his first birthday gathering, he ripped away the wrapping paper and bow, and tore open the box, a shine in his eyes. "Oh," he said, the glint in his irises somewhat fading. "It's a shirt and tie." He held up a solid white, button down shirt in one hand for all to see, and a bright blue tie in the other.

Although it was apparent he was forcing a smile, everyone exclaimed *Ohhhhhh* in unison.

"That's very nice, Simon," his wife commented. "He got you something like that last year, remember? You wore it to all the teachers conventions."

"Yeah, Dad," Penelope interceded. "You told him that you loved it."

That the shirt and tie were a hit at the conventions. Remember?"

"Oh yeah," her father said, examining the tie. "They *were* a hit." The sparkle went back into his eyes. "They'll be jealous again this year!" He glanced at the back of the tie. "What's this horse doing on here?"

"It's Polo, Dad. The shirt and tie are made by Ralph Lauren. The brand is Polo."

"Oh," he responded, laying both the shirt and tie neatly in their box. "Yeah. I think I saw this in Sears."

Stacey coughed for a couple of seconds.

"Are you all right?" Mrs. McAdams hand crossed over the table and touched Stacey's arm.

"I think I was choking," Stacey replied. "But I'm fine now."

Penelope noticed that Stacey didn't have anything left over on her dish to choke on.

"No, Dad," Penelope said to him. "I don't think they sell it at Sears. It's one of the top brands. I think he got it at Macy's."

"Oh, well," her father commented as he closed the box, not appearing overcome with gratitude as he looked on at its cover. "I'll call him later to thank him." He put it aside.

Penelope's mother gave him another present. He read its card. "Oh. This is from Stacey," he said, his sights scouring around the table, ultimately landing on their visitor who kept having trouble focusing on the activities at the table when there was so much commotion going on near their tree. Her father pointed to her. "And you're Stacey, I think," he joked, chuckling aloud.

"Happy Birthday, Mr. McAdams," Stacey said.

He opened her gift and pulled out a blue sweatshirt that had big, white lettering that said "NEW YORK" and underneath it a red apple that had a big chunk bitten out of it."

"See," Stacey said to him, pointing to the apple, "New York is called the 'Big Apple,' and when you come to visit there's a saying – 'Take a bite out of the Big Apple.'"

His face stretched open with surprise and delight. "Hey," he said, "I like this. This'll be fantastic for the Health and Nutrition class I teach!" and quickly threw it on over his overalls.

"Wonderful!" Stacey exclaimed, "And a perfect fit!"

Sure, Penelope said to herself, *that he likes*.

"Next!" he sounded.

Penelope grabbed her present from the pile. It was in a small, blue box that had a pristine, white bow tied around it. "Here, Dad. This is mine," she said as she handed it over.

Her father provided a huge smile as he patted the apple on his sweatshirt and began to open her present. "I like the box," he noted.

When he lifted the cover, he stared into the box for a couple of seconds, looking as though he was trying to mentally register what he was seeing. "Oh."

Penelope eagerly asked, "Do you like them, Dad?"

"What is it, Simon?" his wife asked.

"It's cufflinks," he answered, his lips slightly upturned.

Penelope leaned forward, towards her father. "And they're just not any cufflinks, Dad. They're *Tiffany* cuff links. And they're sterling silver."

"They're beautiful, Penelope," her father remarked, passing the box to his wife so she could take a gander.

"They're lovely," her mother said. "They must have cost you a pretty penny."

Penelope rolled her eyes and laughed. "But yeah, I have *some* money, and what's the purpose of having money if you can't use it to buy presents for your loved ones?"

Her mother gave the box back to her father. He continued to examine the cufflinks with curiosity, as if he was looking at an unexpected lab result in one of his seventh-grade biology classes.

"Aren't you saving the money from Grandpa Ben?" her mother asked.

Becoming quickly agitated, Penelope said, "I am, Mom. At least I'm trying. New York is tough. There's a lot of expenses. And I've bought all this new technology-"

"Technology?" he mother quickly said. "What are you talking about?"

"It's not easy to explain," she replied. "I'll tell you about it in due time. If it ever comes to anything." Penelope turned to her father. "And talking about technology, Dad, if you don't like the presents that Cory and I got you, we can get you something else. We were actually thinking about getting you a cell phone."

He looked at her as if she was from another planet. "A cell phone?"

"Yes. We know that you don't have one. I was going to buy the phone and Cory was going to pay for the contract and monthly bills."

Gathering his children's presents to his breast, her father announced, "I love your gifts! And I don't need a cell phone!"

"But think about it, Dad. You can call anyone from anywhere with a cell phone."

Her father dropped the presents on the table. "I know what a cell phone is. We're not that far into the sticks, y'know."

Penelope realized she hurt his feelings. "I'm-" she was about to say, "I'm sorry," but stopped short of it. She re-thought her sentence – "I'm just thinking that you might want to give Mom a call from wherever you are."

"There are only so many places to go here, Penelope," he said.

She mumbled under her breath, "I know that."

"And everyone knows each other in town. If I need help, they know who your mother is and they have her number and we have phone booths all over if I need them."

Stacey stopped looking out the window. "You have phone booths?" she asked. "I forgot what one looked like."

Penelope's father went on – "And if I'm at home," and he stared directly at his wife and said, "Hi, Anne," and waved – "She's right there ... And if I'm in another room ..." He then proceeded to get up from the seat, moving to the adjacent room, and called out, "Hi, Anne!"

She replied, "Hi, Simon."

He stepped into the kitchen and said, "See. I don't need a cell phone. There's always yelling," and then he turned to his audience, "Polite yelling."

"Of course," Stacey said.

Penelope began to sulk. "I...I just want you to be happy on your Birthday, Dad."

He walked over to her. "I am happy, Pen. I love the presents. And I'm sorry if I hurt your feelings. I just don't want you or your brother to think you have to impress us, that's all. And we don't need much. All we need is you. Seeing you is enough of a birthday present for me."

He leaned over to Penelope and kissed her on the top of her head. Stacey's eyes watered at the scene, and Penelope tried to force a smile. *He doesn't like my present*, she thought.

"Here," he said, and he wound the tie around his neck and placed the cuff links on the wrists of his white-button down shirt that was under Stacey's Big Apple gift.

Penelope examined her father, who was standing in front of his audience wearing a New York City Sweatshirt over his overalls that had a large, half-eaten apple on it; his blue tie was lying atop of the apple's stem, and the sterling silver Tiffany cuff links were practically hanging from the sleeves.

Penelope shut her eyes for a moment, thinking he looked ridiculous.

"I'm very happy with *all* my gifts!" he announced to the three women. "And now I'm going to work on my car in all my gifts!" He was about to turn away when he looked down at the cuff links. "Tiffany's? Is that like Polo?"

"Sort of," Penelope replied.

"So you can't get the cuff links at Sears."

Stacey coughed again.

"No, Dad, you can't."

Her father shrugged and started to walk away from them to the garage. "Glad to have you home, Sugar Pop."

Stacey quietly mouthed to Penelope – "Sugar Pop?" and Penelope's mother got up from the table.

"Anyone want some more cake?" she asked. "Stacey?"

"No thanks, Mrs. McAdams," she responded, rubbing her stomach with a plastic glove. "I'm stuffed," and then she glanced out the window for the millionth time. "I'd actually like to go outside. Get some fresh Elmont air … See what Darvin Svendsen is doing." She paused. "Darvin Svendsen … What kind of name is that?"

"It's Norwegian," Penelope's mother answered.

For a moment, Stacey looked up at the ceiling as if she was thinking real hard. "Norwegian," she commented, putting her napkin down on the table, "that's a good breed," and she got up and walked out to join her Nordic infatuation.

When Stacey left, there was quiet in the room for a couple of moments until Penelope broke the silence, looking up at her mother, who was leaning against the kitchen entrance, cleaning her hands in her apron. "I don't know what to say about Stacey. I know her comments and behavior can be much."

Her mother shook her head. "Stacey doesn't bother me. She's from wherever she's from and she's polite the way she learned to be polite. It's a different way and I understand," she explained. "But it's you that I'm confounded about."

"Mom, do I really have to hear this now?"

"Penelope, I certainly don't mean to be someone who nags."

Penelope threw her arms up. "Well, it certainly seems to be that way," she complained. "And you never were that way before, and all of a sudden there's this yelling in the house. If I'm being impolite in any way it's because I'm not used to all this arguing. What happened to small town politeness and discretion?"

Her mother glared at her. "What are you talking about? We've always had spats here and there. There have always been times when we've yelled. Just like in every other family and just like in any other town. I just think for some reason you've chosen to believe otherwise." She paused and then said, "I don't know. Maybe you wanted to see this place so to the extreme, so you could have another reason to want to break out of here."

Sighing with her eyeballs spinning round, Penelope reacted with — "Oh, come on, Mom. I don't think so."

Penelope's mother sat back down at the table and rested her chin in her hand. She stared at her daughter. "You know, I love you. And I know that you're a grown woman and that you can make up your own mind about how you want to live your own life, but I'd like for you to remember what's important."

Penelope's freckled nose scrunched up. "What? You want me to remember to say that I'm sorry or remember to call you more or buy gifts for Dad at Sears?"

"Admittingly, some of that would be nice, yes. But that's not what I'm talking about. I'm talking about values, I'm talking about identity, I'm talking about character."

"Character?" Her daughter winced. "Character is nothing, Mom. It's worth nothing outside of Elmont."

Her mother looked directly into her eyes. "Penelope, it's worth everything everywhere. I don't care where you're from – Elmont, New York, the Fiji islands," she said, "and if you don't think it's more valuable than the clothes on your back or ... or ... the type of luggage you carry," and she pointed towards the hallway where Penelope left her Gucci luggage, "then you have a serious problem."

A quiet fell over the table, and then Penelope's voice wavered, "I just want to be like my friends. The ones that all those years I saw coming into town from all those great places, who moved forward in their lives while I stayed behind and ..." She was about to say what she actually felt but stopped.

"And?" her mother asked, her expression suddenly filled with compassion. "And? ... You can finish the sentence, Penelope. It's all right."

"No. It's fine."

"Y'know, it's all right to feel anger. Even when it's about someone we love."

"I don't want to talk about it, Mom," she said, her eyes lowering to her lap. "Not when everything is going so well."

"Okay," he mother acquiesced, leaning back in her chair. "But someday you'll find out that what you did was the most worthwhile." She nodded. "What you did, Penelope, was worth a hundred times more than what your friends accumulated during those years. No - thousands more."

Penelope felt a tear well up in the corner of an eye as her sights remained locked on her lap.

"Y'know," Penelope said, "I think I need some air, also. I think I'll join Stacey outside," and then she looked up at her mother. "Unless you need me to help you with the dishes.

Her mother smiled at her, pleasantly. "No. That's all right. You go outside." She jerked her head to the window. "Anyway, I have a feeling Darvin probably needs your help. I don't think he's used to the likes of Stacey."

Is anyone? Penelope mused.

Penelope strolled over to the closet in the hallway, pulled out her parka and put it on, and just at that moment, her father stormed in, still wearing his New York Apple sweatshirt, polo tie, and Tiffany cuff - links. "Need to go into town for a small wrench. The old one isn't holding up well," he said to her as he reached into the closet for his coat. "Want to come with me? I'm sure there'll be some people real happy to see you, Sugar Pop."

"No, that's okay, Dad. I'm just going to step outside for a sec. Talk to Darvin." Without a thought, Penelope casually put her hands in her pockets. "Oh," she said to him, feeling Ted's film canister in one of them and then pulling it out, showing it to her father. "I keep forgetting to develop this film." This was true, she thought. She had been so busy with work and Luke and then learning about technology that she completely forgot to bring it into a drugstore to finally see what was on the roll. "Can you drop it off in town at Mr. Whitmore's to be developed?"

"Sure," he replied, taking it from her hand. "I've got to drop off some of my own, anyways." He read the tape on the canister. "Hannah and Me ... Hannah? A friend of yours?"

"No," she replied. "Not Hannah, anyway."

***

The following morning, strolling through the center of town, Stacey waved her plastic gloved hand around to people as if she was the crowned snow queen at a Christmas parade, greeting her admirers as she passed by on her float.

"Hello!" she yelled out to Mr. Caruthers, Elmont's finest fireman, who was across the street, her hand swaying in the air. "How's it going?" she hollered and fanned her hand towards Miss Fenway, a buttoned-up schoolmarm since the days before the dinosaurs walked the earth or possibly the commencing of the Big Bang.

Being that it was Elmont, everyone gladly and hospitably waved back. Some with a hardy manner, others more demure (depending on genders – except for Mrs. Daily, whose gender, upon appearances, would've been questionable if it wasn't for the fact that she was married to the town's mortician). "Hi there!" Stacey cried out to Mrs. Daily, batting her dark eyelashes.

Stacey turned to Penelope. "Who's the strange looking guy with the unibrow?"

"That's Mrs. Daily."

Stacey shuddered.

As they made way to the grocers with a list of ingredients for the dinner Penelope's mother was planning to prepare, Stacey struck up a conversation that wasn't altogether unexpected – "Do you know that Darvin rides a toboggan?"

"Uh-huh," Penelope answered, looking at her through the corner of her eye, not sure if she really wanted to discuss Darvin Svendsen on a Saturday morning.

"Isn't that cool?"

"Cool? Stacey, do you even know what a toboggan is?"

"I think so."

"It's a sled. Kind of like the ones they use in the Olympics for bobsledding."

"Oh … Really? I thought it was like some kind of sweet bike. Like the Nordic or Swedish version of a Harley."

"No."

Stacey paused and then said, "Toboggan … Darvin … Darvin rides a toboggan … Darvin rides a toboggan." She suddenly laughed aloud. "I think I have a sudden case of assonance."

Penelope thought – *that's another way of putting it.*

Truth be told, Penelope was a little irate with Stacey, and not because she was being staunch and uppity, which was her usual self, or that she was being smart-mouthed like she had always been. On the contrary, he was practically the opposite of who Penelope had known her to be. She was practically the anti-Stacey: pleasant, optimistic, and seemingly elated. And this is what made Penelope itch with annoyance and made her want to swat Stacey away to the other end of the street.

"What's gotten into you?" Stacey asked, obviously noticing her friend's bad mood.

Penelope sneered. "A lot." She wasn't about to mention how Stacey was driving her crazy, and she didn't want to get into all the issues she had with Elmont or with Luke and him not contacting her as of yet, so she chose to vent about her job. "I've got a situation going on at work that I've been thinking about."

"Like what?"

"Like there's an opportunity for a promotion, and I want it, and I don't know if I'll get it, and I shouldn't even care, because I should just concentrate on keeping the position I have now."

"Why what's wrong?"

"Henshaw Tractors is what's wrong. I'm starting to get press placements, but my boss wants me to get a celebrity to endorse the tractors. He's even asked me to write letters to celebrity couples asking for their representation. So far it hasn't been working. He hasn't liked any of my letters."

"Who are you writing letters to?" Stacey inquired as she waved at the town's firehouse, more firemen, and the Dalmatian firehouse dog.

"Brangelina and TomKat."

Stacey put her hand down and snickered. "Penelope, it wouldn't even matter if he liked your letters and you sent them out," she remarked, "because where would you send them to? You couldn't send them to their agents. They'd be hysterical laughing, and they'd throw them out with the rest of the solicitation letters they get. And you couldn't send the letters to Brangelina and TomKat directly, because at any given time does anyone know where they actually are? Angelina Jolie and Brad Pitt practically skip around countries like they were playing hopscotch, picking up kids as they go. And Tom Cruise and Katie Holmes are either in Los Angeles, New York, or uh, Italy, or whatever fancy city they could probably think of going to. Or they're in the

Scientology Temple where they're plotting to take over the universe."

"So what you're saying is no matter what I do, I'm basically, um-"

"Screwed," Stacey inserted. "You're basically screwed."

Penelope thought that she would never use that certain word, but that it probably fit her job situation perfectly. "That's right," she said, and then she glanced at Stacey and noticed she wasn't even walking – she was actually *skipping* through the snow as they were about to go by a statue of Rupert Keller, the man who founded Elmont in the late 1600s; he was holding a large boulder that represented the first stone that was cast to build the town square. "So," Penelope started, "you asked what's gotten into me, so I have to ask - what's gotten into you?"

Stacey waved to Rupert, and Penelope quickly looked over at the statue, almost expecting it to do a return salutation.

"I don't know," Stacey gushed, "it's just wonderful here. The openness, the people. It's so...so...Little House on the Prairie." She swiveled round to Penelope. "Except without the horse and buggies."

"Well," Penelope started, "they only got rid of them recently to make way for automobiles. You should have been here last year." She shoved her hands in her coat pockets. "Y'know, it's amazing to me. You come here and you've become all sweet and relaxed, but my parents have become more irritable and loud. It's as if you cast some strange, magical reverse spell."

Stacey flapped her hand in the air as if to say *stop it*. "Oh, you're really being hard on your parents. Everyone's parents get out of hand from time to time. And your parents - well, they're absolutely great."

"Still."

"Okay. You got me. I spread some Irish-Filipino magic around."

"Stacey, please," Penelope said, sighing. "Why do you talk about being Irish-Filipino all the time anyway? What's so great about it?"

"What's so great about it? It's my identity, and I'm proud of it."

Penelope found her answer oddly pleasant. "That's kind of nice."

"And," Stacey added, "if I came from Elmont, I would be proud of that identity, as well."

Penelope was swift to react – "No you wouldn't."

"Yes, I would," she reiterated, vehement in her statement. "This is like a dream world. It's like being at the dentist and getting sweet air. Only without the dental work, and you get sweet air twenty-four hours, around the clock."

"I think that would do something to your brain cells," Penelope noted, thinking that was one of the reasons she skipped town.

"And why did you leave here?" Stacey asked. "Especially with Darvin Svendsen, the town hottie, in residence." Stacey let out a *whewww* and slid her hand across her forehead like it was a scorching hundred degrees instead of the thirty-five they were shivering in. "That's some kind of man," she panted. "If it'd been me, I would've stayed in Elmont and married him."

"And become the wife of Jack-of-all-Trades?" Penelope inquired as they approached the grocery store.

"Most definitely. I'd throw off these gloves and galoshes and become Jill-of-all-Trades."

Penelope chuckled. "That I'd like to see."

"Don't laugh," Stacey said, plowing a galosh through a mound of snow, "my ancestors were handy. The Irish built rowing boats. And the Filipinos they … they … uh …"

"Rowed in them?" Penelope teased.

"No. I don't know. But they built something."

Penelope pulled open the door to the grocers and asked, "So are you going to ride on the toboggan?"

"Are you kidding me?" Stacey breathed. "I'll do anything to wrap my arms around that alpha body."

"Penelope!" a familiar voice suddenly cried out.

"Hi, Mr. Smith. How are you?" She turned to a bald, older man with glasses behind a register, who she knew to be the brother-in-law of the store's owner and a lower ranking member of the Elks' Elmont, Illinois chapter ("He sits there like a lump," her father would say after an Elks meeting, his furry hat tilting awkwardly to the side. "How can we move a lump up? Half the time we don't even know he's there."). He was wearing a grocer's apron, a red and white striped shirt, and a button displaying a picture of his Calico cat. "How's business?"

"Oh, fine … fine," he beamed. "Holidays were peachy, and we had the best turkeys in all of Illinois. Roy, over at Swenson's farm, got them fresh for us. Meaty and fresh."

Stacey looked sideways at him.

"Oh," Penelope said, "Mr. Smith, this is my friend Stacey from New York."

"Hi yah!" He waved to her and Stacey waved back, having more practice in the gesture that morning than she probably accumulated in all the prior days of her life.

Mr. Smith returned to Penelope. "So, how is the big city?"

"It's wonderful."

"I bet," he said. "Boy we miss you here, Pen. Why, it was just yesterday we saw you ride your first tricycle across the street near the Ice Cream Shoppe."

"Yeah," she said, "I know."

Penelope heard a sniffle from Stacey.

Stacey poked a plastic glove in her eyeball, swabbing away a tear.

"Well, what'll it be ladies?"

"My mother's making her famous stew and Eskimo pies tonight."

Mr. Smith was taken aback. "Ohhh … Eskimo pies….She's going exotic."

"Yeah, well. So she gave us a list of items that she needs."

"Sure," he said, smiling, more than glad to help. "Why don't you give me the list, and I'll get em' for you."

"Great," Penelope responded, and then she nudged Stacey who had the list in her handbag.

"What?" Stacey inquired, wrinkling her forehead at Penelope.

"Give him the grocery list."

"Why?"

"Like he said. He'll get the items for us."

Stacey's eyes grew large. *He will?*

"Yes."

"Everything?"

"Yes."

"You're kidding."

"No."

Stacey shook her head in disbelief and then pulled out the grocery list from her handbag. She handed it to Mr. Smith, and he went on his way. "This place just gets better and better. I can't believe how helpful people are here," Stacey commented. "I swear. If I had lived here, I would've never needed therapy."

Penelope sighed. She had heard enough from Stacey about how wonderful Elmont was and immediately switched her sights to a wall door in the grocers that she recognized. She pointed to it. "That door. It's one of the entrances to the Elmont Museum." She remembered they created the door just in case people wanted to examine Elmont's artifacts while waiting for their items to be pulled or their meat to be sliced.

It had been a while since Penelope ventured into the museum. But she definitely knew what was there.

"You want to go in?" Penelope asked Stacey.

"I don't think so. I think I'd like to go outside. See what the rest of the block looks like – if you don't mind."

Penelope was thrilled to pieces with the idea of their separation for any amount of time. "No," she reacted, trying to keep her bubbling enthusiasm to herself. "I don't mind. But if you need me, I'll be in there for a little while."

They parted ways, one going out the door to the torrid streets of Elmont, and the other, through the door of the tiny museum that boasted the jar from America's "Count the Jellybeans" contest of 1901.

The story of the "Count the Jellybeans" contest: the son of the mayor of Elmont travelled to an adjacent town where the competition was taking place, provided his own estimation of the number of jelly beans in the jar, estimated correctly, and returned home with five-hundred dollars in his pocket (a lot in those days), and the jar of jellybeans, which Elmont proudly displayed in their new museum. In 1950, after some people, including visitors from the adjacent town, claimed they witnessed the jellybeans moving by themselves, the then Elmont health inspector pronounced the exhibit unsanitary and threatened to close the museum unless the jellybeans were removed from the jar.

Penelope went past the famed, empty jar; the head of the largest moose shot in Elmont captivity; the busts of Elmont's city council for two-centuries; and the piece of cloth that, according to legend, Annie Oakley wiped her brow with when she corralled through town.

Eventually, Penleope ended up at the exhibit she knew well. She read the sign – BENJAMIN TAYLOR: A PHOTOGRAPHER'S LIFE – and opened her eyes wide to take in the two walls of her grandfather's landscape photographs.

Suddenly her BlackBerry went off – *Buffalo gals can't you come out tonight - can't you come out tonight - can't you come out tonight - Buffalo gals can't you come out-"*

"Hello?" Penelope answered.

"Hey, Pen?" her brother said through the receiver.

Penelope put her hand to her hip, focusing her eyes on a photo of the Rocky Mountains at daybreak and then the Sahara desert scattered with nomads pulling their belongings behind them. "Cory?" she sounded, annoyance woven throughout her vocal chords. "Is that you? I can't believe you did this to me."

"What?"

"Leaving me alone with Mom and Dad."

"You're not alone. You're with Stacey," he commented, a chuckle partially spurting out from his end of the line.

"That's another thing. Stacey is unbelievable."

"Tell me about it," he said. "What? She's complaining, right?"

"No. She's completely pleasant. It's downright … downright sickening."

"Stacey? Not complaining? *Pleasant?*"

"She loves it here."

"Really?" He paused. "Maybe you should leave her there."

"And you know what? She's got a thing for Darvin?"

"*Darvin? Darvin Svendsen?*" her brother cried into her ear. "The guy who used to shove straw wrappers into his nostrils to see how many he could fit into his nose."

"Oh, that was in first grade, Cory," she said, getting closer to a photograph of a mob of elephants crossing a plane in Africa.

"That was our senior year in high school," he informed. "The guy's nice enough, but he basically grunted his way through school. What could she possibly see in him?"

"I don't know. Perfectly chiseled features, gigantic, strong shoulders, hair that I'd like to have," she replied. "If you think about it, he looks like he jumped off the cover of a romance novel."

"I don't want to think about it."

Penelope quickly looked around. "Cory, I gotta go. I'm in the Elmont Museum, and you know how they get if they catch you talking too much in here."

"Yeah. They'll throw you out, and then they won't let you go in again," he commented. "And you wouldn't want that to happen. Especially since the MOMA and MET don't even come close to the treasures in the Elmont Museum ... Do they still have the jar?"

"Yep."

"Is it still empty?"

"Yep."

"Look, I only have one question. Dad called me last night and left a message to thank me for my gift, and he said that he loved it, but did he really? I mean – I thought he would like it. He liked it last year."

She shrugged. "I think he thought that they were *okay*," she said. "He kept asking me if he could get our gifts at Sears."

"Sears?" her brother copied, sounding floored. "*Sears?*"

"I think both Mom and Dad think we're getting too fancy."

Cory laughed but in a snide way. "Forget it!" he yelled into the phone. "Sears makes them happy-okay! I'll do one better! For their next birthdays and Christmases, I'll go the Salvation Army for their presents! Yeah! That's what I'll do!"

Penelope shook her head and whispered, "Cory. Calm down. There's no need to go crazy about it."

"Pen, I have to hang up now," he said, and she heard a little boy's laughter through her BlackBerry. "Jake's climbing me like a jungle gym."

Click.

Moments later, Penelope perused a photograph her grandfather took of Central Park. *I forgot about this picture,* she said to herself as she analyzed the scenic detail; one particular was glaring: in the center of the image was the Conservatory Water. *Maybe that's why I like that pond so much,* she thought, never having made the connection before.

"Hey, Penelope," Stacey greeted her, her cheeks rosy from the cold and her eyes glowing with newfound, Elmont happiness. "I think our groceries are ready." Stacey's mouth opened wide as if she was suddenly in awe. "I can't believe it. Did you know that the Ice Cream Shoppe makes ice cream from scratch? From scratch, Penelope? Did you know that?" Of course she did. "And I'm not talking about the ingredients being sent from a factory or something. I'm talking about beans and spices from farms and gardens, and *actual* cream from-from-from," Stacey began to stutter from the excitement, "from actual cows – milk then the cream – Y'know?"

"Yes, Stacey. I know. Remember. I lived here most of my life."

"Yeah, but the guy at the Ice Cream Shoppe told me that everything here is natural. No preservatives, all organic, all local! I can't believe it!" Stacey shook her head. It seemed the notion of nature prevailing somewhere had been beyond the scope of her imagination. "Relaxed and friendly people, fresh, clean air, all-natural food-I just can't believe more people don't live here."

"Why? You think that people would want to move here because they'd be healthier?"

"No. I just can't believe people actually die here. " She continued, "I swear to God, if we didn't pass by the Elmont Cemetery, I wouldn't believe it."

Just at that moment, Penelope laid her eyes on a photograph she hadn't seen on the museum walls before. Her face grew sullen. It was a picture of her at about five or six-years-old with her grandfather under a tree at Elmont Park. She was sitting on his lap and his arms were around her. They were both laughing. Penelope's face dropped as she peered into her grandfather's eyes, so full of life. "Well. It does. Death does stop here."

Buffalo gals can't you come out tonight - can't you come out tonight - can't you come out tonight - Buffalo gals can't you come out tonight ..."

"Oh," she complained aloud, "what now?"

She looked down at her BlackBerry. "It's a text," she said.

"From Luke?"

"No."

It was from someone else ...

Ted (Mobile)

March 15, 2008 11:23:03 AM

Hi Penelope! Hope you're having a great time with your folks! Wish your dad a happy birthday for me!
Text me when you get back.

Knowing she hadn't received any voice mail since she arrived in Elmont, Penelope searched through her text messages. Not one was from Luke.

***

It was Sunday evening in Elmont. The next morning she and Stacey would be leaving on a jet plane, heading back to New York, and for Penelope it couldn't come soon enough. As far as she was concerned, the weekend visit went by at a pace such as that of a snail on valium. She had spent two and half days listening to her father go on about the engine he was fixing on an old, red Ford clunker from the sixties, his battle with agitated amoebas during a lab lesson, and his insights on the last baseball season for the Peoria Chiefs, a minor league team from Peoria, Illinois, and his hopes for Elmont to one day soon have their own squad of players ("The Elks and I are getting a petition together," he informed her. "And the Elmont Elks isn't such a bad name...is it?"). She had spent two and half days watching her mother cook, clean the dishes, put them away, sew, and clip coupons, and then cook, clean the dishes, put them away, and then sew and clip coupons (Penelope frequently thought of shampoo directions – wash and repeat, wash and repeat), and then she spent two and half days with her ears filled with funk that had Darvin Svendsen's name all over it, compliments of Stacey who had a crush that had flattened her into a can cover, and two and half days of constantly feeling whooshes of air in her face from Stacey's sighs about how wonderful Elmont was.

Penelope had had it. Although she was happy to spend time with her parents, who she loved with all her heart, her patience had worn thin, and she realized that the togetherness she experienced with them during her past life in Elmont, was just that, a past life. She wouldn't be able to do it now, she thought, she had moved ahead, and she wanted to continue to do so, except that she felt that she may have reached a sudden impasse – there had been no text messages or voice mail from Luke the entire weekend. She was so desperate for his communications that she admitted to Stacey that even a pigeon carrying a message from Luke in its beak would do.

"Then *you* call or text him," Stacey said that Sunday morning. "Why not? You want to be a Manhattan woman? A Manhattan woman is aggressive. She would call."

Penelope shook her head. She wanted to hear from Luke, but she didn't want to be vulnerable with him. The thought of reaching out to Luke first, and showing him that she might be bothered by the absence of his calls or texts, made her feel stark naked. She envisioned her emotions being painfully painted on her breasts and belly, more than apparent for taunting. Would he taunt her? Would he have control over the relationship? Would she take the chance?

"It's *just* a phone or text message," Stacey said.

So it was that Sunday evening in Elmont when Stacey lightly sobbed into Mrs. McAdam's pink, polka-dotted handkerchief and said, "Oh my God," as Penelope looked on at her. They were sitting on the living room couch watching the colorized beta-video of "It's a Wonderful Life." Stacey cracked in the end. "Oh my God," Stacey sniffled into a circle. "I can't believe I never saw this."

"See what you've been missing," Penelope said.

"Yeah, but I never knew," Stacey uttered, pointing a gloved finger at the television screen. "He thought he'd be better off somewhere else. But he was wrong. He really had a wonderful life."

"Well, now you understand the title."

"Yes, and when he realizes it, when he realizes how good he's had it and what life would've been like if he never existed, I like how he runs through the town and wishes everyone a Merry Christmas, even that old movie house!" Stacey moved the handkerchief away from her rosy-red nose. "And even that horrible Mr. Potter! He even wished his arch-enemy, the one who he and everyone else in the town despised, a Merry Christmas!" She threw her arms up, pretending she was George Bailey at Mr. Potter's window – "'Merry Christmas, Mr. Potter! Merry Christmas!' … He was so filled with joy that he forgot his animosity!" She shook her head. "Unbelievable!"

"Uh-yeah," Penelope said, "I never really thought of that part that much."

"Really?" she questioned her. "What's your favorite part?"

Penelope immediately thought of Ted. She had answered this question before. "Zuzu's petals. When he finds them in his pocket after Clarence the angel brings him back to real life. It's just real…."

"Poignant."

"Yeah. I guess so."

Penelope's father suddenly walked in on them. "Oh. Watching 'It's a Wonderful Life' I see," he smiled and then looked at Stacey. "What did you think?"

"Incredible," she replied, rubbing her nose with the speckled cloth and then pulling it away. "And simply heartwarming." She blew her nose.

"Wow," Mr. McAdams commented, "Penelope didn't tell me you were so sentimental."

I didn't know, she thought.

Stacey glanced at her watch. "Oh, I better get to bed. We have an early flight tomorrow," she said. "I definitely need to get some sleep. I can never get it on airplanes."

Penelope went cross-eyed.

Bidding them goodnight, Stacey walked out of the room and up the stairs.

Penelope's father reached into his pocket. "Here, Penelope. I almost forgot," he said as he handed her an envelope and the film canister she had swiped from Ted's closet. "I have to apologize, though. It got mixed in with my film from the town's Christmas party, and I asked for slides. You know how I like to use Grandpa Ben's old Kodak carousel projector. So they made your film into slides, too. Not photos."

"Okay," Penelope reacted, staring at the envelope. "I don't have a projector at home. Can I use yours?"

"Of course? You have to ask?" He walked out of the living room for a second and came back with the projector, which was basically a wheel with slits for slides with a lens attached to it, and a wrapped-up tripod that was a makeshift film screen; he unraveled the screen and placed the projector on the coffee table. "Do you remember how to work it?"

Penelope smiled to herself. It was the one piece of technology, albeit archaic technology, that no one had to show her how to use. Since she was old enough to understand what photos were, which was by the time she was four, her Grandfather pulled out the carousal and went through its mechanisms, slipping Penelope's tiny digits in the projector's slots, showing her where the slides went, and then tenderly grasping onto her index finger, helping her push the button to move the selection of slides forward and in reverse. "Yes. I remember," she answered.

"Good. See you tomorrow morning, Sunshine," her father said and kissed her on the forehead before he left.

"Okay," Penelope murmured as she inhaled deeply and opened the envelope containing the slides, "let's see what we've got," and she dragged the frames out and placed them in the slots of the carousel one by one.

Penelope turned on the projector.

At first, she saw an attractive woman – her grinning head with crinkly eyes lying on the grass. Her honey-blonde hair askew on green, dewy blades.

Okaaay.

Penelope moved onto the next slide. It was the same woman, except now she was on a swing and her locks were flying in a breeze, the sunlight striking the top of her hair, creating a halo effect. She was laughing. Penelope's eyes shifted to the woman's hand that was holding onto the chain link of the swing. She leaned forward and stared at a finger adorned with a diamond engagement ring. It had also caught some sunlight and sparkled on the screen.

Penelope blinked a couple of times. *Alrighhht. This is Hannah. This was the fiancé.* She glared at the woman's happy face. *Horrible woman. Horrible woman to do that to Ted. To break his heart.*

She shook her head at the picture.

And then, she clicked forward to another slide and her mouth dropped open.

It was Ted. It was Ted with his head tilted sideways as if he was trying to do a funny pose in the picture. And it was Ted smiling...with his hair cut short....his bangs cut short. And Penelope could see tiny particulars about him. Like a little scar right above his eyebrow...And she could finally see his eyes.

His wondrous, spectacular, heavenly, big green eyes.

And Penelope fell back in the couch, awestruck; the entirety of Ted's parts – his smile, his hair, the cleft in his chin, and his brilliant, emerald eyes – resulted in the summation of man who was exceptionally handsome. *Exceptionally.*

"What the ...?" she asked aloud in disbelief, fixated on the screen.

Penelope went onto the next frame. It was a picture of Ted holding Hannah. Penelope frowned and her body tensed, and she clicked the button hard to go to the next slide and then stopped and intently examined a photo of Ted in a regular, casual pose, peering through the camera lens; it was as if he was looking straight at her. The corners of his mouth were turned up and his green eyes, alluring and hypnotic, were wide open. Inviting.

So this is what Ted was hiding?

Why?

And from that moment on, Penelope knew what she had to do.

> *George Bailey: Well, hello.*
> *Mary: Hello. You look at me as if you don't know me.*
> *George Bailey: Well, I don't.*
> *Mary: You passed me on the street almost everyday.*

Twenty

Ted (Mobile)

March 21, 2008 10:12:16 AM

Hey Penelope - so great that you keep suggesting (and so diligently) that I should get a makeover for any photo ops that may come my way after your stellar press release and PR prowess generated so much interest (The Washington Times, The Associated Press, and the New York Sun – Wow!)
No one's asked me for a photo or to take a picture of me yet, but I'll consider your advice.
See you soon.

Ted (Mobile)

March 21, 2008 8:01:02 PM

Hi Pen – Interesting news and there's possibly an adventure in it for you…and I may even get that makeover.
Are you curious?

***

"Penelope?" Luke called out as he approached her in the lobby of the Music Box Theatre, his brow furrowed. "What are you doing out here? The second act is about to start."

"I'm just checking my messages. Henshaw Tractors has been on my case about a press interview they want," she fibbed.

He was quiet for a moment, and then asked, "Are you still angry about me not calling you last weekend?"

"No," she answered, even though she was.

"Upset about me not texting?"

"No."

"Because you know it wasn't on purpose," he explained. "I'm having problems with some of my clients."

"Like the one in Boston."

"Yes, and I just got tied up."

"Uh-huh," she said, staring at the BlackBerry and Ted's message – *What did he mean interesting news? Adventure? He might agree to the makeover?* – trying not to take any notice of Luke.

"Look," Luke started, "if you want, I'll buy you that Gucci bag you had your eye on in the catalog," and he pointed to the Gucci cosmetic bag she held under her arm that she magically turned into a clutch.

"No. This is fine," she reacted, the muscles in her forearms tightly squeezing the cosmetic bag-clutch.

"Maybe send a belated birthday gift to your dad? A fruit basket maybe?"

"No, Luke," she glanced up at him and his regal face and stern jaw. "I told you. I'm not upset."

"And we're still going to Hawaii, right?"

"I don't see why not. My vacation time has been approved. Why would you think we weren't going? Because of last weekend?" she asked, shrugging as if she didn't care but she did.

He was quiet and then replied, "I don't know…You've been acting funny since you got back.

"Funny?"

"Kind of distant."

"Really? I guess my mind has been on other things." Penelope decided to cover up her emotions and to forget about Ted and Ted's eyes and his intriguing text message for a millisecond, pushing a smile out to Luke. "It's nothing to worry about."

He slowly nodded, but his expression was one of concern. "Okay," he uttered and then kissed her soft on the lips. "I'm going back in. Don't take too long. You don't want to miss too much," he said, and walked away and through the theater doors.

Penelope couldn't wait for the next text from Ted. "Hello?" she said into her BlackBerry after dialing with fervor.

Ted laughed. "Boy, that didn't take long," he joked. "I'm glad to see that you're becoming quick and nimble with your technology. Not dropping your BlackBerry or anything when you rushed to call."

"How do you know I haven't?" she teased back.

"Ha!" he let out. "I installed a little camera in it."

Penelope pulled the BlackBerry away from her ear and looked at it for a good half-minute.

"Penelope," Ted called out to her through the PDA. "Penelope, I was just kidding."

She sighed and breathed into it – "So what is such a big deal that you had to send me such a cryptic message?"

"You really want to know?"

"Yes?"

"Really?"

"Ted. Stop it," she ordered, trying to put a halt to the volleying.

"An ex-professor of mine from MIT-one that I studied under for my internship and thesis-started an engineering firm a year ago, and he just happened to see the interview I did in the Washington Times."

"And?"

"Well, first he said that he didn't know what happened to me. That he thought I'd fallen off the face of the earth."

"Which you had."

"I'm in the Lower East Side."

"Same thing."

"Be that as it may, he wants me to interview for a job at his firm-a senior position!"

"In D.C.?" Penelope questioned, her face suddenly sinking.

"Yeah," he replied. "He said that if it was up to him that he would just hand me the position, but he's got a partner I have to talk to."

Penelope bit her lip. "Do you want to go back to D.C.?"

There was a pause. "I don't know exactly," he answered, and she could hear the hesitation in his voice. "I haven't been back to D.C. in three years." He paused again. "Maybe it's time to go."

"For good?"

"I don't know," he slowly answered, and then his tone brightened, "But the good news is that I get to go to the interview for free - they're paying for my plane ticket to D.C. and hotel room for the weekend – and they're paying for you, too!"

"Me?"

"Yep. I told them I have a *personal* publicist who handles all my press concerning my present and future opportunities, and that she always travels with me. I made it like you were my Hollywood agent or something."

Penelope finished off his explanation – "And they offered to pay for a ticket for me to go to D.C. with you? And for a hotel room?"

"Yep-can you believe it?"

"Penelope wasn't sure what to believe or maybe if she wanted to believe it – *Ted? Going back to D.C.?*

"Ted? Do you want me to go with you?"

"Of course. I pushed for it didn't I?"

Her eyes wandered across the ceiling. She sucked in some air. "But why?"

There was quiet for a second. "Well, Penelope. You're the reason why I have this great opportunity," he explained. "And besides, have you ever been to D.C.?"

"No."

"Then this'll be a great opportunity for you, too!" he exclaimed. "We'll go next Friday -hopefully you can take the day off - and we'll make a weekend of it! And you'll get to see The White House, The Washington Monument, the Mall, the Capitol Building, and-oh-perfect! They're right at the beginning of the Cherry Blossom Festival."

"Cherry Blossom Festival?"

"Yeah! It's beautiful! There are all these Cherry Trees in the Mall area that bloom this time of year. And the Cherry Blossoms are gorgeous around the Capitol Building." He enthusiastically continued, "And I heard they started to bloom real early this year - two weeks ago - so this is the perfect time to see them. They'll be in mid-bloom." He ended with – "It's spectacular!"

"Sounds like it," she commented, planting her index finger to her lips, pondering.

"It'll be fun," he said. "So? What do you say?"

Ding-Dong. Ding-Dong.

The theater bells chimed for the second act to begin.

Zuzu: Teacher says "every time a bell rings an angel gets his wings."

Twenty-one

The following Thursday evening, close to midnight, Penelope and Ted landed at Virginia's Dulles Airport.

The plane ride was short, lasting a little less than an hour and a half, and during that time Ted was so excruciatingly quiet that Penelope would have preferred the sound of nails scratching on a chalkboard to his silence. He had offered her the window seat, and she declined, preferring to sit in the middle since there wasn't a person next to her, so she could stretch herself out in the span of two chairs. After ten minutes in the air, Penelope wished she could renege on her decision; Ted had become a self-contained unit, steadily staring out of the window into the ebony atmosphere, not uttering a word or sound. This provided her with the unwelcome opportunity to reflect on her ultimate sin for the year so far, which was lying to Luke about the next few days' activities and who she was spending the days with. ("A PR convention in D.C.?" he repeated what she said. "With some of your coworkers? The boss' mandatory requirement? ... Have a good time.") Well, she rationalized, at least she told him she would be in D.C. There was at least a speck of the truth in what she told him.

After some time passed on the plane, Penelope tried to lure Ted out of his shell by talking with him about a variety of topics – Cory's teasing and concern; his girlfriend's unfailing optimism and love for her brother; her strained and strange, yet interesting, visit to Elmont with Stacey, in which she actually watched Stacey hop onto a toboggan with Darvin and screech in terror and pleasure as they slid down a snowy hill a million miles per hour; and how although her parents were a tad uproarious during their stay, remained the same people as they had always been. Through it all, she skillfully managed not to mention Luke – and why should she? Especially now, with the interview and all. And besides, she concluded it was probably already too late to say something about Luke. She and Ted had already been student and teacher for three months, and it all had gone swimmingly – why ruin it now?

While she talked and talked, listening for any vocal recognition from Ted, he just continued to sit like a rock in his seat, sometimes turning around to her, pleasantly smiling as if to say, "I'm not really interested in what you're saying, but I'll smile just to be polite about it." As they waited in front of the airport for a taxi, Ted was doing more of the same, except he was standing, and Penelope shut her mouth, banishing her words to a future scenario when he would be more interested in what she was saying to him. For now, she realized he was more involved in his own emotions. Returning to the D.C. area, a place he had lived in for most of his life, just like she had lived in Elmont for most of hers, appeared to be difficult for him.

When they got into a taxi, she decided that she didn't want the quiet to go on for too much longer. In the back seat, she delicately broached the subject of his mental status. "Ted? Are you all right?"

Ted swept a hand through his hair. "Yeah," he answered, not facing her, and then relayed to the taxi driver, "The Arlington Sheraton. Thanks."

"Are you sure?" Penelope questioned him again as the taxi drove off and away from the airport. "You just seemed really quiet on the plane."

"Oh, I'm just tired. And I'm a little nervous about the interview tomorrow morning.''

Penelope knew better.

"It's interesting to come back to a place you haven't been to in such a long while, isn't it?" She wanted to say "hard" instead of "interesting," but she wanted to throw a soft word at him, not wishing for him to sink further into his sullen mood. "I know how it was when I went back to Elmont after just six months. I can only imagine how it would've been after three years."

He peered out the window. "It's only a place, right?" he reacted like he was trying to get her to agree with him

A hush fell in the taxi, and then the only sounds Penelope heard were the vibrations of the cab's engine and the miscellaneous sounds from the outside – motors running, horns honking, and the multitude of noises from people's everyday living that tended to coagulate into one single hum.

Penelope watched as Ted lifted his finger to the window and began to slide it against the glass. *He's definitely deep in thought. Or*, she said to herself – *maybe something's caught his eye.*

Penelope leaned over a little and looked out his window, into the dark, straining to see what was holding his attention. All she saw was a shopping center.

Ted said, "My brother and I used to ride our bikes to this place." He pointed his finger at the shopping center. "When we were little." He pressed a button on the side of the door and the window went down.

This was the first instance of Penelope hearing about a brother. Ted had always been so private about his life, especially about anything having to do with D.C.

"You have a brother?" she inquired.

He turned to her. "Didn't I tell you?"

She shook her head. He went back to gazing out the window. "He's older. His name is Cal. Short for Calvin. He lives in Sacramento now with his wife and kids."

"Do you have any other brothers and sisters?"

"No. Just the one." He continued, "He's a pretty good guy."

"And your Dad?" Penelope inquired.

"He's in Florida."

"Oh," she sounded. "Everyone's at different ends of the world."

He nodded.

She wanted to ask about his mother, but her instincts told her not to, especially when she mentioned his mother one time when they were in her apartment, and he avoided the conversation altogether.

Penelope gazed at Ted, suddenly wanting to thrust herself towards him to push the hair away from his eyes. Let the real Ted come out. See what he fully was. See those transplendent green eyes. Then, all at once, Penelope quaked – maybe she hadn't looked at the photos correctly. Maybe she had a slight stigmatism the day she saw them and it threw her sight off, so she actually saw his eyes that way, or maybe the person who developed the film over or underexposed it. Maybe his eyes weren't actually green. Maybe they were brown – a dishwater brown. Although he wouldn't be unattractive with brown eyes, she thought, not at all. He would've still been handsome.

The taxi stopped at a traffic light, and Penelope absent-mindedly inched towards him, slow as can be, seeing if she could get a side-glimpse of his eyes through a narrow opening at his forehead, shaped by a collective of voluminous curls. Their elbows practically knocked together.

His head twisted round to hers. "What?" he asked with curiosity, seemingly sensing an invasion of his personal space.

She quickly jumped back to her side of the seat. "Nothing. I was just wondering what you were looking at…So you lived around here, huh?"

His head bobbed up and down. "Arlington," he said and then pointed out the window. "You see that house over there?"

Penelope squinted towards his window and saw a beautiful, two-story colonial with a front porch that was the length of the house, and a yard that was illuminated with floodlights and filled with flowered trees.

Her face brightened. "It's really pretty."

His face turned around to hers. "Yes, it is."

Penelope was immediate – "Do you know that house? Did you live in that house?"

"No. Neither. But that house is a lot like the one I grew up in. Most of the houses around here are like that. Real nice - old and romantic."

Romantic? Yes, that was one of the right words to describe it, no doubt, but Ted talk about romantic? No. No. He was the geeky guy. The MIT, anti-social guy. The guy who lived in a dungeon with the cardboard Mr. Spock guy. He wasn't the "romance" guy. The guy who saw beauty in a house or ... or ... Cherry Blossoms? She thought about it – *What happened to my non-threatening-techno-geek guy? What happened?*

She noticed his index finger again. The same one that had previously grazed the window, began to slowly trace the bottom of the glass, back and forth. Ted seemed to take no notice of what he was doing or where his finger was. She studied him as he gazed out at Arlington, probably pondering his past. She noticed a flush on his cheek and the curls of dark hair that fell on it, and the little cleft in his chin that she had found to be charming from the day she first met him, even though she had thought him to be a completely sorry sight.

Her eyes were drawn back to his finger that continued to linger against the bottom line of the window, and she suddenly imagined his finger slowly tracing the curve of her neck, and then caressing the outline of her lips, oh so tenderly. She stared up at his strong jaw, noticing a bit of a five o'clock shadow sprouting on his one a.m. face, and then she envisioned him taking all of his fingers from both of his strong hands and placing them on the sides of her cheeks, gently pulling her towards him. Penelope felt her spine tingle and that tingle generated a warmth that flowed up and throughout her head, and then, as she imagined him getting closer, ready to press his lips against hers, she trembled.

"Are you cold?" he asked her in real life, putting one of the hands she had just dreamt about on her knee.

Penelope thought she was going to jump out of her skin.

He turned to his open window. "Maybe I should close-" and before he had a chance to finish his sentence, the cab jerked with the force of the speed of light, making a complete stop, hoisting Penelope onto Ted.

"The Sheraton Arlington, Sir," the taxi driver announced as Penelope's heaving breasts pushed against Ted's chest. She looked up at him, her face having landed on the cleft of his chin. She stared at the cleft and the scruff around it. Her heart began to beat fast, and she immediately lifted herself off of his body.

Ted just sat there, in the same position as where he'd been thrown only moments beforehand, seemingly startled. "Sir?" the taxi driver repeated, "the Sheraton Arlington? We're here."

Ted paid the taxi driver and both he and Penelope and their small suitcases (she left the Gucci at home) got out of the cab. They walked into the hotel and immediately headed for the check-in desk, not saying a word to one another.

"Hi," Ted said to the desk attendant, who was a neat and young looking man with side-parted hair and a tie and a vest that matched the peach and mahogany colors of the hotel's lobby. "Hollis, please. Ted Hollis. We have reserved rooms."

"Sure, Sir," the attendant smiled as if he were an attendant at Disney's Magic Kingdom. "Welcome to the Sheraton Arlington." He punched some keys on his computer keyboard and then raised his eyes to Ted. "Yes. Ted Hollis. I see it here. Room 212."

"And?" Ted asked.

"And," the attendant copied, looking at him quizzically and then looking back at the screen. "You have it for two days."

"Wait. What about the other room? There's supposed to be another room reserved under my name."

The attendant tapped on his keys once more. He shook his head. "No. Sorry, sir. There's just the one room under your name. With a double bed."

Penelope's mouth dropped – were they going to share a room? She immediately thought of his finger and what it had provoked in her – *just* in the cab.

What would it provoke in her in a hotel room?

Ted pressed on. "Look. There's a firm that made the reservations – Finch and Stanford. Maybe it's under their name. Can you check?" Penelope noticed that Ted also appeared to be disquieted by the discovery, fidgeting in place.

The attendant played his keyboard like a piano and then replied, "No.

I'm sorry, Sir. Nothing."

Penelope jumped in – "Can we get an additional room now?"

"No, Maam," he responded. "I'm sorry. We're all booked up. This is a busy time of year, you know. People are in for the Cherry Blossom Festival." He provided a toothy grin. "Let me get you some papers to sign and your card keys."

"Thank you," Ted said and sighed as the attendant turned his back to them and Penelope's innards twisted in a knot. He looked over at her.

"Are you okay with this?"

"Sure," Penelope said, waving it off, but shaking in her shoes, but then she thought to herself – *Now, Penelope. Hold steady. This is Ted we're talking about. Ted your technology teacher. It's just Virginia. It's probably just the Virginia air. Like Stacey had become strangely intoxicated by the Elmont air, this is what Virginia air is doing to you, and it's ridiculous. And remember-you live in New York City now. And you have Luke. Gorgeous – and yes, sometimes inconsiderate – but successful Luke. He's everything you've ever wanted.* And then she heard herself yell in her own head – *So stop it, Girl! Don't ruin a great thing!* Penelope regained her senses. "I'll be fine. We're friends aren't we?"

"Yeah." He paused. "Friends."

The attendant returned with the papers. Ted signed them and was handed the card keys.

Ted shook the card keys in front of her. "But I insist you take the bed. I'll ask for a cot."

"Okay." Who was she to argue?

After he asked for a cot, they went up the elevator, and now they were both as silent as Ted had been in the plane and taxi, occasionally smiling at each other until they walked out of the elevator. Once in the hallway, they made idle, meaningless chatter until they entered their hotel room and put their luggage down.

A few words were passed between them about how nice the interior decoration of the hotel was and how comfortable the hotel room seemed.

Penelope glanced over at the bed and then quickly opened her suitcase, pulled out her pajamas, and sped into the bathroom. Only seconds later, she sprung out in her PJs, ready to jump into the bed and hide under the covers. But before she had a chance to leap in, Ted ordered, "Wait." He stared at her. "What's that?"

"What?" she responded innocently, standing in front of him.

"Those pajamas." Ted ginned from ear to ear.

Penelope was wearing her favorite boxer set pajamas that had little red hearts and cows scattered all over the top and shorts.

"What's wrong with them?" she asked, stationing her hands at her hips, defensive.

"Nothing. They're just funny. What's with the cows?"

She rolled her eyes and touched one of the hearts and then one of the cows. "It means I'm in the *moo* for love."

He laughed hysterically.

She waved a finger at him. "Don't pick on the cows, and don't pick on the pajamas! I love these pajamas! I've had them for years, and I'll probably be buried in them!"

"Whoa, whoa," he reacted, raising his arms up in surrender. "Okay, okay. I get it. It's just that they're ...uh...quirky."

"Quirky he says," Penelope huffed as she crawled into bed. "This coming from a man who lives with a cardboard cut-out of Mr. Spock." She pulled the blanket and quilt up and under her chin.

He smiled. "Fair enough," he remarked and then giggled like a preschooler.

Ted went into the bathroom and then came out minutes later wearing only striped pajama pants. "Sorry about wearing no shirt. I'm just hot."

Penelope tried not to look but then couldn't help herself. She peeked over her covers, and caught a glimpse of a tight, muscular bicep as Ted took his place on the cot. Her eyes became fixated on the bicep as it moved along with the rest of his body while he tried to get comfortable on the makeshift bed that squeaked until he found a place and posture he could deal with, his restlessness ceasing.

The room was still, and all she could hear was the sound of his breathing. She could feel her heart beating out of one of the cows on her pajamas. Penelope asked, "Shut the lights?"

"Uh. Yeah."

Penelope rolled on her stomach and reached over to the bright lamp on the bedside table and turned it off. She closed her eyes.

Some minutes passed by and Penelope's heart kept on beating and Ted kept on breathing. "Ted?" she inquired, opening her eyes, looking into the darkness.

"Hmmm?"

Are you asleep?"

He sighed. "No."

She turned her head on the pillow as if she was switching to another part of herself. "Ted?"

"Hmmm?"

"Do you miss D.C.?"

He cleared his throat. "Like I said, it's a place."

"What does that exactly mean?"

"A place is just a place until you have the right people in it."

She thought about what he said. "Are the right people here?" she asked him. For some reason, a quiver crept up in her stomach while she waited for his answer.

"In this room?"

"No, silly," she replied, although she might have wanted to hear the answer to that question. "I mean in D.C."

"No. They used to be," he commented, "or maybe not."

The room quieted down for a second time, and then Penelope asked, "Are the right people in New York?"

There was a silence that seemed to go on forever until Ted said, "Maybe."

Penelope swallowed hard, her heart now beating with his inhaling and exhaling. Beat. Beat. Inhale. Exhale. Beat. Beat. Inhale. Exhale.

She thought about the kiss she imagined in the taxi.

And then she thought about Luke. The flowers. The Gucci luggage. The trip to Hawaii. His Kennedyesque profile and demeanor.

Penelope, wanting to calm herself down, focused on her next project.

"Ted?" she inquired.

"Hmmm?"

"That new laptop I just got. I think I want to go wireless."

She could hear him stirring on his covers. "You're going to need a router."

*　*　*

Sometime in the wee morning hours, Penelope fell into a dream or rather, a nightmare, and in the nightmare was Lorna Lufton, Manhattan Night's actress and fashion designer extraordinaire on the show, in a puffy and glittering gown. She clawed her way up a steep, evergreen hill, her long, polished talons hooking into the earth. She wore a diamond tiara with a large "G" on it.

She was mighty and fierce and determined as she climbed, and as she got nearer to the top of the hill, she found herself periodically stopping, panting and wheezing, trying to catch her breath, but she kept on pulling her body up, until she finally reached the apex, and looked down at her dress and brushed some dirt off of it. She then raised her eyes, and suddenly, out of the blue, she saw a toboggan racing towards her! And Darvin and Stacey were on it crying out – *Wheeeeeee*! And they would have hit her – if it wasn't for the enormous, red apple that pushed her out of the way onto the grass (although a plastic glove did fly off of Stacey, and it slapped Lorna in the face as she sped off into the yonder outdoors with Darvin). But the huge apple practically crushed her, and Lorna couldn't get herself out from under it. It was then that she heard – *Buffalo gals can't you come out tonight - can't you come out tonight - can't you come out tonight - Buffalo gals can't you come out tonight …aaand dance by the light of the mooon* …And the apple was lifted off of her, and she blinked in the sunlight, trying to decipher who or what had performed the miraculous deed.

"Heya Mary!" said a young, skinny George Bailey in his 1930s athletic attire – a striped turtleneck, bloomer shorts, and laced up shoes.

"Mary?" Lorna scoffed as only she could. "I'm not Mary. I'm Lorna Lufton. From Manhattan Nights." She coughed up some dirt and asked, "Who are you?" She examined him from the ground. "And why are you wearing that horrid outfit?"

"You like it, Mary?"

"No, you idiot. And I just told you my name is-"

And before Lorna Lufton could breathe another word, George Bailey peeled the diamond "G" tiara off of her head.

Lorna screamed, "Hey! What did you do that for?"

George Bailey smiled and gestured with the tiara over into the distance to a pretty, two-story colonial with a front porch that was the full length of the house and had flowered trees in the yard. "That house is full of romance."

Lorna struggled to her feet. "That old house? I suppose. But can you give me my tiara?" She insisted, "Sir. My tiara, please. It's a Gucci." She held her hand out. "I need it for when I go to Hawaii."

But he didn't give it to back to her. Instead, George Bailey turned away from Lorna and flung it toward the house, and though the house was miles away, it broke the middle window on the top floor.

"What the heck did you do that for?" she questioned. "And why aren't you pitching for the New York Yankees?"

"I made a wish," he said.

"Yeah?" Lorna looked him over and cocked an eyebrow. "What did you wish for?"

George Bailey turned back to her, but now it wasn't George Bailey. It was someone else. Lorna gasped as she peered into his bright green eyes, and he gently took hold of her arms. "This is what I wished for."

"No! No! But you're Ted!" Lorna hollered. "You're Ted! I don't want you! I want! I want! ..." Lorna searched for a name but couldn't think of one.

"What is it that you want Mary?" he asked. "You want the moon? I'll throw a lasso around it and pull it down for you!"

"No. I don't want to the moon!" she cried out. "And I'm not Mary! I'm Penelope!" And suddenly, it was as if Penelope jumped into Lorna Lufton's body.

Ted smiled and moved closer to her. "I know who you are" he said, his eyes sparkling. "And what did you wish for, Penelope?"

She paused and thought about it. "I wished for this."

Ted slowly leaned over to kiss her, and then, right before their lips were about to make contact, he changed – he changed into her! Penelope was taken aback as her "other" face grinned and said, "Lemonade anyone? Ice cold lemonade?"

At that, Penelope screamed out AAAGGHHHH and threw her (other) self down on the ground, and she and herself fought like cats and dogs, scratching and pawing at one another and grunting until...

Buffalo gals can't you come out tonight-can't you come out tonight-can't you come out tonight-Buffalo gals can't you come out tonight-aaand dance by the light of the moooon! Penelope shot up from her bed, her hair disheveled, some of it askew on her face. She reached over for her BlackBerry on the hotel bedstand.

Into it she croaked, "Hello?"

"Hey, Penelope, it's Ted."

"Ted?" Penelope rubbed her eyes and then her nose, still half-asleep. "Why did you throw my tiara into that window?"

"What? What are you talking about?"

Penelope's lashes fluttered and then she scanned the room – *Oh*, she realized, *I'm in a hotel room. The hotel room with Ted.* She searched around. No Ted. She stared at her BlackBerry and then asked it, "Where are you?"

"I'm downstairs," he said. "I didn't want to wake you up so early. I had some tasks to do before the interview and now I'm going. Thought I'd wake you up now, so you can have some time to go for breakfast and get out before we meet up at the Capitol Building for the Cherry Blossom Festival."

Penelope grabbed her watch from the other bedside table. "What time is it?" she asked aloud and scrutinized the hands on her timepiece.

"It's about nine-thirty."

"I sure hope you're reading that off the GPS locator watch I made you."

"Uh. No," she answered him, feeling bad. She hadn't put it on since he gave it to her. She found it to be too heavy for her wrist and very unattractive. "I don't have it with me." Penelope remembered she had left it in the handbag that she wore that day in Central Park when she was with him, and that handbag wasn't in Arlington, Virginia. It was at her apartment in Manhattan.

"That's too bad."

"Why?"

"Well, I figured it would direct you to where you needed to go today, and you could see how far I was from the Capitol Building when you started to walk over there." He explained, "I never got a chance to deprogram myself from the watch. I didn't fix the computer that day, and then I got a new computer and completely forgot to do it." He continued, "So you can still find me."

She smiled. "Strange behavior for someone who doesn't want to be found."

"Yeah, right," he laughed. "I left some maps and pocket guides for you on my cot. See what you can take in before lunch. I'll meet you after the interview. It should be done by that time. But it'll be a late lunch." He asked, "Is that all right? Can we meet around 1:30?"

Penelope dragged herself out of bed and strolled over to the cot. "Sure," she replied and picked up a pamphlet; a picture of the Capitol Building was on the cover. "Good luck on the interview."

She hung up the phone and sighed.

***

The sun was so bright that day it was as if God himself set up track lighting from the heavens to illuminate the earth, or at least where she was, and much to Penelope's surprise, getting to and around the D.C. area proved easier than she originally thought. The metro train from Arlington to the center of D.C. was a cinch to ride, and the trip didn't take very long. Not wanting to be too far from the Capitol building for her lunch with Ted, she went to the Smithsonian at the Mall, which was right next to it, and wandered into the National Gallery of Art and National Museum of American History for a while before embarking on her tour of the Washington Monument that was just a stone's throw away.

As she took in the Monument that was tall and proud and seemed to look down at her, saying – "YOU DARE PONDER *ME?*" – Penelope looked over her shoulder to the multitudes of people surrounding the Capitol Building. The Cherry Trees generated a pinkish aura around the majestic American icon, and it was so beautiful that she felt a shiver go up and down her spine.

Penelope examined her watch. It was one already. She wondered where the time had gone to. She felt it was only seconds ago that she had awoken from her strange dream only to find herself in a strange hotel room in a strange city. Yet, within the hours, she felt very at home and was amazed at how overjoyed everyone around her appeared to be – tourists, workers, students – all were decked out in a smile, and in turn, she smiled as well.

She sighed to herself as she watched faces and figures pass her by, and then her sights searched around for a restaurant or café. She wondered where Ted was going to take her to eat.

Her stomach rumbled and fifteen minutes later, she headed toward the Capitol Building, now thinking about his interview. *Forget about where he's taking me to eat*, she thought. The question was – would this be their last meal together? Would he ace the interview? Would he feel comfortable living in D.C. again after what happened to him and that idiot-of-an-ex-fiancé, Hannah?

The Capitol Building got bigger as she got closer.

I only want the best for him, she concluded. *If he wants D.C. and he gets the job, I'll be happy for him.*

Her face soured. She realized it would be difficult to say goodbye – but hey, by that time she would have the Streamers Technology account and she would have her Hawaiian vacation with Luke, and all would be well.

Everything would be as it should. Just as she planned. And it would be even better if Ted got what he wanted along the way.

As Penelope reached the front of the building, her eyes widened. She couldn't believe what she was seeing. There were trees of beautiful pink and white flowers decorating the front lawn, and there were people laughing and some couples being amorous under their branches. Her breath was taken away by the rosy and blanched petals that streamed and circled through the air, as if they were performing a magical dance number in the glorious shine of the sky.

Penelope gasped at nature's dazzling show. "Wow." Enthralled by it all, she inhaled deeply, getting emotional, and then she suddenly stopped in mid-breath. "Dogwood?" she said aloud. "They have Dogwood Trees here?" She gasped again, ingesting the fragrant aroma of Dogwood and Cherry Blossoms. She placed her hand on her chest and said, "Out of this world."

Having climbed the hill up to the building, Penelope sat under a Cherry Tree whose only occupants were a pair of playful children, twin boys to be exact, and a woman who was studiously watching them.

Penelope crossed her legs Indian style and put her hands on the grass behind her, striking a casual and relaxed pose. While the petals floated around her, she mused – *I don't think I ever want to leave. It's like a dream* – and then her BlackBerry rang.

Ted, she thought.

Penelope rushed to pull the phone from her bag. "Hello?" she panted into it, her expression aglow.

"Hey, Sweetie," Luke answered. "How's the PR convention?"

She was shocked and dumbfounded. "Oh, it's fine."

"They're not working you hard, are they?"

Penelope glanced down at her watch. It was now almost one-thirty. She knew Ted would be there any minute.

"Oh. Um. No."

"Good because it's not a working trip, is it?"

"No. Not really."

"Good" he said and then paused. "Look, Penelope. I want to apologize."

"Apologize?" She was baffled. After all, it was she that was lying about her trip. He wasn't lying about anything. "Apologize? What for?"

"I've been distant. Busy. Always busy. Not spending enough time with you."

"Well, you've been busy with that Boston client. I understand."

He groaned on his end. "Yeah. But that's over with. I'm done with that client."

Penelope's face screwed. "Really?" *Why was he done with the client?* "What happened?" she asked.

"It's a long story," he answered. "Maybe I'll tell you about it when you get back...The point is that I miss you. And I want us to get closer. And when you come back, I'll make it up to you."

She was confused. "Make up what?"

"What a shit I've been to you."

Penelope's nose scrunched at the word "shit," but she was touched just the same. "Well, it has been difficult at times."

"I know, and it'll be different when you get back. I promise. And Hawaii will be wonderful and oh, I forgot - there's a fundraiser I want to take you to next week. Next Sunday. Will you be free?"

All at once, she felt horrible. Here she was telling him that she was at a PR convention, when all along she was having a weekend holiday with Ted, and now Luke was speaking about getting closer and missing her and taking her out to fundraisers.

What have I done? I'm ruining what I've wished for all along! Luke is everything that I've ever wanted!

"Penelope?" Luke inquired.

"Yes."

"I want to tell you something."

"Yes?"

Just at that moment, a voice called out to her – "Penelope!"

It was Ted with a picnic basket.

"Penelope!" he shouted and grinned. But as he approached her, Penelope noticed it wasn't Ted. At least not the Ted from before. It was a different Ted. A Ted in a sharp, black suit and blaze-red tie. And, most importantly, it was Ted with a short, neatly cropped hair cut, and as he came toward her, through a cascade of swirling flower petals, she could see his sterling, white smile – his handsome face ...and his piercing green eyes.

She almost dropped the BlackBerry, and Luke was still on, saying, "Penelope, I want to tell you that I-"

"Luke," she interceded, "I have to go." Ted was only a few feet from her, and she felt her body and soul melt away from the phone (and she knew it wasn't the sun that was making her melt). "I'll call you later."

Click.

Ted stood in front of her in all his splendor.

Ted," she said, her eyes darting out of her head, her heart pulsating as he smiled down at her. "You look...you look..." She was searching for the words.

"Awesome?" he joked. His mouth broadened to a grin.

She nodded. "Yes, *very* awesome." She had to attach "very" to "awesome," since the latter word alone didn't see to do justice in describing his handsome appearance.

Ted scanned their surroundings, admiring all that was around him. "I know I have my mind on science and space all the time – the heavens - but this on earth? I don't think there's anything like this out there. Beautiful."

She gazed at him and thought – *yes it is.*

He turned back to her. "Time for a picnic." Ted lifted the picnic basket, reached in and pulled out a red and white checkered table cloth. He snapped the table cloth and it rose in the air and then drifted down, landing at Penelope's feet.

Crouching to the grass, he put his hand in the basket and proceeded to take out a bottle of Sutter Home Chardonnay (cheap and good) and Coronet paper plates (the china of paper plates). He was about to pull out something else, but hesitated before saying, "And now, the piece de resistance!" with a pitiful French accent, and all at once, a huge McDonald's bag appeared.

"McNuggets!" Penelope cried out, smacking her hands together in applause and smiling. "Did you get the-"

"About fifteen packets of it," he claimed, and he drew out a small bag from the big one.

"Was that all the honey you could get?" she teased.

"I think that was all the honey they had for a whole year." He placed more of the McDonald's bags on the table cloth along with two empty paper cups. "From the looks on their faces, I have an inclination that no one ever asks for it and this was their only supply for a while. If someone goes in with a gun, demanding honey, they're in trouble."

"I don't think I'll need all those packets."

Ted sat down on the ground. He gazed at her. "You never know what you'll need," he said.

Their eyes locked for a moment before he threw off his suit jacket and pulled off his tie with reckless abandon (which Penelope found so sexy that she felt like pulling off something of her own).

She didn't want to ask, but she knew she had to. "So? What happened? Did you get the job?"

He handed her a cup. "Well, I don't know. I won't have an answer from them until another week or so."

"Do you think you'd like working for them?"

"I don't know that either."

Penelope felt uncomfortable with all this uncertainty. "Ted-is there anything you do know?" she huffed.

"Maybe," he answered, smiling at her. He poured her some wine and then he did the same for himself.

He raised his cup and she followed his lead.

Before he had a chance to say a few words, Penelope put out her own, suddenly wanting to get beyond the unexpected feelings she had in Ted's presence. Feelings she couldn't digest in her consciousness, where Ted was still etched in as her techno-geek teacher – "To moving on and up!" she blurted. (She wanted to say "To Ted getting a new job," but she couldn't get that sentence out of her mouth.)

Ted's face fell. "Is that what you want me to do?" he asked. "Move on?"

Their expressions – his of hurt and hers of bewilderment – embraced.

"I ... I ... I don't know," she stuttered. She peered deeply into his green eyes. His irises reminded her of photos her grandfather took of the ocean when he went to the Turks and Caicos Islands; like that body of water, they were a glistening green and clear and pure and therefore, true, and they were inviting her in. Penelope wanted to kiss them. She wanted to touch his face, and without so much as a thought, she leapt on the trail to following her desires, extending her hand out to his cheek, caressing a sudden blush and the roughness of some overzealous stubble, slowly making way to the side of an eye, peering into a pupil. Ultimately, her hand arrived at his forehead, right above his eyebrow, her index finger touching his tiny scar.

"What's this?" she asked in a hushed voice, caressing the scar with a finger tip.

She could hear Ted swallow hard. "I got into a bicycle accident when I was seven."

She caressed it again. "It left a mark."

Ted's eyes went somber. "It left a lot more than that."

"What do you mean?"

He took in some air and then exhaled, as if sighing. "I got into a bicycle accident when I was seven." His voice began to crack as he spoke. "It was a two-wheeler bike, my first one, and I didn't know how to ride it." He fidgeted. "But that didn't stop me from trying to ride it all by myself, even though I was told not to ... just like most little boys would do." Ted's gaze moved to the side of Penelope, and his pupils dilated like he was staring into a scary void as soft crimson petals drizzled on their picnic. "Right before it happened, I was in the house with my mother, and when the phone rang and she picked it up, that was it. In a split second I ran outside to try the bike out on my own," he said. "And just when I thought I had the hang of it, I went too fast and skidded off the street, into a tree."

"Wow."

"Yeah," he said, appearing distraught and like he was trying to fight back tears. "Anyway, after my mother got off the phone, she found me lying under the tree with blood all over my face." As he told the story, the color drained from his complexion. "She rushed me to the emergency room, crying. She was so upset that I was hurt and that she didn't see me leave the house," he said. "I was all right, though – a slight concussion." His finger swept over the scar. "And this was twenty stitches."

"Twenty stitches and a concussion? That was some accident."

He nodded and then continued, "My father grounded me and told me that it would be a long time before I'd get on that bike. He said that

I had to stay in my room after school and on weekends to reflect on what I did." He paused and rubbed his lips together, nervously. "The grounding started the day that it happened to me, and that night I cried into my pillow. I was so upset ... and my mother came in to comfort me. " He stopped and inhaled as if he couldn't get enough oxygen. His voice trembled as he struggled with his emotions. "She told me everything would be all right. That after a couple of weeks, she would make sure I'd get back on that bike and that she would show me how to ride ... She said she wanted me dream about it." He sighed. "And then she got into the bed with me, and I rested my head on her stomach...And she started to sing." He cleared his throat. He was still looking away from Penelope. "I don't remember what she sang exactly, but I remember how she stroked the scar on my forehead. Like she was trying to get rid of my pain...She did it for so long. It must have been hours... And then I fell asleep."

Penelope gasped. "She sounds wonderful."

Tears welled up in his eyes, but not a single one dropped or rolled onto his face. He went on – "The next morning, my mother went out to the grocers to get some ingredients for my favorite breakfast ... She always did that when I was feeling sad." He shook a little, and Penelope, sensing she was about to hear a horrible ending to the story, tried to contain a long sob by taking in a few short breathes.

Shutting his eyes and shaking his head, he continued, "It was a freak accident ... A woman dropped something in her car while she was driving ... and she reached down to get it and took her eyes off the road ... And she crashed into my mother's car." Ted covered his face with his hands, and Penelope's jaw dropped. "And my mother was killed ... Just like that."

"Oh my God, Ted." The terrible story bore a hole in Penelope's heart, and as she looked on at Ted, so grief-stricken, she wasn't sure if that hole would ever heal. "Ted ..." She felt the sentence come upon her, like a surge. The sentence, the words she hadn't said in so long. That she promised herself that she wouldn't say.... And yet they came to her so naturally as her heart felt his. "Ted ... I'm so, so sorry."

"That picture in my apartment. The one you're always looking at .

That was me with my mother," he said. His eyes were pools of water. "It was taken only weeks before the accident happened."

"She was beautiful."

"She was," he murmured. "I never know where to put it. I move that photo from one place to another. It still just hurts so much." Ted briefly touched his scar again, and then moved onto his eyebrow, smoothing out the sparse, short hairs.

It was just at that moment Penelope realized something. It drifted onto her like the petals from the Cherry Blossoms. Ted hadn't covered his eyes with his hair because he was being messy or that he was trying to hide them. His eyes didn't even matter to him.

"Is that why you were covering your scar?" she asked, knowing she was taking a chance with the question. "Because you were hiding your hurt?"

"What?" His expression was one of surprise.

"Your hair. Before. It covered the scar. Does it remind you of your pain? From what happened with your mother?"

He was quiet for a second, his face still overcast with astonishment. "I didn't think I was...I guess." Although he was speaking in front of Penelope, it was almost as if he was talking to himself. "I mean, I guess it was long like that when I was younger, but then when I went to college it was short, and when I was dating Hannah it was short." Ted went silent for a moment and his eyes widened, as if he had a revelation. "Then after Hannah, I grew it long again."

"Hannah," Ted said, wiping the tears from his eyes. "I thought she was wonderful - smart, funny, pretty. I was so happy with her." He sighed. "I was over the moon about the wedding, but then ... a couple of months before the wedding, I came home, and, like I told you, found her in bed with another man ... But what I didn't tell you was that *the man* was my best friend." He rolled his eyes as if to say *I just couldn't believe it.* He went on with his tale of woe. "I was devastated. I broke the engagement that very moment, put an end to the friendship, left my job, and just decided, off the cuff, to go to New York."

Penelope knew most of the story, but seeing and hearing Ted talk about it after he told her about his mother, witnessing his expressions of sadness, added shades of depth – depth and character – that she hadn't seen before. Not in anyone. "Ted," she said in a hushed and compassionate tone.

Penelope gazed at his scar. She began to realize the mark represented the loss of two of the most important women in his life. The break-up with Hannah was the trigger to hide it away again, just as he had done when he was younger after his mother died, and that's why it hadn't seen the light of day since he left Washington – *until now*, Penelope thought as she sat with him at their picnic lunch at the nation's capitol, his scar in full view.

"She called me afterward," he said. "She called me everyday for months, begging me to take her back. But I just couldn't. And then she was really gone, with my best friend. I thought I'd never be happy again."

"And?"

"And after she stopped calling, I started to think that maybe it was actually something I did that caused her to cheat. Or maybe I was at least a part of the reason. Maybe I should have listened to her. Maybe there was a way to patch it all up so we could be together again." He shook his head. "And I felt that I made a terrible mistake…until…" Ted looked directly into Penelope's eyes. "Until a couple of months ago."

Penelope's intuition peaked. She knew what he was about to say, or at least she thought she knew. But although her feelings for him were growing in strength, she couldn't help but push them aside, not wanting to get caught up in the moment; she didn't want to do anything irrational when she had no understanding of what was going on within herself. It was as if she stepped into D.C. and forgot her life back in Manhattan. The life that she had so desperately wanted. "Ted…"

"Penelope," he stopped her with the sound of her own name. "Did you ever think that you made a huge mistake – maybe the biggest in your life – but then you realized it wasn't a mistake? That eventually, it was the right thing to do?

"Because I have-"

"Ted," she interceded. Penelope didn't know what he was saying, what he meant exactly – she was too involved in her own thoughts to figure all of it out, and she wasn't exactly sure she wanted clarification. "Ted," she felt the need to put a halt to the conversation, and then she found herself unexpectedly divulging her own personal story. It just came out on its own. "I stayed in Elmont for my grandfather," she said, feeling the need to confess some of her own life.

"What?"

"My Grandfather Ben, who I was close with. The one I told you about - the photographer." Her hands clasped together. She was nervous. "He had cancer … First it was kidney and then it was the prostate … He was dying, and I stayed in Elmont to take care of him.

As he listened, Ted's features smoothed out. There was a profound gentleness about him.

She fought back a tear. "I skipped going away to college and having a career out of town, like my friends, to help." Her voice splintered, and she felt as though she was about to fall into a cavern filled with past anguish. "He had years of chemotherapy … Until one afternoon … about two years ago … he passed away in his sleep."

"Penelope," Ted said as a tear rolled down from her eye and perched itself atop of a cheekbone.

A cluster of Cherry Blossom petals fell onto the tear, seeming to want to swathe her pain.

With two of his fingers, Ted reached over to her face, and slowly scooped the tear and petals off of her cheek.

He looked down at both on his finger tips.

"I never told anyone about that," she said.

He tilted his head and gazed at Penelope. "I never told anyone about what happened with my mother."

"You never told Hannah?"

He provided a slight, tender smile. "She never asked."

At that point, Ted and Penelope stared into each other's eyes, and they started to move closer to one another. And closer. The gap between their bodies narrowed as every second passed, and Penelope's body began to tingle as she readied for Ted's kiss and then – "Ted!" A man's voice came out of nowhere.

Penelope and Ted stopped what they were doing, and she looked up and recognized the face right away – the blonde hair and blue eyes – it was the cute blonde boy from the photo and article she found on Ted and his work at the Peabody Firm.

Ted appeared not only surprised, but like he'd been struck with a gigantic mallet. "Dane," he breathed. There wasn't a smile or any gesture to suggest that he was going to rise from the ground for a greeting.

In comparison, Dane smiled at Ted, looking happy to see him, although he did appear a bit restless as he stood in front of them, slightly shifting his weight from one foot to the other. "It's great to see you," he said.

Ted blinked a couple of times before saying, "Yeah."

There was a moment of silence between them, and Penelope felt like she was suddenly intruding on something extremely private.

"Look," the man said in an amiable way, "Hannah's right behind me. She just stopped to pick something up at one of the tables in the Mall."

At that, Ted promptly grunted, pulled himself off of the grass, and grabbed the wine bottle. He stuffed it back in the picnic basket and then proceeded to pick up the table cloth with the food, paper plates, and cups still on it. He gathered it all in a bundle, and like the wine, pushed it back to whence it came.

The man said, "Ted, please …We didn't mean for it to happen." His eyes were pleading. "At least talk to her. So we can put it behind …" He stopped talking.

Ted shook his head with fervor, and it looked as though the man knew his effort was futile.

Ted turned around for a moment to Penelope. His face so striking, and unfortunately, so filled with angst. "Penelope, I'm so sorry," he said, and he charged off with his basket, walking towards the sidewalk that looped around the Capitol Building and walking away from the man, who Penelope realized was the one that Ted's ex-fiancé had cheated with and was his once-best friend, and some new information – he was his once-coworker, as well.

And there was something else – Ted had walked away from *her*. Penelope.

She watched him as he crossed a road, much farther away from the Capitol Building, and she didn't know what to do.

She noticed he'd forgotten his tie and jacket. They were lying on the ground. Remnants of their romantic interlude.

She picked them up.

The man looked at her, his blue eyes sad. "I'm sorry, too."

Penelope thought about it. For a series of words she felt she had overused in her prior life in Elmont, she was certain that they were the most appropriate words for that day.

***

Penelope returned to the Arlington Sheraton an hour or so later, unsure of what she was or wasn't going to find in their hotel room. Or rather who.

Ted's suitcase was gone.

He left behind his Visa card on the cot and a note written on a sheet of hotel stationary:

Penelope,

I hope you can forgive me. Use the credit card for anything you need. Including if you need to change your ticket.

Ted

She picked up the Visa card, sat down on the bed, and stared at the cot. She longed to go back in time. Back to when she and Ted were on the lawn of the Capitol Building ... and they were about to kiss ...

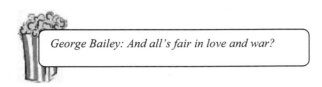

George Bailey: And all's fair in love and war?

Twenty-two

Penelope slogged along on Delancey Street with Sonia at her side. They were heading to the movie set of "Manhattan Nights."

"It's so great that Stacey was able to do this!" Sonia was exuberant. "I just can't believe it!" She clapped her hands in delight. "We're actually going to meet the cast! Maybe even Lorna Lufton! *Thee* Lorna Lufton!" She let out a cackle. "Oh! I can't wait to tell the girls at the office!"

Penelope nodded, her head hanging low. She remained despondent over what happened with Ted the weekend before.

"Hey," Sonia said to her, placing her hand on Penelope's arm. "What's gotten into you?"

"What do you mean?"

"What do you mean 'what do I mean?' You were always the one saying Manhattan Nights this and Manhattan Nights that, and now that we're actually going to meet the cast, you act as though we're going to a funeral. What's wrong?"

"I've just got things on my mind."

"Well, come on," Sonia said and slapped her on the back. "It's not every day that a person gets to meet a star-studded cast of a ridiculously popular TV show."

Penelope raised her drooping eyes. "Yeah. Maybe you're right." She looked at Sonia. "It'll be fun."

"Fun? It'll be a blast!"

"Yeah. And I've also got that fundraiser tonight with Luke."

"Sure! That should be fantastic!"

The fundraiser was for the "Children's Rights Association," a charity that Luke had been involved with since he started his own business, and it was going to be at the Midtown Cipriani restaurant. Penelope had always wanted to go to that restaurant, seeing as how everyone was always talking about it and the events that took place there. And Penelope had always wanted to go to a posh fundraiser. Here was her chance, although, Penelope's mood, if extended to that night, was destined to take the "fun" out of "fundraiser."

"Why are you so concerned about Ted?" Wendy asked right before the weekend began. "You should be more concerned about the dress you're wearing on Sunday to the fundraiser."

"I already have a dress," Penelope answered. She purchased a simple, long, black Oscar de la Renta gown from Saks (not a discount clothing store like Loehmann's or Filene's — a fact she wasn't going to mention).

"So instead of being excited about going to the fundraiser with Luke, you're upset about not hearing from Ted?" she questioned. "What gives?"

Penelope hadn't informed her of the Washington D.C. escapade.

Wendy inquired again — "Did you hurt that poor man again? Did you commit another technology blunder?" Wendy laid her hands firmly at her waist. "What did you do? Press a key on your lap top that you weren't supposed to and send him flying into orbit? Did he finally land, but have to get the NY Fire Department to unhook him from the GW Bridge?"

"*No.*"

"So what gives?"

"Look. I'm just asking you to do me a favor," Penelope said. "Can you just have your ex-boyfriend find out if he's okay?" She glanced at the one press release she wrote up for Ted that was on her desk. Alongside of it was his credit card. "I just haven't heard from him all week, and I'm concerned."

That was a falsehood. Penelope had received a text message from him. But it was just one:

Ted (Mobile)

March 31, 2008 3:32 PM

Appreciate your calls and texts.
Need to be alone for a while.
Hope you're doing okay.

What kind of message was that? And it certainly wasn't enough for Penelope.

Wendy sighed. "I'll see what I could do."

Sonia squinted at the street signs as she passed them by. "Stacey said it was on Orchard Street, a couple of blocks up-I think this way," she informed, pointing to the right.

Penelope looked the other way, to her left, thinking about Ted. When suddenly, he had appeared way across the street. She practically choked on her own air – Ted was with the blonde girl she had seen him with at the bar, and they were walking in the opposite direction.

"Pen?" Sonia immediately turned around to her. "What's wrong?"

Sundays he's busy, Penelope thought. He always told her he was busy doing something, but her never told her what. *So this was it – he was spending time with blonde bohemian trash.*

There was only one thing left to do.

Penelope worked on pulling herself together for appearance sake. "Nothing." She stopped walking, which caused Sonia to stall as well. "Sonia," she said, "I just saw a store across the street I want to go to."

Sonia's eyes widened with surprise. "*Now?*"

"I've been wanting to go this store for eons."

Furrowing her brow, Sonia looked to the opposite side of the block. "Which one?"

Penelope searched the storefronts. "That one." She pointed.

"That one? You want to go to Myrtle's Emporium of Brasseries?"

"Uh-yeah."

"Why do you need to go to a specialty store for bras?" Sonia asked her, giving her breasts the once over. "Aren't you like a B cup or something?"

Penelope grew impatient. She didn't want to lose Ted and the blonde girl while conversing with Sonia about her bra size. Sorrowful as it was.

"Yes," she answered. "But it's not about the size. I'm just looking for something specific."

Sonia stared at her for a moment and then breathed, "Is this private?"

"Yes. Very."

"Luke's not asking you to do anything kinky, is he?"

"No, no."

Arching her eyebrow as if to say *I don't believe you*, Sonia said, "Fine. Just don't be too long....I won't mention this to your brother... And remember it's on Orchard Street, two blocks to the right. It should only be a few blocks from here actually. I guess you'll be able to see it. A movie set is difficult to miss."

"I'll only be a couple of minutes," she said as she ran off, crossing the street at a red light, almost getting hit by a car.

"Penelope!" Sonia yelled out. "Do you need the bra that bad that you'd get yourself killed?"

After Penelope made her way over, she caught up with Ted and the blonde girl who were only a couple of blocks down from her starting point, and she watched them as she kept her distance at a good twenty or so paces behind them.

She noticed that the blonde girl was gabbing away furiously as Ted's head just bobbed up and down.

She made note of what the girl was wearing — cut-up jeans, a navy-blue and white striped top and brown moccasins. *Ech*, Penelope said to herself. *This is what Ted likes?*

They turned a corner and entered into an old building. She stopped at the corner and hid behind the structure next to it, and then peeked around to see if either one of them had decided to turn around and come out. But neither one did.

Slowly, Penelope moved towards the building and then halted in front of its entrance. She asked herself – *what should I do? Should I be doing this?* And then she felt herself fuming. She actually felt fire burning in and out of her ears – *He asks me out for Valentine's Day, he buys me a gift for Post-Valentine's day, he invites me to go on a trip with him where – coincidentally – there's only one room reserved, he makes advances (that never came to anything), and then he leaves, without giving me as much as an idea of what's on his mind. A whole week of wondering! I deserve to know what's going on!*

With a scowl, Penelope stormed through the glass doors of the building and stomped through the empty hallways. Her eyes shot straight ahead as she went on to look for Ted and his blonde mistress, but from time to time her sights veered off to the side, to the walls. The wallpaper was peeling, and in some spots underneath there was crumbling sediment. She wondered why Ted would take the blonde bohemian to such a place.

Even his dungeon apartment is better than this.

Penelope heard voices, and without warning, a non-descript, middle-aged man jutted out in front of her, stopping her in her tracks. "Can I help you?" he asked, his wrinkled face frowning.

Startled, her words stumbled – "I'm-I-uhm-I'm looking for someone."

He grimaced even more. "Well, I'm sorry, but you CAN'T go beyond this point."

"Why?" She felt defiant. "Is there a law against going beyond this point?"

"Miss, I suggest that you go."

At that moment, Penelope heard a recognizable voice. "Wait a minute," Ted said as he walked over to them, his startling green eyes enlarged with surprise. "Penelope?"

The man turned to him. "Ted? You know this girl?"

"Yes. I do."

Ted now stood in front of them. He looked down at Penelope, a confused expression falling across his face.

The man wagged a finger at him and said, "You know the rules. You can't tell people about this place."

Penelope's eyes went from Ted to the man and then back again to Ted. She didn't understand what was going on.

"I didn't tell her. I would never tell. I don't know how she knew…"

"Okay," said the stern man, "but this can't happen again."

Ted nodded. "I understand."

The man grumbled and trudged away from them and into a room saturated with voices. He closed the door behind him.

Ted turned round to her. "Penelope what are you doing here?"

"What am *I* doing here? What are *you* doing here? And what is this place?"

"What am *I* doing here?"

"Yes. What are you doing here with that woman?"

"What woman?"

"The blonde bohemian!"

"What?" Ted looked at her as if she had gone mad.

"Don't look at me that way, Ted," Penelope said. Then her eyes narrowed and her hands became fists, and she began to wave them around as she remarked, "I saw you with that blonde girl that you're having an affair with!"

"*What?*" His eyes flew open and so did his mouth.

"You're having an affair with a blonde bohemian!"

"You mean *Rachel?*"

"Rachel?" Penelope pursed her lips. "Is that her name? *Rachel?*"

"Yes. And nothing is going on with Rachel!"

"You mean to tell me that you're not having an affair with Rachel?" she asked, her voice loud. "*Every Sunday?*"

He crossed his arms and gave her a funny look. "No," he responded, "Rachel happens to be the wife of the director of this shelter. They're neighbors of mine."

"Shelter?" Penelope suddenly felt as though she was going to have egg all over face. Hard-boiled egg.

"Yes, Penelope. Shelter," he said, annoyance written on each of his features.

"What are you doing at a shelter?"

"It's a domestic violence shelter. No one's supposed to know about it. I come here every Sunday to teach the kids how to work on computers."

Penelope shut her eyes tight and groaned. She had made a horrible, horrible mistake. "Oh, my God."

"You thought I was with Rachel?" He moved closer to Penelope, glowering down at her. "What gave you that idea?"

"Well," she said, and she started to breathe heavy; she was sure she was on the brink of having a multitude of anxiety attacks. "Well, Wendy told me you might be dating some blonde girl and then I saw you right afterward at a bar with her-"

"Wait. You saw me at a bar with Rachel?"

Uh-oh. "Yes."

"What bar?"

Penelope meekly responded, "Asia de Cuba."

Ted stopped for a moment and then said, "You saw me? You saw me at Asia de Cuba and you didn't come over? And you didn't tell me that you saw me there?" His face now looked like hers did only moments ago when she charged into the building. Angry as all hell.

"No. I thought you were together. I thought you were having an affair with her," she tried to explain, but then she frowned and plunged her index finger into his chest. "And what were YOU doing with a married woman on a weeknight at Asia de Cuba?" Twice she forcefully poked his ribcage.

"Her husband was out of town," he calmly said, the corners of his mouth still at a downward slope. "I promised him that I'd take his wife out to dinner."

"Oh." She felt stupid.

"And what is this about me having an affair, as you so put it? ... Why would me being with a girl be having an *affair*?" he questioned. "Because in order for me to have an affair, I would have to be cheating on someone. And in order for me to be cheating, I'd have to be having a relationship. A romantic relationship." He paused and then asked, "Penelope? Who would I be having that relationship with? Who?"

She looked up at Ted's green eyes, filled with anger and just a hint of curiosity.

She didn't say a word. She thought about the picnic and the almost-kiss — was she wrong about what he tried to do? Did he really want to kiss her or was it all in her head? Had she imagined it because she'd been swept up by the Cherry Blossoms and the laughing people and the sun and the moment? She kept making inquiries to herself — Did she really have feelings for Ted? Or had she intentionally tripped herself up because she was afraid her wishes were finally coming true? That she was finally getting what she wanted with Luke?

Penelope shook her head, trying to fling the questions from her mind.

He continued, "You said that we were just friends." She shook her head even more. "Penelope," he uttered in a low, soft tone.

And before he had a chance to say another word, Penelope rushed off and away from him.

As she raced down the hallway, Ted called out to her, "Penelope! Penelope!"

Quietly sobbing, she pushed through the doors and hurried across the street, and then ran down what seemed to her to be hundreds of blocks, heading towards Orchard Street. When she reached Orchard Street, she turned right, and through her tears she saw the trucks and the cameras and Stacey and Sonia standing by a set light, and there next to them, in a puffed-out, taffeta gown, throwing back her long, curly hair, was Lorna Lufton.

"Pen!" Sonia cried out. "Over here!" Stacey and Lorna Lufton turned around in Penelope's direction, and they were all smiling until she got closer and they could see what an upset and tearful state she was in.

Before she made it to all three of them, Sonia moved forward and grabbed hold of Penelope's arms, stopping her. "Penelope, what's wrong?"

Penelope let out a little sob, trying to stifle it back. Her voice trembled, "I don't know anymore...I don't know anymore," and then she inhaled deeply, looked over Sonia's shoulder to Lorna Lufton like a mad woman. She threw her pointer finger at the star, and yelled, "You! You!" at her.

Lorna Lufton took a few steps back. She warily glanced at Stacey and asked, "Am I going to have to call security?"

"HOW COULD YOU?" Penelope hollered as some of the stage hands looked on at the scene.

"How could I what?"

"HOW COULD YOU PROMISE ALL THOSE THINGS?" Her arms began to flail around. "Luxury trips! A handsome and successful man! Expensive gifts and restaurants!" Penelope screamed out – "I'm from Elmont!"

"Elmont?"

Stacey jumped in – "Oh, it's the sweetest little town in Illinois-"

"Aaagh!" Penelope sounded and stomped her foot for Stacey to shut her trap, and she did. "I come from Elmont!" she continued. "And you promised me these things!"

Lorna Lufton reacted, "I promised you? You? Personally?"

"You promised me and everyone who watched your show that they would have these things if they moved to Manhattan! You should be ashamed of yourself!"

A pervading hush fell over the entire set, and Lorna Lufton dropped her head, and then, out of the blue, she blubbered, "I know! I know!" The innocent bystanders looked on at her with astonished mouths, as if they were spectators at a freak show. "I am ashamed! I am!" She softly cried and sniffled. "I feel so bad about it! But I wasn't the one who created the character - the writer's did that - but I realize that I breathed such life into her! I'm *such* an incredible actress!" The onlookers – cast and crew – rolled their eyes. "And I really pushed it to the limit with the designer clothes! ... And y'know, I'm from a small town, too!" Her voice cracked, and her bottom lip trembled. "Kalamazoo, Michigan!"

There was an audible gasp from the cast and crew.

"That's right!" She turned to them. "Kalamazoo, Michigan! I lied about being brought up in Los Angeles!" She raised her arms up and exclaimed, "You couldn't figure that out? Who the hell grows up in LA?"

She turned back to Penelope. "What I did was unforgivable. I duped hundreds of thousands of woman into believing that if they moved to New York they would get all that you just said – the fancy restaurants, the well-to-do men, the jet setting vacations. They believed my character. They believed me. And now, I hear it all the time. I hear it when they meet me on the street, I read it in their emails and letters-they relocated to New York thinking they would live like my character, but they didn't get any of it. Just like you." She wiped her wet eyes with her bare arm.

After Lorna Lufton's speech (and if she was faking it, it was an Oscar Winner), Penelope's face suddenly lost its expression of fury. She pondered as she stood there, and then she finally said, "But that's not true with me."

Everyone gawked at her, including Lorna Lufton, who had stopped erasing her tears. "What?" she asked.

Penelope announced, "I got all of it. All of it."

The star's foot immediately hit the ground, creating a loud *thump* sound. *"Then why are you yelling at me?"* she hollered.

Penelope let out a high-pitched squeal – "Because of Ted! Ted! ... I don't know what to do about Ted!" and she swiveled round on her heels and rushed off the set. Where she was going, she had no idea.

"Ted?" Sonia questioned out to her. "I don't understand…The gay guy who's teaching you to knit?"

Stacey clarified, "He's not gay, and he's not teaching her to knit."

Sonia went silent for a second.

"Not teaching her to knit?" – Penelope heard her say. "Really?"

Mr. Potter: Look at you, you used to be so cocky!
You were going to go out and conquer the world!

Twenty-three

Luke followed Penelope into her apartment in his black tuxedo, somewhat on the tipsy side after having a couple of glasses of Vodka straight up at the fundraiser.

"Excellent vodka," he said. "Armadale. Don't forget the name. Best vodka around, and I *know* vodkas."

Penelope sighed as she picked up the hem of her gown that was dragging on the floor. "It was a nice event," she said and turned on the light.

"Definitely," he agreed, "And it's a good tax write-off, and since I donate to the organization, it's good PR for me and my company."

She made the sound *hmmm* in her head. "Well," she said with her arms outstretched as if she was displaying a mansion. "This is it. My glorious abode."

Luke scanned the studio and nodded. "Cute. Compact."

Throughout the evening, he pressed her to show him the apartment since it was so close to where the fundraiser was – closer than his place;

also, he hadn't seen it for the three months they'd been dating. ("Look," he said, "it can't be all that bad.")

She figured it was time for him to see it, and after what happened with Ted earlier that day, she was in no mood to argue with Luke, besides the fact that she also didn't have the energy to do so. The confrontation with her techno-teacher and with Lorna Lufton, along with the strain of her confusion about her feelings concerning two men, had left her depleted and listless.

Luke took his place on the couch, and pointed to a corner. "Why do you have a dumbbell?"

She turned around to it. It was a single five-pounder. "To work out."

"But you only have the one."

She looked over at the Wii console under her television and then at her right arm. "It's a long story." She would never be immobile again, she thought.

Penelope's eyes wandered everywhere in the studio, except to where he was.

"Penelope," Luke said to her from the couch, "come hither." He waved for her to join him.

She slowly made way to the couch and sat down next to him. He grinned and his dimple made a command performance. "You looked beautiful tonight," he commented. "All my friends there, John, Mike, and Sal. They were all admiring you."

"But did *you* admire me?" she asked, peering into his brown eyes.

He jerked back. "Of course. What did you think?"

"I was just wondering."

Luke gently clipped her chin with his index finger and lifted her face to his. "Well, you don't have to wonder anymore," he said and gently kissed her.

Penelope liked the kiss, but other than that, she didn't feel anything. Not like she had before.

He stared into her eyes. "What's wrong, Penelope?"

"What do you mean?"

"You haven't been yourself all night." He paused and then noted, "Actually, you haven't been yourself for a couple of weeks now." She knew he meant since her trip to Elmont. He had commented on it before. *The Elmont trip*, she thought, *the weekend I saw the slides of Ted.*

He drew in a long breathe and then pushed it out. "I guess I deserve it."

Penelope didn't understand what he meant. "Why? What are you talking about?"

Luke took hold of her hand. "Penelope," he said, his voice sounding serious. "I have something to tell you."

"What?"

"You're not going to like it," he announced, "but I promise you that it's over."

"What? Luke? What are you talking about?"

He squirmed on the seat cushion. "Penelope I've been seeing someone else while I've been dating you-but it's over now."

"What?" she asked, her eyes darting out.

"When I was in Boston."

She quickly jumped up from the couch, infuriated. "You mean there wasn't any client in Boston?"

"Yes, yes!" he exclaimed, touching her hand. "There was. I didn't lie about that! It's just that...that... she was there, also."

Penelope huffed, "So-all of those times you went- you were seeing her? Were you there for her or the client?"

He shrugged and looked down at the floor. "It was kind of half and half."

"Half and half? Half and Half?" she yelled with a wrinkled brow and sour face.

He pulled her down onto the couch. "Listen to me. I met her way before you."

"And is this something that's supposed to make me feel better?"

"By the time we met, it was ending anyway. It was just unfinished business."

"If it was so unfinished, why didn't you tell me?"

Luke adjusted himself on the couch, trying to get as comfortable as he could while he was having an uncomfortable conversation. "I don't know. It never seemed to be the right time."

It never seemed to be the right time? Was he kidding? All those dinners, the walks in the parks and in the city streets – he couldn't tell her during any of those times?

Penelope sat there, quiet and subdued. Thinking. And then an idea infiltrated her mind and seeped into her mouth, and then poured out – "Were you planning to go to Hawaii with me while this was going on? Or were you planning to take her to Hawaii?" He didn't respond, his face pale with surprise. "You were planning to go with her weren't you?"

"No, I wasn't."

"That's why the dates for Hawaii were set in stone like they were," she said, narrowing her eyes. "That's it. You planned to go with her a while ago, maybe before you even met me, and when your relationship with her wasn't going as you planned, you gave me that ticket as a Valentine's Day gift!" She shook her hands at him, yelling, "How could you?"

"No, Penelope. That's not it. That's not what happened. Believe me."

"How can I believe you when you lied to me?"

"I didn't lie to you. I just didn't tell you."

With her jaw unhinged and her eyeballs ready to spiral out of her head, Penelope uttered, "Omitting information is still lying." And then, with the finishing of her statement, she quickly understood that she was not only a victim of lying, she was also an offender. After all, she had lied to Luke about being at a PR convention when she was actually with Ted in Washington, D.C., and she had lied to Ted when she hadn't told him she was dating Luke.

My God, she thought to herself, *I'm a multiple offender.*

She wondered if she was worse than Luke. There was only one question she could ask to find out the answer – "Did you sleep with her?"

"What?"

"Did you sleep with her?"

"Honey, we had a relationship before you and I ever met. So, yes, I've slept with her."

"But did you sleep with her when *we* were together."

Luke groaned and then scratched his head. "Well. Yes. What did you expect me to do? A man needs to have sex with someone."

"How could you say that?" she cried out and was about to leave the couch when he grabbed her wrist.

"Penelope. I'm sorry. I've been a jerk and it was a jerk thing to say," he quickly professed, "and I promise I won't be a jerk anymore. But just think of it-I didn't have to tell you. I could have kept it a secret. But I wanted to be honest with you. Because I want to have a serious relationship with you."

"Why?" she assertively asked him. "Why do you want to have a serious relationship with me, Luke? Out of all the girls in the city. Why me?"

He inhaled and then exhaled. "Well-you're cute as a button...So easy to get along with..."

Penelope's stomach turned upside down. "Is that it? Cute as a button? Easy to get along with? Not like the other girls – not like the one from Boston. Maybe she's not cute – she's probably beautiful and probably asks for more." She immediately thought of the women on "Manhattan Nights." "She's not lemonade!"

"Okay. She is beautiful and smart-"

"Are you telling me I'm not smart?" She thought of how ridiculous she'd been with technology. How difficult it was to get use to the gadgets and mechanisms and doo-dads.

"I didn't say that."

"But you omitted it when you described me just a moment ago."

Luke paused. Then he stared into Penelope's eyes and touched a freckle on her face. She didn't move.

"Penelope," he said, "remember that day I was on the phone with you when you were at the PR convention, and then you suddenly had to get off the phone?"

Oh boy did she remember. That was when she was sitting in front of the D.C. Capitol Building and caught a glimpse of Ted – handsome Ted – walking towards her.

He continued, the gravity of what he was about to say lying heavy in his gaze – "I just wanted to tell you," and then he reached into his tuxedo jacket and pulled out a jewelry box and held it out to her. "I just want to tell you that I love you, Penelope. I do love you."

Penelope didn't know what to say. Her eyes were glued to the box and fixated on his words. *He loved me? But how could he? He lied to me.*

"Please forgive me," he said.

Luke opened the box for her. She gasped. In it was a diamond tennis bracelet, and the diamonds were so bright that they were blinding.

So there it is, she thought. *I've finally reached the Holy Trinity – flowers, handbag, and jewelry …Hooray for me.*

Luke took the bracelet from the box and looped it around her wrist, next to her watch, as she mulled him and the bracelet over, remaining lip-locked.

"A gift for you," he told her. "Something to think about."

"Luke," she finally said, "I really need to be alone."

"Penelope."

"Really, Luke. I just need some time to think this all over."

He nodded. "I understand. I'm not happy about it, but I understand."

Luke picked himself up from the couch, his legs active but slow as he marched to the door. Penelope was right behind him.

She opened the door to show him out, and when he stepped into the hallway, she uttered, "I just need some time."

"Okay. Just don't let this ruin everything. What we have," he somberly advised. "I do love you, Penelope. And if anything, we can work this out more in Hawaii. You'll see how different you'll feel once you're in Maui and there's sun and beach. We can start anew there." He gently brushed her face with his fingertips.

"I'll think about it," she said, looking at his bowtie instead of his eyes.

Luke bowed down and kissed her on the lips, and then went to the elevators and pushed a button. Seconds later, she watched as he went in. He solemnly waved to her as the elevator doors closed.

Penelope sighed.

What to do now?

As she turned to go back into her apartment, she suddenly froze. Standing there, in the hallway, was Ted. Appearing stupefied.

Penelope was shocked. "Ted?"

He was silent.

"Ted? What are you doing here?"

He took a few steps toward her and then halted. "I thought I could talk to you about what happened today. But I guess that's a moot point, seeing as how *you're* the one who's having an affair with someone."

Penelope examined his face. In his expression, there was a mixture of shock, anger, and disappointment.

"Ted, I can explain." But she really couldn't.

Penelope's feet left her doorstep, quickly walking to him, but Ted backed up, trying to get away from her.

"I don't know if it's serious of not," she said, now keeping still.

His eyes flew open. "Is that all you can say to me – I don't know if it's serious or not?" He shook his head. "I thought that after D.C. and then after what happened the other day - how you reacted to the possibility of Rachel and I -" He stopped himself and choked on a sob. "I just guess I was wrong," he said and then turned around and went for the elevator.

"Ted." She hurried after him.

"You could have told me about this guy in D.C., at least. Before … Before … " He reeled around and gawked at her. "We were talking about so much. So why didn't you tell me the most important thing?"

She began to cry. She thought about her grandfather, and how he died in his sleep while she was in the next room. "I did tell you the most important thing, Ted!" she sobbed, tears streaming down her face, remembering how sick her grandfather was, and how she told Ted about it that day in front of the Capitol Building. "I did! I did …" Her voice trailed off, and she continued to cry.

Ted's face softened, and the elevator doors opened. He put his hand between them, making sure they wouldn't close as he took one long look at her and then looked away.

He sighed. "I bought you some presents. I put them near your door. I was going to surprise you, but I guess I was the one who was surprised." He turned around to the elevator again, went in, and the doors shut behind him.

Penelope continued to cry in the hallway. In her Oscar de la Renta gown. With her diamond tennis bracelet hanging from her wrist.

"Ted," she wept and then moved back to her door and looked down.

There, on the floor, was a new DVD player with a DVD case atop of it.

She crouched down and picked up the case. *Oh my God*, she thought, her eyes continuing to water. *He remembered.*

Penelope had a flashback to the night Ted first arrived at her apartment, when she told him she had lost it; she perused the cover of the DVD – it was the black and white version of "It's a Wonderful Life."

Penelope dropped to the ground, beside the DVD player, the DVD still in her hand.

She leaned against the wall, bent her legs, and folded her hands on her knees.

And she lowered her face, drenched with tears.

> *George Bailey: I said "I'd wish I'd never been born."*
> *Clarence/Angel 2nd Class: Oh, you musn't say things like that.*

Twenty-four

"**Y**ou're so morose these days," Wendy commented while wheeling her chair over to Penelope's cubicle.

Penelope was performing the task of cleaning her desk before heading off for Hawaii. It had been about a week since she had her volatile discussions with both Luke and Ted at her apartment, and Ted hadn't called or text her since (and that's all that Luke *was* doing).

She didn't try to contact Ted either, acknowledging that he probably didn't want to ever see her again. It was all too difficult anyway, she thought. And, she rationalized, their romantic inclinations for each other were most likely an aberration brought on by too many hours and too many months spent together, not excluding the magnificently beautiful Cherry Blossoms that would render any man or woman helpless to the throes of delusionary love.

Going to Hawaii and sorting out her relationship with Luke was all for the best. *This was the real deal,* she thought. A dream come true, and she wasn't going to chance messing it up again.

"What do you mean-morose?" she asked, condensing scattered papers into a neat pile.

"You know. You're like the walking dead." Wendy got up from her chair, stretched her arms out in front of her, and tilted her face to the side. She then made like she was rolling her blue eyes to the back of her head, letting her tongue out, and she proceeded to march for a few feet.

Penelope touched her elbow. "You can stop now. I get it."

Wendy returned to her chair. "I don't understand. You're leaving for Hawaii tomorrow, and you act as if you're going to Siberia."

"I heard Siberia was nice actually. A little freezing but a gorgeous countryside."

Wendy lunged over to her and grabbed her wrist. "And then there's this," she said, pinching the diamond tennis bracelet between two fingers. "You should be ecstatic about this. You've reached your Holy Trinity."

Penelope sighed, "Yeah, but I'm not even Catholic." She bunched up her pens and pencils that had rolled or fallen behind her computer and placed them in her cup of writing utensils.

"Neither am I. But I sure as hell would be happy as a pig in shit if I got this bracelet and was going to Hawaii." She pointed to Penelope's desk. "I'd be dancing on this desk. In a grass skirt. I'd be doing a hula."

"By all means. Do what you have to do."

Wendy stationed her hands at her hips. "You've become sarcastic," she noted. "You really have become a New Yorker."

"Thank you." Penelope smiled to herself and then blew on her computer keyboard to rid it of dust and food particles that might have plummeted in between the letters.

"It's just that you look a little … haggard," Wendy explained.

"Haggard?"

Well, Penelope thought, *it would make sense if my face appeared to be drawn and pale.* She had been staying up late every night watching old reruns of "Manhattan Nights" and then the entirety of "It's a Wonderful Life" in black and white. A question pervaded her mind – one that Ted asked her months ago – If she had to choose which she liked best – "Manhattan Nights" or "It's a Wonderful Life," which one would win out?

One morning, during a work week, she nodded off at two a.m. and towards the end of "It's a Wonderful Life" when George Bailey yelled through the town "Merry Christmas!" before he might've been thrown in jail (Stacey's favorite part of the movie).

Two a.m.

It was no wonder she looked haggard.

Penelope stopped cleaning her desk, her mind wandering off to Ted and their picnic in D.C., and what he had told her about his mother that was so sad, about his ex-fiancé and his ex-friend that was so despicable, and she thought about their encounter with the ex-friend that was so shocking. And she also reflected on Ted's appearance that day – so handsome. She thought of his smile, his emerald eyes, and the tiny cleft in his chin.

Wendy stared at her with the big blue marbles in her head. "You're acting so weird. Even though you tell me no, I still think you have some secret."

Turning to her, Penelope commented, "This time you might be right."

Just at that moment, Alden Renquist screamed from his office – "Penelope McAdams! Please come in!"

The whole of the office revolved around in their swivel seats in Penelope's direction. She groaned and grabbed a yellow pad and pen off her desk, and tucked a lock of hair behind her ear.

"Sounds ominous," Wendy remarked.

"He knows I'm going to Hawaii today, and that I'll be gone for two weeks. How ominous could it be?" It wasn't like he could ask her to do an activity that was urgent.

Wendy's shoulders lifted. "I don't know. He could ax you?"

Aghast, Penelope glowered at her. "Wendy? How could you say that?"

"I didn't mean anything. But he did basically yell."

"He always yells."

"Yes, but you are leaving tomorrow. It would be the perfect time to let go of someone."

"Wendy," Penelope said, surprised that her closest co-worker would say such a thing.

"I don't wish it. I'm just saying, you never know." She raised an eyebrow. "Just be prepared, in case it does happen."

"But I got all these press placements for Henshaw Tractors-"

"Penelope McAdams!" Alden Renquist hollered again – "I said - can you please come in here?"

Wendy gestured to his open door.

"Coming," Penelope responded and took in a deep breath, twisted round, and headed for his office.

She poked her head in. "You need me for something, Mr. Renquist?"

Alden Renquist sat behind his desk playing with a miniature pool set. He held an itsy-bitsy cue stick in between two fingers, and his eyes were centered a tiny ball as he waved her in.

"Please close the door, Penelope," he ordered.

She shut the door and sat down. *Here we go. He's going to say it*, she worried. *I don't know why he's going to say it but he's going to – Penelope, he'll say, you're fired.*

He raised his eyes from his midget pool table and looked her straight in the face. "Penelope," he said.

"Yes, sir?" she responded nervously.

"Penelope," he said again and then slammed his hand on the desk, "you've been promoted!" He grinned.

"What?" She almost dropped her pad and pen.

"You've been promoted!" His face was now beaming. "I'm giving you the Streamers account!"

She put her hand to her chest. Her heart was pounding fast. She couldn't believe it. "Really?" Penelope thought she was imagining what she was hearing or that she was in a dream state – either at home in her bed or slumbering at her desk.

"Yes, really!" he exclaimed. "I am just astounded, and I have to say, very pleased by your performance!"

Finally realizing that this was actually happening, that she wasn't in an

REM sleep stage, Penelope smiled as wide as the width of the world. "Thank you, Mr. Renquist."

"Call me Aldie." *Aldie?* "You've earned the right." Delight shined from his face as he continued – "You know, Penelope, when you started to get the Henshaw Tractor press coverage, I thought 'Okay, I was right, she has the potential that I always knew she possessed,' but when the agent of a major Hollywood star called me today and said that they wanted to represent Henshaw Tractors-and all because of you-I thought 'This girl has more potential than I even thought-this girl is senior material!'"

Penelope asked herself – *Star? What star? There must be a mistake.* "Mr. Renquist, I never sent those letters out to the Brangelinas or the TomKats-"

He shook his head and slapped the air, saying, "Oh! Who needs the Brangelinas and TomKats! We've got Lorna Lufton!"

"WHAT?" Her entire body shook.

"Yep! You did it! Lorna Lufton's agent called just moments ago, and said that you had a talk with her, and you impressed her so much that she decided to represent Henshaw, and that we should set up a meeting to discuss the particulars!"

Penelope's eyes flew open. *How could this have happened?*

"I know," her boss said, "I know. You're speechless about the promotion. But Penelope-you deserve it. Yes, you deserve it!" He went on – "No one else in this office has your fortitude and talent, and no one else in this office can manage the Streamers account! No one!" He lowered his voice and informed, "And you think I didn't notice that you've been teaching yourself about technology?" He leaned back in his chair. "I've been tasting your coffee – even though I'm not supposed to be drinking it, I've seen you work your BlackBerry quick as a bandit, and I've seen you pressing buttons on your MP3 player and downloading from the internet - I'm impressed." Alden Renquist's finger bolted up – "By the way, since you know so much about technology now, one of the first assignments you have when you get back is to find out who downloaded that virus that ruined all our files last month!"

That would be me, she thought. *That would be me.*

"I'm impressed!" he said again. "Now, don't be nervous-I know that you're not a technology expert, but with what you have learned and with what you did with the Henshaw account, it was enough to put you over the top to hand you the gold prize!"

Penelope didn't know what to say. Words had still vacated her brain from the discovery that Lorna Lufton was going to represent Henshaw Tractors because of their not-even-semi-relationship or conversation. Especially after the way Penelope verbally attacked the star.

Was this how to get ahead in life? she asked herself. *By yelling?*

"You should give yourself a hand! A bow for your performance!" he said, and she knew it was Ted that she should give a hand and bow to, and that he would've been so pleased to hear about her getting the Streamers account, but now she couldn't tell him; she couldn't share her success and joy with the one person who helped her reach the goal line.

Alden Renquist pulled out his bottle of Xanax and patted its cap. "Aaah. Good ole' Xanax."

Seeing as how her boss was so thrilled with her, she easily inquired, "You're still taking that?"

"Oh not for nerves," he answered her unflinchingly. "No - I don't have use for nerves anymore." He smiled. "The proposed alimony payments are no more. It seems that when my wife's private investigator did his research on me, he found out that she indeed was having a delusion that I was having an affair ... But when my private investigator researched her, he found out that I also was having a delusion that she *wasn't*."

Penelope's mouth opened wide with astonishment.

"It was good that I married into money, as well," he said, "Because now it might be coming my way." He nodded and rested his hand on the Xanax bottle. "Now, I'm just taking it for excitement. Excitement that I won't have to pay alimony and that she might have to and about a huge celebrity representing one of our clients."

There was quiet in the room. Penelope was still sitting there with her mouth upturned and happy, even though she felt that her insides had just been hit by a stun gun.

"Well," Alden Renquist said, flipping his hair back. "Just don't sit there! Let's get up and shake hands! Let me congratulate you!"

They both rose from their seats and shook hands. "Thanks so much, Mr. Renquist."

"No. Aldie."

Penelope almost choked on the nickname, trying to hold back a giggle. "Aldie."

"Thank *you*, Penelope really…And have a good time in Hawaii … Oh and by the way, before I forget. I'm doubling your salary."

Her hand went limp in his hand. She felt faint. "Doubling my salary? … Did you say double?"

Alden Renquist beamed and nodded.

Oh my God, she said to herself, *I can move out of my studio. I can move into a one-bedroom overlooking…overlooking…*she couldn't think straight enough to figure out what it would overlook.

"Thank you, Mr.-uh-Aldie." She continued to shake his hand.

"Penelope," he said.

"Yes?"

"Can you give me back my hand now?"

"Oh," she sounded as she let go of it. "Sorry."

With pen and pad in her grasp, Penelope turned toward his door with a big, luminous smile on her face. "Double the salary," she mumbled to herself as she went to leave.

"Lorna Lufton!" Alden Renquist cried out. "Unbelievable!"

Penelope opened the door. "Lorna Lufton," she said to herself in a hushed voice, a question mark hovering above her head. "Unbelievable."

She strolled back to her desk and slowly put her bottom on her chair. Beginning to ponder how or why Lorna Lufton decided to represent Henshaw Tractors, Penelope lost her smile, and it was replaced by a serious expression.

Wendy's head popped over their cubicle wall. She sighed. "There's that look again. I'd love to be a fly on the wall to find out what goes on in there with you and him." She asked, "Did he fire you?"

"No." Penelope couldn't discern how she felt about getting the account now, because she didn't know how it happened. She was drowning in thought, working on figuring how it all came to be, and then she realized she might as well tell her (she was going to find out soon enough, anyway). "I got the technology account."

"No fucking way!"

Penelope didn't cringe at the curse; her brain was too filled with concern to absorb it.

"What the hell is wrong with you? Why aren't you jumping for joy? Why aren't you telling everyone?" Wendy asked, beside herself. "Shouting it out!"

"I don't know," she calmly reacted.

"You need to go tell Ted!" she ordered. "If it wasn't for him, you wouldn't have gotten it!

"I know…but I can't right now."

Wendy sighed. "Well, you have to tell him before he leaves."

Penelope's face and freckles went white. "What?"

"Ted. You have to tell Ted before he leaves for his new job in D.C."

Oh my God, she thought, *Ted got the job. He's moving to D.C.*

Penelope gasped and her heart sunk. "When is he going?"

"Tomorrow. Tomorrow night. My ex told me…he decided to move quickly. Like he did when he moved here…I thought you knew," she said. "I was aware that you hadn't heard from him for a little while, but when you didn't ask about him anymore, I thought you and Ted were talking again."

Penelope felt the blood in her veins pumping exceedingly fast. She decided to do a major cover-up. "Of course. I knew," she said. "I just forgot when he was going. That's all."

"That's something to forget," Wendy said, being sarcastic.

Ted was going to D.C., Penelope thought. And she was going to Hawaii.

Well, she sighed. He didn't call or text to tell her that he was going.

So he made up his mind to leave New York.

Okay, she thought, collecting herself. *Ted would have a nice, new life back in Washington, and she would have the life she always imagined with Luke in*

Manhattan.

Case closed.

Tale finished.

"My ex told me that Ted is looking good," she uttered, "and he also told me that he wasn't dating a blonde girl, after all. He got his information wrong. It was just the wife of some neighbor that he's friends with."

Penelope grimaced. "Thanks, Wendy. Thanks for that information ... *now.*"

Buffalo gals can't you come out tonight - can't you come out tonight - can't you come out tonight - Buffalo gals can't you come out tonight - aaand dance by the light of the mooon ...

Penelope grabbed her BlackBerry from her desk. "Hello?"

"So?" Stacey's voice came from the other end.

"Soooo-what?"

"Aren't you going to thank me?"

"For what?"

"For talking to Lorna Lufton about your tractor account."

Penelope tightened her grip on the phone.

"*You're* the one who got Lorna Lufton to represent Henshaw?"

Stacey exclaimed, "The one and only!"

Smiling, finally having an answer to the Lufton-Henshaw riddle, Penelope asked, "How did you do it? How did you get *her* to do it?"

"It was actually easy," she explained, "Lorna was looking for a way to compensate."

"Compensate?"

"Well. She knew that even though you've been succeeding in Manhattan that she probably made a mess of you anyway. That was evident by how you acted the day you met her." Penelope's face went red. "And to her you represented all the women she screwed up when they watched her on the show and decided to move here and were disappointed." She continued, "I remembered that you were looking for a celebrity to represent Henshaw Tractors, and I thought this would be great-Lorna could help you out by representing them. Then in turn, maybe she could help herself out by feeling that she made up for what she did to all those women. At least in some small way." Stacey laughed and commented, "She jumped at the chance! It turns out that not only did she grow up in small-town Kalamazoo, Michigan, but her family were farmers. She grew up around tractors, so it's kind of sentimental to her. It's a win-win situation."

"Yeah," Penelope said, "win-win … I got a promotion."

"Fantastic!"

Penelope rolled her eyes. "I just wish I could thank you in some way."

Stacey giggled. "You already did." Stacey cleared her throat and announced, "Penelope, I'm moving to Elmont!"

"What?"

"I'm moving to Elmont! I've fallen in love with Darvin and he's fallen in love with me, and he called me last night and asked me to marry him! And I said yes!"

"*What?*" Penelope came close to falling off her seat. "Are you joking?"

"No. Of course not! I would never joke about getting married!"

"But to Darvin?"

"That's exactly what your brother said when I told him." She paused. "But Darvin is wonderful and so is Elmont. Goodbye subways and crowded streets, hello trolleys and green pastures!"

"Elmont doesn't have any trolleys," she said.

"By golly, I'll get one and manage it myself!"

"*By golly?*" Penelope laughed – Elmont had obviously rubbed off on Stacey already. "What about your hand and foot modeling? What are you going to do about that?"

"Oh, that," she scoffed. "I'll give that up. I already reached the big time anyway. I can't do better than being Lorna Lufton's hand and feet – and you should've seen them. She definitely needed my help." Stacey said, "It's time to hang up my gloves and galoshes."

"What are you going to do?"

"For work? Toboggans. Darvin and I have decided to make them– open up a shop." She explained, "It's the wave of the future. No one wants to use gas anymore. Everything is about renewable energy, and then there's talk about driving electric cars. So why not toboggans? Is it a stretch to imagine people riding toboggans around their cities and around the world?" Stacey sounded as though she was running for Mayor of Toboggan Town.

"Yes. I hate to break it to you, but you need definitely need snow for toboggans. And not every place or every season has snow."

"I can fix that!"

"How?"

"I'll figure it out. My ancestors are Irish and Filipino, Penelope. We can fix anything."

Of course, Penelope thought, how could she forget that? And then Penelope's brow crinkled. "But Stacey - Elmont? It can be so … so … quiet … and provincial. Do you think you'll really like it?"

"Penelope," she said, "anywhere he is, I know I'll like."

George Bailey: Zuzu's petals ... Zuzu's petals ...
There they are! ... Burt! What do you know about
that! ... Merry Christmas!

Twenty-five

Penelope heaved her Gucci luggage behind her, stopping a few steps away from Ted's dungeon apartment, just when Ted was walking out. He had a suitcase at his side and his backpack thrown over his arm.

As if he intuitively knew she was there, he looked up.

"Hi," she said, smiling and waving a little.

"Hi," he said back, quietly.

There was an awkward silence.

"So you got the job and you're moving to Washington," she commented.

"Just leaving actually," he lowered his bright green eyes. "How'd you find out?"

"A little bird told me," she joked.

"Ah, that would have to be your coworker, Wendy," he said, raising his eyes. "Word travels fast between those two."

He then gestured with a jerk of his head to the trashcan near his door. It was filled with garbage, including piles of film canisters. "Leaving practically everything behind. Dumped all of my film canisters, except for one."

"Did you keep Spock?"

"What? Are you kidding? Of course." He then looked at her suitcases. "What's with your luggage? You're going to Washington, too?"

"Oh yeah." Penelope provided a half-grin. "That's what I'm doing. That's what I planned all along-to move from Elmont to Manhattan so I can move to D.C." The atmosphere grew quiet and then she said, "I'm just going … somewhere." She gazed at him. "Why didn't you call or even text me that you were leaving?"

He put his backpack on the ground. "Isn't it obvious?" he asked. "All that's happened between us in the past couple of weeks. I didn't think that you wanted to hear from me."

"*Me* not want to hear from *you*? I thought you didn't want to hear from me."

He shook his head and laughed. "I guess we've both been confused."

She slowly nodded, and then she reached into her handbag and pulled out the credit card he left for her in D.C. "Here," she said. "I didn't use it."

He took the card and uttered, "I'm sorry about D.C. I'm sorry about leaving you there like that. I was an idiot. I was just so upset."

"I understand. It was painful for you to see your ex-best friend and then to maybe have to see your ex-fiancé …The memories and the feelings you have for Hannah must have flooded in."

He stared at her with a puzzled expression. "You think I got emotional because I still have feelings for Hannah?"

She shrugged. "There must be something left over."

"No," he said. "I don't care about either of them. They don't matter to me. They don't affect me."

"Then why did you get so upset and go off like that?"

He paused and then answered, "Because of us. I was upset and embarrassed because they were intruding on *us*." He moved his hand back and forth between himself and Penelope, saying, "And what we have … or had."

She didn't know what to say.

He filled in the blanks. "And that probably doesn't make any sense, because really you were right. We're only teacher and student."

"No, we're more than that."

"Okay…we're friends." She didn't add onto his sentence and he continued, "We've acted ridiculous. Getting mad at each other for lying or not telling each other everything about our lives."

"But I did tell you the most important thing," she said to him, tenderly pleading her case, thinking of her grandfather.

"I know," he said, a haze of softness drifting onto his face. "And I did the same with you."

"What does it mean though? What we told each other?"

He thought about it. "It means that we have some depth, some character," he said. "That we're good people."

"Good people." She whimpered. "It sounds so average."

He stared at her. "I don't think it's average," he said matter-of-factly. "Actually, I think it's anything but."

Penelope turned her sights to his suitcase. Whatever she thought of saying didn't matter anymore. He was going. And anyway, she didn't know what she wanted to say. She still didn't know exactly what she felt.

She decided to switch to a less serious subject. "I got the technology account."

It didn't seem to surprise him at all. "That's great," he commented, "but I knew you could do it." He smiled. "After you spent all that time learning about technology and sending yourself to the hospital - how many times?"

"I don't know. I lost count." He chuckled and she said, "But you went one time."

"Hey, you know what they say-you're not a techie until someone hits you with a Wii remote."

She lightly laughed. "Is that what they say?"

"I think so," he teased and then there was silence again. "So," he said, "you got the Streamers account…So it was all worth it."

She peered into his bright green eyes and said, "It was *very* worth it."

For a moment, they just stood there, gazing at one another, until he asked, "Does he know how lucky he is? ... This guy - what's his name?"

"Luke."

His lips tightened and he nodded. "Luke. Like Luke Skywalker."

"No. Not really."

He winced. "Han Solo is so much better."

She tittered a bit at the comment and then he said, "Well. I've got to catch a six-thirty plane. So I guess this is goodbye."

"Yeah. I guess so."

Ted lifted his backpack and swung it over his arm. "Goodbye, Penelope," he whispered, and their eyes locked.

"Goodbye, Ted."

Ted grabbed hold of his suitcase and made way to the curb. He hailed a cab and one immediately came.

She watched him slide into the backseat and then saw something fall out of his backpack, onto the street, right before he closed the cab door.

Penelope went to call out to him that he dropped something, but it was too late. The cab had sped away.

She strolled over to the object. It was a film canister, probably the one he said he decided to keep. She just glanced at it for a moment and then shoved it in her handbag, deciding to hold it for him, just in case he ever came back.

Afterward, downtrodden and not at all thrilled about going to Hawaii, Penelope jumped into a cab and headed to Luke's loft in Chelsea.

"Why did you come here?" he questioned when he met her in the lobby, his own set of couture luggage at his side. "I thought I was picking you up." She noticed he looked very handsome in his sports jacket and tight jeans. Although his appearance didn't seem to affect her as it had in the past.

He provided a dazzling smile, showing off his sexy dimples, as he kissed her.

"I had to go somewhere before the trip and figured it would be easier for me to just go to you from there."

Luke swung his arm around and looked at his watch. "Well, we'll be early but that's okay," he remarked. "Come on. Let's get a cab."

She followed him outside, set her luggage down, and closely scrutinized his movements as he stretched his arm out into the street to signal his need for transportation.

When a cab stopped in front of them, the trunk opened up, and as Luke began to put his luggage in first, he asked, "Penelope, do you have any cash? I have a credit card, but I don't really like to use it with cabs."

"I'll check," she replied and then put her hand in her purse, but instead of pulling out her wallet, Penelope's hand found the film canister that Ted had dropped. She took it out, just to have one more look at it, so she could think of her techno-teacher, and when she did, she noticed the tape wound around it.

Penelope read the tape and quickly opened the canister. When she saw what was there, her eyes flew open ... and she realized she couldn't go through with it. She couldn't go through with going to Hawaii with Luke, and she couldn't go through with their relationship. All the flowers, handbags, luggage, and jewelry in the world weren't enough. Not in comparison to what she really wanted.

She put the lid back on the canister.

"Luke," she said while he groaned from picking up one of his heavy suitcases. He turned around to her. "It's over."

"What?" he asked, startled.

"It's over. I can't do this."

He put his hands to his sides and assumed a firm stance. "Penelope. Please. Not now. Can't we just discuss all of this in Hawaii?"

She shook her head. "No. We can't."

"Look-"

"No you look, Luke," she commanded and his mouth fell open. "I'm lemonade. You were right. And I love being lemonade, Luke! I love it!"

"Fine. You love being lemonade-now can you just get into the cab?"

"No. You don't understand. All this time I've been trying to be something that I'm not. Thinking that if I went somewhere else, other than Elmont, that I'd change. But why? Did I really need to change?" she questioned aloud. "And it's so funny-it took me going somewhere else and finding someone else just like me to realize how proud I am. I'm proud of who I am and where I come from!" She pictured Ted in her head and yelled, "And we're good people, Luke! We're good people!"

The cab driver honked his horn. "Are you getting in or what?" he asked.

Luke raised his hands to the heavens. "Penelope, come on already. What the hell are you talking about?" His hands dropped and he sighed. "Look. If this is about the woman in Boston, please understand that I made an error in judgment. I made a mistake. And I regret it." He sucked in some air and asked, "Haven't you ever made a mistake before and regretted it?"

And then it hit her. She finally realized what Ted meant that day in D.C., and she looked at Luke and said, "I thought I made a mistake, but I don't regret it. It was the best thing that ever happened to me. The best!"

Penelope put the film canister back in her handbag and unlocked her diamond bracelet. She set it on one of her Gucci suitcases. "Here," she said.

Stunned, he just stood there, motionless at the rear of the cab as the cabbie repeatedly honked.

Penelope rushed across the street – *Oh my God,* she thought, *how am I going to find Ted? What airport has he gone to?*

"What's wrong with me?" she mumbled aloud. "I'll just call him." *Hopefully, he'll pick up.*

As she hurried down the block, she stuck her hand in her handbag, searching for her BlackBerry.

"*What the hell, Penelope?*" Luke cried out. "*You're going to leave your luggage on the sidewalk?*"

"Take it all!" she answered. "And take the Gucci luggage! ... I never cursed anyway!"

***

After she failed at hailing a cab and failed at finding her BlackBerry in her messy purse, Penelope blew past throngs of people going towards Broadway, where she knew she could find a taxi. But what airport had he gone to? La Guardia or Kennedy?

Penelope arrived at Broadway, stopped at a corner, and waved down a cab. One finally pulled up, and she hauled herself in.

"Okay. Where to?" the cab driver asked, lowering the volume on his radio.

"Uh-uh," she stuttered, still not knowing the answer to that question. "Wait. Wait a minute."

"Okay. But you're on the meter."

Frantic, she looked for her BlackBerry again, moving around lipsticks, a cosmetic compact, some pages ripped out of a travelers guide on Hawaii, and forgotten receipts in her handbag, until she finally admitted to herself that she didn't know where it was and came up with an idea – she was going to pick one airport – La Guardia or Kennedy – and then she was going to have the cabbie drop her off there, so she could try to find Ted (hopefully, she'd pick the right airport). Once and if she found him, she would then tackle the techno-geek man and tell him how she felt.

"Lady!" the cab driver groaned. "What are you doing back there?"

"Lady!" the cab driver yelled. "You're on the meter!"

She decided to take one more look in her handbag. "Wait a minute," she said to the cab driver, her eyes suddenly drawn to something hidden under her wallet.

She froze.

Of course, she said to herself. *This was the same handbag I had on when Ted and I were in Central Park. The same day he gave it to me.* She pulled out the clunky, yellow-puke colored GPS watch from the bottomless pit that was her purse.

But was it still working? Could she still find him? The last time they talked, he told her he'd forgotten to take himself off her watch's locator program – was that still true?

Penelope quickly put it on her wrist, where her diamond bracelet had previously been, and pressed some buttons. She smiled, elated as it lit up like the city's skyline. She was amazed that it still worked without some kind of charger. *The battery must be incredible,* she thought. *Leave it to Ted to create a battery that could last this long-probably hundreds of lifetimes!*

She pressed some more buttons and there, on the face of the watch, was the a little red blip moving around. "Ted!" she cried out, her heart beating quickly under her blouse.

"Lady!" the cab driver hollered, impatient with his pick-up.

Penelope scrutinized the red blip. Which airport was it heading to? She gasped. It wasn't heading to any airport. She saw the blip going up 42nd street, near 3rd Avenue.

What was he doing?

"42nd and 3rd!" she commanded.

"Finally!" the cab driver reacted and pulled away from the curb like a race driver and continued driving up and down the city streets like one.

When he finally got to 42nd and 3rd, he said, "That'll be thirty even."

"Thirty-dollars?"

"You were on the meter."

"That's crazy."

"Welcome to New York."

"Fine," she said, not having time to get into a fight about cab fees. She threw the money at him and leaped out the door.

Penelope pulled her wrist to her face and watched the blip. It was now on 42nd heading towards Broadway. "Where is he going?" She noticed there was a darkness beginning to fall upon the city. Dusk was only moments away. "Great," she said aloud as her feet moved expeditiously down 42nd Street, "just what I need. To look for him in the dark."

But even though she knew the night would make it more difficult to get to him, she knew with his magical GPS locator watch and the fact that he hadn't left for the airport – that he was still in Manhattan-that she had every chance to catch up to him and spill the beans. Tell him all that she wanted to say, and specifically, one important thing.

With newfound, unbridled enthusiasm, Penelope picked up speed and she started to run, and now she was at 42nd and Lexington. "Ted! Ted!" she cried out, raising her arms in the air once again. People on the street looked at her as though she was a danger to the city, including a homeless man who was muttering to himself.

As she hurried, panting along, she analyzed the watch. The blip was going towards Broadway. "Ted?" she asked the blip. "What are you doing? Where are you going?"

She quickly turned around and found herself next to the famed AT & T store, where her story had first begun on New Year's Eve a little more than a year ago.

Penelope moved over to the store and peered through the window, hyperventilating and exhausted from the energy she had expended in a mere twenty minutes, and there, in full view, was her AT & T salesman – still skinny and still mustached – and with a female customer; he was looking down at her, displaying the same condescending expression that he had on when Penelope had met him.

Penelope zeroed in on the long strip of hair under his nose. Her lips swerved up and the brown in her eyes twinkled as she saw him twitch his mustache.

She realized she owed him since if it wasn't for the AT & T salesman – snotty and cynical Mr. AT & T – she would have had her texts from the beginning, and she wouldn't have needed to recover them.

When I said I didn't want the text messaging service, he could have impressed upon me how important it was to have it. He could've talked me into it. He could have demanded that I get the service. But he decided to be true to his "I-could-care-less-about-you" nature and let it go, and sent me into the bustling and technologically connected city of Manhattan without it.

Thank heavens!

Penelope, not able to keep her emotions of gratitude and excitement to herself, banged on the window to get the salesman's attention.

The entire AT & T store turned around to her, including the AT & T salesman, and she grinned so large that the grin took up her entire face. She lifted her hands up a mile high. She felt as though she could have touched the top of the Chrysler Building. "Thank you, Mr. AT & T salesman! Thank you!"

The AT & T salesman looked at her as though he was trying to make out who she was, and then, if she was crazy, but then he smirked, seemingly remembering her.

Penelope immediately had an image flash in her mind – it was from "It's a Wonderful Life," and it was George Bailey yelling, "Merry Christmas, Mr. Potter!" at the tail end of the movie, stopping at Mr. Potter's window before he went on and through the town of Bedford Falls, wishing all people and edifices holiday joy.

Why not? Penelope asked herself, but she realized it was early April, way beyond St. Nick's time to provide a Christmas salutation, so she thought of the next best thing; she raised her arms up in the air once again, waving them around, and shouted, "Happy Easter, Mr. AT & T Salesman!" and she was about to look down at her GPS locator watch to see where Ted had gone to, so she could find him and then run off like George Bailey, her now hero, when suddenly the lights went out in the AT & T store.

Penelope turned around. Her eyes trailed the lamps on the street as they darkened in the dusk, along with the traffic lights, leaving the city at a virtual standstill.

Manhattan was having a blackout.

She looked at all the people scattering on the city blocks in a tizzy, her brain being attacked by the sounds of honking car horns and pedestrians yelling questions to one another, asking what was going on.

In the pitch black, Penelope glanced down at her GPS watch and gasped. The little red blip was gone from its screen along with the rest of the map of the city. The watch had stopped working.

She immediately realized that not only had the electricity gone out, but whatever had caused the blackout must have knocked out the signal that made all the futuristic communications in Manhattan possible.

Her eyes went back to into the AT & T store. All the customers frantically punctured the buttons on their cell phones and BlackBerrys, shaking their heads.

Oh no, she thought – *Ted – how am I going to find him now? What am I going to do?*

She watched as Mr. AT & T salesman scurried throughout the store and practically threw himself on a display of PDAs, spreading his arms out like he was protecting the items from looters.

"Wait a minute," Penelope said to herself aloud as she witnessed his valiant attempt to protect technology. She thought about what the salesman said to her the day she came into the store and he found out that she knew nothing about technology – "When you go to Times Square, those objects and people you see floating in the air - that's technology ... I just wanted to tell you that before you saw them and decided to pray to the signs like they were gods. Like a caveman would." Then, in her head, she heard Ted's voice saying – "You know where my favorite place is? ... 47th and Broadway... The Times Square area ... Duffy Square ... Those bright billboards ... The bursts of light. All that energy ...When I feel low. Need to think, that's where I go. And somehow, suddenly, it all doesn't seem so bad."

Penelope connected the dots.

"That's it," she said to the air as people rushed past her in the dusk, not knowing what was going on. "That's it. 47th and Broadway. At the signs in Times Square. That's where he is!"

Penelope's feet nearly leapt off the sidewalk as she started to run up Lexington Avenue, crossing over 43rd Street, going beyond 44th, knocking into people on the way, unable to discern their bodies in the dark, as she hurried towards her destination.

As Penelope cornered 47th and Lexington, making a sharp left in the direction of Broadway, hoping that in the blackout she could recognize the street, she had a series of flashbacks of her moments with Ted – the day she met him at his apartment and how he treated her with respect and recovered her texts; the day she ran into him in Best Buy where he offered to help with her technology problem in exchange for public relations services (but what about those PR services? She hadn't done much, even though she tried ... Did he really want her services or did he just want to be around her?); the evening he hurried over to her apartment in the middle of the night to help her with her new flat screen TV (all the way from downtown on his bike!); and then there were all the other times they spent together – including their picnic in Washington, D.C. in front of the Capitol Building during the Cherry

Blossom Festival. She remembered the smell of the Dogwood Trees and all the petals falling all around and on top of them while she gazed into Ted's emerald eyes and his handsome face, waiting for him to kiss her...She knew he wanted to kiss her.

"Ted! Ted!" she cried out, racing, and when she finally made it to 47th and Broadway, she crossed the street, and looked around at her surroundings, but she couldn't see much since the blackout hadn't lifted. She scrutinized the outline of people's faces, but she couldn't make out if any one of them were Ted's.

"Ted! Ted!" she called through the crowd, hoping he would answer. Hoping he was there. "Ted!"

Penelope raised her eyes to where the Broadway billboards were *supposed* to be; of course, she couldn't see them either. Broadway was a virtual slab of ebony.

She squinted, and she could see the faint delineation of the bleachers that were in Duffy Square under the signs of Broadway that were usually lit up; they didn't lead to anywhere except for a platform that could double as a stage.

Maybe he's up there. It's worth a try, she said to herself as people plowed into her, feeling their way around in the void.

Penelope knew it would be tricky climbing the bleacher stairs in the dark without tripping, but exhausted and exasperated, she decided to do it and that her best bet was to go up the stairs slowly, making sure to look down to try to distinguish one step from the other, until she made it to the top, and she could holler out to him, as if she was on a mountain peak; Ted's name reverberating like an echo in the city.

Nodding to herself, she started up the stairs, step by step, tripping on one or two, and then a couple of steps later, almost falling over again, and then steadying herself. There must have been more than twenty steps, but she wasn't counting. All she wanted to do was achieve her goal – to get to the top.

When she finally did, Penelope caught her breath and stopped in place on the platform, staring into nothingness.

Oh, she sounded off in her brain. *What was I thinking? He's probably not up here.*

As a last resort, she looked at her watch again, wishing it would start up. But much to her chagrin, the GPS locator watch remained kaput.

With fervor, gasping for air, Penelope started to shake her wrist, but no matter how much she jostled the watch, it still didn't work. "Ted!" she cried to the watch. "Ted!"

The watch made a rattling sound as she shook it, and then, a familiar male voice came out of the night – "Uh … Are you trying to get that GPS watch I gave you to work? Because I don't think it's happening." It was Ted's voice. "You know, when technology fails, there's always yelling."

"I tried that," she said in the direction of where his voice was coming from, still not being able to see anything, including his face. "Ted?" she said, and then, all at once, the lights at the bottom of the staircase flipped on, and from there, the bulbs on each step followed suit, upwards, one by one, as if someone had ignited a match to a fuse – the fire, the illumination, trailing right to the platform. Right to them. And she could finally see his face; he was only a couple of feet away from where she was standing,

Ted slowly walked over to Penelope, smiling.

She said, "I decided not to go…wherever I was supposed to go to."

He stopped in front of her. His green eyes fell down to her face, and she could feel his hot breath on the top of her head.

"I can see that. Your luggage is gone."

"Yeah. I left it all behind."

He nodded. "I decided to come back here…to think. I wasn't feeling …." He was trying to find the words and came up with – "very well."

Penelope raised her GPS-watched wrist. "You forgot to take yourself off."

"Yeah," he smirked. "Sure … I forgot."

"Ted," she said, "I have to tell you-I have to tell you the most important thing."

"But you told me already."

"No. This is new." She continued, "I want to tell you that I now understand what you meant that day we were in D.C., in front of the Capitol Building. When you asked me if I've ever thought I made a huge mistake, but it turned out that it wasn't a mistake at all. That it was right, and the best thing that ever happened."

"And?"

She paused, her heart racing in her blouse. "And I have been in that situation," she told him. "I thought I made a huge mistake when I didn't get that text service. But now I realize if I had the service, I wouldn't have needed to get my missing texts, and then we wouldn't have met." She ceased talking again and then went on, "That mistake of not getting the text service was the most important thing in my life… because it brought me to you."

His eyes softened. "Interesting," he said. "That day in the park I was going to tell you that I once thought it was a big mistake leaving Hannah and D.C. … not staying and working it out. But it was actually the best mistake I ever made." He smiled and breathed, "Because if I hadn't moved here, I would have never had the privilege of knowing you … and falling for you … And that would've been tragic."

She raised an eyebrow.

"And you don't think me putting you in the hospital is tragic?" she asked, grinning.

"You've got a great right hook."

They both laughed, and then Penelope reached into her handbag and took out his film canister. "You dropped this when you got into the cab."

She looked at the tape wound around it as she had done before. It read: PENELOPE'S PETALS.

A sob crept up in her voice. "It's like Zuzu's petals."

Ted shook his head. "They're Penelope's Petals," he whispered and took the canister from her and pulled out her hand.

He turned the canister over and out came a cluster of dried, pink Cherry Blossom petals; they floated onto her open palm.

Penelope started to cry. "I can't believe you saved them." Her mind drifted back to their picnic in front of the Capitol Building and the Cherry Trees.

His fingers brushed her face. "They were the ones I took off your cheek, along with a tear. I couldn't help myself," he told her. "My memory of you and I in D.C., at our little picnic. I couldn't let that go."

Ted leaned over to her. Their mouths were almost touching, and just when they were about to kiss, Penelope moved her lips away from his mouth, and made her way up to his forehead, near his eyebrow, and kissed his scar, the mark of his sorrow, tenderly.

All at once, the signs above them lit up, and then the rest of the lights in the city went on as well, and they could hear people screaming "hoorays" and "thank Gods" and clapping.

Penelope and Ted raised their eyes to the flashing billboards above their heads. One of them brightly flickered – WELCOME TO NEW YORK!

"*Ahhhh,*" Penelope sighed and smiled as she stared up at the billboard and as Ted reached over to hold her, "I love technology."

Ted lowered his gaze to Penelope's face. "Penelope," he said, his voice cracking, "thank you for finding me."

Her heart quickened.

"And see what happens when you use my GPS watch?" he remarked, looking down at her wrist and the heavy, very unfashionable accessory. "Now will you wear it?"

She smiled and replied, "Now, yes. Later? Mmmmm … we'll have to talk about it," and they both grinned and he pulled her close, and they shut their eyes and their lips touched as a strange wind flowed between them, carrying Penelope's Petals away from her palm, up through the air, way up into the rays of light coming from the billboards – tiny pink specks from the nation's capitol illuminated by the bright signs of the nation's Big Apple.

Harry Bailey: A toast. To my big brother George.
The richest man in town!

Epilogue

TWO YEARS LATER

"**C**an I help you with something?" Penelope questioned a young girl who was wandering around Best Buy, appearing totally clueless. She was scanning the BlackBerrys and then the MP3 players with wide eyes.

She was a tiny thing, probably about the usual size of Penelope herself, and maybe a couple of years younger.

Penelope thought she might be of some assistance. "Are you okay?" she asked.

The girl was startled. "Oh," she questioned, "do you work here?"

"Oh no. I just browse here. I like to keep up with whatever's new in technology."

"Good for you," the girl reacted, her eyes revolving in her head. "I don't even know what I'm looking at sometimes." She spread her fingers on a cherry red iPod. "My boyfriend is a whiz with technology, and we just relocated to Washington - we moved in together - and I figured, y'know, a fresh start. Learn something new." She added, "Since he's so big on gadgets, I figure learning more about technology would be a good place to start."

"Well then-good for you," Penelope said. "I've been there, that's for sure. It can be difficult-getting acquainted with technology, but you'll get the hang of it. I did."

A Best Buy employee passed them by and gave Penelope the fingers-paired-and-separated, Star Trek Vulcan salute. In return, with straight and proud posture and an expression of joyous accomplishment, she did theVulcan salute, fingers raised more than high.

The girl asked, "So you know people here? You come to this Best Buy a lot, huh?"

"Yeah. It's convenient. I mean, I don't live in Arlington, but my job is close to here. It's in D.C., but it's on the border of Virginia and D.C." She added, "I do PR for the local Meals on Wheels chapter. I used to work for them in my hometown."

"That's great."

"Yes. The job is very purposeful."

"We live in D.C. Do you?" the girl asked.

"No, my husband and I live in Old Towne,Virginia," she replied, "and we moved here from New York City."

"Old Towne is beautiful," the girl cooed. "But it must be difficult moving from such a big city like New York to Old Towne. It's such a small town."

Penelope smiled. "No. I mean New York was wonderful. And I owe Manhattan a *great* deal. But it really hasn't been that difficult. Ted-that's my husband-got a job in D.C. at an engineering firm, and I liked it here. So the relocation was pretty easy." She continued, "And Old Towne is not too far from D.C. proper, so it's like a little bit of small town and a little bit of city ... It's perfect."

The girl nodded and then looked around with a confused expression.

Penelope felt empathy for her. "Are you sure that you don't need some help?"

"Well," she responded, "that would be great. Only if you have the time. I don't want to put you out."

"You wouldn't be putting me out. It's my pleasure." *After all,* Penelope thought, *it was the Elmont way.*

"Oh," the girl clapped her hands together, "that is so sweet of you."

"No problem. I was going to get my husband a gift - a digital camera. It's kind of an anniversary for us. He does some freelance photography. But he can't seem to let go of that old Canon SLR camera of his." Penelope knew the girl wouldn't understand what an SLR camera was. "That's a film camera," she remarked. "Anyway, my father keeps telling me to let it alone, but I don't know why I would listen to him, he won't let go of anything either. He keeps working on this old Ford that was manufactured God knows when." As the girl listened to her in a congenial manner, Penelope chattered on – "And I swear that car is so finished with that…" Penelope suddenly paused. A flood of water was streaming in between and down her legs. "Oh my God," she mumbled.

The girl grabbed her arm, concerned. "What? What? Should I call for a doctor?

"No, no. Not yet." Penelope advised, "But can you please go into my purse and find my BlackBerry?"

The girl hopped to it. "Sure," she replied as she did what she was told, rummaging through Penelope's handbag. Seconds later, she found the BlackBerry. "Who should I call?"

Penelope thought about it. "No one. Don't call anyone." She took the BlackBerry from her. "I think this would be more appropriate," and Penelope wrote the following text message:

To my techno-geek husband:

My water broke. Going to the hospital now to have our techie-baby. See you there.
… I love you very much. Penelope (just in case you didn't know)

Oh - on a side note: I think Spock will be so pleased.

Penelope passed her BlackBerry back to the girl but not without saying, "It's so funny. I still have the same BlackBerry from New

York." Her eyes began to well up with tears as she touched her round, pregnant stomach and smiled to herself, wistfully. "You can call the hospital for me now. I'd really appreciate it."

"Sure!"

Looking sentimental herself, the girl started to push the buttons on Penelope's BlackBerry and cried, "This is so wonderful! You're having a baby! I'm so happy for you!" She put the phone to her ear. "You've got to give me your name. So I can friend you on Facebook, and you can send me pictures of the baby!"

"Okay," Penelope replied.

Yep, she thought, giving herself a mental pat on the back, *I know what Facebook is.*

"Or you can just attach a picture to a text - I can get it that way!"

"Okay," Penelope said.

Yep, she thought, *I know how to send a photo via a text.*

"Oh, and my boyfriend has an iPad, and it's fun seeing things, like photos, on an iPad!"

iPad?

Penelope's smile disappeared, and she looked on at her, perplexed.

The girl continued, "Supposedly you can read books on it – at least that's what he tells me, but he just got me one of those eReaders, and it's actually kinda cool reading on it, so I think I'll just stick with that for now … "

eReaders?

Flustered, Penelope's face turned red. "iPad? … eReaders?

The girl said, "Yeah. My boyfriend shows me these things as much as he can … Wait. You don't know what an iPad is? Or an eReader? They're the most popular forms of technology around, everyone is using them now … "

Penelope rolled her eyes. *Oh no,* she sighed, *and I thought I was doing so well …*

ABOUT THE AUTHOR

Alisa Dana Steinberg is a novelist, poet, and blogger, and back in the day, she was a practicing psychotherapist (and now she frequently thinks she's the insane person in the room). She lives in Manhattan but doesn't own a pair of Jimmy Choo shoes or hangout at Bungalow 8 like Carrie Bradshaw (although she wouldn't be adverse to either). Steinberg is a lover of great literature, good jokes, romantic movies, and the frequent shopping excursion for fabulous clothes at bargain prices (where she doesn't have to fist fight a fellow shopper for a Juicy Couture sweater). She's the author of "Text Me, a Tale of Love and Technology" and "Notes from Ellen Wasserfeldman" (a comedic novel, the first of a trilogy, coming out in the Fall of 2010). Steinberg has been a writer since the age she first played hopscotch (which wasn't yesterday).

Author Photograph by Rob Tannenbaum/First Frames Photography.

Made in the USA
Lexington, KY
11 April 2011